THE REAL DEAL

A DUBLIN NIGHTS NOVEL

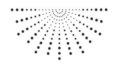

BRITTNEY SAHIN

EMKO MEDIA, LLC

The Real Deal

By: Brittney Sahin

Published by: EmKo Media, LLC

Copyright © 2019 EmKo Media, LLC

This book is an original publication of Brittney Sahin.

Editor: Deb Markanton

Line Editor: Arielle Brubaker

Proofreader: Judy Zweifel, Judy's Proofreading

Cover Design: LJ, Mayhem Cover Creations

Paperback ISBN: 9781699210154

❀ Created with Vellum

To Deb M. -
This one is for you. Thank you!

PROLOGUE

Positano, Italy - Six Years Ago

Sebastian

"Thank you for meeting with me."

My gaze moved from the amber liquid in the glass to the Englishman sitting across from me.

Henry Cuthers. A rich and entitled arse. Dressed in a herringbone check suit circa the Al Capone days, he looked about as vintage as the clothes he was wearing. A .38-caliber revolver hidden in a shoulder holster beneath his jacket would complete the look.

But no, a man like him wouldn't carry. He had his bodyguards to protect him so he wouldn't break his manicured nails.

Cuthers stiffened with my eyes set on him. His pale skin reddened from the base of his throat to the tips of his too-big ears, letting me know his tough guy look was an act. He was a businessman with too much time on his hands, and now he was showing his cards, his fear. And he should be afraid.

"I assume you're calling in a favor, one that violates the rules?" My patience dwindled with every passing second as I waited for him to speak.

A slight tremor appeared in his hand when he slid half a piece of paper across the table. "My wife wants a divorce. She left me a three-line note to say goodbye before she took off to Rome with another man as if ten years of marriage meant nothing."

I didn't touch the paper as I observed him.

The whites of his eyes overwhelmed the green color. Lips drawn tight. Fingers curled into his palms on the table.

Grief and sadness? No.

Anger and betrayal? Hell yes.

"And this is a problem because . . .?" I remembered his wife, a classic beauty. She was reminiscent of Sophia Loren in the prime of her career. I'd never understood why she married a man like Cuthers, not even for his wealth.

"She left me for my competitor. I'm worried she'll sell company secrets. Screw me over in more ways than one."

"What do you want?" I leaned back in the seat, catching a brunette's eyes at the table off to my left.

"We've worked together in the past, my friend. I heard you were in the area and hoped you would agree to help. You did accept the meeting." Cuthers motioned to the bodyguard standing nearby, a briefcase clutched at his side, beckoning him to the table.

The man popped the twin gold locks and flashed the money, then quickly snapped the briefcase shut.

"Three hundred grand now. Another three after the job is done. Make it look like an accident. An extra hundred if you can set up her new lover, too."

"I'm not a hitman." The words came out like the blunt tip of an unpolished knife.

"No one would have to know." The nervous sweat at his brow journeyed down the sides of his clean-shaven face. "Think of the money."

Patience now exhausted, I angled my head and brought my gaze to the black-and-white checkered floor for a heartbeat. With swift movements, I rose and lunged toward him before he could react. Before his bodyguard would even know what happened.

With Cuthers' lapels in hand, I yanked him to his feet, then twisted his arm behind his back and slammed his face onto the table.

My hand remained steady on the back of his neck as I held him in place. I swept my gaze from left to right. The red-lipped brunette caught my eyes and smiled.

Conversation in the room abruptly stopped but only for a moment.

Most people were well acquainted with who I worked for, so they wouldn't attempt to intervene. Cuthers' idiot bodyguard didn't seem to understand because he pressed the muzzle of his gun against my temple.

"I suggest you remove your weapon before I kill you and your employer."

Cuthers lifted his hand in the air, signaling to his guard to lower his weapon.

"It wasn't smart to go around the rules." I leaned forward and brought my mouth to his ear. "Your membership has officially been revoked. Consider yourself lucky that's the extent of it."

"You're only a fixer. You can't—"

Grabbing a handful of his hair, I lifted his head and slammed his cheek back down onto the table, then bent his arm even farther back, on the verge of dislocating it from the shoulder. "I speak for every leader, not just for *La Lega dei Fratelli.*" The arsehole needed a reminder that the rules applied to The League of Brothers here as well as elsewhere. The rules were sacred. "No League protection from now on."

He moaned when I punctuated my words with one last twist of his arm. "Understood."

I released him with a shove and stood to my full height.

His bodyguard stepped in front of me, a 9mm rested against his abdomen, jaw locked tight. He was itching to exchange blows. And it'd be a waste of his time.

I wasn't armed, and I didn't need to be.

I snatched the scrap of paper off the table and glanced at Cuthers. "If you send anyone else after your wife, if anything happens to her, I'll find you, and I'll kill you." I held the paper between us. "Do you understand?"

"Why does her life mean anything to you?" He massaged his shoulder and grimaced.

I ignored him and tucked the paper into my back pocket, and he flinched when I stepped close again. "Don't make me come after you."

Once outside, I sent a quick message to Signore Calibrisi, the leader of *La Lega dei Fratelli* in Italy, to let him know Cuthers had been taken care of.

I hopped onto my red Ducati Monster 696 and slipped on my helmet.

The sun had set two hours ago, so the village off to my left and the pebble beach that lay at its feet were barely noticeable. During the day, the whitewashed houses appeared stacked vertically, nestled into the weathered cliffs like a carefully constructed puzzle. But hidden by the night sky, the only clue they existed were pinpoints of light glowing from within houses here and there.

Darkness draped my shoulders like a blanket. A comforting sensation. A feeling of home.

My sins were easily hidden when the sun slept.

And as I took on the hairpin curves of the twisting roads on my bike, traveling along the Amalfi Coast toward my home—a boat docked at the marina—for one moment . . . one small moment of time, I allowed myself to dream my life was different.

Dreams were for those who were able to live in the sun— to live in the light of day.

Those dreams would be wasted on me.

Besides, I was far too comfortable in the dark.

"YOU'RE A HARD MAN TO FIND."

I removed my helmet and tracked the female voice behind me.

The orange glow of the marina lights revealed a woman wearing a tight-fitting leather jacket leaning against a red BMW convertible.

Her voice—American?

"I'm surprised you found me at all." I set down my helmet and approached the brunette who held herself with the kind of confidence I didn't see in most men. I certainly hadn't seen it in that arsehole, Henry Cuthers.

She pushed away from the convertible and closed the space between us with self-assured strides.

She reminded me a little of Signore Calibrisi's daughter, Emilia, with her long dark hair and almond-shaped eyes, but there was something else familiar about her I couldn't quite map out in my mind.

"Do you know who I am?" Her voice was softer this time.

Hesitant, as if she were fearful of my answer. An interesting contrast to the way she held herself—shoulders squared and chin lifted.

"No," I said, even though something inside of me wanted to answer yes. "I'd sure as hell like to, though." I dragged my eyes from her brown riding boots, doubtful the woman ever rode horses, before my gaze moved to the snug fit of her denim jeans.

"I would advise against checking me out."

I scratched at the scruff on my jaw. "And why is that?"

"Well," she began, "because we're related." Her words carried a hint of amusement, but I still stumbled back as if I'd been punched in the face by a heavyweight boxing champ.

"Did Luca put you up to this?" I grinned, trying to find my bearings again. "He's notorious for his antics." I'd gone out with Luca in Milan a few weeks ago, too. He probably wanted to get back at me since I'd left the club with the blonde he'd had his eye on first.

"I know it sounds crazy, but it's true." Her tone had changed, less soft and more pleading.

And now this wasn't remotely funny at all. "You have me mistaken with someone else." I turned, needing to get the hell away from her.

Whatever game this woman was playing, well, she could find someone else to rope into her sick kind of fun.

"Wait," she called out as I continued down the dock, striding past other yachts until I reached mine.

She was a beauty, my boat.

A Hatteras Flybridge 53 ED. 1983 model. After I restored her, she ran as good as new, too.

I climbed aboard, unlocked the cabin door, and moved into the galley.

When I turned around, she was taking a seat on the couch

on the starboard side. She'd drawn a hand at the base of her throat as if struggling to loosen her words free.

Her fierce confidence had been left on the dock. Inside here, she looked like a lost young girl.

Now, in the light, I realized she was barely legal. Twenty or twenty-one, at most.

Dark brown eyes. Brown hair with streaks of red flowed over her shoulders. A strong but feminine jawline. Straight nose. High cheekbones.

Shit, I did recognize her. "Alessia Romano."

Italian in name. American by birth. Richer than rich.

Her father, Anthony Romano, had died a few months ago. It'd been all over the media. The death of a billionaire always made the news.

Romano wasn't League even though, as a billionaire, he would have qualified. League leaders were required to have the kind of wealth most men would never see. However, The League of Brothers had chosen to refrain from crossing the Atlantic to the Americas. They were strictly on the European and Asian continents.

"You said you didn't know me." Disbelief shredded her tone into something small and weak.

"You're a Romano. I didn't notice outside." I grabbed a bottle of my favorite American drink, Maker's Mark, and poured two glasses. "Here." I took the two steps from the galley to the couch and handed her the drink. Eyes locked warily on mine, she brought the glass to her lips and sniffed.

"It's not poison." A Maker's neat could take getting used to, though, I supposed.

And when a tiny smile touched her lips, I realized the corners of my mouth had flipped, too.

She took a careful sip. I downed mine in one quick swig.

"It's true, Sebastian, I'm your sister."

She knew my name. My *real* name.

How in the hell . . .?

Her words had me feeling like I was twelve again. A kid with everything to lose. And now all I could think about was the moment I'd found my mother lifeless on the floor of our flat in Paris. Drained of color. Too still to even be breathing. I'd screamed for help first in English then French. The medics were too late. She'd been gone before I'd even found her.

"No, it can't be true." I ripped my focus back to the boat and out of Paris.

I didn't know anything about my father, except he'd been in Dublin on business when they met, and I was the product of an affair that went on for years before I was born, and it was an affair that ended the moment I came into the world.

He caused her to become a drunk. The alcohol led to pain pills. And those pills caused her death. *He* killed her.

So, no, it wasn't possible I was his son because if my father was already dead, he'd stolen my chance at payback, which was unacceptable.

"You're lying." The words came out hard and gritty like I'd put them through a meat grinder first.

"I didn't know about you, not until my father was on his deathbed, and he told me about the son he abandoned in Dublin." She stood and dipped her hand into her pocket and produced a photo. "Colleen Ryan is your mom."

I was three in the photo. Sitting on my mother's lap with a smile on my face. We were still living in Dublin at the time.

"Where'd you get that?" I set my empty glass down and snatched the picture.

My ma's blue eyes stared back at me. And the pain of losing her crawled back into my chest.

"It was the last time your mother sent our father a photo.

She gave up trying to reach out to him after that. Well, that's what Dad said. And he let her give up." The word *sorry* was written all over her face as if she was somehow to blame for her arsehole father.

But no, I couldn't be Anthony Romano's son.

I turned, refusing to look at her. Unwilling to risk seeing someone who did, in fact, look similar to me.

I set the photo down and moved to the wall alongside the small fridge. I pressed my palms to the cool surface and bowed my head. My heartbeat pumped wildly when it should've been steady. Resolute. Un-fucking-breakable. I was facing a woman who was trying to rip my world apart, and my heart was betraying my mind as it beat a desperate, imploring rhythm . . . *You have a sister.*

"I've been looking for you since the day he died. We have a family friend in the CIA. It took a few months, but, well, clearly he tracked you down."

If the CIA knew my location, I'd have to get the hell out of Italy. I couldn't let them discover my allegiance to The League.

"No one else knows who you are, and he vowed he wouldn't tell anyone about the favor I'd asked to find you," she said as if reading my mind, a hint of sadness in her voice that I think she was trying to mask.

I knew a thing or two about favors. "Yeah, and what else did this CIA guy tell you?"

"You were arrested three times while living in Paris, all before you turned eighteen. Then you disappeared from the grid. The arrests and stuff, is that because of what happened?"

"What happened?" I whirled around, my anger spiking. I snatched the glass she was still holding and tossed the bourbon back, swallowing hard. "How my mother died, you mean?" I seethed. "How I got bounced around in the system? Lived on the streets?" I slammed the glass down on the counter off to my side.

She stepped back, fear in her eyes. Smart girl.

"I'm sorry about everything. I can't even imagine." Innocence and a sweetness I didn't deserve flooded her tone.

How could she not understand I could destroy her and her rich self in the blink of an eye? And if she dared to continue to talk about my mother, I might throw her into the water and let the Tyrrhenian Sea carry her away.

"I suggest you find that confidence you had when you first got here, and use it to walk the fuck away right now."

She lifted her hand toward me—a plea to give her the chance she seemed to desperately need.

"I don't want to leave." Her eyes became wet. "I'm so sorry for the hell you've endured because of him. But I want to know you. Please."

A single tear fell down her cheek.

For a second, I saw my mother's memory in that tear as it slid down her tan skin.

"You don't want to know me," I said gruffly. "Trust me."

"Maybe." That word had me going absolutely still. "Maybe you're dangerous since it took a high-ranking official in the CIA to find you." Her shoulders lifted before she slowly let them fall. "So, it's entirely possible I'm making a mistake by being here. But I couldn't live with myself if I didn't try."

I quickly invaded her space, leaning in so we were eye to eye. On instinct, she threw her palms against my chest to protect herself.

"There's a question on your mind. Ask it," I bit out.

Surely she belonged in the sun. Not in my world.

Her chin wobbled. "No."

"Ask." My demand carried more intensity than it deserved, but she needed to hear the truth. To know how dangerous I was to her and the ivory tower she most likely lived in.

"Have you ever hurt anyone? K-killed?"

"Yes," I hissed without hesitation, and her hands slipped free from my chest. "Time to go."

"No." Her perseverance continued to catch me off guard, and she quickly continued, her voice unwavering and confident. "I sold all the shares of our father's companies. I'm unloading his assets. I'll give you the inheritance you deserve." She drew in a shaky breath as if she'd run out of steam. Her next words released on a sigh. "I can help you. Please. You'd have access to anything you could ever want or dream of."

"My dreams died along with my mother!" My jaw briefly locked tight at my words. At my slip of the truth I worked so hard to bury behind steel walls and a titanium coat of armor.

"It doesn't have to be that way." More tears fell. I'd admitted to her I was a killer, and yet, she wasn't running away. "I want to know you. I thought maybe you'd want to get to know me, too. Maybe we can even run a business or something together."

Optimistic. Idealistic. Her youth and innocence were fragile.

I'd only crush her dreams.

I bared down on my back teeth, opening my lips just enough to unleash my words. "I'd rather spend a lifetime in prison than touch his money."

This girl—barely a woman—wasn't my problem, and I had to remember that.

I couldn't be her brother or her hero.

"Go."

"No!"

My hand went back to the wall as I willed myself not to turn around.

How was she standing her ground, and to me? Someone who made grown men weep.

"I won't go anywhere. You're my brother." The tears were gone now; I could tell by her tone. "And I think you need me."

I wasn't sure what the hell possessed me to turn, but I did.

She lunged my way and threw her arms around my waist and held her cheek to my chest.

She was hugging me. Fuck.

My arms were locked at my sides because I didn't know what to do. How to act.

She was going to try and pull me into her world, wasn't she?

But she'd fail.

And she might even end up dead.

CHAPTER ONE

DUBLIN, IRELAND - PRESENT DAY

HOLLY

EIGHT POWERFUL MEN SAT AT THE LONG, SLEEK SILVER TABLE in the boardroom, but only one board member was responsible for provoking my silence, captivating me with his dark eyes.

Still on my feet, I brought my palms to the metal in front of me as I struggled to get my voice to work, knowing everyone was waiting for me to begin since my brother had given me the floor.

Get it together, damn it. You're a McGregor. But the man across from me, Sebastian Renaud, had the power to muddle my thinking and rob my speech. My throat tightened as sweat bloomed between my breasts beneath my black chiffon blouse.

This was only the second board meeting with Sebastian

since he'd acquired a seat at the company. I didn't have to worry about bumping into him at work, but we did keep running into each other outside of the office.

We'd collided on Drury Street last week, my newly purchased lingerie spilling onto the footpath, and I swear he'd gotten a kick out of dangling the sheer nude bra on his finger as I'd shoved the pink tissue and the rest of my purchases back into the bag. I'd never been so flush in my life.

And just this Monday night, I'd been leaving my favorite Italian bistro with my sister-in-law, Anna, as he'd been entering. He didn't have a date on his arm, but knowing him, he'd have met her there, too much of an arse to pick her up first.

And those stories only covered the last nine days. I had months' worth of similar run-ins. I was beginning to think I was trapped inside a comedy, and everyone was having a great laugh but me.

Dublin should've been big enough for the both of us, yet somehow, we kept entering each other's personal space. Today, at least, I'd had time to anticipate and prepare.

But apparently all that preparation sailed out the window with him directly across from me.

Sebastian's lips twitched. The hard look on his face a contradiction to that near smile. It was as if he knew what I was thinking, well, more like *who* I'd been thinking about.

In a fitted two-piece black suit, black shirt, and no tie, he looked devastatingly handsome—charming, at ease in the boardroom—and just as dangerous as well. Of course, a man known as The Deal Maker had to be ruthless, and I'd do well to remember that.

I'd been the one to seek him out first, to bring him into our lives. I'd gone to Sebastian in May for help to try and prevent the sale of our media group to a shrewd (and now deceased) businessman. But I'd had the good sense to walk out of his hotel before I did anything I'd regret, including making a deal with him.

I certainly never expected Sebastian to wind up in the middle of an investigation shortly after that night, one that involved my brother Adam's then-fiancée and now wife, kidnapped on their wedding day.

Now in November, we were all still recovering from the events that had happened. Fortunately, my brother and Anna got their happily ever after, but we were also now stuck with Sebastian in our lives.

When I'd stormed his office in Paris this past summer, after discovering he'd bought our stock and scored a seat on our board, he'd claimed he did it to help.

Sure . . . a man like Renaud wouldn't help anyone unless it benefitted him. He had to have ulterior motives, which meant I sure as hell shouldn't be sitting here wondering what it'd be like to have his lips pressed to mine. I shouldn't be imagining the expression he'd make if I were to remove my blouse and let him see I was wearing the bra he'd dangled on his index finger last week.

"Holly, are you ready?" Sean was at the head of the table. It'd once been our father's seat. Our grandfather's before that. And now my brother held the position of CEO and chairman of the board of McGregor Enterprises whether he wanted it or not. "Holly?"

"I, um."

My brother knew me well. He'd taken one look at my face and realized if I ever managed to speak, I'd most likely fumble my way through talking, just like the last time Sebastian sat across from me.

"Our stock prices have taken a turn for the better in the past few weeks," Sean spoke up, and I nearly collapsed with relief back into my seat. "I believe we owe Holly for our latest stock increase."

The Reed deal. Right.

"You're referring to the fact that word is out we're in negotiations with Reed Productions?" Cole's brogue had softened from his time living in New York. My uncle was on the board as well, but he'd had to stay back in Manhattan, so he'd sent my cousin in his place.

"I'm still not quite understanding how a relationship between McGregor and Reed would benefit the company. Or, for that matter, how it benefits Reed," Leeland Green, one of our eldest members on the board, commented. His silvery-white brows lifted when his eyes moved from Sean to me.

"I do wonder what Reed really wants with the McGregors." Sebastian's deep voice had the hairs on my arms standing beneath my sleeves. "Reed may not have the company's best interest at heart."

And you do? "Harrison plans on filming a movie here in Dublin and—"

"First name basis already," Sebastian interrupted.

Arsehole.

Harrison Reed and I had become friends during talks about a possible deal between our companies, and I'd sure as hell trust him over the devil sitting across from me.

"He wants to partner with our media group to ensure the film is as authentic as possible. I think it's a solid move on our part to get involved with him." My gaze flicked to my brother and away from Sebastian. "Harrison's flying in Sunday night. I'd like to finalize the deal next week."

"Good," Sean said with a nod, a touch of pride in his blue eyes.

In the last six months, I'd gone from running HR to managing our media group, McGregor Advanced

Communications. And despite the stress that came with the transition, I was doing a damn good job.

"You should let me join you in that meeting." Sebastian's insane suggestion brought my gaze back to him. "I'll make sure we get the best possible deal."

"I think I can handle Harrison Reed." I matched his low tone with one of my own.

"I'll make sure Reed doesn't take advantage of you." He narrowed his gaze on me. Midnight lashes framed his brown eyes, which were the color of expensive, dark rum. He pinned me with his pensive stare, and I was helpless to look away while the cliché, but oh-so-real, chill of goose bumps erupted across my skin.

I bit down on my back teeth and gripped the chair arms.

Sean coughed into a closed fist, an attempt to draw the board members' focus to him. "If our stock can benefit from the mere mention of working with Reed Productions, then closing this deal will do wonders for the company." My brother kept his tone level as his eyes journeyed around the table, attempting to come across as confident as possible. Filling Da's shoes was no easy feat, especially since our brother Adam had first made the attempt then bowed out. They'd been hesitant about him taking over, and I was sure Sean felt like he had something to prove, even if he'd never admit it to anyone.

"I'm still not sure if getting in the movie business is really what we should be doing." Leeland Green should've retired eons ago. I wouldn't hold my breath for it to happen. Too damn stubborn to go.

Our media division was involved in everything from magazines to talk shows. Movies were a natural progression. Leeland wasn't one for big ideas, though.

"We'll see what Reed has to say. A deal with Reed will

require majority vote, same as always," Sean answered. "Moving on." He looked to Cole after he'd gone through a few more items on the agenda, topics I was supposed to present and discuss. "What's new in our Manhattan office?"

My mobile vibrated in front of me, and I snatched it when Cole began to talk.

Renaud: *Hi.*

My attention whipped to Sebastian, but he was casually observing his mobile as if he hadn't just texted me.

Me: *What do you want?*

Renaud: *I was curious if you had my number saved.*

His thumb went beneath his chin, his forefingers at his temple as he sat. His blackish-brown hair was shorter on the sides and longer at the top. Messy strands, like a work of art, were pushed to the side, no gel in sight to keep his hair in such a manner. The man was sinfully good looking.

Me: *What do you want?*

Renaud: *To tell you happy birthday.*

Was there a company memo sent out? How'd he know? Then again, this was Sebastian I-Know-Everything Renaud.

Renaud: *You shouldn't be working today.*

Me: *The world doesn't stop spinning because of me.*

I don't know why I even bothered to respond, to participate in whatever game he was trying to play.

Renaud: *It should.*

I inhaled at his words, doing my best not to let them visibly affect me.

Me: *Well, thanks for the message, but it was unnecessary. We're not friends. We're . . . business acquaintances. And barely even that.*

I was done with this conversation. I flipped my mobile upside down on the table to let him know.

When I looked up, he was in the process of stowing his

iPhone inside his jacket pocket. I stole a look at his face, the dark scruff covering his cheeks and jawline. Not a full beard. He'd most likely gone a week without shaving. It would make most men look lazy or unkempt, but on Sebastian it was just plain sexy.

"Any other topics on the agenda?" Sean asked, which meant Cole must've already finished with his report. And shit, I had no clue what Cole had even said.

"I have one item I'd like to discuss." Sebastian set his attention on Sean, and he grew quiet for a moment before he peered my way. "Why are we not accepting the offer from Paulson Incorporated to sell them the land in Limerick?" He rested his elbows on the table, bringing his fingertips together.

"That land has belonged to the McGregors for over a hundred and fifty years," I rushed out. "We promised the people of Limerick we'd keep it as a preservation for wildlife. A natural habitat."

"We're losing tens of millions of euros by withholding from the sale," Leeland added, which was the last thing I needed. I wasn't surprised he was on Sebastian's side, though. He cared more about money than an oath, and he'd pushed for us to sell in the past to previous buyers.

"Leeland, I'm well aware we're losing millions. As I'm aware Paulson Incorporated is hoping to expand their reach into Ireland and build new commercial and residential developments, which would give an economic boost to the area."

There had better be a but coming and soon.

"Selling the land would definitely be in our best interest." Before I lost my mind, Sean added, "But we made a promise. We can't go back on that promise. I'm sorry."

"Shouldn't we at least consider a vote?" Sebastian asked.

"We voted on this matter twice before you joined the board, Mr. Renaud, when two other companies made a similar offer. The majority ruled in favor of keeping the land," I informed him.

"Well, like you said, that was before I joined, Ms. McGregor." The powerful way he held himself, the straight brows that gave nothing away, and the depth of his eyes as they looked straight through me . . . I was almost compelled to agree to whatever the hell he wanted.

"I think we should vote again," Leeland added. "How about we meet in three weeks?"

Shit. That was too bloody soon.

"Fine." Sean shot me an apologetic look. "I can't stop the vote from happening, but I urge you all to keep in mind the McGregors gave their word about preserving that land thirty years ago. Then again just last year."

"And there are only three McGregors at this table," Sebastian stated as if we needed the reminder.

What *I* needed was to learn to throw a punch so I could box the head off this guy.

"Please remember that there are six other board members," he added.

Before I could summon a comeback, Sean declared the meeting adjourned and pivoted in his seat to face his executive admin, Bella. "Since it's already past four, you can hold off on sending the meeting minutes until Monday."

I knew Bella had been conspiring with my brothers to throw me a surprise birthday party tonight, so there was that, too. But now that the future of our property in Limerick was uncertain, I wasn't in much of a mood to celebrate.

I gathered my things and stood as the room began to empty.

"Renaud, a minute?" Sean requested.

"I'm late for an engagement. Another time, perhaps?" He casually tossed out the words, not bothering to look our way before he left.

Cole stepped alongside Sean, his eyes moving from the doorway to my brother. "I wasn't at the last meeting, but damn, you were bang on about Sebastian." He patted Sean on the shoulder then left.

Sean braced his temples with his middle finger and thumb. "We need to get rid of Renaud somehow."

"What's up with his newfound friendship with Leeland?"

"I don't know." Sean lowered his arm and braced the table. "Next thing you know, he'll have the board voting us off."

"Maybe that's his true intention." I wouldn't put anything past him.

"We won't let this Limerick vote go arseways," Sean promised. "You have my word."

"Da should've filed for government protection of the land." Which was exactly what I intended to do, but three weeks wouldn't be enough time to complete the process. "Sorry I choked up today," I added. *Like last time.*

"He makes us all uneasy." Sean gently squeezed my shoulder. "Maybe we shouldn't talk about this right now. It's your birthday."

"It's twenty-six. Not the big thirty. And whatever you have planned tonight—"

"Happens at eight. So be on the lookout for a text from me at seven thirty with the address."

"Just promise me . . . no strippers jumping out of a cake."

"That may have been Ethan's idea, but no worries, I shot it down."

Ethan was the wild child.

Sean, the charmer.

Adam, the fighter.

And me? I'd been dubbed the responsible one. Sometimes I wished I could trade my role in for a new one.

"See you tonight." Sean kissed me on the cheek before leaving.

I sank back in the chair and messaged Sebastian before I could stop myself.

Me: *I'm just letting you know you won't win. You won't get the votes.*

I stared impatiently at the phone as three little bubbles floated up and down while he typed.

Renaud: *It's just business.*

Me: *And it's my business. Back off.*

Renaud: *Then your father shouldn't have taken the company public. You have a board to answer to now, and I'm on it. Get used to it.*

After I'd all but slammed the mobile back onto the table, embarrassment flooded my cheeks when I saw that Bella had caught my burst of anger.

She leaned into the doorway of the boardroom, her glasses dangling in hand. "You okay?"

"No," I said on a sigh. "What's up?"

She pushed away from the doorframe, her lithe body straightening to its runway model height, then she slipped on her frames and tucked her neon blue hair behind her ears. This was her third new look in the last two months. I loved her for her vibrant spirit. And I was a little envious, too.

"You have a visitor. Hollywood Handsome. Mr. Sex on a Stick. Harrison probably-delivers multiple-orgasms Reed." She fanned her face, her glittering 1-carat princess cut engagement ring catching my eye. "The man is even better looking than his Instagram profile."

Wait. What? I jumped out of my chair, chills sweeping up, down—hell, everywhere that I had skin.

She shrugged. "What do you want me to do? I can occupy him if you'd like." She waggled her brows, her deep blue eyes fixed my way.

"You're getting married, remember?" I would've laughed and teased her with some inappropriate comment if I wasn't so jumpy and nervous to finally meet Harrison in person. "Send him to my office."

I slipped inside the nearest lavatory and checked myself in the mirror.

I fixed my blouse, ensuring it was neatly tucked into my red skirt. Blotted a touch of shine off my forehead and cheeks. And thankfully, I hadn't sucked the gloss dry from my lips during the meeting with Sebastian.

I stared at my reflection. A mini pep talk needed. *I can do this. I can face Hollywood Handsome.*

A minute later, I found myself standing in the doorway to my office, taking in the sight of Harrison Reed's perfect backside. He was facing the floor-to-ceiling windows that overlooked a bank of trees outside.

"Hi," I whispered, the word clinging to the back of my throat as he slowly turned to face me.

He was in jeans, and his white button-down shirt was untucked. Sleeves rolled to the elbows to show strong forearms. Brown suede oxford shoes. No watch. Must've been how they dressed in California, much more laid back.

"Hi." His gray eyes combed the length of me as if he were indulging in a slow and decadent journey, one that'd end with sex and multiple orgasms. Bella was probably right about the man.

He crossed the room to get to me since I'd remained stuck in place, still in shock by his early and unannounced visit.

How was I supposed to greet him?

Handshake? Too formal.

But could I hug a man I'd only just now met in person?

He gathered me in his arms, taking charge of the decision, and I was grateful.

"What are you doing here?" I murmured into his chest before breathing in his heavenly cologne.

Mint. A touch of vanilla and spice. And sex. He smelled like someone who, let's be honest, knew how to give a woman a proper time in bed.

"Happy birthday. I thought I'd surprise you." He stepped back, his focus narrowing on me. "You okay?"

I blinked. A few times, maybe.

Harrison Reed should be off-limits for a lot of reasons.

Twelve years older than me.

A possible business partner.

Playboy celebrity.

Lives forever and a day away from Dublin.

Also . . . not Sebastian.

I squeezed my eyes closed at the last item on my list.

Sebastian didn't belong on my "Reasons not to fall for Hollywood Handsome" list—not for a bloody second.

And yet, it was like Sebastian's name crushed every other item and towered at the top no matter how much I willed *his* face, *his* smell, *his* deep and sexy voice to go away.

"Holly?"

At the feel of his firm hand wrapped gently around my arm, more protective than possessive, I opened my eyes.

"Words," I sputtered. "I need to use them now."

He smiled. "Words are overrated."

I laughed. That was probably a line from a movie. "I'm truly surprised is all. And it's just twenty-six. My birthday is nothing."

"Should I have called first?" He closed one eye and winced as if he were afraid of my answer and let go of my arm.

This man was a titan in his industry. He ran one of the most well-known movie studios in Hollywood, and he was uber hands-on when it came to his passion projects.

"No, I'm happy you're here," I admitted. "Had a rough meeting just before. Sorry."

"You want to talk about it?"

"No, just work stuff. Thank you."

Sebastian was an off-limits subject matter. I had to protect the company, and I couldn't let Harrison know I had concerns about one of our board members. I didn't want to lose a chance at a deal with Reed Productions.

Partnering with Reed to film a movie in Dublin and employing more people because of it—it'd be the boost our company needed, as well as our city.

"Can I get you something to drink? Tea? Coffee?" I motioned for him to sit, but he shook his head.

"I gotta hit the hotel and shower, but thank you."

And if Bella were in the office, she would've offered a play-by-play of what shower sex with Harrison would probably be like—after he left, of course.

I wanted to close my eyes. To be rebellious. To think of this man naked and wet.

But I knew what would happen if I did.

He'd turn into Sebastian in my mind. It'd be The Deal Maker not Hollywood Handsome who'd wind up in my thoughts. Because ever since I met Sebastian, he seemed to take control of every one of my wild fantasies.

"You're blushing." Harrison's lips teased into a grin.

I'd forgotten the art of the English language again, hadn't I? I was taking tongue-tied to an all-new level. I really needed to get laid. The vibrator wasn't cutting it these days.

"What'd you say?" Great, and now I needed him to repeat himself because I'd taken a trip to la-la-orgasm-land.

"Blushing." His oxfords carried him closer to me. Slow, almost cautious steps.

And he should be cautious. If we were in one of his movies, I'd be the heartbreaker, since I was the one who wouldn't be able to commit.

"Your cheeks are turning pink," he added when I'd still yet to, you know, S-P-E-A-K. "I had planned to take you out for your birthday, but word is there's a secret party—one you already know about—happening tonight."

"Come with me. And this weekend, we can get a head start on all the touristy activities I had originally planned for next week."

"You sure you don't mind?"

"I'd love to spend the weekend with you." The color, no doubt, deepened on my cheeks. "That probably didn't sound right."

"It sounds perfect to me."

CHAPTER TWO

HOLLY

"Do you like it?" Anna asked as we stood in the entranceway to the grand ballroom at the hotel in Dublin, which overlooked St. Stephen's Green across the way. Two of the three walls of towering windows offered a gorgeous view of the city park.

"I've always loved this place." My hand went to my heart as memories caught in my mind. "My parents would throw these lavish masquerade balls here when I was growing up, and they were adult-only, but one year I snuck out and hid"— I pointed across the room to the pool of silver fabric —"behind the drapes and watched everyone dance." My mood lifted at the memory, the frustrating day at work taking a very distant backseat. "And when they took their masks off at midnight, it was like a fairy tale."

Ma and Da had been so in love then. I was just ten, but I could see it in the way they danced and moved, how they interacted with each other. I could only hope they'd reconcile, to remember the love they once had and refrain from getting a divorce.

"I take it Adam told you?" I turned toward my brother who had his arm wrapped around his wife's waist, his palm resting at the side of her pregnant belly covered in a long, flowy silver gown.

"I was the one who found you that night," he said with a smile, looking handsome in an effortless way in his black tux, a contrast to the clothes he normally donned these days at his fighting gym.

I closed one eye and poked at his chest. "You weren't supposed to be there either."

"I followed you. I couldn't let my sister roam the city by herself."

Anna pulled herself free of Adam's arm and moved to a small table outside the ballroom, which had dozens of silver and black masks on it. "Your mask, my love." She handed a simple black eye mask to Adam. "And this one is for you since you're the birthday girl. Handmade in Venice."

I held the work of art in my hands. Intricate details and beading like small, glittering diamonds with touches of white lace atop the silver base. A small crown-like feature at the center. "It's perfect. Thank you." She helped me put it on, tying the silver ties around the back of my head. My hair flowed wavy and loose over my shoulders tonight.

"My lady." Adam offered Anna's eye mask next. A simpler version of mine. "Everyone is here. Ma and Da even arrived together."

There was optimism buried in his words, the same hope I shared that our parents would reunite. "If ever a place to get a reminder of their love, this party just might do it."

"I do think Bella may have invited your entire office tonight, though," Anna said a moment later. "She was in charge of invites, and she said something about hitting control-all accidentally when the party invitations went out."

Adam laughed. "Bella make a mistake? She used to work for me before Sean, and trust me, she doesn't make mistakes."

"True," I agreed, surveying the room, trying to see who actually showed up. The masks hid a few identities, but for the most part, I could tell who was who.

"I was hoping Bree would be able to come. I miss her and Jack." It would've been a nice birthday surprise if my cousin and her son had managed to fly in from New York. She would've loved this party. As kids, we used to throw our own pretend balls while our parents were at the event, well, up until she moved to Manhattan with Cole when I was eleven.

"She really wanted to be here." A scowl crossed Adam's lips. "The divorce with Derek . . ."

Mr. Baseball. I'd never liked her pro-ball husband, but he was still little Jack's father, so I'd always done my best to be polite around him. "I wish she could move back here with Jack."

"Derek will never let that happen." Adam's shoulders dropped, and I could feel his mood growing dark and protective.

Anna caught on as well, and she smoothed a hand up and down the side of his arm. "How about we go mingle? A ton of people want to say their hellos."

"I just want one more second to take it all in. Go ahead."

Adam kissed my cheek and whispered, "Happy birthday, Sis," then he and Anna moved into the room.

I remained still, relishing in all the details. My throat thickened as memories continued to float to mind. A time of youth and innocence, when I believed a man would one day sweep me away and marry me. My dreams were a touch different now, but there was still a princess in all of us, even when we grew up, right?

And this place was fit for royalty, too. The room was seamlessly divided into three sections: a dance area where men and women in their masks moved before a full orchestra, high-top cocktail tables with the staff serving hors d'oeuvres, and lastly, a lounge-like area near the windows overlooking the park with several couches and a bar. The bartender even had on a mask and bow tie.

The only windowless wall in the room glowed in silvery hues as if the lights were moving slowly over the wall in a rhythmic dance.

But my favorite part had to be the immense hand-forged chandeliers suspended from the coffered ceilings. It was as if strands of diamonds, or crystals, dripped from the heavens above.

"We couldn't have done this without Anna," my brother Ethan said from behind, and I whirled around to face him as he placed on his black mask.

"You wore a tux for me." I nearly clapped a hand to my mouth in surprise. Ethan was never much of a suit-and-tie kind of guy.

"For you, anything." He kissed my cheek and hugged me. "Happy birthday." He held on to my hands as he stepped back to observe me. "Ma buy that for you?"

"Yes." Now I knew why she had insisted on giving me the dress and shoes as an early gift. The color theme of the party was silver and black.

The floor-length dress was strapless and only when I walked could you catch sight of my silver heels peeking out. The black leather bodice of the gown was an alluring contrast to the silk chiffon asymmetric skirt, and it'd been designed by one of Ma's favorite designers, Brunello Cucinelli.

"You look like heaven itself." My brother had adopted some of Sean's charm, so it would seem. "Come on. Let's get the hellos out of the way so we can get a drink and loosen you up a bit."

I scoffed. "I'm loose-ish."

"Sean told me about your meeting earlier," he muttered into my ear as we made our way into the room. "And I'm thinking you might enjoy something strong to drink."

Good point.

After an hour or so of chatting with family and friends, I finally made it to the bar. "Something strong and delicious," I ordered, rubbing the tip of my heel against the back of my calf muscle over the fabric. "Surprise me."

"Sure thing, Birthday Girl." He grabbed a martini shaker and went to work, and I lifted my chin toward the ceiling and closed my eyes, allowing the music, the Italian lyrics, to move right through me to my very soul.

I honestly couldn't have asked for a better birthday.

"Sorry I'm late."

I opened my eyes at the sound of Harrison's voice. "How do you know it's me?" I teased. "You can only see me from behind."

He wrapped a hand around my elbow and urged me to face him. "Such beauty is hard to miss."

"Mm, you're smooth, I should've known."

The black mask made his gray eyes even more exquisite, and the well-fitted tux was a rather nice look on him. "I bet you attend a lot of Hollywood parties like these."

"We do like to play dress up out there." His head tilted ever so slightly, his gaze thinning a touch as he lowered his chin, quickly taking in my dress.

I wanted heart palpitations and to feel a greedy need of

desire, but I was coming up empty in regard to him, and it was all because of another man.

"Would you dance with me?" He stepped back and extended his hand, and I glimpsed the freshly made drink out of the corner of my eye.

"I'll be back for that." I slipped my hand inside his and allowed him to escort me to the dance floor.

My first dance of the night at a ball I'd always dreamed of attending . . .

Harrison placed my hand over his shoulder and held my other firmly in the grasp of his left hand. He moved with a gentle grace, a sophisticated understanding of the music.

He dipped me then asked, "Are we still on for tomorrow?"

"Of course."

"I can pick you up, and we can go from your place."

"Well," I began, mid-twirl, "I just moved out of my flat in the city to the suburbs. Boxes are everywhere, so I'd be embarrassed to have you over and not actually invite you in."

"Understandable."

He was so agreeable. And easy to talk to. The kind of man who should make me feel all the things: butterflies, racing heart, lightheaded.

We'd had a few late-night chats (my time zone), and I'd slowly learned more and more about him, from his favorite Al Pacino films to the character quirks of his siblings, and he'd discovered I was more of a Julia Roberts in *Pretty Woman* fan than an action-flick kind of girl. I was also from a decent-sized family, so I had plenty of my own sibling stories to share with him.

. . . But all I could feel for Harrison was friendship.

"You okay?" he asked when I stilled, my heels becoming rooted in place.

A rush of unease traveled up my spine and goose bumps scattered across my skin.

It was insane, but I could feel him there.

HIM, as in Sebastian Renaud.

I shifted out of Harrison's arms and turned to confirm the truth of what I'd felt.

Sebastian advanced through the room, long strides carrying him my way in his fitted, black tuxedo trousers. The black leather mask on his face was perfect for a man whose very presence screamed danger, authority, and sex. He sure as hell looked like he belonged in a high-class BDSM club, in the role of a Master, of course.

"Holly?" Harrison placed his hand on my elbow, seeking my attention, but I remained frozen in place.

Right now, I was that young girl with dreams of her prince stalking toward her to claim her as his in a room full of whispering onlookers.

But my prince wasn't the hero. He was the villain.

And yet, I couldn't help but want the bad guy.

"You came," I whispered, surprised by my ability to speak with Sebastian now at arm's length, his brown eyes cutting straight through me as if he were capable of peeling back my layers and exposing every grain of truth about me. The little pulses of need, the desire to do naughty, erotic things with him.

"I was invited," was all he said before setting his focus on Harrison. "Reed," he greeted.

Harrison offered his hand. "Renaud?" A touch of surprise graced the tone of his voice, and my heart leapt off the proverbial cliff of oh-shit at the fact Harrison knew him. Well, maybe *of* him. The man's reputation probably crossed oceans. "I was hoping to meet you while I was in town."

Harrison folded his arms in a defensive stance, confirming he knew Sebastian was trouble.

"And you're in Dublin early," Sebastian noted.

"I couldn't miss Holly's birthday."

"Same," Sebastian responded tightly, his eyes locked on mine. "I'd like to dance with you."

It wasn't a request. It was an order that slid across my skin and penetrated my bones. I had to stop myself from lifting my arms like a marionette willing my puppet master to guide my next move.

"I need to catch up with your brother Sean," Harrison said, offering a polite withdrawal from an increasingly awkward situation. I wasn't sure if I wanted to thank him or beg him not to leave me alone.

Sebastian didn't waste a beat. Hell, he didn't even wait for Harrison to part ways before he pulled me into his arms as if I belonged to him. No formality or delicate grace. A possessive hold with my body tight against his, his hands skirting closely to my arse.

I looped my arms around the back of his neck, no other place to go aside from his back, which felt too intimate, even though he was holding me in just such a way, and I hated to admit how much I enjoyed it.

"The mask suits you," I whispered without thinking.

"I'm used to them." His brows remained straight, giving nothing away. No indication of a joke, but I had a feeling he was referring to the more metaphorical type of mask than literal, and even I felt the same every once in a while.

We were barely moving. Right left. Right left. About as simple as we could get. But it didn't seem to matter.

"You own anything aside from Brioni?"

His custom tux was timeless and sophisticated. The black, single-breasted jacket enhanced his broad frame. But it was too elegant for him, for a man who had rough edges. It was as if the fabric could barely contain his raw strength and power.

"You know your designers."

"Once upon a time, I wanted to be a fashion designer. I probably can't even sketch a stick figure now, let alone draw clothes."

His Adam's apple moved with a hard swallow, drawing my eyes to the sun-kissed, tan skin of his throat.

How was he tan this time of year? I was so pale compared to him. Maybe he spent his weekends on tropical islands having orgies?

"What happened, why aren't you following your dreams?" His eyes, once again, snatched my focus, and his mouth became a white slash.

"Forced to grow up," I admitted, a bit too easily. But it was also true. "But hey, I also wanted to be a backup dancer for Madonna. And headline my own Vegas magic show."

When his lips actually quirked into a smile—a real one, not the I-make-you-wet-and-I-like-it one—I matched the smile with one of my own.

"Silly childhood dreams. That's all they ever were."

"And now? What are your dreams now? You must have some." A simple sincerity glided through his tone so effortlessly I didn't even question whether or not he had a hidden agenda.

"I have a tendency to look at only what I can see right in front of me," I said softly.

"Sometimes that's not such a bad thing." He held me a little tighter, and I considered asking about his dreams, but I was growing lightheaded in his arms.

I drew in a deep breath to ground myself. But his cologne, the dark notes, so smooth and rich, teased my senses.

He was getting to me. Under my skin like always. Being

this close to him, with his hands on my body, it was confusing.

I was supposed to be mad at him, especially after he pulled that shit about the Limerick sale in the office earlier. I shouldn't be smiling, thinking about my dreams. Thinking about how this fairy tale night now felt complete with him there, even if it didn't make any sense.

"My parents had a masquerade party here every year when I was a kid," I admitted as if I needed to explain the sudden pull of my lips into the smile I shouldn't wear around him.

His eyes moved to the side, and I tracked his gaze to find my parents dancing. My heart jumped in my chest, and I nearly bowed my head to his chest as liquid gathered in my eyes at the sight. When I'd seen my parents dancing at Adam and Anna's wedding in the summer, I'd assumed it was for Adam's benefit, a bit of a peace treaty on a sacred night. But there was something different in the way Da held Ma in his arms tonight. Love anew, maybe. Well, a girl could dream.

"They'll be okay," he whispered into my ear. For the life of me, I couldn't fathom how he knew the right words to say, or why he'd care to make the effort.

Something about the sincerity in his tone, in his words, had me locking up. Was he trying to play on my emotions? Manipulate me?

I couldn't let him hurt my family. We'd already been through far too much this year for more damage. I needed a break, a moment to breathe.

"I know what you want," I whispered, forcing the words to the surface. The truth had to exist between us. If I buried it, I'd lose myself in his eyes and his embrace.

"And what is it that I want?" He tipped his head just a hair and gave me a familiar look, one that only he could pull off. Casual and commanding at the same time. A predator, like a venomous snake, luring an unsuspecting prey.

I stepped back, removing myself from his hold. His arms hung at his sides for a moment before he slowly deposited his hands into his trouser pockets.

"You want our company. And I think"—I wet my lips, the taste of cranberry-flavored gloss on my tongue—"you also want me."

He was quiet for a moment. "I did come with a date," was all he said, his expression blank.

I followed his eyes to a leggy blonde in a tight silver dress near the bar, her hand on Ethan's chest. My brother was leaving on Monday to work out of our New York office for a few weeks. Da thought it might motivate him to finally get involved in the business by giving him a change of scenery. I highly doubted the trip would encourage Ethan to get serious about his life, though. Women and having fun were his main priorities.

"She looks really invested in your relationship," I said when resetting my focus back on him.

"She's not my girlfriend." A raw bite of need traveled through his tone, emphasized by the flare of his nostrils and a stormy look directed right at me. I could feel it between my legs.

"I, um, I can't do this." I hated the crack in my voice—the obvious earth-shattering effect he had on me.

I felt beautiful and sexy in this gorgeous gown and fairy tale mask, and with him looking at me like he already owned me—I might give in. It was very possible I'd let him claim me as his, at least for one night. And regret would fill every crevice of my being afterward.

"I . . ." Suddenly, it was as if someone had wrapped a hand around my throat and squeezed. "I need air." I grabbed the hem of my dress and started for the exit as if I had to escape before the clock struck twelve and my chariot turned into a pumpkin.

I had to get far away from The Deal Maker, or I might be tempted to trade my integrity for an orgasm.

Sean stepped in front of me, bringing my escape to a halt. "You okay? He say something to you?"

"We danced. That's all. I was being polite since we have so many eyes on us."

So many lies.

Honestly, I'd wanted to dance with Sebastian, to have an excuse for him to touch me.

I'd wanted to savor the moment and keep it for later tonight when I'd imagine his hands dragging slowly over the curves of my body.

I'm going to hell, and great, Sebastian's the devil, so we'll be together for eternity. Twenty-six years of being rational and calm flew out the door when this man came into my life.

"Holly?"

"Huh?" I blinked my focus back to Sean's face.

"Want me to kick him out of here? You look ghostly. You sure he didn't upset you?"

"No, please." I shook my head. "It wouldn't look good with Harrison here. I think he already suspects something is off with Sebastian, and I'm worried that could cause issues."

His mouth tightened momentarily. "I wasn't expecting Reed in Dublin today, let alone at your party. You said you'd been chatting with him these last few months, but are you two—"

"No," I said a bit too loudly.

"I know his reputation. You should be careful."

"He's like you." Dislike of my brother's playboy attitude burned through my words.

He looked heavenward for a moment. "This is your birthday, Sweets."

Sweets, his nickname for me because of my childhood sweet tooth. Wasn't I too old for that name now? And was I all that sweet anymore given the inappropriate thoughts racing through me lately?

He squeezed my arm. "I just want you to be happy."

"And I am." I pulled him in for a hug, hoping he'd let this go. I didn't need him stressing about me. I was doing a damn fine job of stressing about myself already.

"If you change your mind about Sebastian, let me know."

"I won't, but thank you." I patted him twice on the chest, then cut through the crowd to get out of the room.

I set my mask back on the table outside the ballroom, then grabbed my jacket from the coat check and exited the hotel. The chilled air nipped at my face, and it was exactly what I needed to reduce the heat inside of me.

Heading for the park, I crossed the street, doing my best to avoid twisting an ankle by keeping my heels from getting caught between the cracks of the cobblestone.

I passed under the Fusilier's Arch and started for the ornamental lake. The park had been well maintained, with walls of trees and other greenery. It was a perfect escape from urban life while still being in the city.

A place to reset my focus.

I had to figure out why the hell I was so attracted to Sebastian aside from his gorgeous looks. Handsome men didn't routinely turn me into a timid and shy girl with stars in her eyes.

Was his effect a result of sex deprivation? It'd been a year, so maybe. The last time had been with my brother's best friend, Les. *Och, what a horrible mistake.* And it could best be described as trying to play naked Twister. Les had been hitting on me for years, and I'd finally given in after too much to drink. But nope, we'd never work at all.

Before him . . . I couldn't remember. I was too young to be having such a dry spell.

Maybe I worked too much. More likely, I was just too picky. And as luck would have it, I seemed to have a thing for dangerous men. Well, *one* dangerous man.

Surely Sebastian would have sex tonight. Probably rip that woman's dress off in one fast swoop. Provide her with so many orgasms she wouldn't be able to see straight.

And good for her. I didn't need his mouth between my legs. I didn't want that sexy scruff scraping inside my thighs as his tongue teased my clit.

Nope. Not at all.

I stopped walking once I reached the lake, my shoulders sagging from the weight of the jealousy flowing through me.

There was a time I probably wouldn't have roamed the park at night alone, but the city had been safer lately. Crime at a minimum.

One of the reasons was probably the death of Donovan Hannigan. The local crime boss had been the cause for so many problems in our family, not just for the city. It'd been a relief he was gone, but his murder had dragged our family's name into the spotlight with the Garda wondering if we were behind his death given our grudge against him. Either way, the man who'd once had a firm grip on Adam was dead. I should say *God rest his soul,* but I hoped he was rotting in bloody hell.

I buried my face in my palms, trying to get a grip, but at the awareness of someone behind me, I began to turn, expecting it to be Sean. I was wrong—because *Don't move* was whispered into my ear, followed by, *Give me your purse.*

Was this really happening? This wasn't how a fairy tale

masquerade ball was supposed to end. Swept away by a prince, yes. Not robbed by some punk.

I lifted my hands in the air and faced him anyway. "I don't have a purse, as you can see."

He wore a black hoodie, but the hood around his face did nothing to disguise the fact he was probably only a teenager.

I didn't see a weapon, so I started to lower my hands, but he lunged my way, and I stumbled back and fell.

"I said don't move." He cursed as he crouched next to me and began going through my coat pockets.

He won't hurt me, I told myself.

I carefully placed my palms on the ground on each side of me and sucked in a breath, holding still as he searched me, hoping if I didn't move he'd just leave me the hell alone.

"That coat. It looks expensive," he said. "Take it off."

I stood, my hands trembling as I fumbled with the buttons.

"Now," he barked out.

I quickly finished, but as I moved to shrug the coat from my shoulders, I caught sight of someone closing in on us.

It all happened so fast.

Quick movements. Almost like a dark shadow had come out of nowhere.

The boy flew to the ground and landed hard on his back, groaning. Sebastian knelt over him and punched him across the jaw, then fisted his hoodie, lifting him up a little, before his fist connected with his face again, sending him flat on his back.

"Do you know who I am?" Sebastian seethed, leaning in.

"Stop," I begged when he pulled the boy to his feet as if weightless.

He clutched the material of his hoodie with both hands,

bringing his face closer, and I rested a palm on Sebastian's back. His body steel beneath my touch.

"Sebastian. Let him go," I urged. "He's only a kid."

"You ever touch another woman again, and I'll . . ." He dropped his words as if now realizing there were people in the park watching the scene unfold. He released his grip on the boy, and the kid stumbled and fell before getting back up again to take off.

"Are you okay?" He turned to face me, the harsh intensity of anger written on his face and in every taut line of his body. Mask gone as well, although he didn't need it to intimidate because the anger he'd been wearing was far scarier than black leather.

"What were you thinking? You could've killed him." My attention flitted to his hands still bunched at his sides.

He stepped closer, the nearby lamppost dragging a shadow across his face, hiding his eyes. "Why were you alone in the park at night? Don't you know any better?"

"I thought I'd be safe." Dublin really had been better since Donovan turned up dead, plus one of the other leaders of a gang had wound up behind bars this year.

The few people around us began to disperse, and honestly, I wasn't sure if I wanted to be left alone with him.

Less shaken up now, I managed out, "He probably needed money for food."

"Or drugs." Sebastian turned, swiping a hand over the back of his dark head. "And he should never have touched you."

"I fell. It was an accident."

He looked in the direction the boy had run and said something under his breath. A curse in French, maybe. "I shouldn't have let him go. If he hurts someone else because I set him free . . ."

"Thanks for the assist, but he wouldn't have hurt me."

"You can't know that." He whirled to face me.

"You're much scarier than him," I murmured, my throat dry. "I promise."

"You're right about that." He tipped his head in the direction of the hotel a moment later. "Let's get you back to the party."

"I don't want anyone to know what happened. They'll worry. My older brothers are too protective. I don't need more of that from them right now."

He peered at the starless sky. A pull of angry dark clouds above us. Rain imminent. "Your brothers are right to protect you. The world is a dangerous place." When his eyes reached mine again, my heart nearly stopped.

The look in his eyes wasn't a dark one. Nor was it lustful. It was something I'd never witnessed on him.

A deep, cutting sadness.

The tight clench of his jaw wasn't fury, either. Well, at least not in this moment. It was almost as if he were combatting a horrible memory and trying to keep whatever emotions he was holding inside of him at bay.

"You lost someone?"

"Yes," he answered without hesitation, his honesty taking me by surprise.

I hadn't expected to feel sympathy for him, but it was pouring out of me at an alarming rate, even if I didn't want it to.

"Let's go."

"I'm fine on my own."

"If you think I'm going to let you walk alone back to the hotel, you're mistaken."

Darkness had reclaimed both his tone and his eyes. He'd

eliminated whatever moment of pain he'd let slip to the surface.

"Nothing will ever happen between us, you know that, right?" I had no idea what possessed me to say that, now of all times, but . . . maybe it was more for my own benefit. I'd needed the reminder. He wasn't my prince. This was no fairy tale.

His eyes moved to my mouth, and his lips tightened.

"Sebastian?"

When he reached forward, brushing my hair off my shoulder, the back of his hand caught my cheek, and the heat from his touch sent a quiver down my spine.

He leaned in closer. "Nothing will happen," he said, his mouth near the shell of my ear. "It *can't* happen."

CHAPTER THREE

Sebastian

"What the——"

I grabbed hold of the kid's Led Zeppelin tee—at least he had good taste—then shoved him back inside his flat, kicking the door closed behind me.

"How'd you find me?"

I tossed the kid's wallet onto his chest in answer, and his focus narrowed on the worn-out leather before shooting me a murderous glare.

I remained casual and pointed out what he clearly already knew. "This place isn't habitable, Declan."

A leather couch that appeared to have been clawed at by an animal was against the wall, and it probably doubled as a bed. Only a stove and small fridge for the kitchen. Pizza boxes were stacked on the only table in the room, and hopefully, they were empty. Of course, maybe that'd explain the godforsaken rotten stench in the room.

He started to rise, but I held out my hand, a warning for him to remain on the ground. "How'd you swipe my wallet?"

Yeah, well, in a previous life I'd once been a thief, and I hadn't forgotten the art of taking something without notice.

"Do you make it a habit of attacking women in parks?" I crouched before him and cocked my head, trying to get a read on the eighteen-year-old, and why he'd tried to mug Holly last night.

I thought he might piss himself seeing me there, but instead, his jaw tightened, and he appeared to be growing a set of balls.

The kid had shaggy, light brown hair in need of a cut and style. A decent beard for his age. And his glacier-blue eyes tightened with every second I remained studying him.

"Don't do it," I warned, realizing he was on the verge of attempting to attack. "I'd prefer not to hurt you again."

"You think you can?"

And his balls are getting bigger by the minute. "Are you expecting someone?" I asked instead, wondering why he flung open the door without checking who was there first.

"My brother, and if you lay a hand on him, I'll—"

"You'll what?" I raised a brow, genuinely curious.

"I'll kill you," he seethed.

I stood. "Where are your parents? Do they know you accost women at night?"

"They'll be back soon, so you should go. My da will fuck you up." He rose to his feet, and this time, I allowed it.

"Yeah, and where do they sleep? All of you on that one couch over there?" There was only one other room connected to the living room, and it was a lavatory.

"How long has it been just you and your brother?"

"I don't owe you anything, let alone a conversation." He walked over to the bed slash couch and dropped down, tossing his wallet next to him, not bothering to check if I'd stolen the three euros he had inside.

I folded my arms across my chest. The beats of my heart picked up as I remembered a time when I'd lived on the streets, and a place like this would've been like a palace to me.

"I have no intention of leaving until I get answers." I remained in front of the thin, hollow-core excuse for a door.

He picked at the hole in the knee of his faded denim jeans. "Our ma comes and goes. She's been gone for a few weeks, though. She's normally back by now. I needed money for food." His lips bunched tight and his nostrils flared. "You happy?"

"And do you make it a habit of stealing from women?"

"Rich people who—"

"Ah, you think yourself Robin Hood? But let me guess, you don't redistribute the wealth." I stepped closer to him, catching his eyes zero in on my silver watch as I let my arms fall to my sides.

"Please go before my brother gets home." He quickly redirected his gaze back to my face.

"And where is he?"

"Playing ball across the street." He stood and faced me. "You gonna go hit him, too?" Anger turned his light blue eyes into something dark. Protective.

I recognized that look. The desire to keep your family safe.

My hand went to my unshaven jaw as I tried to wrap my head around the offer I was about to make. "Have you considered getting a job instead of stealing?"

I'd been asked that question each time the French police had arrested me in Paris when I was even younger than him, and I'd given the same bullshit promise to try and clean up my act when they'd let me out of jail.

"Not many jobs for people like me. And then who'd look out for Samuel?"

"You can't live here. This place is fucking filthy." I met his cold stare, not ready to leave. "How old is Samuel?"

"No, man. No more information." He brought a finger to my chest, pushing against the material of my coat. "Get the feckin' hell out of my life! You want my word I won't steal from another rich woman? Fine. Just don't come here again."

At the feel of my mobile vibrating in my pocket, I stepped back and glimpsed the caller ID. "Yeah?" I answered, ignoring the daggers the kid shot my way.

"Luca's at the bar. Thought you'd want to know."

"Thanks." I ended the call with Ola and pocketed my mobile. "I have to go."

"Good," he said as his eyes dropped to the card I'd extended him. "What's this?"

"An opportunity." I sure as hell hoped I wouldn't regret it.

He took the card, his eyebrows pulling together. "Nah, man. I don't swing that way, so if you're propositioning me for—"

"Shut the bloody hell up." I pointed at the card. "I own the hotel. Get your brother and meet me there in two hours. I'll get you two a room to stay in." And if he needed to hear it, I added, "And not with me."

"I don't understand." Suspicion clouded his face.

"You can't live in this shithole. And I don't want you on the streets bothering people for money. You can work at my club to earn your stay."

His head jerked back, shock in his eyes. "You punched me in the face last night. And you're here offering me a job and a place to stay? You happen to hit your head on the way over?"

You'd think. "Does your brother go to school?"

He swiped his free hand up and down the back of his messy hair. "I won't let him drop out like me."

"Good." I nodded. "I'll have one of my drivers bring him to and from school next week." I started to turn, but he captured my arm.

"I don't understand why you'd do this."

"Because maybe you remind me of myself."

"Sure, you were once like me?"

I didn't answer. How could I?

"Well, thanks for the offer, but I'm gonna have to pass. My ma could come back, and I gotta be here when she does." He pushed the card at my arm, but I didn't turn and accept.

"And if she doesn't?"

"She will. She always comes back."

No, they don't always come back. "Why don't you hang on to my number? If you change your mind, call me."

* * *

"I see the beautiful Ola ratted me out." Luca caught my eyes in the mirror behind the shelves of liquor as he leaned against the bar in my nightclub.

It was late afternoon, so the place wasn't open, but he was never one to pay attention to normal business hours.

I glanced at Ola, my best bartender, restocking the shelves. The bottles were color-coordinated with lights illuminating from behind. Alessia and I had disagreed on the arrangement of the bottles when we'd opened the place together. I wanted the liquor sorted by type, but she clearly won, and I couldn't help but smile at the memory of her little victory dance.

"You okay, Boss?" Ola set her palms on the acrylic resin bar-top counter, the burnt wood finish beneath the liquid bar top shiny. Her bright blue nails were chipped, and they tapped with annoyance. Luca, most likely, the cause.

"Can you give us a minute?" I requested.

"Sure thing." Her nose crinkled, the few freckles there disappearing with the movement. A silent I-hate-him in her pale green eyes as she threw a glance at Luca before leaving.

A moment later, the door at the side of the bar swung shut, affording Luca and myself privacy. "What're you doing here?"

"What? No hug?" His brownish-blond hair flipped up at the back collar of his leather jacket, and he swept a few long hairs out of his face.

"You know I don't hug." I removed my coat and tossed it over the back of the bar chair, which was covered in a red fabric with gold buttons. The seats looked like they belonged on the set of a French cabaret show. *Moulin Rouge*, Ma's favorite. Alessia had known that, too. "Why are you here?"

Luca was a top-tier fixer for The League of Brothers like I'd once been. Sort of like a general in command of an army. Only the battleground was off-the-books and we played by a different set of rules.

"Here on vacation. It was a last-minute trip, and I didn't want you to hear it from someone else I was in town."

Luca's idea of a vacation was stealing a priceless artifact for the hell of it, parachuting into a jungle to see if he could survive (so far, he had), and participating in wild weekends of sex with too many women at once on islands in the Mediterranean. Needless to say, trouble usually followed wherever he went, especially lately.

So, if he was in my city, I'd need to keep an eye on my friend.

"You could've called." I took a seat, still a bit out of sorts after my talk with Declan.

He was a thief, but I'd been one, too. And I'd been a kid who had his ma disappear on him whenever she went to score drugs. And I had a feeling it was the same for Declan.

"Call you? That'd take the fun out of the surprise." He collapsed onto the chair next to me and snatched his scotch.

"So, who'd you bring with you on this last-minute trip?" I asked after a few seconds had passed, hoping I could trust he was telling the truth about his visit. "You don't ever travel alone on vacation."

He side-eyed me. "I'm taking time off from women for a while. It's just me."

"What? You dating men now?"

"Shit, maybe I should. I keep getting burned by women." He finished the rest of his drink and set the empty tumbler back down. "Nah, forget that. I love pussy way too much." He repeated his words in French. "So anyway, I'm between jobs, and I thought maybe it'd be the perfect time to get to know the real me."

"And this journey of self-discovery brought you to Dublin, huh?" Too many scenarios of how his trip could go seriously wrong latched hold of me.

"Okay, truth? I missed my friend." He slapped a hand over my shoulder. "You seeing anyone? Like for more than one night? Or are you still obsessed with the one you *think* you can't have?"

"I'm not obsessed," I grumbled.

Only Luca knew about Holly McGregor.

I never actually admitted to him I wanted her, but he'd figured it out, and what pissed me off was the fact he'd read me so easily. I wasn't normally such a fecking open book.

"Why don't you just sleep with her and get her out of your system?" He got off the stool and circled the bar to grab the Glenlivet and refill his drink.

"Make yourself at home, why don't ya?"

"Always do." He grabbed a second glass and poured me a scotch, too.

"I can't be with her, and you know why."

But the problem was I didn't want anyone else. I'd sent the blonde home, orgasm-free to her dismay, after Holly's birthday party last night.

I was a man who needed sex like I needed air to breathe, and I wasn't fucking having any. And it was because of Holly.

I couldn't have her, and the sooner my dick realized that the better. But the fucker kept holding out for her. A stubborn son of a bitch.

"Wow." Luca's mouth tightened as he fought a smile. "You have it bad." He was grinning now and loving every minute of my pain.

"I don't—"

"Shut up," he said before pouring the scotch down his throat. "She's gorgeous. Any man or woman would want a piece of that ass." He set his forearms on the bar and leaned forward. "But men go absolutely nuts over a woman they can't have. That's all it is. *Ce n'est pas de l'amour.*"

"I never said it was love." I wish it were as simple as screwing Holly and moving on, but no, of course not. It had to be complicated. "Don't you have someplace you need to be?" I stood. "Trouble to stay *out* of?"

I had somewhere I needed to be.

I needed to head to my hotel and jerk off. I was going to be seeing Holly tonight, she just didn't know it yet.

I rarely lost control. My actions were always in check. I'd mastered the art of managing my emotions years ago. But when it came to people I had a soft spot for—my mother, Alessia, and now Holly (even if she didn't know it), my thinking wasn't always clear.

And with Holly coming to the club with that Hollywood arse tonight, I'd very possibly lose my shite and slug the guy.

Or worse, I might even tell Holly the truth about how I felt.

CHAPTER FOUR

DUBLIN, IRELAND - FIVE YEARS AGO

SEBASTIAN

"You're sure this is what you want?" I asked my sister, not sure how I felt about owning a nightclub in the city I grew up in, or anywhere for that matter.

Alessia shifted on the leather to better face me. We were sitting at a booth on the second floor of a three-tiered club. Lasers and bright lights flashed around the room. Some Swedish house DJ was spinning in front of a wild crowd on the first level.

We were waiting for the owner of the club to join us so we could give our answer as to whether we wanted to make the purchase.

"We agreed on hotels to start off with, but"—she held two excited fists in front of her lips, her eyes widening—"this has always been my dream. The music. The energy. Can't you feel it?"

Yeah, well, Alessia was twenty-one. So, her idea of a good time was a bit different than mine. I'd been in these places, with these types of crowds, long before I'd even turned eighteen.

"But like the hotels, this place would have to be solely in my name. Are you sure you're okay with that?" No one could know we had a connection. If anyone ever found out she was Alessia Romano instead of Josie McClintock—we'd both be in trouble.

"Of course." She threw her arms over my shoulders and hugged me.

I wasn't quite sure if I'd ever get used to being hugged, but she seemed to like it, and I'd do my best to handle it. And maybe someday I'd figure out how to be the one to hug her first.

I still couldn't believe a year had gone by since she came into my life, turning my world upside down.

I'd been hesitant to let her in, but she'd refused to give up on me. And then she'd spun her grand idea of us working together and putting the inheritance to good use.

Alessia had wanted to use the money to build our own empire.

We'd purchased three hotels in the last few months, all currently in the process of undergoing a facelift. Dublin, London, and Paris.

But the nightclub business?

I wasn't sure I wanted her around a bunch of arseholes hitting on her and attempting God knew what. I'd begun training her in self-defense moves a few months ago for whenever I wasn't around, but still.

She looked happy, so how could I deny her? Plus, the money was hers. It'd always be her inheritance. She'd pleaded with me to be part of her life, and so here I was, trying to act like a businessman when I barely knew how to be a brother.

"I have another surprise for you when we leave here." She pulled away from me, her bottom lip firm between her teeth. A nervous look in her eyes, even visible in the shitty lighting.

"Do I even want to know?"

"I think so."

"Sorry to keep you waiting," Lydia, the owner, joined us.

She recently married a guy from Dubai and was in a rush to sell to be with her new husband. Alessia had jumped at the chance the second she'd seen the ad, practically poetic about the "rare gem" of a place it was.

"What do you think?" Lydia's lips spread into a wide smile. She was pretty young to own the place. Barely forty from where I sat. Then again, Alessia was twenty-one, and she'd be handling the club. "I know what Josie thinks, but what about you, Mr. Renaud?"

I'd still have to get used to that last name. Alessia had chosen both of our identities without consulting me first. A surprise gift, validation she believed we could make working together possible.

She'd even managed to find the best hacker money could buy on her own to create our identities. He'd scrubbed my previous life as Sebastian Ryan from existence, too.

When she'd presented her plan with a plea in her eyes and hope in her voice, how could I say no and break her heart? I'd tried. Several times. But here we were. I'd caved. If she could convince a man like me to do whatever she wanted, she'd bring the men of Europe to their knees in a boardroom. I was pretty damn proud of her skills, to be honest.

She'd really thought of everything. Well, almost everything.

"I like it." More importantly, Alessia wanted it. The location was at the heart of the city, the size was impressive, and it didn't need much work. "Need to upgrade the selection of whiskeys," I added with a smile, "but yeah, we'll take it."

Alessia tapped a finger at her lip. "Maybe color code the bottles, too."

Lydia held her forefinger in the air. "One question."

And here it is.

"How come I've never heard of you before, Mr. Renaud? I obviously ran a background check on you before our meeting, but I was surprised to discover there's absolutely nothing about you prior to your thirtieth birthday. Not even a record of your birth. No former addresses."

Alessia had planned everything down to the smallest detail with one exception. She'd neglected to have the hacker create a past life for me. Talk about a red flag.

I could feel my sister's eyes on me, curious as to what in the hell I was going to say. She hadn't thought about this before, and I'd never brought it up because she'd been so excited about what she'd done on her own without my help.

The hotels we'd acquired were sold to me by men I'd made deals with in the past to avoid such questions on my background.

I coughed into a closed fist and directed my focus on the woman. "Truth?"

"That'd be ideal," Lydia answered.

"If I tell you, I'll have to kill you," I said in a low voice, offering her my most intense look before grinning. "Kidding," I quickly added, and this produced a smile from her. "But honestly, I worked for the government, and I can't really divulge my past. It's classified."

Her mouth rounded at my bullshit. "What government?"

"Also classified." Maybe I was better at spinning this new me than I thought because she appeared to be buying it.

She studied me for a few more seconds. "I guess the club will be in good hands then. And since you're paying in cash, it's a deal." She extended a hand, but I motioned toward Alessia. It was her club. She should shake on it.

"Wow. I, um." Alessia rose from the table when Lydia stepped away to take a call. "I messed up on your identity, didn't I?" She moved to the railing, which overlooked the dancers below.

I strode up next to her. "It's fine."

"Why didn't you say anything before?"

"You were excited about us working together, and I didn't want to—"

"Disappoint me?" She faced me and reached for my forearm, but I didn't move. "For the record, you could never disappoint me."

She really had no idea how wrong she was—I was disappointing her every second of the day, she just didn't know it.

I was still in The League even though I'd promised her I left my old life behind when we started working together.

I focused back on the crowd below, my gaze falling upon a group at the bar. More specifically, one woman.

I couldn't take my eyes off her. Long dark hair. A gorgeous body. And when she turned to talk to someone, it was then that I saw all of her. And she had the face of an angel.

"Sorry for slipping away like that," Lydia said upon return.

"You know who that is?" I pointed to the angel at the bar who was now laughing at something the guy to her left was saying, and for some inexplicable reason, I wanted it to be me standing next to her, making her laugh.

Maybe there'd be benefits to owning this club after all.

"Ah. The McGregors. Holly's having her twenty-first birthday party, and she's the reason why we have one of the hottest DJs in Europe spinning tonight."

That was a shot to the balls. Twenty-one was too young for me. Twenty-one was my sister's age, so . . .

Alessia followed my focus to Holly. "Are the McGregors important people or something?"

"Their family business provides a lot of jobs here," Lydia explained. "They're also billionaires, so there's that."

I flipped through The League members in my head, trying to remember if the McGregors were on it, but I didn't think so. There wasn't even a League leader in Dublin.

"I know a Cole McGregor. I'm sure he's not related to them, though. He lives in Manhattan." Something in her tone . . . she was sad, wasn't she?

"Oh, that's their cousin. He's probably down there with them. They always celebrate together." The way her lips twitched into a smile and her eyes seemed to gleam with pride, had me assuming the McGregors were most likely not of the arsehole-variety, which was surprising for a bunch of rich kids. "How do you know Cole?"

A connection to her past life. Great.

Alessia stole a glimpse at me out of the corner of her eye, then moved back and out of the line of sight of the people down below.

The last thing we needed was for this Cole guy to recognize her.

"Should I give you two a minute?" Lydia was more perceptive than I'd given her credit for.

"Yes, please." I watched her retreat before returning my

focus to the McGregors. Well, to the woman I wished I could take to bed tonight.

When Holly's gaze lifted, as if she could feel my eyes on her, I stepped back next to Alessia and into the dark where I belonged.

"That guy gonna be a problem?"

I also wanted to know whether or not they'd dated and if I needed to break his legs, but I kept those thoughts to myself.

"We lived in the same building in New York." Her lips drew into a tight line.

"That all?"

Silence stretched, and it had me worried.

This brother thing was still new to me, and I wasn't sure how long it'd take to get used to.

"A close friend as well. He watched out for me. Helped me when my mom died." Her words were drowning in regret, filling the space between us.

Was her sadness due to the loss of her mother, or the life and friends I'd forced her to leave behind?

She blinked a few times and waved a hand between us. "Come on, let's finish with Lydia. I still have that other surprise." She grabbed hold of my arm, and I'd opted to let the topic of Cole and her past go.

We wrapped up the deal in Lydia's office, which would soon become Alessia's, then we left for part two of the night —whatever she had planned.

Ten minutes later, the limo parked outside of a French restaurant, and Alessia turned in the backseat to face me.

"What's special about this place?" I glanced at the sign above the door. *Les Fleurs*.

"I've asked a lot of you," she said in a soft voice. "But one of the reasons I wanted to get the club in Dublin, the hotel here, and now this place, is because I wanted you to feel like you're home again. This is where you're from, and I want to get to know the you before . . ."

I gripped the bridge of my nose and inhaled at the comment I knew was coming.

"The you before you became one of *them*."

She didn't know anything about The League of Brothers, including their name. I'd been intentionally vague. No reason to go into detail about my job as a fixer and the things I'd done.

"Dublin was your mom's home, but you said she also loved Paris, which was why you moved there as a kid," she began when I didn't speak. "She took you every Sunday to get croissants, and I thought it'd be nice if you owned a French restaurant here sort of as—"

"Alessia." My chest tightened. I didn't know how to handle emotions like these. I'd shut off the ability to feel the day Ma died. And I'd needed to become even harder, colder, as a fixer for The League.

Part of me wondered if my heart would still work if I attempted to flip on the emotion switch again. Did I have it in me to love? To feel?

I also didn't know why I'd told her so much about my ma. I guess when she'd been walking down memory lane with stories of her mother before she'd passed away in a car accident, I'd felt some need to defend what happened with my mother. To let her know Ma wasn't just a junkie.

"We're going to get through this. Together. We have each other now," she said, tears in her eyes.

"I know." I kissed the top of her forehead and forced a smile to my face, even if something in my gut told me that no, we'd be far from okay.

CHAPTER FIVE

PRESENT DAY

HOLLY

"TODAY'S BEEN AMAZING. THANK YOU." HARRISON'S LIPS parted into a devastating smile as we sat across from one another at dinner.

We'd hit up so many places, including Guinness Storehouse, The Church Bar, Dublin Castle, and Trinity.

"You came at a great time when there aren't so many tourists here."

"Are we that bad?" He smiled.

"Nah, we love you Americans." I squinted. "For the most part."

He eyed the half-eaten bowl of traditional Irish stew. "And since we tried a drink at every place we visited, I don't have much room for food." He lifted his glass to mine.

"Enough room for more beer, though?"

"Always." He winked.

"Sláinte." We clinked our glasses together.

"This pint of Gat is pretty damn good." His eyes thinned, probably noting the amused look on my face as he tried to sound like a local. "Did I say that right?"

"You're bang on." I returned the glass to the table. "You could also order the black stuff and your server would know to bring you a Guinness."

He let go of his drink and reached across the table and placed his hand over mine. "Thank you for today."

I welcomed the warmth of his touch. The slightly fuzzy feeling coursing through my body right now wasn't from the beer or the Jameson whiskey we'd had earlier. I was pretty sure I was finally relaxed. It'd been awhile since I'd felt at ease, too.

After walking around the city and seeing Dublin through Harrison's eyes, it'd also reminded me how much I truly loved my home.

The city had a certain kind of energy I always missed when I traveled. And yeah, maybe it rained a lot here—but bright side? Ireland was pretty damn lush and green because of it.

We'd started our day early, and part of that had to do with my guilt about how I'd ended last night. After Sebastian walked me back to the party, I hadn't been in the mood to dance or do much socializing with anyone, and since Harrison had come to Dublin early to spend time with me, I'd wanted to make it up to him this weekend.

"What was your favorite part about today?"

"Easy." His smile reached his eyes. "Spending it with you."

I sucked in a deep breath, the lingering smell of ciggies buried into the ancient wallpaper at my side stale and bitter.

I'd have to exhale at some point.

But damn if I'd know what to say once I could breathe again.

I'd never be able to fall for him, even if I wanted to. It was nice to push inappropriate thoughts of Sebastian out of my head for a day and be present with someone who wasn't so dark on the inside, but I didn't want to mislead Harrison either.

"What else should I know about the city?" His lips were still pulled into a smile. "Or is there anything I should or shouldn't say while I'm here?"

"Well, don't ever ask a Dubliner to say, '*top o' the mornin' to ya'*—we really don't say that here. And never get into a conversation with a taxi driver unless you enjoy losing an argument. They're debate experts, and believe me, they'll win." I tapped at my lip. "We use the word feck or fuck liberally, and which one can depend on our mood. Same with shit and shite. Ass and arse."

"I noticed that, and I gotta admit, hearing you say those words . . ." He cleared his throat, and a touch of red moved up the column of his neck.

I quickly sputtered a few other words we used as well as their meanings, then asked, "You need a pen to take notes?"

He tapped at his temple. "All here."

"There might be an exam later," I teased.

"Anything else?" His eyes traveled to my mouth for a quick second.

"Yeah," I said, trying to save myself from the continued rise of color I could feel crossing my face, "you've probably heard someone say by now *craic*. Sounds like the word crack in America."

"And that means fun, right?"

"Right, but if you use it, you'll probably still come across as a tourist."

"Got it." He checked the time on his watch. "We should probably get you home to change for part two of the evening."

I had no idea where he was taking me tonight, but he'd said he owed me the surprise this time since I'd spent the day as his tour guide.

"You sure you're up for spending the night with me?"

And now my cheeks were on fire.

Bloody hell.

* * *

"Honestly, I couldn't think of anything that someone like you hasn't done before." Harrison's arm was looped with mine as we started across the Ha'penny Bridge over River Liffey. The lights from the nearby buildings blinked on the river, different colors popping. "Hope you enjoyed tonight."

"You kidding? A helicopter ride over my city? It was amazing. It's been a few years since I've been in one, and I rather enjoyed your company."

He stopped midway on the bridge and moved to the white railing overlooking the water. My brother had planned to propose to Anna here, but he ended up being spontaneous instead. This bridge was a staple on postcards tourists sent home to loved ones. For me, it'd always be the place where I'd come to try and clear my head. And I'd been doing a lot of that lately.

Of course, I might rethink walking alone at night after what happened in the park.

"Let me guess, your family owns a chopper?"

I nodded. "My brother Adam learned to fly."

"That guy sounds like a man of many talents."

"Something tells me you're similar."

Harrison took a step closer, gently placed his hand on my bicep, and skated his fingers along my coat up to my head. He moved in and threaded his fingers through my hair, which fell in soft waves over my shoulders.

He wanted to kiss me, didn't he?

"I've had an incredible time." His hand remained at the back of my head, fingers still caressing my hair, and I didn't know what to do or say. "I'm glad I came early."

"I'm honored to be the one to show you the city, and I, um, look forward to us working together. If you're still thinking of partnering with McGregor Enterprises, that is."

My talk of work had him lowering his hand back to his side.

Was it a cold slap of reality?

"About that."

His two words struck a nerve. Nothing ever good followed *about that.*

He scratched at his trimmed beard. "I do have some concerns about one of your board members."

"Oh." The word was more like a drawn-out breath. I knew what was coming. How could I not?

"I was hoping you'd come with me tonight to talk with Renaud."

Sebastian I-Hate-Him Renaud. Of course.

"I really do want to work with you and your family, Holly, but—"

"You don't trust him," I interrupted, my shoulders sagging.

Sebastian was going to ruin everything.

He'd already ruined me for every other man, and he'd never even kissed me.

But this impacted our company. First, the land deal in Limerick. And now the movie with Reed Productions.

Sebastian's mere presence at McGregor would be enough to destroy us. He wouldn't need to even lift a finger.

"Renaud's expecting us at his club tonight. He's agreed to answer a few of my questions."

This was a shock. Sebastian open up?

"Why didn't you mention him to me before?" A touch of distrust painted a fine line through his tone, and I regretted hearing it, even if I deserved it.

"He's our newest board member, and I'm still trying to wrap my head around his intentions," I admitted. "I'm sorry I didn't bring him up to you whenever we've talked. I don't even know much about him." Aside from rumors. Apart from the fact I wanted his body pressed to mine and his tongue in my mouth.

I reached for Harrison's arm this time, resting a palm on the material of his overcoat. His eyes tracked the movement of my hand and remained there for what felt like forever before he looked back at me.

"You must already know what our family has been through this year, not just with Anna's abduction."

We'd been questioned for the murder of Donovan Hannigan.

Da had a heart attack.

During Anna's abduction, Da had been arrested (and cleared) for the murder of the businessman who'd been blackmailing Da to try and force the sale of our media division.

I discovered my parents had separated and lied to us about it.

Da resigned as CEO and chairman of the board, and Adam had stepped back as well.

The media had pushed and poked. They'd done damage. Drew blood.

This year had been a whirlwind. But at least my brother finally got his happily ever after. He deserved it.

"Sebastian, well, he seized the chance to buy our stock when investors began dumping it because of all the bad luck we'd had," I explained, "and he somehow got himself onto the board. But—"

"I'm the last person you have to worry about in regard to the media's spin on the truth. I'm used to ignoring them given my profession." A small smile met his lips. "And I wouldn't have asked for your help on this movie if I didn't think we could make this work."

"But?"

"*But,* I didn't do a thorough check of your board members until this past week when I'd made the decision to come meet with you."

"Oh." My hand plummeted to my side.

"I just want to clear a few things up." He brushed the pad of his thumb over my cheek. "I need to have a better understanding of Renaud's intentions before we move forward."

"Understandable." It took all my strength to allow that word to slip from my lips, though.

He motioned for us to walk again, taking my arm with his as if we'd been friends, or maybe lovers, for years. "You should know I called my sister today," he said in a low voice. "I asked her to have her husband look into Renaud. If anyone can find out the truth, it's him."

I stopped at his words and pulled my arm free of his.

If our friend, who was former MI6, couldn't find anything on Sebastian, how would Harrison's brother-in-law have any luck? "Why talk to Sebastian tonight then?"

"To get a read on him myself and also . . ." He took a breath. "I have more than one sister, and if anyone was a threat to one of them, I'd stop at nothing to keep them safe." His lips crooked at the edges.

"You think of me like a sister?" If that was the case, I'd completely misread him.

"God, no." He briefly covered his mouth with his hand. "There's something about you. And I have this desire to—"

"Protect me?" I whispered.

"Is it crazy?" His broad shoulders arched back as he stood tall before me. A wall of masculine strength. A man who could keep me safe if I wanted him to.

His mouth edged near mine like an invitation for a kiss, one he was waiting to see if I'd accept.

"We shouldn't, right?" he asked without losing sight of my parted lips.

I stepped back, needing a second to breathe. To think.

"I'm sorry." His voice was low and forgiving.

"Don't be."

I could do this. I could get through this night.

Yeah, sure. And there are really leprechauns with pots of gold at the end of rainbows.

CHAPTER SIX

HOLLY

THE LAST TIME I ENTERED THIS CLUB HAD BEEN THE NIGHT OF Anna's bachelorette party. The place was the hottest spot in the city, even if I didn't want to admit it.

It had once been a textile factory, and the interior remained a tribute to its former days with all the iron and steel. Now the industrial look was draped in elegance and gleamed with sophistication. Chrome tables and satin couches, overflowing with gorgeous guests in their designer labels, circled the exterior of the dance area.

The dancers bumped into each other as they crowded the main attraction, the dance floor, moving to the pulsating beats of the DJ, who tonight was spinning actual vinyl instead of CDJs, a great selection ranging from Calvin Harris to the more old-school beats of New Order. Every few minutes, a touch of fog burst from a machine filling the area as the lights flickered and flashed in rhythmic beat with the music, too.

Chic and posh. Too-tall heels. Champagne flutes or martini glasses in hands. A lit-up mirror behind the wall of liquor at the main bar. Yeah, the place was amazing. But . . . it belonged to the man I wanted to hate. Correction, *did* hate.

I stood from the chair at the high-top table we'd been sitting at while we waited for my brother to join us. "He's here," I announced at the sight of Sean entering the main doors into the club, a woman attached to him as well—her arm tight with his as they strode toward us.

Harrison had invited Sean last night while I'd been at the park nearly getting mugged.

"Did you mention your plan for tonight to him?" I looked back toward the bar, wondering if Sebastian had made an appearance yet. Of course, I usually felt the man before I saw him.

"Yeah, I did." He stood once Sean was before us.

"Hey, Sweets." Sean pulled me in for a hug and kissed my cheek, then shook Harrison's hand. "This is . . ."

Oh please God, remember your date's name. Don't be that guy anymore.

"Trisha," he said as if he'd worked damn hard to remember. "We just met in spin class this morning," Sean explained as if reading my thoughts.

"Since when do you do spin class?" I tried not to laugh at the picture of my brother on a stationary bike inside a gym.

"I think he may have followed me in there." Trisha's white teeth flashed when her red lips spread into a wide smile. Her lips matched the tight red dress that wrapped around her body like it'd been painted on, barely covering much of her legs. "He had no idea what to do."

"Or how damn hard it'd be to ride a bloody bike," Sean said with a laugh.

"Spin is pretty big in Hollywood. Hot yoga, too," Harrison spoke up.

"Oh?" I stole a look at him. "You do hot yoga?"

"Of course." The flashing lights crossed his face, making his gray eyes glimmer. "Don't you?" he teased.

"Six a.m. classes before work a few times a week. Helps relax me before I start my day."

"Maybe I'll join you on my next visit," he offered, and I could feel Sean's burning gaze on us. His intense scrupulous stare. He didn't like what he'd heard regarding Harrison's reputation. The man reminded him too much of himself.

We all approached the bar area after exchanging a few more words.

"Can I get you two anything to drink?" The bartender was pretty, and totally Ethan's type. Light blonde hair in a high ponytail, a black scoop-neck tee with the words *Bite Me* in red letters below her cleavage, and blue lipstick to match her nails.

"Bottle of Armand de Brignac, please," Sean ordered, palms on the counter, eyes straight on her.

The bartender placed a chilled bottle on the counter, and the signature Ace of Spades at the center of the gold bottle held my eye.

"You have good taste," she said with a European accent, which was deep and sexy. And apparently like candy to my brother, because he couldn't seem to wipe the stupid grin from his face. Guess she was also his type.

She smiled at him while opening the bottle, but there was something more playful than sexy in her expression, like she was teasing him into believing he had a chance with her. And I instantly loved her for that.

"We should celebrate. A toast to new friends," Sean said while passing out the flutes.

I quickly guzzled the expensive liquid, not giving the bubbles time to tickle the back of my throat.

"A word?" Sean asked a moment later and tipped his head to the side. I silently allowed him to lead me away from the bar and off to the side of the dance floor. "You seem tense. You okay about tonight?"

"Harrison may cancel the deal because of Renaud. So no, I'm not okay," I blurted, hoping he could hear me over the sudden changeover of songs to one that had a deeper bass, and I waved away the fog that began to fill the space between us.

"Don't worry. We have a plan."

Wait, what? Before I could ask more, my skin prickled with awareness.

My cousin Bree's young son, Jack, would call these "Spidey" senses. I was caught up in an insane web of desire —every inch of my body consumed by tingles, every hair standing on end whenever Sebastian was in the same room.

"He's here," he said, and I turned toward the bar, waving away more fog to get a clear view. "We shouldn't leave Harrison alone with Sebastian." Sean took hold of my elbow as if he'd known my knees were about to buckle.

Sebastian had also brought a date. Of course. A woman that could be Heidi Klum's younger sister. Tall. Blonde. Long legs that went down to nude slingback heels. A barely there, glitzy silver dress. Her arm was around his waist, and although it was hard to tell from my vantage point, his hand was most likely positioned on her ass. She probably didn't just take hot yoga, with her figure, she could instruct it, too.

I bet he had a little black book filled to the brim with women's names and phone numbers. Maybe more than one book.

But when his mouth opened, and he laughed at something someone said—dear God in heaven, I stopped in my tracks.

His white teeth flashed, and the column of his throat tightened with the movement, and if I didn't see him laughing myself, I never would've believed it.

"Holly?" Sean urged me to move, but how could I?

Sebastian was so close. Legs encased in dark trousers, an untucked, black button-down dress shirt with sleeves rolled at the elbows, and a simple watch. If Bella thought Harrison was Mr. Sex on a Stick, then dressed in this semi-casual but still sophisticated outfit, Sebastian looked like Mr. He Giveth All The Orgasms God.

When Sebastian's eyes grabbed hold of mine, his laugh died. And I was the reason, wasn't I?

"What's wrong?" Sean whispered into my ear since I was still glued in place.

All I could think about was how Sebastian's hands had felt when he'd held me while dancing, and how his eyes had pierced right through me as if, as crazy as it sounded, he truly cared about me.

But the man he'd been last night in the park, moving so fast, effortlessly taking down the mugger—punching and punching—I had to remember him, too, didn't I?

I just wasn't sure which version of Sebastian was more dangerous to me. Most likely both.

"It's nothing." I went for the thin strap of my black dress when it slipped from my shoulder to my arm and secured it back in place.

One hard swallow. And two quick breaths. Now I was ready to walk. Sort of. Maybe.

But this time, Sean wasn't prepared to move. He tugged at my arm and turned me toward him. "I'm worried. What's going on?"

What would he think if he knew I desired a man no one trusted? I had to get a grip. "I'm fine."

"You sure?"

"Of course." I rejoined everyone, and Harrison placed his hand on the small of my back. The dress I wore fit my body like a glove and stopped just short of my knees. And I had on my strappy and very sexy heels.

Sebastian noticed the position of Harrison's hand, and he removed his palm from his date's back and placed it on the counter at his side. His palm flattened, and his fingers seemed to flex and arch almost aggressively like he was resisting an urge of some kind. The veins in his forearm tightened along with the fit of the material around his bicep.

"I'm Holly." I reached for Sebastian's date's hand since he hadn't bothered to introduce us.

"Ainsley." Her gaze moved over my body. Assessing me as competition, even though to everyone with a pulse at the club, it appeared I was there with Harrison.

"I have a private room upstairs reserved for us." Sebastian lifted his hand from the bar and pointed to the second level. "You ladies will excuse us?" He didn't wait for an answer from Trisha or Ainsley. "Drinks on me," he informed my new favorite bartender. "Anything they want."

"Be back soon." Sean leaned in to press a kiss to Trisha's cheek. I wondered if Sebastian would do the same with his date, but he didn't even say a word.

We followed him up the spiral staircase off to the side of the main dance area. The second level shared the same music as below, the speakers built into the walls, but the ambiance was a touch different. Black leather horseshoe-shaped booths with brass tables and dimmer lighting. A more laid-back feel, one that screamed private lap dances welcome.

We strode past the booths, then stopped outside a room while Sebastian swung open the steel door.

No stripper pole inside, just a leather couch and table in front of it, which had actually been a surprise.

Sebastian dimmed the harsh lights to a warmer setting as I sat on the black leather sofa, which was up against a red-painted wall.

"The glass enables us to see downstairs, but prevents others from seeing in here," Sebastian explained when Harrison walked toward the picture window. "Soundproof, too. Speakers can be turned on and off if you want to hear the DJ. I thought it'd be easier to talk here."

My brother sat on my left and Harrison on the right. I felt safe. Protected between them.

Sebastian remained standing after he shut the door, his towering frame overwhelming the room, which was the size of a jail cell, not that I'd been in one before. "So, what is it that you want to know?" Straightforward and unexpected.

How much truth would we actually be able to get out of this man? How many lies, too? And how would I know the difference?

"I'd really like a partnership with McGregor Enterprises, but I do have some concerns given your presence on the board." Harrison stood as if he felt the need to be on the same level as Sebastian, and I could hardly blame him.

"I think I speak for Reed as well here," Sean added. "What's your interest in our company? And who the hell are you for real?"

Sebastian's lips crooked into a slight smile. "Let me ask you something." He stepped closer to Harrison, but he didn't remove his hands from his pockets.

"What is it, Renaud?" Harrison's question had my heart skipping even higher.

"What do you need from me to make the deal happen?" Sebastian peered my way, his body stiff. Well, when was it not?

Harrison mimicked his position, his hands diving into his pockets. Spine straight. A commanding presence as well. "Sell your shares. Give up your seat on the board."

I pressed my back to the leather in surprise, trying to wrap my head around his bold demand. Was this the plan he and Sean had discussed without me? And what the hell . . . why wouldn't they clue me in on this ahead of time? As far as curveballs go, this was huge.

But no way would Sebastian give in to him, and after what I'd witnessed him capable of with that mugger, he might box Harrison's head off, too.

"That's the only way you'll make a deal?" Sebastian's dark brows pulled together. "And you think dumping all my stock onto the open market will be wise?"

Shit, he was right. It'd be a crushing blow. But we could repurchase some of the stocks, I supposed.

"It's only a movie," he said on a sigh. He looked at me as if seeking my opinion, which didn't make sense because he did what he wanted and didn't give a damn. "And this is what you really want?"

I glimpsed Harrison before setting my focus on my brother, and Sean nodded. "Yes," I managed when I found Sebastian's eyes again.

His jaw tightened as he remained quiet for excruciatingly long seconds. "You have my word then. I'll no longer be involved in the company by the time you begin filming. That's the best offer I can make."

Shock pushed me upright and onto my feet. Sean stood as well.

"You're serious? How can I trust you?" Harrison lifted his hands from his pockets.

"I've never not followed through on a deal before." Sebastian offered his palm.

Was this really happening?

I stood next to Harrison, my heart racing in anticipation of what he was going to do, and my eyes widened in surprise when he took Sebastian's hand.

"It's a deal," Harrison said with a curt nod.

Sebastian glanced at me for a brief moment, and there were a million ways I could interpret the blank expression on his face. But my gut feeling said it was sadness. And then, he up and walked out of the room without another word, the door softly closing behind him.

"I'll, um, be right back." I fled before they could stop me, catching sight of Sebastian striding away. "Wait," I cried, my voice barely registering above the loud music popping around us. But somehow, he'd heard, because he stopped.

He looked back, then at the door off to his right. "In here." He jerked open the door, and I found myself inside a room with the same setup as the last. Only, this time, he locked the door.

I crossed the space in a hurry to get to the glass wall and pressed my palms to the smooth surface.

I got what I wanted. He was going to leave my life before filming began, and hopefully, that wouldn't be too far into the future. So, yeah, I'd won. But the victory felt too easy. Something was off.

I caught sight of Sean and Harrison descending the winding staircase, probably heading for Trisha and Sebastian's plus one.

"What do you want?" He was close. His warm breath like a caress on my skin.

"Why are you giving in?" I whispered.

"Because you want this deal." His voice was steady. Always in control. Why couldn't I be like that around him? "And you want me gone, yes?"

A deal with Sebastian Renaud always came with a price.

"And what do I owe you for this? What kind of favor or debt will I have to repay?" A touch of defeat gripped my words, and I hated the sound of it. "I can't vote in favor of the Limerick deal. I won't do it." I whirled around to face him.

"That deal will happen with or without your support." For a moment, I would've sworn guilt glided through his tone, but then he rasped, "You're powerless to stop it."

I poked at his chest. "You arrogant, son of a—"

I dropped my words at his quick movement. My back hit the glass, and his hands went to my shoulders, caging me in place.

His eyes moved to my mouth as if he were expecting a protest from me. I should demand he release me. I was so mad at him, and yet, I couldn't tell him to back off.

"You can have your movie deal with Reed, but don't sleep with him."

"Excuse me?" I lifted my chin. "Who the hell do you think you—"

This time, it was his lips that stole my words.

They slanted over mine in a hot, almost angry, and crushing kiss. His tongue entered my mouth and took control, and I tried so, so hard not to moan. Not to kiss him back. But the warmth of his touch, the confidence of his kiss, the demand of his mouth for my lips to obey . . . I was done.

His strong hands slipped behind me, cupped my arse, and he lifted me in one swift movement. He guided my legs around his hips, all while keeping me pressed against the window, his lips never losing hold of mine. And that's when I kissed him back. When I gave him my absolute everything. More than I even knew I had inside of me.

My fingernails bit into his shoulder blades as I hung on for dear life.

He tasted like spice and vanilla, hints of something exotic as he killed me in the best possible way with his mouth, delivering a seduction of senses with every sweep of his tongue.

I felt . . . free as he kissed me, even though his physical hold of me contradicted the very meaning of the word.

And I nearly choked out a "Don't stop!" when our mouths parted. But his whispered words at my ear prevented such insanity. "This can never happen again." And like that, he let go.

The back of my hand raced across my slightly swollen lips as I regained my composure. My chest was too tight. The pressure between my legs unbearable.

The erection in his pants said it all. He was hurting as much as I was.

"Why'd you kiss me?" I repositioned the straps of my dress, hoping when I returned downstairs, no one would be able to see the evidence of my lapse in judgment.

"I'm sorry." His words sounded almost genuine.

"You don't seem like a man to apologize."

"I'm not." He started to turn, but I grabbed his bicep, and he halted. He was hard as a rock beneath my palm.

"You should let go." His voice was a cool whisper over my skin, which served to take the edge off the explosive heat raging inside of me.

"You're confusing." I lowered my hand. "You refuse to pull back on this push to sell the land in Limerick. You're agreeing to walk away from McGregor for the sole purpose of helping me secure a deal with Harrison. And yet, you don't want me romantically, or physically, involved with him."

"That's not true." He faced me straight on, his eyes thinning. "I don't want you with anyone."

"And that includes you?"

He leaned in so close that all I'd have to do was press up in my heels to touch his lips with mine. "Especially me."

CHAPTER SEVEN

SEBASTIAN

I LEANED BACK ON THE COUCH OFF TO THE SIDE OF THE dance floor and clenched my free hand into a fist on my lap. I was nursing a scotch and doing my best to stay seated while Holly danced in my line of sight. I shouldn't have been watching her, but she'd slammed back shot after shot, and I couldn't have some arsehole trying to take advantage of her, which included Harrison. Honestly, I was surprised she could still stand, let alone dance.

Ola swapped my empty drink for another a moment later, and after I thanked her and she left, I waved off a brunette who'd attempted to join me on the couch.

"Do you enjoy pain?"

I forced my eyes off Holly and tracked the voice to Luca standing alongside the couch in his usual club clothes. Jeans and a white, untucked dress shirt, paired with a gray blazer and matching oxfords. His hair was gelled back away from his face, but he pushed at it anyway as if expecting a piece to fall into his eyes.

"Sometimes pain is the only way you know you're alive."

"Is that some existential shit?" He dropped down next to me and slapped a hand between us. "I don't know how you do it, *mon ami*."

I didn't have a choice. She could never be mine in the way I wanted, but I also knew it was insane to demand her not to be with anyone else, including Reed.

The idea of that man in bed with her—his mouth on her . . . I wanted to kill him. To wrap my hands around his neck and choke the life out of him.

"You have no intention of taking my advice, do you?"

"No." I'd just tasted her lips. Had my tongue in her mouth. My hands on her. It wasn't even close to enough. I'd never get enough of her. I had become an addict like Ma. My addiction: Holly. "Christmas," I said. "After Christmas, I'll be out of her life for good."

That had been the plan all along, but Reed didn't need to know that. McGregor Enterprises was back on its feet, and there was only one deal I needed to close, then I'd be out of her life for good.

"I have a hard time picturing you walking away."

Holly shoved her hands through her long, dark locks as she moved seductively to the song. Her hands then followed the lines of her body to her full tits on display in her fitted black dress, her cleavage making my mouth water. She continued to work her hands down her hips, and I dragged my gaze to her long, shapely legs in those fucking redder-than-red heels.

"Where's your date? If Holly's here, you must have brought one along," he joked, but the man knew me well.

I spotted Ainsley on the dance floor, not too far away

from Holly, grinding up against some other guy. She was only a friend and had been well aware of the fact that I had no intention of hooking up with her. And Luca was right; I'd brought Ainsley along to try and maintain a distance from Holly. A clear failure.

"If you don't have sex with someone tonight, I'm worried you'll kill a guy." I glanced at him out of the corner of my eye, and he pressed a hand to his chest. "I'd prefer that guy not to be me." He smiled. "And is that Harrison Reed at your bar?"

I shifted on the couch, uncomfortable at the mere mention of his name. "You know him?"

"He's famous, so yeah, everyone knows him."

"Right." I set the glass down on the table in front of me and rolled my neck from side to side, trying to loosen up.

"That's some luck. She with him?"

"Co-workers," I rushed out.

"Yeah, sure." He motioned for a nearby server and ordered a vodka tonic. "I—"

I shook my head, warning him not to continue when I spotted Sean on his way. "Can you give us a minute?" I asked Luca.

Luca lifted his chin my way, then left.

Sean remained standing in front of the couch, blocking my view of Holly. "Are you serious about leaving the company?" A drawl of suspicion moved through his tone.

"Yes, but I'll give your family advanced notice, so you have a chance to purchase the stock back at a fair price," I spoke up so he could hear over the song blasting through the speakers.

"What do you really want in return?"

He didn't believe me, and maybe I didn't blame him, but I was telling the truth. "Nothing."

"I don't believe that. If you think this little stunt will get you into my sister's—"

"I'd stop now," I warned, now standing.

"If anything ever happens to her, I'll end you."

"I'd count on it, or you wouldn't be much of a big brother, would you?"

His forehead tightened, but then he surprised me by turning and walking away.

I approached the bar and motioned for Ola's attention. "No more shots for her."

She nodded, but then tipped her chin as a signal to stop talking.

"You really didn't just do that, did you?"

I hung my head at the sound of Holly's voice. "You shouldn't drink so much. Not at my club, at least."

"I can make my own decisions."

I turned to face her, finding the tight draw of her angry lips and her squared-back shoulders ridiculously sexy. "Apparently not, or you wouldn't have let me kiss you."

"I didn't *let* you." She wrinkled her adorable nose in dispute to my claim. Her embarrassment was cute. "You didn't give me a choice."

I leaned in closer and brought my mouth near her ear. "Says the fingernail marks on my back."

If I hadn't been wearing a shirt, she would've drawn blood, and if the lighting wasn't shit in here, I'd surely see the familiar rise of heat up her neck and into her cheeks.

She was always so damn confident and collected *except* around me. I shouldn't love that fact, either, since I was supposed to stay away from her, but I did.

"Like you said," she bit out, "it'll never happen again."

"Everything okay?"

Reed. "She was just saying goodbye. Make sure she gets home safe."

"Planned on it." I could tell he wanted to say more, and so did I, but there were no more warnings to dole out, were there? And so, we had no further reason to discuss Holly.

She wasn't mine.

I reached into my pocket at the feel of my mobile vibrating.

A message from someone at the Garda—the police. Most Dubliners referred to them as The Guards, the protectors of the city. But without me, I wasn't sure how much success they'd have in doing just that.

"I have to go." I held her eyes, and for a moment, her lips parted as if she might protest my departure. But then that full, luscious mouth of hers thinned, forced into a tight line. "Good night."

* * *

"Thank you." I gave the officer a nod as Declan shoved past me and started for the exit. "Pretty damn ungrateful considering I bailed your arse out of jail," I said once we were outside. "What were you thinking?"

"I didn't know he was Garda!" he hissed.

"That's not the point. I told you to stop stealing."

He whirled around and threw an angry finger in the air. "Women! You didn't say I couldn't steal from anyone else."

He was shivering, so I removed my gray wool coat and handed it to him. It was colder than normal, below five degrees Celsius.

"No way!"

"Don't be a stubborn arse." I pushed it his direction. "And where's Samuel?"

"Sleeping." He snatched the coat and muttered a *Thank you*, but didn't put it on.

"Thank you? Did I hear ya right?"

"Yeah, well, it won't happen again." He turned, but I caught his arm.

"Damn right. We're getting your brother, and you're going to the hotel. You can leave a note for your ma to call me when she comes home."

He remained still. Contemplative.

"You worried she'll come home and not care?"

"No," he yelled.

"Then what?" I cocked my head.

"She's never been gone this long. I-I don't think she's coming back." His voice was barely a whisper.

I pinched the bridge of my nose. "I'll find her, okay?"

"Why do you care?" His shoulders sagged, and it was obvious he was puzzled. He'd never had help from anyone before, and I didn't think he knew how to accept it. "I don't understand."

"I told you I was once like you." I let my arms fall heavy to my sides, the cold night air chilling my body, a much-needed change after being around Holly, where I'd almost let the depths of hell consume me with my need for her.

"I need more." He was back to being the tough guy.

"And I don't talk about my past, so you're just going to have to be satisfied with whatever I choose to tell you." I didn't mean to lose my cool, but after the night I'd had . . . I was on the edge of control, not a place I was comfortable.

"I can't repay you, though. I—"

"Work at the club, remember?"

"That doesn't seem fair."

"Life isn't fair, so if someone gives you something, don't turn it down. Don't be stupid." The rage cut through my tone again no matter how much I tried to crush it. "I don't give out third chances."

My own regrets bled through my words.

"If not for you, do it for your brother." If he was anything like me, he'd stop at nothing to protect his family the way I'd once desperately tried to do.

I may have failed, but with any luck, his story wouldn't turn out the same.

CHAPTER EIGHT

PARIS, FRANCE - FOUR AND A HALF YEARS AGO

SEBASTIAN

"ALESSIA ROMANO IS YOUR SISTER, AM I CORRECT?" THE abrupt switch from French to English didn't throw me, it was his words that were like daggers to the heart.

I stood from the other side of his desk and braced a hand in front of me for support as I wrapped my head around Édouard Moreau's words. Moreau, the leader of *La Ligue des Frères* in France, knew my secret. And now I knew why he'd really summoned me to his office in Paris.

"The wealth you inherited. You lied to me, Sebastian." He unbuttoned his jacket, removed it, then began working at the sleeves of his dress shirt. "You're like a son to me, how could you?"

More knives to the heart. I was going to be butchered at this rate.

He'd been the man to bring me into the organization. To take me off the streets and give me a new home. A cause to believe in. A reason to live.

I'd stolen his Ferrari out of his garage when I was eighteen. His fortress-like mansion had been dubbed impenetrable, but I'd gotten into his garage without breaking much of a sweat. Of course, Moreau had his men find me, but instead of hurting me, he made an offer.

"Anthony Romano was your father, am I right? The American billionaire." He looked out the window that had a perfect view of the Eiffel Tower in the distance. The tops of the trees down below filled my line of sight when I joined him to share the view.

Paris. Ma's favorite city. Then again, she'd never traveled much to see the rest of the world. But she'd loved the air of romance in the city she claimed wrapped her up like a comforting blanket on a cool night. Of course, her obsession with France began after my biological father broke her heart, so it was quite possible she needed to find a new love to fulfill her, and that love had been for me and this city. And then for pills, and those damn things won in the end.

Anthony Romano. No, he wasn't my father, just blood.

Édouard Moreau had been the closest thing to a father I'd ever had. He was caring, compassionate, and he'd been a loyal husband before his wife was murdered. He never had children. Never married again. He'd chosen to devote his life to his work as leader of *La Ligue des Frères* after his wife was killed on the streets in a mugging he couldn't stop.

"One of my men saw you with Anthony Romano's daughter," he explained when I'd yet to speak. "A few times." He slowly faced me, and my pulse raced. "She calls herself Josie McClintock." His pale gray-blue eyes tightened. The deep lines on his face aged him more than his sixty-five years.

I knew we should have been more careful about being seen in public together. We'd scrubbed her previous life from the Internet the best we could, but even a new name would be ineffective if photos from her life as Alessia Romano still existed.

Cole McGregor had taken the ones down from his Facebook profile recently, and I wasn't sure if he'd been pissed she left, or the pictures were too painful of a reminder of her absence. I actually felt sorry for the guy. Alessia had been as vague about their relationship as I had been about the organization I worked for and supposedly quit.

"I'm sorry." What else could I possibly say to make this right? "I was trying to protect her from our enemies."

"And does your sister know who we are?" Still no anger like I'd expected given my lie. Luca usually got scolded like a petulant kid when he messed up, and what I'd done was worse than any of his antics.

"I told her I once belonged to a group of sorts." I kept my voice low. "I was vague."

"She thinks you quit?" he asked in surprise, and I nodded.

This conversation was going to get worse, wasn't it? And I deserved whatever he threw at me given my betrayal.

"And is this what you want, to leave The League?" His tone dipped lower, nearly void of emotion, and it had the hairs on my arms standing.

"I don't know," I admitted. I couldn't risk another lie. I didn't want to further hurt him as I knew I had with my omission of the truth already.

"Why'd you lie? Why break the rules? We would've protected her like family, same as you." No change in his voice and it had me on edge as to what he was thinking, what he was planning to do.

"I wanted to keep her away from this life. Keep my worlds separate." I faced the window again, bringing my palm to the glass, focusing on the Eiffel Tower. The last time I visited was when I'd had a picnic with Ma at the foot of the towering structure. That lunch had been a week before she died. "I didn't want her to know who I am."

I'd admitted to Alessia when we first met I was a killer, but she never asked more, and I didn't feel compelled to explain it to her. *A fresh start,* she'd said. And I wanted that, too, but if I left The League, what would happen?

"And what? You think you're a bad person?" he asked, surprise in his tone, his question forming a knot in my throat. "You're now worth one point eight billion dollars," he went on when I couldn't get the words out. "You do understand what that means?"

I blinked, not sure I fully comprehended what he was suggesting. "Are you serious?" Was he offering me a second chance, one that came with a reward?

I slowly turned, my heartbeat kicking up higher at his unexpected words.

"You know how I feel about you." He brought a fist over his blue dress shirt, covering his heart. "I am more of a father to you than whatever some DNA test would suggest. This is what I've always wanted for you." His lips drew together as he paused for a moment. "I'd always thought that I'd turn my inheritance—the leadership position of France—over to you, but now there's no need to wait. Say the word. If you want Ireland. It's yours."

Ireland. Mine. It was too hard to believe.

Pierce Danforth, the leader of The League in the U.K., had attempted to control the Republic of Ireland as well, but he'd been stretched too thin. My country had become even more vulnerable lately, especially to the vultures of The Alliance, a criminal network that spanned all of Europe and Russia.

The League in Ireland needed its own leader, and it'd been a dream I'd never thought I'd be able to obtain.

"The League of Brothers in Ireland. Me in charge," I said first in English, then in French. My statements broken like my thoughts.

"I will overlook this lie about your sister, for you, my son. I will forgive you."

Forgiveness. How could he after I'd lied to him?

I wanted to believe it was true, but there had to be a catch. I didn't deserve this.

"The League assembles next week to discuss a pact with The Alliance. We can vote the leadership position then."

The idea of any type of pact with our enemies had my blood heating.

"I know how you feel about that. But you'd no longer have to worry about The Alliance coming after you." He paused. "Or Alessia."

Alessia's safety was everything to me, but the cost would be high. We'd be aligning ourselves with the very men we'd been going after for years.

"We may be able to work something into the deal, perhaps a promise they'll curb their activities in our cities." He closed his eyes, remorse cutting across his face. "*C'est une trêve.*"

"How can we trust they won't break a truce? Send their assassins after us when our guard is down?"

His lids slowly lifted. "I don't think we have much of a choice." He wrapped his hand over my shoulder. "And if you take the position in Ireland, it'd make us stronger."

I blew out a breath and turned away from him, and he retracted his hand. "I need time to think about it."

"You're one of our best men. *The* best man. Even The Alliance fears you. You belong at the top. Money does not bring you power or security. We provide that. Without us, you'd be a powerless man in a suit like I was when my Diana died. Are you sure that's what you want?"

"I didn't say I want to leave The League, I just don't know if I can accept this position."

His mouth pressed into a firm line as he assessed me. "You have until Sunday."

* * *

"You missed the grand opening. You knew how important this was for me, and you didn't show." Disappointment slashed through Alessia's tone and brought lines across her forehead.

She collapsed onto the chair across from me inside the bar. We were at our hotel in Paris.

I glanced at my watch. Eight p.m. I had four more hours to provide my answer to Moreau. I still wasn't sure what in the bloody hell I was going to do.

"I'm sorry." I lifted my head, my eyes catching sight of the white gold Celtic cross she always wore before my attention landed on her face. "I don't think we should be seen together in such a public place anymore. We shouldn't even be here together right now." It pained me to say those words, more than she'd know.

I had enjoyed getting to know my sister and all her quirks. She was also a savvy businesswoman, and I'd been impressed with her negotiating skills, but her love for partying worried me, and running a club would most likely feed into that.

Partying could also lead to drugs, and I was goddamn terrified I'd lose her the same as Ma.

"Sebastian?"

Had she said something? I hadn't heard a word. "Yeah?"

"I thought my identity as Josie protected me from anyone finding out we're related. Why do we need distance?"

"Because it's no longer safe," I snapped, unable to hide the anger in my tone. Angry at myself for being so careless as to allow anyone to discover my relationship with her.

She snatched my 12-year-old Redbreast whiskey and tossed it back in one quick swallow.

"You don't need me at the club, anyway. You can run it just fine without me."

Even if I was beginning to regret buying the club, it was with her money. Everyone believed "Josie" was management and not the owner. But officially, the club was hers in every other way possible.

I'd been damn foolish to think I could keep her identity from The League. And worse, what if The Alliance ever got wind of my sister? Maybe the pact was the only way to keep her safe from them?

"I want you there with me. The point of us running these businesses was to do it together." She set the glass down. "What is it you aren't telling me?"

"It's nothing." More lies. And I'd have to keep them coming if I wanted to keep her safe. "Why don't you tell me more about this guy you're dating?"

"How do you—"

"Spies," I said with a wink.

"Funny."

I wasn't even remotely kidding.

"Well, if you'd come to the opening last night, you would've met him."

Meeting some guy she was sleeping with wouldn't be a grand idea. "Would I like him, at least?"

"You'll never like anyone I date." She lowered her voice. "No leg-breaking if you ever do meet him." She waved a dismissive hand. "But really, he's a notorious flirt and not the kind of man to settle down."

"If he hurts you, I'll do a lot more than break his legs." I meant every word. If anyone ever so much as touched her the wrong way, I'd torture them to death.

"The scary thing is that I kind of believe you." There was a touch of humor running side by side with a hint of serious.

She should believe me, though.

And if I accepted Moreau's offer, I'd be more feared than ever.

Powerful. Unstoppable.

A deal maker.

A fecking devil among men. Well, that's how people would perceive me, at least. They wouldn't know the truth. They couldn't.

She reached for her necklace and clutched the cross, and her lids dropped. "Your protectiveness reminds me of someone I used to know. He liked to play big brother."

Cole McGregor? "I like him already."

"You probably would." She tucked her necklace beneath her top and opened her eyes. "You know, you can try dating, too. Maybe it'd help you relax. Stop being so broody and tense all of the time." Her lips quirked into a grin. She was becoming an expert at hiding her emotions like me, but I wasn't sure if I wanted that for her. "I'm sure you're hooking up, but maybe you should try something real? Find someone who'd put little hearts in your eyes. Someone who gets your blood pumping."

"I really don't want to talk about my sex life with my

little sister." I drew in a deep breath and let it go. "But I'm also just not capable of more. I'd feck it up." The honesty from my mouth surprised even me.

"Sebastian." Her voice grew small.

I snatched my mobile when it vibrated. Another message from Luca. He'd been blowing up my mobile all weekend after he'd learned "Josie" was my sister. "Sorry, I have to make a call."

"You sure you're going to be okay?"

I didn't answer, because I honestly had no idea.

CHAPTER NINE

PRESENT DAY

HOLLY

MY HANDS WERE GOING TO HURT TOMORROW. I HAD absolutely no idea how my brother used his knuckles like weapons daily, jabbing and punching not only heavy bags but people.

Then again, I was there to wear myself out to the point I'd be too tired to continue obsessing about Sebastian's kiss. After an hour, no such luck. I was beginning to worry the touch of his lips would remain a ghost in my life forever. And I wasn't into threesomes, so how could I ever date someone new with Sebastian lingering, even if only in my mind?

Adam slipped off his puffy gloves and tossed them aside before catching the heavy, swinging bag between his palms to stop me from killing it.

I was panting. I didn't ever pant. I thought hot yoga was hard, but this was next-level stuff.

I rolled my shoulders back a few times and turned toward him. Behind him, two fighters were pummeling each other in one of two cages, and a few other guys were doing some Kung Fu-like moves on a mat a few meters to our left.

"I need to learn self-defense, and I want you to teach me." I hadn't come to that realization until I'd watched the guy on the blue mat get flipped onto his back and pinned beneath someone nearly half his size.

"Why now?"

My gaze drifted to the back wall, where *McGregor's Gym* was painted in red letters, and beneath it in ancient Gaelic were the symbols for family. Those same symbols were also part of the tattoo inside of Adam's forearm.

"Well, I got to thinking, and I've started traveling more for work, and what if I'm ever, I don't know, mugged or something when I'm out of town."

There were plenty of valid reasons to want to hit something and to learn to self-defense, but I couldn't tell him most of what was on my mind. He'd go crazy with worry.

Adam and Anna were expecting a baby in a few months, and after everything he'd gone through—Anna's abduction, making the difficult decision to leave the family company—I didn't want him shouldering any more responsibility.

"If someone ever laid a hand on you, I'd feckin' kill them."

Sebastian almost did on Friday.

What was it with the men in my life wanting to kill people?

Shit. No, Sebastian wasn't a "man in my life." He was the enemy.

"You're not that man anymore," I reminded him, hoping I was right.

Anna had saved him. She brought him out of the dark hole he'd been hiding away in and helped him realize he was a good man.

"When it comes to family, you know I'd do anything to keep you all safe."

"You wouldn't kill."

He grimaced. "Yeah, well, I almost killed Anna's ex."

"That was different, and you didn't go through with it."

"If Anna hadn't stopped me, I would've," he admitted, his voice steady. The events of the past still clinging to his mind even though it'd been two years.

"What's your point?"

Adam wasn't Sebastian. Sebastian barely knew me, and yet, he'd almost murdered a kid for trying to steal my coat. Adam protecting the love of his life from her abusive ex wasn't a fair comparison.

"The point is that I won't let anything happen to you, even if—"

"You have to kill someone for me?" I tightened the knot of my ponytail and eyed the heavy bag again. If he wasn't going to teach me any moves, may as well go for round two.

"Holly." The plea in his voice had my focus skating his way.

"Adam. You're going to be a father. Your son needs you. Your wife. You can't shadow my every move and keep me safe. You won't always be around to watch over me."

You weren't on Friday. Then again, I probably shouldn't have walked alone in a park at night, even if our city was much safer than it used to be.

His blue eyes narrowed as he studied me. "Is there something you're not telling me?"

I lifted my hands between us, making fists. "Just teach me."

"Fine." He grunted, or maybe it was more of a snarl. "But do me a favor?"

"What?"

"If you're really worried about your safety when you're traveling, maybe hire a bodyguard to go with you?"

Great. I didn't need Adam to become even more overprotective. "I'll be fine." I forced a smile. "Now, show me what in the bloody hell to do."

He shook his head. "Yeah, okay. But so help me, if anything ever happens to you—"

"I get it. I get it."

"Stubborn." He flicked his wrist, motioning for me to follow him to one of the other mats off to the side of the two men fighting.

"Where do ya think I got it from?" I asked before he surprised me by sweeping his leg beneath mine, bringing me down flat onto my back in one quick movement.

"First lesson," he began. "Always expect the unexpected."

* * *

AFTER DABBING THE TOWEL AT THE BACK OF MY SWEATY neck beneath my ponytail, I grabbed my mobile from my purse and checked my messages.

Harrison: *I've been calling but you must be busy.*

Harrison: *I need to fly to Amsterdam and put out a few unexpected fires. I'm so sorry.*

Harrison: *I'll be back Thursday or Friday. Deal and a celebratory dinner after?*

"You okay?" Adam pulled a black tee over his head and stepped in front of me.

I clutched the mobile between my palms, almost grateful I had more time before I had to see Harrison again. "I'm fine."

"You don't look fine." He cocked his head. "This about that Reed guy?"

How'd he . . .?

"Anna saw you and Reed dancing at your party. She thinks you two would make a good match."

My brows shot up in surprise. "And what do you think? Never mix business with pleasure, right?"

He brought a hand between us, cutting it through the air with one eye closed. "Never talk about you and a man like that around me. I'll—"

"Nah, you're all talk these days." I grinned.

"Don't try me." He wrapped a hand around my waist, and I leaned into my big brother. "Also, I'd be a hypocrite if I said don't date the guy because of work, given Anna was an intern at our company."

"True."

"But."

"Isn't that one of your least favorite words?" I tipped my chin to the right to look up at him.

"This *but* is important."

"Why is that?"

"Because I don't think you two should date, and it's not because of the deal."

"Why?" I stepped out of his grasp to face him.

A contemplative look crossed his face. "I don't like Renaud, you know that."

"*But?*" I almost choked on the word.

"I've seen the way you act around him, and how off-kilter he seems to make you." He lowered himself onto a folding chair outside the second fighting cage, which was empty.

"That's anger, not anything else."

He smiled. "Liar."

There was no way Adam was suggesting I date Sebastian, so what in the hell was he getting at?

"There might be attraction," I admitted since I hated lying to him.

Might was such a shit word. There was an insane amount of sexual chemistry even after he'd informed me the Limerick deal would happen no matter what.

His elbows went to his thighs. "Sean told me Renaud will relinquish his seat on the board and get rid of his shares—at some point—but can we trust he'll do that?"

"The only thing I know about him is that he seems to be a man of his word. If he makes a deal, he sticks to it." He had his reputation to maintain, I supposed. "I don't understand what this has to do with my not dating Harrison, though. I'm fairly certain he does want more than a friendship or a business deal, but—"

"Yeah, well, you shouldn't lead Reed on. More importantly, you're my sister, and I don't want you to get hurt. Dating a guy who doesn't make you feel, whatever it is that Renaud does, would weigh on your conscience."

Sean had been worried Harrison would hurt me given his reputation with women, but here Adam was concerned I'd do the heart breaking.

I didn't think any man, not soon, at least, could ever make me feel even a tenth of what I'd felt when Sebastian had kissed me last night.

Growing up, I'd rarely gone to Adam for dating advice. Sean had always been my go-to. He wasn't the best at giving advice, given his lack of long-term commitments, but I'd felt safer talking about the opposite sex with him. Okay, more like the guys I dated would be safer. I didn't need Adam scaring my dates to pieces with a bunch of not-so-empty threats.

But somehow, Adam could read me better than even Sean could when it came to Sebastian.

"For the record, I don't want you with Renaud, or anyone like him for that matter. I just want you to find someone who"—he waved a hand in the air, uncomfortable and not practiced in talking about such matters—"makes you . . ."

"You're right," I cut him off, saving him from having to talk about sex with me. "Harrison and I should only be friends." And hopefully, he wouldn't hate me for it.

"And Renaud?" He rose and braced a hand over my shoulder.

"Easy." I squeezed my eyes closed. "We shouldn't be anything at all."

CHAPTER TEN

HOLLY

THE LOBBY IN SEBASTIAN'S HOTEL WAS AS ELEGANT AND gorgeous as one of his Brioni suits. The place also had a touch of Rome in the architectural design. Columns, arches, and other breathtaking reminders of one of my favorite cities. But the Celtic music softly playing in the background was a reminder of where I was.

I didn't want to like the place. To feel at home in a building he owned. But I did.

I planned to head straight for the lift and go to his suite, demand he drop the Limerick sale, and leave the company now. I didn't want to wait even a day. I needed him gone from my life. To reclaim a sense of who I was before he took over my every thought.

But before I reached the lift, I spotted something, or rather someone, that stopped me dead in my tracks.

"You." I forced my boots to carry me to the eating area off to the side of the bar.

Hoodie Kid, without the hoodie right now, sat at a table with a younger version of himself. Same messy light brown hair. Blue eyes, too.

"What are you doing here?" I stepped up to their table and crossed my arms, trying not to feel bad at the sight of the bruises Sebastian had left on his face.

"Do I know you?" He glared at me, his eyes tightening.

Oh, he recognized me, but he didn't want to acknowledge the fact in front of the kid.

"Do you take me for a fool?" I rolled my eyes. "Cut the act."

He stood and tipped his head to the side, motioning for me to follow him away from the table. "You his girlfriend or something?" He tucked his hands under the armpits of his long-sleeved shirt. A much better quality material than the hoodie he'd been wearing on Friday.

"No, I'm definitely not." Never would be.

"But you know him?"

I nodded. "And do you?"

"He's not giving me much of a choice." His hands fell to his sides when he glimpsed back at the boy sitting at the table eating a sandwich.

"What do you mean? Did he hurt you?"

"He's making me live here and get my shite together."

I took a step back, surprise winging through my body so fast I nearly lost my footing.

"He threatened me."

Now that sounded more like it. "You need me to get you out of here?"

"What's with you people wanting to help me after I tried to steal from you?"

My hand went between us. "He's helping you? I thought you said—"

"He's basically blackmailing me. If I behave, he'll give us room and board and won't go to the Guards about what I did to you."

Us? The kid was probably his brother.

"Making me work at his club, though. So, it's not all a handout."

Sebastian nearly murdered the kid in the park. No way would he give him a home and a job. "How'd he find you?" My hand went to my forehead and I applied pressure, a headache stirring.

"He stole my wallet mid-punch on Friday." A hint of a smile, as if actually impressed by Sebastian's quick hands, touched his lips.

I would have laughed if this situation wasn't insane.

"Says he used to be like me."

My jaw about fell all the way to the pretty marbled floors. "What?"

"He wants me to have another chance." He held his palms open. "Like I said, it's crazy. But my brother needs this place, so I'll scrub these rich arsehole's floors with a toothbrush if I have to."

"I, um." I had to talk to Sebastian. "Stay out of trouble."

"If I hurt you on Friday," he began when I'd sidestepped him to get to the lift, "I'm sorry."

"Thanks." I entered the lift a few seconds later, clutching the handles of my Prada bag and mulling over what the kid had shared as the lift quietly climbed floors.

I rapped at his door a minute later. Then two more times when there was no answer.

I checked the time on my watch. Five o'clock.

He wouldn't be at his club at this time on a Sunday, right? Of course, he could be at *Les Fleurs.*

I knocked one more time and nearly fell inward when the door opened.

And shit.

Sebastian shirtless was going to wreak havoc with my ability to speak around him.

He also looked pissed to see me.

I should have looked away. Not only because his glare could've cut me to ribbons, but because he was half-naked. And the man was ripped. Muscles upon muscles. Every part of him rigid, even . . .

I started to stumble back, but he reached out and caught my arm, holding me in place.

His black sweatpants were tented. Rock. Freaking. Hard.

I cleared my throat. "You always answer the door like this?" I kept blinking as if that'd stop the shocking surprise.

"No, but you kept knocking." He released his hold of me and arched his shoulders back, effectively positioning his amazing chest in my face. I wanted to reach out and touch him to see if he was real. And did he feel as hard as he looked?

Hard.

Yeah.

That brought me back to the erection he was sporting.

"I didn't mean to interrupt you." My chest painfully tightened at the idea he'd been having sex. "Tell whoever is here, I'm sorry."

"I'm alone." He shifted to the left to let me inside.

"Oh." Why did I feel so relieved?

I also couldn't seem to move yet. How could I go into his suite with him so hard in, well, so many places?

Had he been getting himself off? "I should come back." I started to turn, still in a daze from this display of masculinity in front of me, but he quickly secured a hand around my waist, stopping me.

It took me a moment to realize that a good portion of my body was now pressed against an equal portion of his, which included that throbbing intensity between his legs.

"You came for a reason. What is it?" He abruptly let go and strode inside his suite, making it impossible for me to miss the black Celtic cross tattooed between his shoulder blades. Simple in the design. Sort of like my brother Adam's ink.

The devil was Catholic? Then again, wasn't Lucifer a fallen angel?

I finally got my feet to move. "You want to get dressed first? Maybe, um, decompress. I can wait out here while you finish."

His brows lifted. "Oh, sure."

Okay, I could work with sarcasm. I had three brothers. "You use porn or have a great imagination?"

His hands settled above the waistline of his black sweats, showcasing his hip bones and those muscles Bella referred to as *sex lines*. The material sat so low, it was obvious he had nothing else on beneath.

His hard-on was no longer saluting me, but the bulge didn't exactly go away.

And now I also noticed he had scars on his body. Like he'd been in a knife or gunfight one too many times.

"What happened to you?" I couldn't stop myself from asking as I circled his body like he was some sort of art exhibit, searching for more wounds.

His back was worse than his chest. His golden skin had been marred by blades and bullets.

"It's nothing," he said brusquely.

"You call that nothing?" I held in a gasp as I glanced at

one particular scar along the side of his torso. It was like someone had taken a knife and tried to slice him open from armpit to hip bone.

Six injuries that I could count. How many were beneath his sweats?

"Holly." His dark brown eyes tightened on me.

I dropped my Prada bag and untied the belt of my Burberry raincoat. "I, um, ran into the kid who mugged me downstairs. What's he doing here?" I draped my coat over the barstool off to my right in the kitchen area.

"That's none of your concern," he answered as I turned to face him, his body far too close.

"He did try to steal from me, so yeah, I'd like to know what's going on."

He lowered his chin, eyes seeking mine. "You shouldn't have come. You shouldn't be seen here with me."

"That makes no sense." Nothing ever made sense with him, so why was I surprised? "You're on the McGregor board. I was at your club last night."

"That's business. You being here, alone with me . . ." His eyes deepened in color to a grittier shade of brown, like a dark soil you'd bury your treasures in to keep them hidden from your brothers when you were kids. "I don't want anyone to get the wrong idea."

My eyes widened in surprise. "God forbid anyone thinks we're having sex. You have a reputation to maintain." I snatched my purse and coat, prepared to leave, forgetting why I'd come to begin with, but when he snapped out my name, I froze. "What?"

"There are things you'll never understand about me, and—"

"How could I when you won't tell me anything?" I whirled back around to face him. "Let me guess, I wouldn't want to know, right?" Irritated, I tossed my belongings again, this time letting them fall on the floor. I peeled my cream cable-knit jumper over my head and flung it, too.

He took two quick steps back as if I were a threat. How insane was that? "What in the bloody hell are you doing?"

Honestly, I wasn't so sure. But I had to get through to him. To get him to not just listen to me, but to open up for once.

I wasn't always so "responsible" and "sweet" as my brothers had labeled me.

My hands went to the hem of my black, long-sleeved cotton shirt, and he bit out my name like a plea this time.

"Have you lost your mind?" he asked once I was out of my shirt.

"Yes," I hissed. "You're making me crazy." That part was true. "I came here for a reason, and I'm not going until I get answers." I lifted my chin, trying to hide a wobble of nerves there. "If you're going to be a pain in my arse, then I can play the same game."

I knew he wanted me. I'd had his tongue in my mouth and his hands on me last night to prove it. So, I could make him squirm right now, too. I'd probably regret this later, though.

His eyes dropped to my breasts, which were still hidden, but the bra was nude and sheer—practically transparent. My nipples peaked with his gaze on me, and my abdomen muscles tightened.

"We need to talk."

He dragged a hand down his face and let go of a deep exhale. When his arm was back at his side, his granite-like jawline locked even tighter. "The last thing I'll be doing is hearing a word out of your mouth with you like that."

And how did he think seeing him shirtless with an erection had made me bloody feel?

"Then get dressed, get focused, and come back out here and let's have a proper conversation." I huffed. "I'll be clothed and waiting."

"And what is it that you want?" Defeat wrapped around his words, and it was satisfying, warming me in all the right places.

Mission accomplished.

"To talk about the land in Limerick. And renegotiate the terms of the deal you made with Harrison."

His lips curved at the edges. "You want to negotiate with me?"

"Yes." I waved my hand. "Now please, take care of that problem you have." My gaze dipped to his sweats, his hard-on had reappeared. "Maybe shower, too. Then come back out here."

"You always conduct business like this?"

"Apparently only with you."

His lips tipped into the slightest of smiles, the small movement catching me off guard. The sight of a smile on his face was almost painfully beautiful.

"Shower. Clothes. Then talk," I reiterated, letting my commands sit between us for a moment.

"Don't forget about the jerk-off part." He was close now. So close, I almost thought he might dip in for a kiss. "Be right back, love."

Love? Oh for feck's sake. I whirled away from him and waited until I heard the bedroom door close to drop my face into my palms and yell on the inside.

After getting my shirt and jumper back on, I went to his bar for a drink. Whiskey wasn't my normal go-to, but there was an immense collection of bottles from all over the world.

I went with an eighteen-year-old Jameson Bow Street

whiskey. The older, the better, right? A touch of toffee, hints of leather. Toasted oak and spice. The complexity . . . it reminded me every bit of Sebastian, down to the way he'd tasted when we'd kissed. Yeah, if Sebastian were a drink, he'd be this one.

I settled into one of his armchairs, relishing the taste by consuming it slowly. And after five or so minutes—must've been a quick orgasm and shower—the door to his bedroom opened.

"Thank you."

"For what?" I played dumb, of course.

"For helping expedite my shower with your little striptease." He winked, and my jaw dropped.

His mouth twitched, the threat of a smile nearly exposed. His lips were irritatingly perfect, the kind even a Renaissance sculpture would envy—sensual in fullness, yet unquestionably masculine. My temperature spiked at the memory of those lips on mine.

"Well, thanks for"—I raised my glass and gestured toward him—"the clothes." I cleared my throat, hoping to kill the embarrassment with it. "Being dressed, I mean."

He was in dark wash denim and a white, long-sleeved cotton shirt. Bare feet. Mussed-up wet hair. Handsome as bloody ever.

"Anytime." Another smile. God, help me.

"You have a thing for whiskeys?" I needed a new topic. "I may have poured myself one that's been maturing for almost two decades."

He cocked his head, his dark brow lifting. "I'm a bit of a connoisseur."

I tapped a finger on the glass and closed one eye. "I would've taken you for someone to organize your bottles by, at least, country of origin, or brand. But color?"

His eyebrows flat-lined, same as his mouth, and pain cut through his rum-colored eyes.

"You'd be right in your assumption." He didn't make sense, and I wasn't going to go down some rabbit hole doused in whiskey. I was there for a reason. "Early for something so strong, don't ya think?"

"Early for a lot of things," I snapped back, my eyes falling right to the crotch of his jeans.

He smirked.

Damn it.

"Tell me about the kids first," I demanded.

He sat in the leather armchair across from me. "I spoke to the man who tried to mug you. Well, kid," he said after the longest minute of my life had passed. "He was remorseful. Also living with his ten-year-old brother in this godawful shit hole. They were alone."

Finally. The truth. I took a mental victory lap. "And you set them up here?"

He nodded.

"Why? I mean, that's what I would've done, or someone with a heart, but not you."

"You're right. It's out of character for me," he said in a low, almost hollow tone. "Want me to kick them out?"

I closed my eyes for a second. "I'm sorry."

"For what? Being honest?"

"For being mean."

"You could never be mean."

His words and the soft tone in which he'd spoken, had my lids lifting to seek his eyes. "With you, I am. I'm always so angry at you."

His attention moved to the window, which overlooked the city. "That's how it should be. You need to keep your distance." He slowly carried his focus my way. "Because whatever you think about me, I promise you, I'm much worse."

"See, the thing is," I began and set the tumbler on the end table off to my side, "I'm not so sure I can believe you." I stood and moved to the window. "Horrible people don't help kids." I caught his eyes in the reflection of the glass. He was standing behind me now, but not close enough to reach out and touch me. "You keep warning me away, but it's because you're trying to protect me, isn't it? And that's another notch in the I-don't-believe-you're-bad belt."

I faced him, and his hands were tense at his sides as if he wanted to grab hold of me but resisted. "Don't do this." His brows drew together. "You'll only be disappointed."

"I won't—"

"You will," he said, the anger in his tone harder than I'd ever heard from him, and I backed against the window.

"Fine," I sputtered, needing to focus on why I was even there. "I want you gone from the company long before the movie with Harrison begins filming, and I also want you to know I'll stop at nothing short of going to London and telling off this investor that we'll never sell the land."

"You can't go to London." It was less of a demand and more a desperate plea. "I need you to trust me when I say don't try and stop the deal from happening," he added, his voice even softer this time.

"Do you owe someone a favor? Did you make them a promise, and since you always keep your word about deals, you're being forced to do this?"

His silence was the only answer I needed.

I was right.

Him and his deals.

But this was one deal he'd have to lose.

"I'm not backing down. And you think I'm stubborn?

Good." I lifted my chin. "I'm a McGregor. We don't lose." I maneuvered around him, worried he'd follow, but he didn't.

I had to get out of there and as far away from him as possible.

I snatched my coat and purse and hurried for the door. When I flung it open, I nearly collided with someone's fist mid-knock.

The man retracted his hand and tossed it through his wavy, brown hair. "*Excusez-moi. Je suis désolé.*" The guy had a James Dean meets Johnny Depp thing going for him. Cleft chin. A nose that looked like it'd been broken once or twice.

I didn't bother with pleasantries or a smile. If he was a friend of Sebastian's, I had no desire to get to know him.

"Luca Moreau." His eyes were a lighter brown than Sebastian's. The color of the whiskey I'd drunk, but there didn't appear to be anything sweet about him.

"I have to go. Sorry." I maneuvered around him and rushed for the lift.

Once downstairs, I sought out the two kids, hoping I wasn't too late.

I approached the teenager who'd mugged me. I still didn't know his name, did I? "Can we talk?"

A pair of light blue eyes peeked over the magazine. "What?" He lowered his reading material to the table.

"I don't think you should stay here. I can put you two up in another hotel." Sebastian may have offered this kid a second chance after he'd attempted to mug me, but he had to have ulterior motives. I didn't want this boy to ever have to owe him a debt. "Please."

"Why?" He looked at his brother across from him before bringing his eyes back to me.

"I just think you'd be better off away from him." I motioned to his black eye as one reason.

"I can't go." He shook his head. "Sorry."

"But he's . . ." I didn't want to say more with his younger brother's curious eyes on me.

"The way I see it," he began in a steady voice, "there's probably no place safer to be than under his protection."

CHAPTER ELEVEN

SEBASTIAN

"YOU FINALLY GET HER OUT OF YOUR SYSTEM?" LUCA poured himself a drink as my gaze moved across the room to Holly's half-full glass on the end table next to the chair she'd vacated five minutes ago.

What in the hell had she been thinking coming here? And getting half-naked in front of me?

Luca strode my way a moment later. "Judging by that angry look you're wearing, you didn't screw her."

"What do you want?" I asked, irritated for so many damn reasons. "I have a meeting in thirty minutes."

"I went to the bar, and Ola said you were here." He took a sip of his drink, eyes set on me. "Mind if I take Ola out?"

"You go on a date? What happened to your vacation of self-discovery? Staying away from women?"

"But Ola is a hot one. She acts like she hates me, but I think she's playing hard to get."

Not a chance. "I'd prefer you keep your dick in your trousers."

"Just because you're not getting any doesn't mean I can't."

I snatched Holly's glass and took it to the kitchen sink. I needed to remove all reminders she'd ever been here.

This woman was going to destroy me, and I was okay with that as long as she didn't get hurt.

Getting off three to four times a day to thoughts of Holly wasn't enough. I wanted her. *More* than just wanted her.

It could never happen, and I'd have to keep yanking one out whenever I got the urge to tell her what was on my mind.

But for her to show up while I was mid-stroke, and then to take her goddamn top off, letting me see her tits beneath that sheer bra . . .

"So, why was the lovely Ms. McGregor here?"

"Don't change the subject. Ola's off-limits." She was perfectly capable of handling herself, but I didn't want her to be in a position to have to.

"Why?" He glared at me. "You want her, too?"

"No," I snapped. "But she's a good person."

"And I'm not?" He laughed.

"You're League."

He scoffed. "You're kidding, right? Being with me would make her much safer than her being alone." He finished the rest of his drink and set the glass on the kitchen counter.

Luca's words were a cruel reminder of a choice I'd made and would regret every day.

"I don't know why you let women do this to you."

"What the hell are you talking about?"

His eyes darkened, but he shook off whatever he was thinking, then smiled. "Make you crazy. Doing the same

119

thing over again and expecting a different result—definition of insanity, right?"

"I don't know what you're getting at."

Of course, Holly was making me insane. And apparently, I was pushing her to walk that line as well.

I'd flirted with her when I'd ordered myself not to.

Then last night I'd kissed her, had my hands on her tight body.

And tonight, I was seconds away from pinning her to the window and burying my face between her thighs to see if she tasted as sweet as that mouth of hers.

But Limerick. Damn the deal that had to happen for reasons I could never reveal to her.

I checked my watch. "I have to go."

"You didn't answer my question about Ola," he said as I grabbed my coat and put it on.

"Because you already know my answer," I responded once we were out in the hall and heading for the lift. "And since when do you seek permission, anyway?" I stabbed a bit too angrily at the call button outside the lift.

"Respect, *mon frère*. Your kingdom." He was a bit more flippant than normal, but I ignored it. Too much on my mind. Hell, like the smell of the lift.

Jesus. It even carried Holly's scent—flowers and vanilla. I snatched my mobile from my pocket as the doors closed. We needed to finish our conversation about Limerick. I couldn't have her running off to London and getting herself into trouble.

"Messaging her already?" He smirked.

I shot Luca a scolding look before reading over the text I'd just sent.

Me: *I'll leave the company after the board votes in favor of the Limerick sale. I won't wait until next year.*

I knew that wouldn't be enough for her, but it was a start.

Holly: *You can leave after they vote against the sale of the land. Or before. Either way, I accept those terms of the deal.*

I pocketed my mobile, parted ways with Luca, and ten minutes later, my driver pulled up in front of *Les Fleurs*. The meeting tonight with a group of investors had been scheduled weeks ago, and I wasn't one to bail at the last minute. But how could I sit through a business dinner when Holly might already be packing her bags for London? The answer was easy, I couldn't.

My eyes locked on to the purple cursive script of the sign above the door of the restaurant, which had a hand-painted bouquet of wildflowers next to it.

Alessia. My chest tightened at the memory of the last time we were together here and parked in this very spot.

"Change of plans," I told my driver. "There's somewhere else I need to be."

CHAPTER TWELVE

DUBLIN, IRELAND - FOUR YEARS AGO

SEBASTIAN

"NICE PLACE YOU HAVE HERE." DONOVAN HANNIGAN SAWED his steak in half, the blood oozing from the center in the process.

He was the type of crime boss who probably laughed while his lackeys broke legs and cut off fingers. A fecking arsehole who believed himself untouchable.

Chop shops. Dealing drugs. Blackmailing small businesses. Illegal fight clubs. The list of his offenses went on and on, and I hated that I had to let him continue living and breathing. Even if I had accepted the leadership role of Ireland, because of the deal we made with The Alliance, I couldn't take him out. That didn't stop me from envisioning ways to kill him as we sat here.

I shifted back in my seat, leaving my dinner untouched as

we sat at a table in *Les Fleurs*. Seeing this piece of scum inside the elegant restaurant my sister decorated didn't sit well with me. But this conversation had to happen on my turf, not his. And taking him to the club with Alessia there tonight was out of the question.

"The fight club you run on Church Street, I need you to relocate it."

His menacing dark gaze crawled up to my face. "You're kidding, right?"

"Do I look like a man who'd make a joke?" I angled my head ever so slightly, and my lips drew tight.

"What does it matter where my club is?"

"Because I said so," I rasped. "You know who I work for." Who I *still* worked for.

He shoved a huge bite of steak in his mouth, his eyes never leaving mine. "And you know whose protection I'm under, so I'm not sure why we're even having this conversation," he said after he'd taken his damn time chewing. "One call to my brother-in-law, and you're done."

"You may have Alliance protection, but—"

"And your League's pact with The Alliance means you can't touch me." He winked. The fucker actually winked at me.

"A new flat complex is under construction next to your fight club, and the property owner has concerns the proximity to the club will drive down prices."

"Too bloody bad." He tossed his linen napkin on his plate. "I won't do any such thing."

"Just because I'm not allowed to kill you, doesn't mean I can't make your life a living hell," I seethed.

Moreau had been right, we needed a stronger League presence in Dublin. Even though I wasn't in charge, I'd still do my damn best to save the city from completely falling to the likes of this arse.

"You have forty-eight hours to relocate your fight club, or you won't have one at all. Am I clear?"

"I don't take kindly to threats. The Alliance will have your head."

"This isn't a threat. It's a promise." If someone like Donovan was negatively impacting League business, I had every right to handle it (without killing him, of course), as laid out in the deal.

He pointed two fingers at his eyes then my way. "You want to fight me, don't ya? I can see it on your face. Why don't we step outside and handle this like men?" He was still fairly jacked for someone in his late fifties. A heavyweight boxer in his younger days who'd turned to illegal ways to make money when he stopped winning fights. "I think you're a scrapper beneath that suit. You could use a good fight."

He ran a hand over his slicked-back black hair and lifted his chin, his gaze sharp on something, or someone, behind me.

I glanced back to see Alessia on approach. What in God's name was she doing there?

"Oh, I bet that one likes it rough in bed."

"Say a fecking thing to her, and I'll pick up that steak knife and slice your tongue off, are we clear?"

"And break the precious rules?" He grinned. "Nah, you won't do it. But thanks for letting me know she's someone you care about."

Motherfucker.

"Go near her, and you die. Slowly and very painfully," I said in a low voice before rising to face my sister. To hell with the pact.

"Sebastian." She kissed both my cheeks. She'd adopted

more and more European customs since she'd been away from the U.S.

Her gaze darted to Donovan before journeying back to me, concern crossing her face. She knew him, didn't she?

"What are you doing here?" I asked her. "I thought you were at the club."

"I was trying to get ahold of you, and you weren't answering your phone. I called around. Your people said you were here."

"How'd you get here?"

"My driver. Like always."

"Wait in the car. I'll be right outside."

"But—"

"Now," I ordered, not wanting her anywhere near this arsehole. I didn't want her to even breathe his toxic air.

She glimpsed Donovan again, concern etched in the lines of her forehead, then whirled around, clearly upset I'd dismissed her, and she hurried out of the dining room for the exit.

"Forty-eight hours." I leveled the smarmy bastard with a look that promised retribution should he ignore my warnings, then I left the table and got into Alessia's limo.

The partition between the driver and back was already up, affording us privacy. "How do you know Donovan Hannigan?"

She lifted one shoulder. "Word is he's responsible for like half the crime in the city. And if you were meeting with him . . ." She let go of her words as her voice broke. "Tell me this isn't what you used to do, who you used to work for. He's not in that mysterious group you were once part of, right?"

"No. It's people like him who ruin cities, not me."

"I don't understand."

And how could she? I'd kept her sheltered and protected

from my world the best I could. And maybe if I'd been honest about who I was to begin with, she'd understand that—understand the dangers most people remained ignorant of . . .

I scratched at the back of my neck. I didn't know what to say or how to explain. "Let's get you back to the club. Or home."

"No." She shook her head. "I want answers. Tell me to my face—are you still working for them?"

Them. How could I ever define "them" to someone who grew up in a world where money literally rained down upon her like a gift from God? It'd never matter how much cash I had in my bank account, I didn't come from money, so I'd always know the extent of what people would do for it.

Theft. Bribery. Murder.

"I never left," I finally answered.

She slid farther away from me, her back hitting the other side of the limo. Of course, she'd fear me. Hate me. Maybe she was right to.

"How could you lie to me?" she whispered. "You don't need the money. It makes no sense."

"I can't walk away. It's not so easy."

"Then explain it to me. Tell me why you can't leave. Why you want to keep hurting people?"

"I'm not . . ." I sucked in a sharp breath and let it go. "I haven't killed anyone since you came into my life." And that was the truth. I hadn't left The League, but I'd kept my commitment not to kill.

And were we really going to have this conversation in the back of the limo tonight? And could I ever tell her the truth about The League without further endangering her? The more she knew, the larger the target on her head.

"How can I trust anything you say?" Liquid coated her eyes. "Is this the real reason you've been keeping your distance from me lately? Were you worried I'd find out you never left?"

"No, it's always been about keeping you safe."

She swiped the backs of her hands across her cheeks, wiping away the tears. "I-I can't do this. I can't handle secrets and lies. You're either with them or you're with me. I gave up someone I cared about to be here and—"

"Maybe you shouldn't have," I snapped and regretted it immediately.

She was talking about Cole McGregor, and I was an arse for stealing her from her old life. But I wasn't sure if I could give her up. She'd managed to open my heart, to show me it was capable of functioning, and the pain of her loss would destroy me. I hadn't been able to say *I love you* yet, but in time, I might get the words out—words I hadn't spoken since Ma died. "I don't want to lose you."

"Then don't," she murmured.

My shoulders slumped. "It's not that simple."

"And I think it is." She scooted closer and reached for my hand, her gesture causing my throat to thicken with regret at how everything had gone arseways.

I could send her away for a while. Not to New York but somewhere safe while I got things straightened out, then maybe I could officially trade in my old life for a new one.

The *maybe* felt like a gigantic boulder obstructing my airway.

Feck maybe, I decided when peering at my sister. "If anything happens to you because I leave—"

"It won't," she said with a sniffle. "Because I've got you to keep me safe."

CHAPTER THIRTEEN

PRESENT DAY

SEBASTIAN

THE RAIN HAMMERED THE STREETS AS THE DRIVER ROUNDED the final bend leading to Holly's new home, a place I'd never been to and sure as hell shouldn't be going to now. But her safety trumped my comfort. Being in her home would be hell, though.

The place wasn't what I expected. Small for someone of her wealth. A white two-story with stucco exterior. A copse of trees enveloped the home on the property and gave it a cottage-like feel. No other houses in sight.

It was like her oasis. Wildflowers. A fairy tree at the center of the land. A pond without a fountain. Simple and calming. Maybe it was similar to the land in Limerick she was desperate to keep.

The idea of her alone out here made me a bit crazy.

"I'll get you the umbrella," my driver, Nick—who'd been Irish Special Forces before joining me—offered.

"No need." I gripped the door handle. "I'm not sure how long I'll be."

"No rush, Mr. Renaud. I'll wait right here."

I walked with slow steps to the front door, despite getting blasted by wind and rain. I was fecking nervous. A strange and unfamiliar feeling.

Standing in front of her red door, I lifted my hand to knock, but she swung it open before I had a chance.

Security cams. *Good.* I wouldn't need to lecture her about the danger of living alone out in the middle of nowhere.

"What are you doing here?" Her eyes were wide, her lips parted.

It took me a moment to remember because I was too hung up on her casual look. It was one I'd never seen before.

Her face was clean of makeup. So fresh and beautiful. Her hair in a messy bun at the top of her head, a few strands wild. Light denim jeans, bare feet, and a loose-fitting cream-colored jumper that hung off one shoulder. No bra strap in sight.

"Can I come in?"

She blinked a few times and hesitated before stepping back. She was obviously reluctant to let me in. Were it not for the pouring rain, I'm not sure she would have.

But I'd stand there forever just to look at her.

I removed my coat and swiped both hands over my hair, which was now soaked. The coat had kept the rest of me dry.

"Shoes off," she ordered. "I don't wear them inside."

I toed off my sneakers and left them beside the door.

"You know you could hire someone to help you do that?" I said at the sight of boxes stacked in the living area.

There was a TV, which judging by the strewn wires, had

yet to be set up. A dark brown leather couch at the center of the room off to my right in front of the TV stand. One matching armchair and a coffee table.

She went to the boxes on the table and lifted a knife.

"Gonna cut me?"

She rolled her eyes and slid the blade along the seam of the box, allowing the tape to part. "I'm not the dangerous one, remember?" Her gaze flicked my way when she discarded the knife next to the box.

Her eyes moved to my abdomen, and I could see the question in her gaze—the curiosity about the marks she'd seen on my body earlier.

I'd been stabbed. Shot. Burned.

The injuries came with the line of work and certainly weren't typical of a billionaire businessman.

Not exactly explainable unless I offered a lie about being Special Forces like my driver, Nick. And lying about being military didn't sit well with me.

"Why are you here?" She lifted something from the box and unwrapped it. A picture frame. I wanted to steal a closer look, to get to know more about her, but I refrained.

"You know why."

"The deal? I'm not up for renegotiating my terms," she said with a stubborn lift of her chin.

"I never agreed to your terms."

She unwrapped another picture frame, then reached for a glass of red wine beside the box she was unpacking.

The movement of her throat as she swallowed had my mind going to a no-fly zone: her mouth wrapped around my cock with her hand beneath those lush lips moving up and down.

"Look who's the one getting red in the face now." She

crossed her arms, still holding the wine glass. "What's on your mind?"

"I don't get red."

"Right. You're too tan." She brought the glass back to her mouth, the rim hovering near her lower lip. "Where do you get color like that this time of year?"

I still owned the Hatteras Flybridge I'd had the day Alessia came into my life, and I took it out every chance I got.

"What if we both can get what we want?" I asked, abruptly changing the subject.

I'd had an idea on the drive over. I wasn't sure if it would work, but I'd give it a try. For her. Anything. Well, anything as long as it didn't compromise her safety.

She set the glass down. "I'm listening."

"Well." I sidestepped a stack of boxes to get closer to her. "The buyer is looking for land in Limerick. You happen to own the largest plot of undeveloped land. But what if we can find the same amount of acreage he's looking for somewhere else in Limerick."

"You just said—"

"We get more people to sell in the same area and combine that territory," I explained. "Then we sell that to Paulson Incorporated."

"I'm sure the investor tried that, and clearly, no one sold to him," she countered.

I doubted that, but I replied, "Because I wasn't involved."

"What makes you think they'll sell to you?"

"I can be persuasive."

She brushed loose strands of her silky hair away from her face, probably buying time as she contemplated my proposal. "It may work, but I should be the one to go to Limerick. The

McGregors have a solid reputation there. The people will trust me. And you shouldn't be involved."

I shook my head. "I already am involved," I reminded her. "And the property owners won't make a deal with you."

"Because I'm a woman?"

"No, because you're not me." I strode closer to her against my better judgment. "I can offer them something you can't."

Her hand brushed down the column of her throat. Her skin was so soft. Delicate. "And what is that?"

"I'd owe them a favor."

"And why would a favor from you matter to them?"

"A debt owed from someone like me would give them power they can't get anywhere else."

"They're mostly farmers, I don't think—"

"Please trust me," I interrupted. "And know this might be the only way you can keep the land you so desperately want while also making this investor happy."

"And you need him happy, do you?" Her tone softened. "You also owe this man a favor?"

"Yes," I admitted.

"And you'd be willing to owe more favors to help me?"

I brought my palm to her cheek without thinking. She immediately leaned into my touch and closed her eyes. I don't think she meant to do it, but God, did I like it. We fit together. Crazy as it was.

"For you, I would."

"Why?" The word came out like a whispered breath of air, and it struck me in the heart, reminding me we were too close. I was physically and emotionally too close to her.

"Yes or no?" I asked instead. "Do we have a deal? I can't promise you it'll work, but it's the best chance at keeping the land."

"And Paulson Incorporated"—she stepped back, and I had no choice but to lower my hand to my side where it belonged—"will bring jobs to Limerick? Ultimately, Paulson will boost the economy there?"

"Yes," I lied. "The company will help the city."

And when Holly found out the truth . . . it would kill me. Rip open the wound in my side, and I'd bleed everywhere because she'd never forgive me.

She let go of a breath. "My land remains protected, and the city can still flourish." She lightly nodded. "Then yes, it's a deal."

She offered me her hand to confirm the agreement. I stared at her long, slender fingers and swallowed hard. If I took hold of her hand, I'd pull her against me so fast she'd need to brace her palms against my chest. But like the arsehole I needed to be, I left her hanging.

She lowered her arm. "I'll try and get a flight to Limerick for Tuesday. Stay a night there. Scope out the land in person and see what might work."

"I'll rearrange my schedule to come with you."

"You sure you should be seen with me?" she asked sarcastically.

"Business is fine, but what about Reed? Don't you need to finalize the movie deal with him?"

She dropped her gaze to the wood floor. "He had to leave to attend to a work issue. He'll be back at the end of the week."

When her light green eyes returned to mine, I couldn't help but ask, "Does he know you're only going to be friends?"

"And how do you know that's what I want?" she challenged, the defiant lift of her chin sexy as hell.

"The way you kissed me," I reminded her. "The fact you let me see your tits earlier."

Without makeup, it was that much easier to see her blush. "I had something on."

"It was see-through." And did nothing to hide her swell of flesh that would fit perfectly into my palms.

I glimpsed the doorway to the kitchen down the hall. I should go now that I got what I'd come for. I shouldn't go find her open bottle of wine and pour myself a glass. But I did.

"You think about asking first?" She leaned against the doorway of the kitchen, observing me as I brought the glass of red to my lips.

I leaned my hip against the white marble kitchen island. "You didn't seem to have a problem drinking my alcohol earlier."

"You can drink my wine if you tell me why you're really helping those kids. And why you're helping me. If you're as heartless as you claim to be, you wouldn't give a damn."

"There's a difference between being a bad person and—"

"No." She padded into the kitchen and stood on the other side of the island. "Bad people rarely do good things." She heaved out a breath. "He said you stole his wallet Friday, and that you used to be like him. What did he mean?"

"Sounds like he talks too much, thanks for letting me know." I added more wine to the glass. I was going to need it.

"Sebastian."

The sound of my name rolling off her tongue made me happy Alessia hadn't changed my first name, too.

"We have three more weeks until the vote. Three weeks to get this new deal finalized. And that means we'll be working together for twenty-one more days, so help me out here. Help me hate you a little less."

I set the glass down and circled the counter to stand in front of her. "You only hate that you don't hate me." And I knew that because I was on the same damn page.

Her lips parted, but she didn't speak. How could she? She wasn't a liar, and she wouldn't be able to deny the truth.

When she bowed her head, I hated myself a little more.

She'd begged me to open up, to help her understand why she should stay away from me. I'd behaved like a prick when all she really wanted was to know me better.

But how could I give that to her? I'd only opened up to one person and . . .

"You ever been to Dún Laoghaire?"

"Yeah, coastal town in the suburbs." Her eyes lifted. "Why?"

"It's where my mother was born." I turned and started back down the hall to her living room, then dropped onto the armchair opposite her couch. "I spent my childhood at the bay. Staring at the sandbanks and those rocky outcrops," I said once she'd entered the room and sat on the couch. "From Howth to Dún Laoghaire, we'd spend our weekends traveling the coast, and she'd tell me stories about our ancestors. About the shipwrecks there."

She placed a brown throw pillow against her chest and held on to it as she listened to me, remaining quiet as if she feared I'd stop talking.

"I used to walk the pier back in Dún Laoghaire all the time and imagine I'd grow up to be a pirate." I smiled at one of the few happy memories I still had. "You told me you'd dreamed of being a lot of things, but I'd only ever had one dream. Probably not the best idea."

She returned my smile, and the movement of her lips— the happiness there—quickened my pulse.

"As much as my mother loved Dublin, she was obsessed

with Paris," I continued for some crazy reason. The last person I'd shared my stories with had been Alessia, and it felt strange, but also right, to talk to Holly. "We moved to Paris when I was eight."

"So, you're not French? I thought—"

"No, just lived there," I admitted, even though my manufactured identity declared I was part French.

"What about your father?" she asked, keeping her voice soft.

"I don't have a father. He didn't want us. I never met him. I didn't even know his name for the longest time." Anthony Romano gave me his blood and a sister, but he'd never be more than that in my mind. "The kids," I said, remembering why I was telling her about Ma. "Declan and Samuel—their ma isn't around much. They didn't tell me, but I think she's got a drug problem. Declan was stealing to take care of Samuel."

Her mouth tightened as if she couldn't find the right words to share.

"After my ma died of a drug overdose in Paris, I was placed into the system, but I hated it. I ran away. Lived on the streets. I stole so I could buy food. Clothes."

"I'm so sorry." Her green eyes glimmered with unshed tears.

She didn't need to cry for me. If she knew the things I'd done, she'd beg me to leave.

"That's why you're helping them," she said. "Because of what you went through."

"Only I'm hoping to find their ma before they experience the same fate as me. Declan is eighteen, but I doubt he'd win custody of Samuel. I can't have the kid ending up in the system." I stood and went to the window, the rain continuing to glide down the glass outside. "What are you thinking?" I faced her, worried she'd be looking at me as if she could fix me.

"I'm thinking you had a difficult life." She set the pillow aside and stood. "And you must have worked very hard to get to where you are today."

I didn't earn the money, though I couldn't tell her that part. My openness would have to end now.

"Would it make you feel better if I tell you something no one knows?"

It'll make me care more, and I care too much already. But I kept my mouth closed, desperate just to hear the sound of her voice.

She stood alongside me but kept her gaze out the window, and I turned around to share the same view.

"When I was in high school, my boyfriend wouldn't take no for an answer, and I hadn't been ready to give up my virginity."

My hand became a fist, and I set it against the windowpane as I bit down on my back teeth at her words. This was not what I was expecting to hear.

"Sean stopped him long before he had a chance to do anything."

Relief struck me, but the anger didn't subside.

"If it'd been Adam there, he probably would've—"

"Killed him?" Same as me.

"But that's the part my family knows." She faced me, bringing her eyes to mine. "What they don't know is that I grabbed my father's gun and went to him the following week, and I threatened him. I held the gun on him and said if he ever tried to force a girl to do something against her will ever again, I'd know, and I'd come back for him and kill him." Her lower lip trembled. "I still check on him, too. Like some insane stalker. Making sure he keeps the promise he'd made while he pissed his trousers." Emotion choked her words, breaking them in half.

Holy hell.

This woman.

"Holly." I pulled her into my arms, brought her cheek to my chest, and held her tight against me.

Was I hugging her? *Oh, God.* And she was allowing it.

"Am I crazy?" she asked after she'd let go of me. The fact she was asking that question was a reminder she had absolutely no idea the kind of man I truly was.

"You're not crazy at all," I said, resisting the urge to caress her cheeks between my palms.

I'd be needing this man's name, but I'd find it out on my own. I'd make sure he did live up to his promise. There were indeed worse punishments than death. Fearing me would be a start.

"Your secret is safe with me." I forced myself to step away, and she swiped the backs of her hands across her cheeks, discarding the evidence of her tears.

"This, um, wasn't how I was expecting the night to go." She grabbed her glass of wine and finished it before grabbing her knife and slicing open the packing tape on another box— as if she hadn't shared her secret with a man she was supposed to hate.

Instead of leaving as I should have, I went into the kitchen, refilled my glass, and helped her unpack.

"You didn't really do that?" she asked a few hours and three more glasses of wine later.

She pressed her hand to her abdomen, laughing so hard she doubled over.

I set the empty box aside as she tried to stop herself from fits of laughter. "True story," I admitted.

Five years ago, when I first saw Holly laughing at the

club, I never would've believed there'd be a time when she'd be cracking up at one of my stories. "I'll never forget the first time I saw you."

She took a deep breath, setting aside her laughter. "Outside your restaurant when I nearly collided into you this year?"

"No," I admitted.

What was it about her home that had me opening up?

"I saw you the night I bought the club. You were celebrating your twenty-first birthday, and I just . . ."

"You saw me back then?"

"How could I not notice you?" My voice was nearly hoarse. We'd been talking for hours, and I wasn't exactly someone who spent much time having conversations, so this was all uncharted territory for me.

"I don't know what to say." She blinked a few times, gathering her focus, and I wondered if I'd killed the moment we'd been sharing.

This night had been like catching a glimpse of an alternate reality, a look at what my life could've been like.

"I want you, Sebastian," she said in a rush.

Those three words combined with the sinful sound of my name from her lips had me rooting myself in place even though I should've backed the hell up.

"I wanted you before tonight, even though I knew I shouldn't." She wet her lips, allowing her confession to sit between us. "But now—"

"Nothing changes." I hated the words. I wanted to destroy them. To be with her.

My chest constricted at the drop of her eyes to the floor, the pain I'd inflicted with those damn words.

"I thought I was only attracted to you. A physical thing."

Now I stepped back. This statement far more dangerous.

"I'd give anything to have you touch me. Feel you inside of me." Her voice dipped. It cracked. Her desire bled through, and I could feel it. "I wanted you to see me earlier. I loved your eyes on me. And you were right about what you said—I hated myself for wanting you. For wanting to sleep with you even though there's so much I don't know and don't trust about you."

Hated. Past tense. Fecking hell.

"But now I think that maybe whatever this is between us isn't just about sex."

"It is," I lied as I ate up the space between us and tipped her chin, demanding she look me in the eyes. She needed to see the darkness there. To remember it. To never forget it. "It would only be sex." I brought my face closer to hers, doing my best not to give in to my own wants and needs. "It'd just be fucking. And yes, I want it. More than you could possibly know," I rasped. "But I'd hurt you. You'd end up hurt. I need you to understand that." Her eyes began to close, but I begged, "Look at me."

Where's the fear? You need to be afraid of me. But it wasn't there. I'd let my guard down, which I hadn't done since my sister came into my life, and now Holly was looking at me as if I weren't a bad guy.

"Okay," she whispered.

"'Okay' what?"

"It can just be sex."

She was going to kill me. Bury me so far down that even if the ground flooded, I'd remain deep within the earth forever.

"One time won't ever be enough." I brought my chin to the top of her head and held her against me, bringing her arms around my body. Hugging again. Twice in one night. A bloody record.

"Then it doesn't have to be." Her words vibrated against my chest.

I closed my eyes, struggling to maintain my resolve with her so close. "I have to go." I peeled her arms off me and started for the door before I did something I'd regret. "I'm sorry," I said once my shoes were back on, and the door was open. "But you're much better off without me."

CHAPTER FOURTEEN

HOLLY

"You've been staring at those papers in a daze. You okay?"

"What?" I looked up to find Bella standing in front of my desk in one of her bright blue pantsuits.

Her dark brows slanted with worry. "You need me to get you something, love? Coffee? Tea?"

"No." I forced away thoughts of Sebastian and last night. We'd spent the night talking and drinking. Laughing and sharing stories. It almost felt like the start of something, a relationship. Well, up until he fled my home, declaring I should have nothing to do with him. "You get the jet booked for Limerick?"

"Wheels up tomorrow at eight a.m., and I reserved two rooms at a great little hotel in the city." She tapped a pen at her bright red lips. "Sure you don't just need one?"

"Not funny," I responded, even though I knew she was joking.

"Not funny at all." Bloody hell, I hadn't even heard Sean enter. "She's going there with Renaud, and I don't understand why."

"I explained it to you already." My attention swerved to Bella. "Can you—"

"Yup. Leaving."

Sean sank into the chair in front of my desk once Bella closed the door and raced a hand over his short, dirty blond hair. "Why are you trusting him? How do you know he's not lying?"

Because he opened up to me last night. Because I'm beginning to understand him better. The fact he was so afraid I'd get hurt by associating with him outside of work meant he cared. Cared a lot. And if he was as evil as people made him out to be, he would have taken me to bed when I all but begged him to have sex with me.

"You ever stop to wonder why he's so hell-bent on us selling the land?"

Another question I couldn't verbally answer. Great.

Yes. He made a deal. The terms unknown. And frankly, I didn't need to know. Probably didn't want to.

"Fine. You won't talk about Renaud, what about Reed?"

"What about him?" I finally responded. I wasn't playing dumb so well, was I? "He's in Amsterdam, and he called me an hour ago. We've rescheduled for Friday at three. I put it on your calendar."

"Yeah, I know that. I'm referring to the conversation you had with Adam and how Reed might want more but you only want friendship."

Twins. Freaking twins. They weren't identical, but they still seemed to know what the other was thinking. And did they have to tell each other everything?

"Does Reed know this yet?"

"No, but surely a man with a reputation like yours won't mourn my loss."

"You're not just anyone." He loosened the knot of his blue silk tie. "But back to Renaud, we—" He let go of his words at a knock at my door.

"Come in," I called, thankful for the distraction.

"Speak of the devil," Sean muttered.

My heartbeat soared at the sight of Sebastian standing in the doorway.

Rather than one of his signature Brioni suits, he was dressed in jeans and a khaki-colored cable-knit jumper, a hint of a white tee beneath showing at the neckline. Brown suede oxfords. He looked like he'd just stepped out of a men's catalog instead of the dangerous man he claimed to be.

"Hi." I was on my feet immediately, palms atop the desk for support. My heart flew out the window the moment his eyes cut sharply my way as he ignored Sean's presence.

Last night had been . . .

He'd told me about his ma and his childhood, and I'd told him my dark secret. There was a bond between us now whether Sebastian wanted to admit it or not.

"I got your text. You asked me to stop by?" His brows lifted, curiosity with a touch of conflict in his eyes.

"Yes, thanks for coming."

Sean rose from his chair and moved to stand before him, getting way too close for my comfort level. "I have meetings I can't get out of tomorrow, but if you so much as lay a hand on my sister or say anything to upset her in Limerick . . ." He left his threat hanging in the air, allowing Sebastian to fill in the blanks.

Sebastian kept his hold of my eyes, continuing to ignore Sean and his threats. Sean peered back at me, shook his head in disapproval, then left my office.

"Charming guy." Sebastian's lips crooked at the edges, giving me one of his rare smiles again. I swear those smiles were gifts.

"Holly?"

I hadn't talked yet, had I?

"The flight and hotel room, er, rooms are booked," I informed him. "But there's somewhere I'd like to go tonight, and I was hoping you'd come with me." I held a hand up, sensing he was going to protest that we couldn't be seen outside of work. "With Declan and Samuel."

"The McGregor Youth Foundation? Not a bad idea."

"I think it'd be a nice change to sitting around a hotel room or lobby. Plus, it'd be a great place for Samuel to hang out while Declan's working at the club."

He remained near the door as if he was afraid to get too close. "It's a grand idea."

"You know where it's at?"

"Yeah. Will your other brother Adam, also not one of my biggest fans, be there?"

"Not tonight." I'd checked. "Seven work?"

"Sure." He turned to the side and pressed a palm to the interior doorframe. "And, Holly?"

"Yeah?"

He smiled. "Thank you."

CHAPTER FIFTEEN

HOLLY

"RUGBY AND AMERICAN FOOTBALL AREN'T ALL THAT different, are they?" My sister-in-law stretched her legs out in front of her and brought a hand to her belly. "Maybe hotter, though. When Adam plays rugby . . ." Her lips quirked into a full smile, blush on her cheeks and all.

"When Adam does anything, he pretty much kills it. He's damn competitive." I looked back at the boys playing rugby in the large gymnasium at the youth center from where we sat against the wall watching.

"Sebastian looks like he's enjoying himself," she added a moment later, and I side-eyed her. I could hear the question in her voice: *Have you fallen for him?*

Sebastian had the ball clutched beneath his arm as he ran, pulling Samuel and two other boys, about ten and eight, along with him. He gave in and fell, and I was pretty sure it'd been on purpose.

On his back with his knees bent, the boys laughed and more piled on top of him.

God, the man was even more gorgeous like this. Carefree. Hanging out with kids and playing rugby. I'd never thought it'd be possible to see him in this light, and when I'd suggested we bring Declan and Samuel to the center, I hadn't imagined Sebastian would actually participate in the nightly activities.

"You think the boys would want to try horseback riding when the weather is warmer?"

"Maybe."

Anna had grown up on a horse farm in Kentucky, and when she'd first come to Ireland a few years ago, she'd immediately had a connection with the kids at the center, and she'd taught them to ride.

She'd been a godsend for the kids, same as Adam.

Sebastian stood to his full height and tossed the ball to Declan, who actually looked like he was enjoying himself, too. When Sebastian's hands settled on his hips above his jeans, I couldn't help but imagine the happy trail beneath his navel. He'd removed his jumper, and the white tee was damp with sweat, molding to his muscular frame.

"You know, from everything Adam has told me about Renaud, I have to say, he doesn't look so evil."

Sebastian shot me a quick smile before the boys purposefully tackled him again for no reason, and he went down without a fight. My chest tightened at the sight. "I don't think he is." I turned my focus her way. "And I can only imagine what my brother has said."

"Aside from his concern you've got stars in your eyes whenever you look at the man?" She lifted a brow. "I see the stars in your eyes now, too. I guess I was wrong in my prediction about Harrison being a good match for you."

There wasn't any judgment in her gaze. No creases of concern on her forehead or around her eyes.

"You know, your brother thought he was a bad choice for me, too." She smoothed a hand over her stomach and winced as if she got kicked in the ribs.

"Is he kicking?"

"Yeah," she said, rubbing her abdomen. "Want to feel your nephew?"

I nodded eagerly, and she placed my palm at the side of her stomach. I felt a quick flutter of movement. "Wow." Life was amazing. Growing a person inside of you . . .

"You want kids?" she asked when I brought my hand back to my lap and focused on the game again. Declan had just kicked the ball between the goalposts, and I clapped.

A shy smile slid to Declan's lips, and he tipped his head in appreciation for the applause.

"Kids?" I drew in a breath as I studied Sebastian again, wondering why in the world I was now envisioning him as the father of my children. His child in my womb. And yet, the idea had my body warming, my pulse picking up. "Yeah, but maybe not three boys like my parents. Not sure how they handled all of them."

Anna was from a big family, too. Sisters, though.

"Any idea where Declan and Samuel's mother may be?" she asked a few minutes later after the kids on Sebastian's team scored again.

"Sebastian has people looking." That's what he said, at least. "I'm sure if anyone can find her, he can." Hopefully, it wouldn't be too late. I couldn't imagine losing a parent the way Sebastian had, and he'd do everything in his power to prevent that happening to the boys.

Declan strode my way during a quick break a few moments later, looking more like a relaxed kid than the angry teen in the park. "Samuel is having a great time," he said, his voice a bit breathy. "Thank you for this."

"Of course. Um, do you like to eat?" I was attempting to further insert myself into their lives, and it had me nervous. I wasn't used to working with teens like Anna, but I wanted to help, to support them in any way I could.

He laughed and folded his arms. "On occasion."

"You and Samuel want to come over Sunday night for dinner? Home-cooked meal?"

He grinned. "You don't have to ask me twice. Thank you." He nodded once, then went to grab a water.

I looked back out to where the twenty or so kids were gathered at the center of the room. Sebastian was on his hands and knees with the younger kids climbing onto his back, and he was making a show of struggling to stand. His eyes moved my way, and he held me there at that moment, completely frozen.

"Yeah, the man has it bad for you," Anna whispered.

When Sebastian finally tore his gaze away, my spine bowed because yeah, I had it so damn bad for him, too.

CHAPTER SIXTEEN

LIMERICK, IRELAND

HOLLY

"THAT WAS ALMOST TOO EASY." I UNZIPPED MY BOOTS AND pulled them off inside the hotel room in Limerick. "If I wasn't so tired from running around today, I'd say we could fly home tonight."

When we'd been standing at the edge of the land I desperately wanted to save a few hours ago, memories from when I was younger had come to mind. Memories of running through the fields surrounded by nature, a time when I was young and carefree, not so damn responsible, and I'd teared up. Sebastian had taken me by surprise when he'd held my hand, and we'd simply stood in silence. It'd been exactly what I'd needed.

When I looked up, Sebastian's back was to the hotel door, his hands tucked in his trouser pockets. Eyes on my legs.

"You handled yourself well today. I was impressed."

"You doubted me?" I asked in surprise.

"Never." He pushed off the door and strode closer to where I stood at the foot of the bed.

The quaint hotel we were staying in didn't have any suites, and I actually enjoyed the cozy feel of the room, even the outdated bedspread printed with pink roses.

"You, um, also amazed me out there." We'd visited four sites, and all four landowners had barely put up a protest when Sebastian requested they sell the land. Of course, each owner had, in turn, requested to speak to Sebastian alone and out of earshot from me, so I honestly didn't know what else was said, but deals had been made. Mission accomplished.

Well, almost.

We still had to try and get the CEO of Paulson Incorporated to agree to the new pitch. It was clear Sebastian needed to make this man happy for some reason. I shouldn't trust him so blindly on this issue, and if anything went arseways and I was pressured to sell the land we'd designated as a wildlife preservation, then I'd change my opinion of him, but for now—he had more checks in the "good" column than "bad."

"They were intimidated by you," I admitted.

Sort of the way I was feeling now with his dark eyes positioned on my mouth.

"People fear me." His gaze traveled to mine. "As they should."

I wanted to protest, but it'd be a been-there-done-that kind of thing, and I was too tired. My feet too achy. "I'm hungry. There's a place downstairs. Feel like eating?"

He was less than a meter away, but it felt like we were a world apart in that moment, as if he were mentally distancing himself from me.

Jaw clenched?

Eyes broody?

Body rigid?

Check. Check. Check.

"You should eat."

"But not you?" I swallowed, placed one foot in front of the other—that's the way it's done, right?—then lifted a hand to his chest when I reached him.

"I'm not in the mood to eat." He sounded grouchy, which didn't make sense given the pretty successful day we'd had.

"Drink then?" I needed something to take the edge off, to unravel all the knots in my stomach. "I'd say we should celebrate our success, but I don't want to jinx it until we get this investor to sign off on a new deal." I removed my hand from his chest and turned. "I'm gonna get more comfortable. Meet you downstairs in five?"

I felt his gaze on my body as surely as if it were his hands roaming over my backside. Heat consumed me, and for a brief moment, I wondered if my clothes might light on fire.

"Yeah, okay," he finally responded, his tone husky. "Holly, do me a favor?"

I spun to face him, finding him already at the door, his focus gathered over his shoulder as he clutched the knob.

"Yeah?"

His eyes flicked to my legs. "Please wear trousers?"

"Why?" I couldn't hide the smile that snuck up on me even if I wanted to.

He slowly pulled open the door. "I'm trying to do something, and you're not making it very easy for me."

"And that is?" My fingers swept to the column of my throat.

"Behave."

* * *

"Proper Twelve," Sebastian ordered as we sat at our table tucked off to the side of the bar area near the window. Rain slid down the glass. Darkness had fallen over the city, and with the lights half-dimmed, the setting felt romantic.

"Make that two whiskeys." I settled all the way back in my seat and crossed my *jeaned* legs. If he wanted to behave, I'd do my best to try as well, even if I wanted to be bad—to have sex with him and finally release all of the tension that'd been months in the making.

"You becoming a whiskey drinker now?"

"I happen to like this brand."

"Because it's McGregor's brand?" He smiled.

"It's not like I'm related to the famous Connor McGregor." And even though I wasn't a fan of MMA fighting, I was a fan of him.

He thanked the server for our drinks a moment later and quietly watched as I brought the whiskey to my lips. "A smooth blend of grain and malt. Hints of vanilla and touches of honey. It's good."

"You know your drinks like you know your menswear. Did you want to distill whiskey as a kid, too?"

"Funny." I rolled my eyes. "I just have a highly sophisticated tongue."

He lowered his glass to the table with such force the thud could be heard over the soft local instrumental tunes playing overhead.

He was fighting back a quip about my tongue, wasn't he?

"Can you tell the difference between all those whiskeys you have back at your place in Dublin?" I challenged.

"Of course."

I brought my right elbow to the table and rested my chin

in my hand, then I circled the rim of my glass with my left fingertip, watching my light pink nail circle around and around. "Care for a test?"

"Are you serious?"

I lifted my eyes to his face. "Absolutely," I said with a smile.

He motioned for the bartender and whispered something into her ear. She nodded and smiled before walking off. He turned a seductive gaze to me. "I always imagined if I were to be blindfolded with you, it'd be for a much different reason."

I swallowed, and my heart beat harder and faster.

"Are we wagering?" I slid my thumbnail into a deep groove in the table alongside my glass, unable to look into his eyes.

"I don't think making a bet with you would be the best idea."

I was sure he was right.

"Here you are, love." The bartender set a whiskey flight in the center of the table—a wooden tray on which sat three one-ounce glasses. "American, Scottish, and Irish. Not in any particular order." She winked a blue eye my way, then her hands went to her slender hips.

The place was rather busy, and yet, I'd swear it seemed as though we were the only ones in the room.

"Since I don't have a blindfold on hand, this work for you?" Sebastian asked as he waved a hand at the wooden tray.

"I suppose." My tongue hit the roof of my mouth and remained there as I waited and watched.

He brought the first glass to his lips, closed his eyes, then took a drink. "Jack Daniel's. Tennessee."

The bartender nodded her confirmation.

"That's pretty specific. Bet you can't do it again," I

challenged when his lashes lowered again as he lifted the second glass.

"Dead Rabbit. Irish."

"You're a freak of nature, love," the bartender said with a laugh. "Bloody hell."

He nailed the Scottish drink as well.

I leaned back in my seat after she'd taken the board of empty glasses away.

"Like I said, one of my passions."

"And your others?"

"Boats," he was quick to respond. "Not modern ones. They need some age to them. Fixer-uppers."

The idea of him working on a boat was hotter than hell.

My lips stretched, and he matched my smile. "You know, it's kind of ironic," I began, "but I always compare your eyes to that brand of rum that has a pirate on the bottle, and yet, you like whiskey."

"Well, the pirate part makes sense." His smile moved to his eyes, and God help me.

I downed the last drop of my whiskey. "Weather is looking mighty fierce out there," I sputtered as our server reappeared at our table and positioned the bottle of Proper Twelve at the center.

"In case you want more," she said.

He remained still when she left. Well, most of him. There was a slight twitch to the hand that was palm down on the dark wooden table.

I poured more whiskey into my glass, hoping I wouldn't regret that decision tomorrow since I hadn't eaten dinner.

Maybe a drink with this man hadn't been the best idea given my desire for him. Desire I could no longer chalk up to being the only reason why I wanted him.

Harrison had called while we were out today, and I'd

almost not answered with Sebastian in the limo. Harrison had been checking on me. Graciously apologizing again for having to leave.

Guilt had shredded me, and Sebastian had looked about as uncomfortable as I'd ever seen him while I'd been on the mobile, too.

He didn't want me with Harrison. He'd made that pretty damn clear.

When Harrison returned to Dublin, I needed to set the record straight. We could only be friends. Even if nothing ever happened with Sebastian, Adam was right. I'd be unfaithful to my own feelings by being with anyone else until I could shake this thing I felt for the man sitting across from me.

And it would shake . . . eventually.

It had to.

"What are you thinking about?"

"Harrison." I hadn't meant to speak so honestly, and I didn't expect my response to have such an obvious and immediate effect on him, either. "How I need to make sure he understands we're only friends," I quickly added before he broke the glass he was holding.

His eyelids dropped at my words, but his body didn't relax. He looked even tenser if that was humanly possible.

"I'm sorry. I didn't mean to share my thoughts."

"I asked," he said, his tone almost gentle. "I imagine he won't take the news well."

Harrison had nearly kissed me on the bridge Friday night, but he'd refrained from making a move after the club Saturday. Maybe he'd gotten the message—he'd seen my physical response to just being in the same room as Sebastian. Hell, everyone seemed to notice.

"Honestly," I said, not sure what in the world I was doing,

"I wish I wanted him. It'd complicate things at work, but it'd make my personal life easier." *And it's been forever since I've had sex,* but I kept that part to myself.

His eyes opened at my admission, and he released his glass. His palm went flat on the table next to it. "Holly."

The way he said my name this time served as a warning and nothing else.

I took another drink, buying myself some time to recover. "He wants me, but I—"

"I want you," he interrupted, his voice gruff, loud enough to draw attention from the patrons at the bar. And if we were in a movie, somewhere a violin would have stopped playing.

He cursed in English, then French, and stood. He dipped his hand into his pocket for enough euros to cover everything ten times over. He tossed the money onto the table, snatched the bottle, and left.

"You okay?" Our server strode to the table once Sebastian had fled, and I was still glued in place, not sure what to do or say. My goal wasn't to make him jealous. I was trying to vocalize my thoughts, open up about my guilt. And . . . it hadn't gone so well.

"I'm fine." I tucked my hair behind my ears, gathered a few calming breaths, and stood. "Thank you," I said with a smile before leaving for the lift.

Sebastian was only two rooms down from me. A short distance.

I wasn't even sure if he'd gone to his room, but if he had, he wouldn't want to face me.

And maybe I'd poked him enough for one night, even if that hadn't been my intention.

I exited the lift and walked past his room, prepared to leave him alone. But the sound of something breaking inside made me involuntarily flinch, and I quickly backtracked to stand in front of his door.

I should've turned and left, but I couldn't seem to get myself to move.

"Sebastian?" I knocked.

"Please go," he replied a moment later.

"Are you alright?"

"I'm fine."

"Can I see you?"

"No," he shot back right away.

I wasn't about to beg, so I turned to leave, but at the sound of the door opening, I pivoted back around. "I thought you said *no*."

Shirtless again. Wearing only trousers with a black belt. Bare feet. Messy hair as if he'd clawed at it.

He'd been up here for a few minutes, and he'd managed to get half-naked and break something in that space of time.

"What happened?" I pressed up on my toes to try and peer behind him, but he was too tall for me to see inside, and his broad frame filled the doorway.

"I'll need to pay for a mirror." He stepped aside, hands in their normal pocketed position, so I sidestepped him and moved with tentative steps.

A bottle of wine lay shattered, shards on the dresser and floor. The red liquid dripped down from the dresser to the carpet. "At least you didn't throw the whiskey. That'd be a real crime." I eyed the mirror, unable to see my reflection even though the pieces remained splintered but in place. "You always use mirrors for target practice?"

"Something like that," he grumbled.

"Might need to pay for the carpet, too." I crouched and picked up some of the broken bottle and tossed it into the rubbish bin.

"I can afford it."

His tone had lightened, but when I faced him, the tense frame of his body remained.

"Don't do that," he said when I picked up more of the broken bottle off the dresser. "You might cut yourself."

"I have experience with this." Adam had once used a mirror in a similar way in the past.

"You shouldn't be here." He reached for my arm, urging me to stop what I was doing.

"And yet, you let me in."

"My mistake. You need to go." He released his hold of me and started for the door.

"I didn't mean to upset you downstairs. I shouldn't have mentioned Harrison." I also didn't realize my words would trigger a Hulk-like reaction from the man.

"This isn't about him." Instead of opening the door to let me out, he leaned against it and bowed his head.

I should've felt better hearing that, but broken mirror and all, I didn't.

With his focus not on me, I took the chance to study his scars. There was more light in the room than there'd been in his suite back in Dublin on Sunday. I desperately wanted to know who hurt him, but then, what would I do with that knowledge?

Knowing wouldn't make me feel any better, but some part of me wanted justice for him. To hurt whoever had hurt him. It was crazy but true.

"I'm mad . . . at myself."

I strode to stand in front of him, even if he didn't want me near him.

The broken mirror—he didn't like what he saw, did he?

"I'm not normally weak." His eyes captured mine, but he

didn't move away from the door. "And I don't like it. Weakness is dangerous."

"And I don't understand." I couldn't stop myself, I reached out and brushed the back of my hand over his jawline, touching the dark scruff there. A two- or three-day-old beard. The look he always had.

His jaw tightened beneath my touch, but he didn't remove my hand. So, I stepped even closer.

"I told you that I can't be with you."

"But you do want me?" I knew the answer to that, but I wanted to hear the truth from him.

His lips drew into a hard line, and he nodded.

"And you're struggling to maintain your control around me?" My eyes narrowed. "If you did lose your control, if you did take me into your arms, would you hurt me?"

"Never intentionally," he said in a low voice.

Intentionally? "Are you, um, into pain during sex?" I was way too out of practice in the bedroom for anything beyond vanilla.

His biceps flexed, the muscles tightening before my eyes.

"No." He swallowed. "I'm not into pain."

My longing for this man grew by the second.

Sex. Three letters that never meant so much until this moment. Three letters that, when strung together in such a way, could make even the strongest-willed person falter.

And right now, I didn't want to be in control. I wanted to be free. I wanted to be like Ethan for just one bloody night.

My hands went to his belt buckle. I unfastened it and popped open the top button of his trousers. His pecs, his abdomen—there were little twitches of movement at my touch, but he didn't stop me when I lowered his zipper.

He stared deep into my eyes as if he could see both heaven and hell there, and he had a decision to make.

When he secured a hand around the small of my back and pulled me tight to his body, I realized he'd made up his mind.

I gripped his biceps at the feel of his hard length against me.

"This is a mistake," he said when his free hand cupped the back of my head. "But I'm done fighting you."

My breath hitched. His mouth locked on to mine, and I surrendered to him. I'd submit every part of myself if he wanted me to. In the bedroom, at least.

His firm lips softened, and his tongue eased into my mouth slowly. I moaned, my yearning for him beyond the breaking point.

My body went lax, and I kept hold of him, so I didn't wilt like some delicate flower.

"Holly." My name on his tongue this time was still a warning, but it was the good kind. The I'm-going-to-screw-you-now kind.

He spun me around and pressed my back to the wall alongside the door, and I knocked into a picture on the wall.

His hands framed my face as he brought his lips back to mine, stealing my breath, my sanity.

My palms dragged down his hard wall of muscles, and I yanked at his trousers in an attempt to get them to fall.

He kissed me like something fierce and wild, and it was better than I'd ever imagined, even in my fantasies. His trousers and boxers dropped a moment later, and he kicked them to the side.

"You're still dressed, love." His murmured words had my nipples pebbling, and my desire spiking to new heights.

He backed away, his chest rising and falling with deep breaths. Lust darkening his eyes. "Strip for me like you did at my hotel."

I could barely move with him naked before me. He was

carved like a marble statue of perfection. And his cock was massive—thick and veiny. Heat pooled between my legs, a sticky wetness against my thong.

But . . . the scars . . . there were more on his muscular thighs.

"Don't look at them," he said, clearly knowing my mind had shifted to worry.

My heart hurt for whatever had happened to him.

"Look at my eyes," he said when my attention jumped to another tattoo on his leg. Before I had a chance to analyze it, he gathered me in his arms and kissed me again, redirecting my focus.

And when his mouth seized mine, my mind emptied of everything except for how he made me feel. I brought my hands to his chest and pushed him back so I could give him what he wanted. Me naked.

His hands tightened at his sides as he observed my movements.

Boots off. Jeans next. Jumper after.

I wasn't exactly a stripping pro, especially with someone like him watching, but I'd do anything to evoke the devastating look of hunger in his eyes.

His gaze dipped once I was completely naked, moving from my breasts to my smooth center.

"Turn around," he commanded.

I moved with slow steps and faced the wall, eyeing the photo of the city of Limerick I'd knocked into before. But when a large, warm hand connected with my skin and trailed down my spine, my lids snapped closed, and my knees buckled.

His hand went to the curve of my arse cheek before traveling to my sex. To my very wet sex.

I wouldn't be able to stand much longer. The need was

too great. Hot pulses of desire had me clenching my thighs together with his hand wrapped around from behind, touching my clit.

He released me but only for a moment to change his position. He pressed his body tight to mine, bringing both hands around the front of my body. One hand massaged my breast, the other feathered over the sensitive area between my legs.

"You're perfect," he said into my ear, the sound of desire heavy in his tone. "I want to take my time, to appreciate you." His voice deepened when he pinched my nipple. "But it's been a long time. A long time wanting you, too."

A long time? No way had he not had sex recently. He had women with him everywhere he went. I'd even spotted him with women—*plural.* I didn't want to think about that, not with his hands on me and us so close to finally giving in to our desires.

I turned toward him, losing his touch in the process, but then I draped my arms over his shoulders and stared deep into his heavy-lidded and lust-filled eyes, probably a mirror of what mine looked like.

"You don't have to be gentle."

"I want to be. For you." His brows pulled together.

"And I just want you to be you," I whispered. He lifted me into his arms and deposited me on the bed before I even knew what the hell happened.

"Fuck," he rasped as he climbed on top of me, our naked bodies pressed together exactly how we were meant to be. Somehow he managed not to crush me with the weight of his muscular body.

His kiss turned rougher, and God, did I love it.

With his hands now propped on each side of me, his

biceps tightening, I shimmied against him, desperate for him to fill me.

He worked his mouth down my body, and my hands went to his thick, luscious hair.

"Gorgeous." He licked and sucked my breast. Took my nipple between his teeth, and, oh wow . . .

"Sebastian." I arched off the bed, and he brought his palm between my legs and lightly slapped me there, then rubbed the sensitive nub. I was going to scream—lose my mind.

And when he worked his mouth even lower, pausing at my belly button to swirl his tongue around, my legs squeezed, my knees bent, and I fisted the bedding at my sides.

Want greater than I'd ever experienced in my life surged through me.

But nothing would've prepared me for when he positioned his mouth over my sex.

Absolutely nothing.

He parted my thighs, spreading me open as if he could look at me forever.

We were in the light. He could see all of me. And I wanted him to.

"Beautiful." I think I died a little the moment his mouth dropped down.

When his tongue slid along the seam of my sex, I came. Right freaking then.

I cried out his name, my entire body wrecked. Shattered. Destroyed for life.

But he didn't stop. He continued to punish me with his tongue in the best possible way, and I rode the orgasm.

I wanted to screw my eyes tight from the almost painful bliss I was experiencing, but I also couldn't take my gaze off him.

He squeezed my hips when I lifted my arse off the bed,

ensuring he kept his mouth on me, never losing hold of me for a second.

"Sebastian, please," I begged. "I need you inside of me." I couldn't take it any longer.

I needed my mouth on him, too. I wanted to trail my lips along his body. To kiss his wounds in an attempt to heal. But I was greedy, too greedy with the desire for us to be one.

I took a second to catch my breath when he stood to grab protection. His backside was as hard as every other part of him. The tattoo of the cross at the center of his back held my eye.

Once he was wrapped, he repositioned himself on top, and his eyes connected with mine. He dipped in for a kiss. A long, sensual one. Whiskey mingled with sex.

He didn't ask if I was sure. He didn't check if I wanted to change my mind. And he didn't have to.

I'd secured my hand around the root of his cock and guided his tip to my center, and he held my eyes as he thrust in with one hard movement.

I swore louder than I'd meant to, my body lifting off the bed as he claimed me.

Sounds, not words, continued to leave my lips. Incoherent beats of breathy noise.

He pushed into me with deliberate strokes. He moved harder than I think he'd meant to, burying himself so deep inside of me.

"I'm sorry," he said, starting to slow down as if he'd been worried he'd hurt me.

I shook my head, and my fingernails bit into his biceps. "Don't stop. Please."

I lifted my hips and moved with him, letting him know I only wanted more. More of whatever he'd give me.

Hard. Soft. Rough. He was perfect. This was perfect.

"Sebastian," I cried when I couldn't hold back another orgasm. It was a the-world-tipped-off-its-axis kind of moan that ripped from deep within my chest, and the sound impacted him because his jaw locked tight as if he were biting down on his back teeth . . . and he came, too. I could feel it happening.

He bowed his head, his forehead touching mine, and he hissed.

"What's wrong?" I whispered.

He lifted his head, a mix of guilt and longing in his deep brown eyes. "I'm gonna want to do this again."

CHAPTER SEVENTEEN

SEBASTIAN

SHE WAS ASLEEP. THE SHEET COVERED HER LOWER HALF, AND her beautiful tits lifted with each soft breath she took. I should've covered her, kept her warm, but I was a greedy bastard and loved the sight of her.

When I'd first seen her that night at the club, I'd thought she looked like an angel. And I'd been right.

She was heaven in a bottle, and I wanted to savor her. To keep her for myself. Forever.

I stood from the armchair by the bed, allowing the bottle of whiskey to rest against the side of my leg.

I didn't get drunk. Not ever. I couldn't afford to weaken my senses or control. But I'd fucked up. I'd crossed the line I shouldn't have. I'd tried to resist her, and I'd failed.

And now that I'd had her, I didn't have a damn idea how I'd ever be able to walk away. But when she discovered the truth, she wouldn't walk—she'd run.

She moaned and rolled to her side. Her eyes opened, and

she blinked a few times, attempting to adjust her focus in the dark. "Why are you drinking?"

I brought the bottle to my lips and took a long swig. I wasn't drunk yet. But I wanted to be. I needed to dull the pain of a loss I knew was imminent.

"Sebastian?" She positioned her back against the headboard, sheet covering her beautiful body, as I set the bottle on the bedside table and sat next to her.

She'd had her tight arse up against my cock while she'd slept. Her back to my chest. The heat from her had made my normally hot skin feel like it was on fire.

And now, I wanted her in my arms again. Her body pressed to mine.

"I'm fine," I lied.

She reached for my hand, allowing the sheet to slip, then shifted on top of me, straddling me in my upright position. She moved her hips in circular motions, grinding her pussy against my very awake cock. If she wasn't careful, I was going to slide right into her, because she was already drenched.

"I want you." She leaned in and captured my lower lip between her teeth and pulled.

"I'll always want you," I admitted, choosing to let her decipher my words how she wanted. I wasn't about to follow my statement with a *but*, not with her in this position, ready for me to claim her again.

She leaned back, and her finger circled the bullet wound at the side of my abdomen.

She had questions. A lot of them. And I couldn't provide any answers. Especially not about the scar that ran from my armpit to my hip—the time I was sliced open at the side and nearly bled to death.

"What is it? What are you thinking?" She moved off of me, her concern trumping her desire to come.

She truly was a woman with a pure heart.

I stood and found my trousers on the floor near the bed and pulled them on without anything underneath. I zipped the fly and lowered my hands to my hips, leaving the button undone.

She brought the sheet back to her body like a shield.

"The thing is," I said, the knot in my stomach turning into a hardened fist, "everyone I ever care about—well, they die."

CHAPTER EIGHTEEN

Paris, France - Three Years, Eight Months Ago

Sebastian

"Who killed her?" My hand trembled as I held the 9mm at my side, the weapon I'd taken from the guard who'd tried to stop me from storming Moreau's mansion unannounced. Fuck protocol. Alessia was dead.

I lifted my hand, biting down on my back teeth, as I raised the gun in the direction of the man who I considered a father since I was eighteen. He and Drake Anderson, one of the ten leaders of The Alliance, were sipping whiskey in Moreau's opulent study.

I shifted the gun toward Anderson. "Your people?" Spit and fury accompanied my words as they flew out of my mouth. "Who feckin' killed my sister?"

Moreau held a hand in the air. Catching sight of a bodyguard in my peripheral view, I whirled around to find two more men approaching, their weapons drawn. "Lower your guns," Moreau ordered. "Sebastian's not a threat. He's upset," he added in a calm voice. "Leave us be."

"You sure that's a good idea?" Anderson stood from the red armchair, his arms tense at his sides.

"He's here about his sister." Moreau rose as well. "And so are you."

"Excuse me?" Anderson snapped out.

"I wanted your assurances The Alliance had nothing to do with the death of Alessia Romano, now known as Josie McClintock."

My heart stuttered. I'd thought Moreau had ordered her death as reparation for me leaving The League. I was wrong to have ever suspected it, but when I'd heard Anderson was meeting with him . . .

"Of course not." Anderson's denial wasn't very convincing.

Moreau returned his attention to me, his eyes focused on the gun still pointed at him. "You know I didn't hurt her, my son." He slowly left the study to join me in the foyer area. "I'd never do such a thing. Nor would I break one of the most sacred rules."

Rule Two: *No killing women—not unless they were assassins sent to kill you.*

I sucked in a breath, knowing no matter who killed my sister, this was my fault. Her blood would forever soak my hands.

Moreau gently brought his palm over my hand that held the gun. After a moment, I released my grip and let him take it, then dropped to my knees on the tiled floor.

"She's dead." I never allowed myself to cry, but for her I would. She was an innocent dreamer with a heart too damn big. "It should've been me."

He crouched before me and set the gun on the floor, then placed his hands on my shoulders. "When I lost my wife, I wanted to kill everyone. I understand how you feel, and it's not easy. But say the word, and you'll have the full weight of *La Ligue des Frères* backing you. We'll find out who killed her, and we'll seek justice."

I dragged my gaze up to his to ensure I could believe him. His eyes were sorrowful, almost as if he shared my pain.

"I assume we'll have your support as well?" Moreau asked Anderson. "When Sebastian left The League, we made a deal."

"What deal?" I stood, as did Moreau, but my legs were fucking rubber.

"That The Alliance wouldn't touch you even though you were no longer in our organization," Moreau explained. "I told you that you're like a son to me. Even if you're not League, I-I couldn't let anything happen to you."

"We made a deal, yes," Anderson said. "No one on my payroll killed Alessia Romano."

The Alliance. The League of Brothers. If neither were responsible—then who?

"What do you know about her death?" Moreau pointed to the study. Two armchairs sat in front of a lit fireplace off to the side of a desk.

I took a minute to try and pull myself together. It'd only been a day since I met with the coroner. There had been nothing left of her body but ashes. Dental records had been a match, though. I reached for her Celtic cross in my pocket and gripped it. Somehow, it had survived the fire.

"She, uh, was in my home in Paris," I whispered as I sat, physically unable to speak any louder. I was too gutted. Too shocked.

I drew in a shaky breath, then recounted one of the worst days of my life.

I'd received an anonymous text informing me Alessia was inside my home and that it was currently burning to the ground . . . I hadn't believed it.

I called her immediately. No answer. Called another three times.

I'd phoned members of The League in Italy to try and locate her as I raced from my hotel to my home, hoping to hell the text had been a sick fecking joke.

When I'd pulled up to my street, both levels of my home were engulfed in flames. I'd barely noticed the crowd of people eyeing the fire, the squawking of walkie-talkies, the high-powered spray of water, the shouting firemen. It was all a blur.

I'd tried to get inside and confirm she wasn't really there. It took seven men and a pair of handcuffs to hold me back.

"I need to know who did this," I appealed to Moreau. "Whatever it takes."

Moreau waved Anderson off, and once we were alone, he declared, "Rejoin The League. We'll have everyone, including The Alliance, working toward finding justice."

"I don't want anything to do with The Alliance," I rasped, still not sure if I could believe they were guilt-free in this matter. I'd racked up a number of enemies in their organization before The League had issued a truce.

My heart was fucking broken. The heart I thought I'd lost when my mother died. Alessia had helped to remind me it'd never been lost, it was merely damaged.

"You must join us again."

The sight of Luca running down the stairs into the foyer caught my eye. Glock in hand, he rushed into the room but came to an abrupt halt when he saw me. "Sebastian."

My best friend looked both relieved and heartbroken. I'd ignored his calls since it all happened.

"What do you need?" he asked. "Name it."

I had no doubt Luca, also Moreau's nephew, would help me seek revenge.

"What Sebastian needs to do is take his rightful place as a leader like he should've done a long time ago," Moreau said in a steady voice. "We'll find who did this to her. We'll get vengeance." He nodded, his eyes growing dark. "It's what we do."

CHAPTER NINETEEN

PRESENT DAY

SEBASTIAN

"HOW WAS YOUR TRIP?" LUCA WAS SITTING AT MY BAR WITH a devious smirk on his face when I arrived. "You look both relaxed and on edge at the same time." He shook his head. "I swear it's a look only you can pull off."

I cursed under my breath and grabbed a bottle of whiskey, prepared to drink far too much even though it was only seven at night.

"You were with Holly last night in Limerick, right?"

He wasn't going to let this go.

"Is she going to sell the land?" He stood and strode closer, his eyes narrowing on me.

"She doesn't have a choice." I decided not to let him know about the new deal I was hoping to propose instead.

I opened the bottle and brought it to my lips. Two times in

less than twenty hours I was drinking straight from the damn bottle. Luca would know something was wrong just by that behavior alone.

"You fucked her, didn't you? Took you long enough." Normally, I ignored Luca's crass behavior, but in this instance, he was talking about Holly. His chuckle came across as lewd, his words vulgar.

My jaw clenched tight, and I did my best not to snatch his shirt and yank him close.

He wasn't just Moreau's nephew, and my friend, he was almost as dangerous as me. I didn't need bad blood between us because I'd been the one to mess up and sleep with Holly.

"So, you're remorseful about it, huh?" He brought his hand to the counter off to his side and closed one eye. "You know," he added, his voice dropping lower than normal, "you haven't been the same since Alessia died. Always so angry."

"Do you blame me?" I roared, grateful we were alone at the club.

We were closed on Wednesdays, so Ola and the others wouldn't be there prepping for the opening.

"You shouldn't have gotten out, you knew the risks."

He'd never spoken like this to me before. He'd never openly admitted the truth—that Alessia's death was my fault.

I'd hoped by distancing myself from Alessia after I left The League she'd be safe. I explained to her the only way I could get out was to put space between us.

I made her give up the club, leave Dublin and move to Sicily—a place run by Signore Calibrisi. I thought she'd be safe there. No enemies would dare step foot in his territory and kill a woman.

I hadn't counted on anyone being crazy enough to abduct Alessia and bring her back to my home in Paris to be burned alive. It'd been an eye for a fucking eye. My sister gone because I'd once taken the life of a man's brother.

When I'd gone after the bastard, seeking my own vengeance, I almost died that night, too. Almost bled to death.

I'd been lying on the ground, eyes on the sky, and thinking about dying. Justice had been met. I didn't need to live anymore.

But something, maybe it was Alessia's voice in my head, wouldn't let me give up that night.

And if I had died, Holly would be dead now, too. I'd managed to save her life, even if she didn't know it. But now that I was falling for her—hell, I'd already fallen—I could be the reason she ends up dead.

The world was messy. Entirely too complicated.

"You run Ireland now. You have every League leader's devotion no matter what you do. And now you have Holly. I say stop mourning and living in the past, brother." He grabbed hold of my shoulder, but I stepped back and out of his reach.

"Don't ever tell me what to do," I said through gritted teeth. "Or our friendship won't protect you."

He cocked a brow and held both palms in the air. "I'd hoped getting laid would loosen you up. Guess I was wrong." He saluted me. "*Au revoir, mon ami.*"

I set the bottle down and pounded the bar with my fist once he was gone. A moment later, my mobile vibrated on the bar top.

A text from Holly.

Holly: *I'm worried. Can we talk?*

What would I say? I'd barely spoken a word to her since we left the hotel in Limerick this morning, and then I dodged her calls all day.

Holly: *I'm home now. Can you come over?*

Holly: *Please.*

I stowed my mobile in my pocket, dropped both palms onto the counter and bowed my head, not sure how in the hell I'd gotten myself into this situation.

I was the bloody League leader of Ireland. I was feared by everyone who knew my name. And all it took was one woman to bring me to my knees.

* * *

"You came." Holly stepped out of the way and motioned me inside. Against my better judgment, I entered her home, slipped off my loafers, and tossed my coat.

I knew what would happen, too.

I'd be powerless to stop it—to stop myself.

She stood before me in black sweats and a white tank top, no bra. *Fuck,* I could make out her nipples. Her glossy lips parted as she prepared to speak, but I didn't let her get that far.

I gathered the fabric of her tank top and guided her arms up to free her of it before I seized her face between my palms and kissed her.

She didn't push me away and demand answers—ask me the meaning of the words I'd delivered at the hotel in Limerick. No, she kissed me like her life depended on it.

She wrapped her legs around my waist, and I carried her down the hall and into the kitchen, never losing hold of her mouth.

I set her down in front of the kitchen island and reached back to pull my shirt over my head, then hastily discarded the rest of my clothing while she did the same. I slapped a condom onto the counter and snatched her into my arms, bringing her legs back where they belonged—tight around me, her body pressed to mine.

In seconds, I had her against the wall, her arms around the back of my neck, hanging on as she kissed me.

I was going to take her right there in the kitchen. Then in the living room. Her bedroom. Every room in the house.

I would make her mine, even if it was forbidden. Even if this wasn't why I'd shown up.

I couldn't wait any longer to be inside of her. And when her legs suddenly dropped to the floor, and she pushed me away, only to sink to her knees before me—my heart stopped working.

My back hit the kitchen island, and I grabbed on to the counter edge as she worked her mouth over my hard cock. She wrapped a hand around the root, and teased her tongue along the edges of the head.

I clenched my teeth as I watched her nearly choke, tears in her eyes, as she took all of me.

The loud knock at the door, followed by a buzzer, should have stopped her.

"Holly," I warned when the buzzer went off again.

"Not until you come." She lifted her chin to look up at me, her gorgeous eyes dilated, her lips swollen.

I nodded, unwilling and unable to tell this woman no—even when a thunderous voice came from outside the front door.

"Who's here with you? Holly, can you let me in?" A pause. Another set of raps hammering at the door. "Are you okay?"

Her brother Adam. Just grand. That should've killed my mood, but I was too close to coming in her mouth, and no way could I back down now.

She continued to suck harder but not quite faster,

followed by slow, torturous swirls of her tongue around the head of my cock.

My fists met the countertop on each side of me, my entire body shuddering as I came inside her mouth. She sucked the life and every last drop out of me.

"Holly!"

Adam's voice. Right.

"Get dressed." She stood, smiling. Reluctant to let her go, I grabbed hold of her and kissed her swollen lips. "Go in the other room."

I grabbed my clothes and went through the connecting door, only to find more unopened boxes. Her brother wasn't some gobshite; he knew she wasn't alone. My driver, Nick, was parked out front for feck's sake. So, I got dressed and went back into the kitchen before Adam broke down doors to find me.

I caught a glimpse of him heading my way, quickly snagged the unopened condom off the counter and tucked it into my back pocket.

His eyes seized mine from down the hall. "What the hell are you doing here?" He barreled straight at me, ready to swing.

"Adam, don't you dare!" Holly yelled from behind and fisted his jacket in an attempt to pull him back.

Adam's mouth was tight, his eyes on me, ready to unleash the fighter he kept caged inside.

I rested my palm on the kitchen island off to my side, my energy totally spent after she'd drained me of it. "What do you want?" I asked him, trying to maintain my cool.

"Why is he here?" Adam turned as Holly came around to stand between us, stretching her arms out as if trying to prevent the exchange of blows.

"And why are you here?" she asked instead.

"I've been calling you. I wanted to make sure you were okay after being alone with this arsehole on your trip."

"I'm fine." She lowered her arms only to cross them over her chest.

Now, with her brother present, she wore a jumper over her tank top to hide her nipples—nipples I still needed to lick and bite.

My cock twitched at the thought. Apparently, my energy for round two had already returned, even with her overbearing brother in the kitchen with us.

"You shouldn't be alone with him in your house. Why is he here?"

"None of your bloody business," she returned, her voice steady and confident.

She turned and brought her back flush to the marble island where I'd been standing only minutes ago. Images of her kneeling before me would forever haunt my mind long after we'd have to part ways.

Adam stepped closer and glared at me. "You should go."

"I think that's up to Holly." I cocked my head, noticing the angry tic of muscle at his jawline.

"Adam." She reached for his arm. "We're—"

"Here for work," I interrupted. "I was dropping off papers."

I didn't need her putting ideas in his head about there ever being an us. An "us" was impossible given the life I led.

"You expect me to believe that?" Every flexed muscle in his body indicated he wanted to rip me to shreds. If I'd ever found some bloke I hated alone with Alessia, I probably wouldn't have had his restraint.

"I don't really give a damn what you believe." Holly extended her arm, pointing to the door. "Now go."

Damned if part of me felt guilty I was putting a wedge

between her and her brother. I'd give anything to have my sister back.

"You know he's dangerous." Adam's voice dropped about as low as it could go.

"Adam, we talked about this. You know how I feel . . . you called me out on it," she said, her tone softer than I expected. "Don't act so surprised to discover we slept together."

Damn it.

"I thought I knew you," he said, disappointment in his voice, "but I guess I was wrong."

He turned on his heel and left the kitchen, the front door banging shut behind him.

She placed a hand on my chest, embarrassment coloring her cheeks to a soft pink. "I'm so sorry."

She was so beautiful. Her stunning, soft green eyes lifted to mine and pulled me into her world, a place where I wanted to live, even if I didn't belong.

I held her face between my palms and dipped in, prepared to kiss her, but my mobile began vibrating. My *other* mobile. The one provided to me by The League that only leaders held.

I released my hold of her and stepped back. "I have to take this, I'm sorry."

She nodded and turned. The sag of her shoulders, the slope of her spine—classic guilt. But before I could figure out how to help her, I had to answer the call.

"It's Calibrisi," Moreau said straight away. "He's dying. One day tops. We're assembling in Sicily tomorrow. He's named his replacement, and we need to vote."

I hung my head, my heart heavy at the news. "I'm on my way." I ended the call.

"What's wrong?"

"A friend of mine is dying. I've gotta go to Italy," I admitted, unable to lie to her.

Her eyes thinned with concern. "I'm so sorry."

"I knew it was coming. Lung cancer. But I didn't expect it so soon." I cupped my mouth, trying to digest the truth.

Calibrisi had been one of the founding League members.

"I need to leave tonight." I brought my lips to hers and stole that kiss I'd wanted before the call, knowing it could quite possibly be our last.

CHAPTER TWENTY

HOLLY

I LOOKED AROUND MY BROTHER'S GYM AS I DRAPED MY WOOL coat over my arm, careful not to trip in my heels.

"You can't fight in that get-up."

I looked to my left to find my brother's best friend, Les, exiting the cage. His barrel chest was more muscular than I remembered when I'd made the tragic mistake of sleeping with him. He tossed his gloves onto a folding chair, his eyes moving over the length of my cream-colored wrap dress.

"Not gonna happen again," I scolded in response to the slow journey of appreciation he'd taken of my legs before landing on the V-neck of my dress.

"I know, and would ya keep your voice down?" He patted the air. "Your brother is already in a shite mood. You want my blood all over the walls if he finds out?"

I contemplated a response but decided to get to the point. I was in a bad mood, too. "Where's Adam?"

He jerked his thumb behind him toward the hall that led to Adam's office.

Once outside his office, my purse vibrated before I could knock.

A text from Harrison.

Harrison: *I'm coming back today instead. I'll be at the office by 3.*

Me: *Everything okay?*

Harrison: *No. See you this afternoon.*

"Grand," I mumbled and deposited my mobile back into my Prada. "Adam, it's me. Can I come in?" I set my coat and purse on the chair outside the office door.

"Go away," he called out, his voice deeper than normal.

"We need to talk. Please." I hated being in a fight with him, and I hadn't been able to sleep last night thinking about how things ended before he left. I had to make it right. "Adam," I said with a plea to my voice.

A minute later, the door opened, but it was Anna standing on the other side.

Oh, holy hell, they'd been having sex in his office, hadn't they? And Les had known and decided it'd be great not to give me a heads-up first.

Anna tucked her strawberry blonde hair behind her ears and smiled before pulling me in for a hug. "I'll give you two the room."

I nodded and waited for her to leave, then shut the door and faced my brother.

He folded his arms across his chest and leaned back in the leather chair behind his desk. The angry draw of his lips into a tight line and the crease in his forehead were pretty damn good indicators he thought he had every right to be mad at me, not the other way around.

"You always have sex in here?" I deflected, hoping to ease the tension. No such luck. He didn't move a muscle. Adam was far more stubborn than me, but he'd never admit it.

I kept my back flush to the door, reluctant to enter his office space. It was fairly small, with only a maple desk in front of the dark painted wall and a floor lamp off to the side.

There was nothing on his desk, not even a pen. Thinking back to the other times I'd been in his office, the desk had been empty then, too. Now I knew why—he made love to his wife in there.

"I don't want to be in a fight with you."

His shoulders dropped a touch, but the rest of him didn't move. And he didn't seem ready to speak.

"I thought you of all people would understand. At one time, you believed you were bad for Anna. Dangerous. Look how that turned out." Married with a kid on the way. Never happier.

"There's a big difference between Sebastian and me." He stood and dropped his fists to the desk. "And you told me nothing would happen between the two of you. I believed you because I thought you were too smart to let attraction cloud your judgment and your good sense."

"I don't always make the best decisions," I admitted, thinking about my horrible hookup with Les last year. And then I remembered another mistake I'd made. "I did try and offer Anna money to leave you two years ago."

"You were trying to protect me. And her." He drew out an exaggerated sigh. "And are you, at least, admitting that sleeping with Sebastian was a bad decision?"

I wasn't ready to admit to Adam, or myself, that being with Sebastian had been wrong. "I don't know what will happen. Maybe it was a mistake. Maybe not. I have no idea." And that was the truth.

"I care about you, Holly. If I somehow brought this on because I mentioned it was obvious that you . . ." He shook his head and gripped his temples, clearly uncomfortable with the idea of Sebastian having sex with his sister.

"I can't handle any friction between us, Adam." And then I opened up. Not exactly easy for me. "I need you to trust me, to trust that I'm strong enough to handle the consequences of my decisions. Right or wrong."

He circled the desk after the silence stretched for a solid minute. "What happened in Limerick that made you change your mind about him? You've been spouting your hate for him for months."

I smiled as I carefully considered my answer, then whispered, "I got to know the man beneath the suit." When I took a hesitant step closer, he didn't back away. That was progress. "You let Anna get to know the real you. And once you did, you had no regrets." I shrugged. "You and Sebastian, you're both billionaires in suits, but underneath there's so much more."

He smirked, and thank God for that. "I'm not a billionaire anymore."

"Right." After he and Anna married, Adam signed most of his shares of the company over to Sean and me. And then he'd donated the majority of his fortune to charitable foundations. "You're a philanthropist."

He tucked his hands into the pockets of his gray sweats. "Listen, I'm sorry for how I acted last night, but I don't want to see you get hurt. I'd die before I let anything happen to you." He reached for my forearm and pulled me in for a hug. "I love you."

"But?" I murmured against his chest.

He freed me of his embrace. "No conditions." He closed his eyes, seized hold of a deep breath, then let it go. "*But* if he ever does hurt you, in any way, I don't care who he is, I'll end him."

CHAPTER TWENTY-ONE

HOLLY

"Can I come in?"

I looked up from my laptop to see Harrison standing in the doorway in one of his Tom Ford suits. Navy blue. Crisp white shirt and dark tie beneath the jacket. No smile. His gray eyes cold and hard. I'd been expecting that given his text this morning.

"What's wrong?"

He shut the door, then eyed the glass wall with a view to the hall. "Can I lower the blinds?"

Yeah, this was going to be a shitty afternoon, wasn't it? "Of course." I stood and braced the desk, not ready to leave the safety of the solid structure. Hell, I needed to keep my palms flat to the surface, or I'd probably lose my footing, nerves too tangled.

Once the motorized blinds scrolled down, Harrison moved to the desk and placed a USB drive in front of me. "You need to look at that. It's information on Renaud."

I dropped back onto my chair at his words and stared in a daze at the small, black object bearing his initials, HR, on the side.

I wasn't sure if I was ready to open Pandora's box, to download the files and let them infect my thoughts about Sebastian. "Harrison, you're an amazing friend, and I—"

"Fell for the devil instead?" When I looked up, his lips were pressed tight, the look in his eyes still cold. "I think it was obvious I wanted more than friendship, Holly," he began, then held a hand in the air between us, "but it would never have worked. The distance. The fact that I'm no good at relationships." He paused for a moment. "But we have become friends, which means I care about you." He pointed to the USB. "And Renaud is more than dangerous. He's a killer."

I blinked at his words, at the harshness of his statement.

Sebastian's past may be dark, but a killer?

"My sister's husband—well, his private security company is the best at finding intel on people throughout the world. Believe me when I say what they found out is not only true, but . . ."

"What is it?" My hand went to my chest, a lame attempt to slow my heartbeat.

"Renaud is associated with a very powerful and deadly group known as The Alliance."

The Alliance? I guess just because I'd never heard of it didn't mean they didn't exist.

"The organization is mostly this side of the Atlantic, so the CIA hasn't had much reason to get involved in pursuing their criminality. But agencies from Interpol to MI6 . . . they've tried and failed to take them down."

I pressed my fingers to both my eyes, a headache blooming.

"You need to stay as far away from Renaud as possible." The concern in his voice had me dropping my hands, and I finally reached for the USB.

"I'm surprised my friend didn't discover this when she looked into him for me." I stuck the drive into the side of my laptop and downloaded the files.

"This group has more influence than you could possibly imagine. Officials at every level in government who help ensure The Alliance doesn't go down."

"Then how'd your brother-in-law's company make the connection?" I stared at the little blue folder on my computer screen with Renaud's name beneath it. I couldn't open it, not yet.

My hand hovered over the mouse, my palm growing sweaty.

"I don't know. Like I said, they're the best at this kind of stuff." He came around behind the desk to stand next to my chair. "Take a look. Please."

My heart stuttered as I clicked open the folder. "Who is this?" The first image was a blond man with two different-colored eyes. Yeah, he looked like a killer. His hollow gaze void of emotion. No soul.

"Drake Anderson, the CEO and owner of Anderson Industries. He's one of the three men who have been identified as top-level members, or maybe leaders, of this Alliance organization. There's believed to be many more, but the reason why I'm sharing his name with you is because he's the one trying to buy your land in Limerick."

"What?" I took shallow breaths as I peered over my shoulder at him. "No, Paulson wants the land."

"A shell company of Anderson's. And it gets worse, Donovan Hannigan was Drake Anderson's brother-in-law, the man you said was a crime boss here."

I shut my eyes, feeling like I'd had one too many whiskeys. My head was fuzzy, and the room was spinning.

At the feel of his hand on my shoulder, I drew in a deep breath to calm down, to get my heart to beat at its normal pace.

"Sean told me Renaud is responsible for pushing the land sale. That can't be a coincidence."

Sebastian needed me to sell the land . . . but to Drake Anderson? What in God's name?

"There's more you should know about Renaud." I opened my eyes and watched with trepidation as Harrison took control of the mouse to reveal more of the awful facts he'd discovered.

"This man jumped out of his tenth-floor flat after Renaud paid him a visit." The screen displayed a photo of a man who looked vaguely familiar, and I quickly remembered hearing about his suicide in the news a few years back. If Harrison was suggesting this was Sebastian's doing, I refused to believe it. "Holly, Sebastian *is* capable of such things. This one, however, may scare the shit out of you. The manager of Renaud's club, here in Dublin, died when his home in Paris was destroyed by a fire. She was the only one inside. Arson." He paused to let that sink in. "The name of his manager was Josie McClintock, but the dental records matched an Alessia Romano. Heiress to the American billionaire, Anthony Romano."

Alessia Romano? Why did that sound so familiar? Surely, the death of billionaires made the news, but it felt like more than that.

"Renaud's net worth matches the amount of money Alessia inherited when her father died. Renaud also buried the truth of who really died in that fire and made sure it never got leaked to the press."

"No," I snapped.

"He's been arrested multiple times in the last few years in different countries," he continued anyway, "never remained in jail for more than a day. Charges always dropped."

"Then he's innocent."

"Or corrupt," he countered, the deep timbre of his voice cutting.

"Nothing you've said proves he's guilty. There has to be another explanation." I lifted my hands and stared at them as they visibly trembled.

"His real name is Sebastian Ryan. His mother died in Paris when he was twelve. He was arrested three times before eighteen, then he disappeared. No known addresses. It was probably when he joined The Alliance. Looks like five years ago, he decided to take on the alias Sebastian Renaud when he became a billionaire."

He told me he was dangerous, but this? It didn't add up. "I need to talk to him." I reached for my mobile, but Harrison covered my hand with his.

"I have to tell Sean. He needs to know the truth about Renaud."

"This is speculation. Please, wait. Let me talk to Sebastian and see what he says." I swallowed, forcing down the lump in my throat.

I didn't make love to a killer. I hadn't had a murderer's hands on my body. No, it couldn't be true.

"I'm trying to protect you." Harrison's voice softened, like he was consoling a child.

I stood and faced him, prepared to hold my ground. "I don't need anyone to keep me safe." I brought my balled hands to his chest, fighting back tears. I didn't want to believe Sebastian had managed to manipulate me, but if it was true, I'd never forgive myself for falling for his act.

Harrison gripped my shoulders, then pulled me to his chest and held on to me as I let go and cried.

"It's gonna be okay," he promised, and I wished more than anything I could believe him.

* * *

"This stuff really is good." I hiccupped. Drinking at work wasn't the best idea, but it was after hours, at least. "Want some?" I held up the bottle of Jameson and leaned across my desk, intending to hand it to Cole, but his gaze was pinned to my laptop.

"I was heading for the airport when Sean called," he said, a hard grit to his tone. "Is it true?"

"Which part?" I didn't have a damn clue since Sebastian was currently in Italy and hadn't answered any of my calls.

"Alessia Romano—she's really dead?" His eyes were bloodshot as if he'd either been crying or was on the verge of losing his mind with rage.

I set the bottle down as he circled the desk to view my screen. "Wait." A memory tugged at my mind, and I closed my eyes to latch on to it. "She's *your* Alessia? The friend slash neighbor you and Bree used to talk about?" My eyes flashed open, the news sobering me up some.

His mouth tightened briefly, and he nodded.

This was too much. "I'm so sorry." I pulled up the files Harrison had provided and offered him the laptop.

He lifted it and began pacing the office in front of my desk. "Josie McClintock."

"I guess Alessia was pretending to be Josie, but I have no idea why." Or if that was even true. What if Harrison's brother-in-law got the information wrong?

He slowly closed the laptop and placed it on the desk, the

muscles in his jaw locking tight. "I'm gonna kill him. Where is he?"

"Italy," I said after hiccupping again. "I don't know when he'll be back, and I don't know exactly where he is." Sean had stormed in and asked. Adam, too. My family was out for blood. And now Cole. And me? I just wanted to hear his side of things. I refused to believe he was a monster.

"Alessia was . . . she was a good person. She didn't deserve this. She was younger, and I always looked out for her." His gaze was on the floor, his brow furrowed as if pulling up memories in his mind. "Her dad was never home, and after her mother died, her nanny took care of her. We, umm, became close."

"Were you more than friends?" I asked softly.

"No," he said straight away, but I wasn't so sure. "After her father died, she told me she'd discovered she had a brother, and she wanted to find him. Share the money."

I remembered now. Bree had said that one day Alessia just vanished from New York. Cole had been so upset. I'd tried to talk to him at the time, but he wouldn't take my calls, and eventually, he refused to even mention her name.

"Brother?" The effects of the Jameson were wearing off quickly.

"Alessia was a mess after she found out. Desperate to find him. I didn't think it was a good idea. She finally located him and took off." His voice was thick with emotion, bringing more of his native brogue into his speech.

"Where'd she go? What happened?"

"I tracked her flight to Italy, and I went after her."

"Did you find her?" But I already knew the answer, didn't I?

He shook his head. "I tried, but no luck. Two weeks later, she emailed me. She said she wouldn't be coming home, and she was sorry, but I wouldn't hear from her again. I was so bloody angry."

"And you didn't want to talk about it, I remember." I tried to stand once more, my body weak, my senses still dulled by alcohol. "Did she tell you her brother's name?"

"No, and the email account had been shut down. I hired the best IT people to trace the origin of the email, but the signal had bounced around all over the world." His eyes became glossy. "I lost her. And to find out she'd been in Dublin at the club, and I . . ."

"If she's really Sebastian's sister, you have to believe he'd never be the one to hurt her."

"This is my fault. I should've found her before he got his claws into her." He looked up at me, fire in his eyes. "Alessia didn't deserve to die." He started for the door. "And I'll do whatever I have to do to get justice for her."

"You're not a killer." I stretched my hand out as if I could stop him.

"If it takes being a killer to take one down," he said while catching my eyes from over his shoulder, "then that's exactly what I'll be."

CHAPTER TWENTY-TWO

SICILY, ITALY

SEBASTIAN

LEAGUE LEADERS FROM AROUND EUROPE AND ASIA WERE assembled at Signore Calibrisi's mansion. Calibrisi had passed away this afternoon. I'd always been closest to him and Moreau, and I'd mourn his loss for quite some time.

Édouard Moreau eased up next to me and offered a glass of whiskey, his gaze surveying the assembled men. A bunch of black suits, with a net worth of seventy billion, filled the study.

During affairs of this sort, as well as League meetings, one leader was randomly selected to stay behind. Similar to the designated survivor protocol in the United States. In case a coordinated attack by our enemies or some other catastrophic event were to happen that wiped out the majority of the leaders, someone would remain to ensure The League's survival. Tonight, the leader of Japan remained in his country.

"Gentleman." Pierce Danforth, The League leader in the U.K., stepped forward. "Signore Calibrisi asked me to speak on his behalf. He wanted this vote for his successor to happen tonight, and then after, for everyone to toast in celebration."

I'd said my goodbyes to Calibrisi an hour before he'd taken his last breath, and he made me promise I'd always look out for his daughter, Emilia. It was a promise I hoped I could keep, but protecting women I cared about didn't always go as planned.

I lowered my glass to my side and waited to hear the announcement of Calibrisi's chosen successor. Twelve votes were needed. It wouldn't be a done deal without most of us agreeing.

"What is it, my friend?" Moreau asked when Danforth had yet to speak.

Danforth flicked his wrist, and the men parted when Emilia started through the room. "Emilia Calibrisi has been chosen as the successor."

The crowd grew quiet, and I was pretty sure everyone was thinking the same damn thing. Would they allow a woman in charge of *La Lega dei Fratelli*? There were no official rules about it, but this was the first time they'd encountered the subject.

Emilia stopped at the center of the fourteen of us. Black leather fitted pants, a red silk blouse, and dark heels. Her long black hair was pulled into a tight bun, and her eyes were made up with heavy liner, dark eyeshadow, and mascara. She was twenty-eight, but her age wouldn't be an issue. It was the fact she was a woman.

"I appreciate the condolences you've provided my family today," she began, slowly moving in a three-sixty to make eye contact with each and every one of us. Her attention fell on me last. "I understand that this might come as a shock to you, but this is not only my papa's wishes but mine as well." She turned her hand into a fist and held it close to her chest. "I truly believe in the code of The League, and what it represents, and I think we can continue to grow and prosper, to do what my father and the rest of you originally set out to do."

She had balls to stand before these men like she not only belonged there, but she could lead them as well. She probably could, too. She'd always managed to get her father to do or give her whatever she wanted growing up, and that was no easy feat.

"We must now vote in private," Danforth said after Emilia offered a few more convincing reasons as to why she should join as leader.

"Before we vote," I began, stepping forward, "I propose we change the name of the organization to simply The League. It's time we're inclusive of women as well."

The League had originally been designed for the purpose of keeping women and children safe. To protect our cities. But there were a hell of a lot of women capable of protecting others, too. Emilia could go head-to-head in a battle with almost everyone there tonight, and I knew that since I'd helped train her.

Emilia glimpsed my way, her red lips drawing together as she nodded her thanks.

"I have to agree with him," Moreau said. "The name is not nearly as important as our honor and what we represent."

"Let's vote then," Danforth said a moment later. Emilia left the room with a nod to everyone.

It would be an anonymous vote, but I was fairly confident it'd go in Emilia's favor. Calibrisi was one of the most respected League leaders, and if he wanted his daughter in power, he'd most likely have his dying wishes granted.

* * *

"THANK YOU FOR WHAT YOU DID."

I was on the forward deck of my boat, a bottle of Glenlivet in hand, staring at the messages from Holly when Emilia boarded. "You deserve it."

I'd never forget the first time I met my sister, and she followed me onto my yacht in Positano. Everything changed the day she walked into my life.

"You okay?" Emilia zipped up her black leather jacket. "Papa said you haven't been happy lately, with The League in particular," she went on when I'd yet to answer. "Is that true?"

"The League," I said with a smile. "I like the sound of that."

"Mm. You've always been amazing at deflection." She snatched my bottle. "Every time I brought up the subject of us dating you always changed the topic so quickly."

I looked toward the sea instead of meeting her eyes. I hadn't anticipated this conversation, not tonight of all nights.

"When we'd train, and you had me pinned beneath you in defeat—why didn't you ever kiss me?"

"Your father *was* in the room."

I looked back her way, squeezing the mobile even tighter in my hand. I missed Holly even though I had no right to.

"True." She chuckled. "But really, Sebastian, what's going on? Papa asked me to look out for you."

Now I was the one smiling. "Funny. He asked the same of me for you."

"I figured. You're the only one he trusts with me."

"Probably has to do with the fact that I always turned down your advances."

"Mm." She took a sip, then added, "You do have a point."

"After he nearly killed Luca for sleeping with you, I think most men are terrified to even go near you."

"Luca would've deserved it," she rasped. "But Papa is not the reason you refrain. So, who is the woman that has stolen your heart from all others?"

Holly. It'd always be her. The woman owned me long before she ever knew it. But I controlled her safety, and it came with a heavy fecking price, one that would make her hate me.

"I want to do things differently. Be a better leader." She handed back the bottle, and I set it down at my side. "I fear we're starting to lose our way. Greed has corrupted some members, and even leaders, in the organization. And this pact with the enemy . . ."

"I couldn't agree more," I admitted. "But it feels like a no-win situation regardless of whether we break the truce or stay aligned."

Her dark lashes fluttered, and her eyes zeroed in on me. Something possibly dangerous whirling around in her mind.

"I don't know about that."

"Emilia."

"We could restore The League to our old glory days. Go after The Alliance like we used to."

"At what cost?" I whispered. "How much blood would be shed?" Now I sounded like Moreau, making excuses for why we let such evil people remain in existence.

"Just consider it. I won't make a move without you."

"It's not that simple.

"I think it is," she answered with a determined lift of her chin.

Her words reminded me of my sister, of Alessia's hope. Her optimism.

"I'll think about it," I said, but I'd never do anything to jeopardize Holly's safety, and if I were to go against The Alliance, a target would land on Holly's head—so no, how could I ever discuss this again?

My sister died because of me. Like hell, I'd let that happen to Holly, too.

CHAPTER TWENTY-THREE

Sebastian

The club was busier than normal, even for a Friday night. "You good?" I asked Ola after I'd rounded the bar to make myself a drink.

"This new DJ certainly has brought in a big crowd tonight." She wiped down the counter before her attention moved to someone shouting out multiple drink orders.

I snatched the Proper Twelve from the shelf. I'd never be able to drink this again without thinking of Holly and our night together in Limerick. She didn't even know I was home since I hadn't responded to any of her calls or messages. Being an arse came easier than I liked to admit.

"You serving drinks now?" Luca scooted one of the chairs out of his way and slapped his palms on the bar top.

"Not for the likes of you," I joked and joined him on the other side of the counter.

"A woman in charge, huh?" He pressed his back to the bar and folded his arms, his eyes moving to the dance floor.

The DJ had switched to a hardcore electronic song, and the crowd was going wild. "Hope she doesn't order my balls cut off."

"You shouldn't have slept with Emilia, and then left her naked and alone in bed the next day."

"Actually, we never made it to a bed. That one is wild." He sought my attention from over his shoulder. "But seriously, I'm concerned The League of Brothers—"

"The League," I corrected, and he grimaced.

"They've gone soft." His attention landed on two blondes dripping in diamonds, and not much else, approaching the bar. "Looks like I just found what I'm doing tonight." He tipped his head their way. "Want to join me?"

"No, thanks."

"Your loss, *mon ami*," he said before moving in on the women.

"Hey, just a heads-up," Ola said from behind, and I pivoted to face her. "Someone called asking if you were in tonight, and I'm getting the feeling they're not a friendly. They hung up before I could get a name." She swept her blonde hair up into a messy bun. "Should I have interrupted your conversation with Fuck Face and told you sooner?"

"I see Luca failed to win you over," I said instead. "Again."

Ola's eyes moved over my shoulder in Luca's direction. "I know he's your friend, but I really don't like him. Just be careful, okay?"

"Looking out for me, huh?"

"You've always looked out for me. Maybe let someone return the favor?" She winked, then turned toward the shelves of liquor.

I met Ola a few years ago when I was in Poland on business. She was tending bar in a dive of a club, and I happened to catch the owner smacking her around. I lost my cool and nearly killed the guy that night. When I checked on her the next day and discovered that the arsehole had come after her for payback, I offered her a new life in Dublin.

Now she took nursing classes during the day and worked at the club a few nights a week.

I turned back toward the club-goers and scanned the floor, a bad feeling creeping up the back of my neck. A few minutes later, I knew why when I spotted Cole McGregor heading straight for me.

"You son of a bitch." He reeled his fist back when he was within striking distance and swung.

I dodged his punch and slammed him face-first onto the bar counter in one fast move, then twisted his arm behind his back. Seething, I brought my mouth to his ear, "What in the hell are you thinking?"

"Need help?" Luca asked from behind, his voice casual.

"No, stand down," I ordered.

Ola peered at me, alarm in her eyes. "Call the Garda?" she mouthed, and I shook my head no.

I let Cole go and backed up a step. "What's your problem?"

"You," he hissed and lunged my way.

I blocked his efforts and flung him to the ground, the nearby patrons scattering.

He stood and came at me again, but I grabbed hold of his forearm in time and kicked him in the abdomen, bringing him to his knees.

The DJ stopped spinning, and security started our way. "I'm fine. Back off." I didn't need bouncers to handle Cole McGregor for me.

The fight could easily turn into a spectator sport, though.

Men and women were already crowding around us, eager to see what would happen.

Every punch and effort Cole made, I deflected and stopped, responding on instinct.

I tried not to hurt him, but I'd been conditioned over the years to fight. Trained by some of the best instructors in the world.

He leaned forward now, breathless.

I looked around at the crowd gaping at us, wishing they'd all just fecking leave.

Cole took the chance to come at me, but I knocked him across the jaw. The switch inside had been flipped, and I hadn't been able to stop myself. I threw a few gut shots as he attempted to defend himself, then secured a firm hold of the lapels of his jacket and flung him with all my strength, needing him to stay the hell down this time.

I turned toward the crowd, my breathing deep, blood boiling. "Go!" I yelled, and they got the message.

Cole sat upright, but his shoulders sloped with defeat, and he wiped the back of his hand across his mouth, drawing blood on it. "Alessia's dead because of you," he said, his voice breaking.

I went completely still, but before I could come up with a response, Holly and Adam burst through the main doors of the club.

"Sebastian," she cried, her eyes set on me as she slowed her pace, then her attention drifted to Cole on the ground.

Adam removed his overcoat and tossed it to the floor, then began rolling his sleeves to the elbows as he confidently strode my way. "You want someone to fight?" He pressed a hand to his chest. "Fight me."

"What'd you do to him?" Holly rushed to Cole and crouched alongside him.

"I didn't mean to," I said under my breath, not sure she even heard me.

"You shouldn't have come," she chided as she tried to help Cole stand, but he collapsed back onto the ground, unable to get up.

I stood near the bar, not sure what the bloody hell to do. Adam rotated his neck from side to side and shook out his arms as if loosening up for a fight. It was the last thing I wanted.

Sirens wailed outside, and the Garda would be there soon. Ola hadn't called, but clearly someone had.

"We know who you are." Adam lined himself directly in front of me, arms hanging loosely at his sides.

I lifted my hand between us to find Cole's blood on my knuckles. "You should go."

"Is it true? Did you kill Alessia, your own sister?" It was more an accusation than a question. I wanted to look at Holly, but I needed to keep my eyes on the undefeated fighter in front of me. "You take her money? Is that how you got so rich?"

I lowered my hand to my side and remained silent. When Adam swung, I knew it was coming, but this time I didn't defend myself.

My head snapped to the side, the movement giving me a glimpse of Cole now on his feet next to Holly, her arm looped around his back.

"Stop," she pleaded to Adam, but he came at me again, and my back hit the edge of the bar as he struck me.

It took every ounce of self-control I possessed to let him hit me. A gut shot followed by a left hook. And now I knew why fighters feared his left. It hurt like a son of a bitch.

I stood tall again, palms in the air. "I'm not going to fight back. So, you want to hit me, go ahead."

Adam lifted his hand, but Holly wedged herself in the tight space between us like a shield, facing her brother. "Stop, please."

"I want you out of our lives for good!" Adam slowly lowered his fist and sidestepped her to view me.

My shoulders relaxed with his hand at his side. "I would like to, believe me."

Holly faced me, panic in her eyes. A million questions probably racing through her mind, but then she looked back at Cole taking a seat on the couch, clutching his side.

Had I hurt him that badly?

"Did you work with Donovan Hannigan?" A slight stammer of trepidation cut through her tone. "Are you with The Alliance?"

Jesus. How in the hell did she learn about them? "You have no idea who I am or what I've done." She needed to hear me. Understand me. *Fear* me. It was the only way to protect her.

"You belong in jail," Adam said, and my attention snapped his way. "And with any luck, you'll end up there soon."

Before I could respond, five officers filtered into the club. "Everyone get down!" the Garda at the center of the men yelled.

"We're fine." I moved away from Adam and Holly. "I'm not pressing charges." I held my hands up to show I was unarmed. "There was an accident, that's all."

The Garda in charge looked my way and tipped his chin in recognition. His gaze moved to the couch where Cole sat in a hunched position. "You sure, Mr. Renaud?"

"Just an accident," I repeated, hoping none of the McGregors spoke up.

The officer nodded, then flicked his wrist, motioning the men to follow him out.

"You should all go." I slowly walked to the bar, brought my palms to the counter and bowed my head. I wanted to hurt someone. I just didn't want it to be any of them.

"Sebastian, talk to me." She was so close, I could feel the heat of her body behind me. After everything she'd apparently learned, why in God's name did she give a damn what I had to say?

"This isn't over, Ryan." Cole's use of my real name had me turning around in shock. "I won't stop until I have my revenge."

His dark eyes held a murderous glare. I could understand that. I lived and breathed hate every day, well, except when I was with Holly. She was the calm in my storm. My pain and anger ceased to exist when she was in my arms.

I looked at her still standing too damn close, her hands fisted at her sides as if she was trying to keep from reaching out for me.

I gathered a deep breath and let it go. "You should know the men responsible for Alessia's death have been handled." The truth. No reason to keep it hidden now. They knew too much, and it was clear that Cole, in his misguided belief I was responsible for her death, was willing to die to avenge Alessia.

"What are you saying?" Cole stood but faltered and braced the table by the couch.

"Just back down." My command sounded like a watered-down plea, my energy fading fast. "I didn't *want* to be in your lives." My voice broke even more as anger sank its sharp teeth into my words.

Adam circled Holly and stood in front of her, blocking

my view of the woman I wanted to spend my life with. But what kind of life could I give a beautiful dreamer like Holly?

I grew even angrier, wanting to blame Adam for making me fall for his sister. "You didn't give me a fucking choice. This"—I closed the space between us and stared him down—"is your fault."

His brows tightened. "What in the hell are you talking about?"

I leaned in. "Everything I've done has been to protect your family. Did you really think you could out a crime boss in front of the city without consequences?"

Adam staggered back, and his gaze dropped to the floor. He raked both hands through his hair, then gripped the back of his neck.

I glimpsed Holly to see a look of shock on her face at my words.

"I'm the reason you're alive right now." I turned away, unable to look at them, especially the woman who made me feel far too much, and at the moment, it was all pain. "Now leave. And don't mention The Alliance to anyone, especially not to the Garda, or I won't be able to keep you safe."

"We don't need your protection," Adam hissed.

"And if you hadn't have gotten mixed up with a crime boss," I began, my tone dropping lower, "maybe you wouldn't." I pivoted to face him. "But it's too fecking late."

CHAPTER TWENTY-FOUR

DUBLIN, IRELAND - TWO YEARS AGO

SEBASTIAN

"I HATE BEING IN THIS GODDAMN PLACE." I GLIMPSED LUCA out of the corner of my eye as I gripped the railing on the second level of Donovan Hannigan's fight club.

"Maybe you'd rather be in the ring, I know I would." Luca smirked and looked back to the cage where two fighters were squaring off.

We were in a closed-down industrial building. People of all socioeconomic statuses were at the club, but the most well-off spectators were on the second floor, which offered the best view and more space compared to the cramped and crowded area below.

I wasn't sure how the hell Donovan had managed to get Adam McGregor, a billionaire businessman, to fight in his ring, but there he was going up against Frankie Donahue. From what I'd heard, neither had ever lost a fight.

Maybe Adam was like me and needed to get his rush from sources other than money and power. I was a privileged dick for saying money wasn't satisfying anymore, especially since I'd grown up poor. You'd think I would be more grateful, but even power didn't do much for me at this point.

When I took over as leader of The League in Ireland after Alessia died, I'd been given everything a man could want, but I still felt dead inside.

With Alessia gone, none of it mattered. Even after I'd found the man responsible for her death last year, nothing could assuage my guilt over her loss.

The Alliance hadn't been culpable, but that didn't change my hate for the criminal organization. They would always be the enemy. And The Alliance was the reason I was in this fight club right now. Drake Anderson needed a fucking favor. He had concerns his brother-in-law might be in trouble.

I wanted to bulldoze this building and everything connected with Donovan. He was the reason Alessia had discovered I'd never left The League. That night outside *Les Fleurs* changed everything, and the chain of events that followed had led to her death.

"Well, I think all of this fighting stuff is hot." My date sighed and tightened her grip around my arm. Luca had insisted on making the arrangements for the night. Twin sisters, both too skinny and too blonde. Neither remotely my type.

"I could take down anyone who stepped into that cage with me," Luca bragged, his date hanging all over him.

"We're not here to fight, or to watch the fight," I reminded Luca in case he got any damn ideas. We were there on business.

"Damn," Luca said a moment later. "McGregor's losing."

"Knowing Donovan, he's probably forcing him to throw the fight." I dragged my gaze in search of the crime boss, but the sight of Holly McGregor approaching the cage, alongside another woman, caught my attention instead.

My eyes snapped closed for a second as the memory of the night I first saw Holly invaded my thoughts, the night Alessia and I had purchased the club.

"*Ça va, mon frère*?" Luca gripped my shoulder. I opened my eyes and focused on her again, ignoring his question.

The woman was exquisite. So damn beautiful. *Elle était belle.* Still as angelic looking as ever. Maybe my dark soul craved her light?

"Is that Adam's sister? Hannah? No, Holly, right? Who's the woman with her?" Luca asked.

I shouldn't go to her no matter how much I wanted to. I'd sooner die than pull another innocent woman into my world.

"*Putain de merde*! Adam just won," Luca announced. I hadn't noticed, too captivated by Holly's presence.

"Donovan Hannigan is a lying, thieving sack of shite," Adam said a moment later. He pointed to the other side of the second-floor balcony, but Donovan wasn't there. "Looks like Donovan has already taken off—and with all of your money."

The murmur of angry voices shot around the room on both levels.

"I better find where Hannigan took off to," Luca said.

"Keep him in your sights when you do." Luca nodded and disappeared into the crowd. I gripped the railing again as Adam continued to speak. My heart pumped harder with each ounce of truth he revealed about Donovan.

Adam was calling out the crime boss for the piece of shit that he was. Did he have any idea of the consequences of such an action? He most likely had no clue Donovan was protected by The Alliance. Hell, it was doubtful a man like Adam even knew The Alliance existed.

"You ready to go? All this fighting turns me on." My date tugged at my arm, but I ignored her, too invested in Adam's words.

When he finished denouncing Donovan, the audience slowly dispersed, and I had a better view of Holly as she and the other woman waited for Adam to join them. If Holly were to raise her eyes, she'd see me looking at her. She didn't know my name. Not yet, at least. I mostly stuck to the shadows when I was in town. But she'd learn it soon, and she'd come to fear me as everyone else did.

"Come on, baby." More pulling on my arm.

"No," I snapped, not losing sight of Holly.

"Baby, it's only a party if it's with you. Come on, Luca left. You can have us both to yourself."

"Not interested," I snarled, whirling to face her. She staggered back, no doubt terrified of the fierce look on my face. Those looks came naturally to me now.

The women quickly took off after that. I pivoted to look over the railing at the McGregors, reaching into my pocket for my mobile in the process.

Holly's gaze floated up as if she could feel my eyes on her, and I stepped back out of sight.

"I'm following Hannigan now," Luca said once the line connected. "He left the club. What do you want me to do?"

"Stay on him. McGregor just made his family a target. The Alliance will be out for blood."

"And?"

"Nothing happens to them." I kept my eyes steady on Holly. "Put the word out there—let everyone know that the McGregors are now under my protection."

CHAPTER TWENTY-FIVE

PRESENT DAY

HOLLY

"YOU AREN'T SERIOUSLY DEFENDING THAT MAN, ARE YOU?" Sean threw his hands between us. I patted the air, motioning for him to keep his voice down. We were in the living room of Cole's hotel suite, and he was asleep in his bedroom.

He'd refused to go to the hospital to make sure he didn't have any fractures. Stubborn, like my brothers.

"I don't know what to think," I replied softly.

"You're letting your feelings for the man cloud your judgment."

How could I not? "I think he may be telling the truth."

Sean dropped onto the couch, a similar setup to Sebastian's hotel suite: bar, armchairs, and a couch off to the side of a kitchen area.

Sebastian in league with an evil organization? No, I didn't

buy it. "Because"—I glanced at the closed door of the second bedroom where Adam was on the mobile with Anna—"he didn't want Donovan coming after us. You weren't at his fight two years ago. You didn't hear what Adam said about Donovan that night." I'd felt someone watching me from the second level that night, and when I'd turned to look, no one was there. I'd bet my inheritance it'd been Sebastian in the shadows.

"Why would Renaud give a damn about us? Protect us?"

I didn't know how to answer that, so I kept my mouth shut.

"And what about the Limerick deal? Anderson and this Alliance group are behind that, which means Renaud must be connected with them. He joined our company to manipulate us."

"He was probably—"

"Don't say it." He looked up at me. The lights were dim, but the disappointment was still obvious in the lines of his face and in his eyes. "Please, just don't."

Was I letting my feelings for Sebastian cloud my judgment of him?

I'd drunk myself to sleep Thursday night after Harrison and Cole dropped their bombshells.

I'd missed work today to keep an eye on my cousin, to make sure he didn't do anything crazy if Sebastian returned. But since Sebastian hadn't answered any of my voicemails or texts, I hadn't even known he'd come back from Italy until Cole took off for the club.

But tonight? After witnessing Adam punch Sebastian, and Sebastian standing there taking it all . . . I'd probably cry myself to sleep. Every swing of Adam's fist was as if he'd grabbed hold of my heart and squeezed.

Maybe Sebastian had only been fighting Cole in self-defense, but with my presence, he'd refused to do the same with Adam.

And there went my thoughts again, rallying around the idea he was a good man, no matter what anyone said, including himself.

"I want you to stay at my place until we get this thing resolved," Sean continued, but it wasn't a request.

"Someone should stay with Cole to make sure he doesn't go after Sebastian. Next time, he could end up in the hospital."

"I'll stay the night. And then he can bunk with me at my place tomorrow," Adam said, and I hadn't even heard the bedroom door open. "But Sean's right, you shouldn't be all the way out at your place alone."

"I don't need you to protect me from Sebastian." Their insinuation he might hurt me was ridiculous.

"He's dangerous," Adam snapped out in a low voice.

"We should go to the Garda." Sean stood.

"You saw how the Garda walked out of the club tonight without even challenging Renaud. They must be in his pocket." Adam pressed his back to the wall of windows overlooking the city, his gaze moving back and forth where I sat in the armchair and where Sean now stood in front of the couch. "We need to let MI6, or whoever is investigating The Alliance, handle this."

"That could take months. Years. Who knows how long?" Sean shook his head. "Plus, it looks as though they haven't had any luck."

"And what, we're supposed to single-handedly take down a massive criminal network?" I scoffed.

"All I know is that Cole wants Sebastian dead. He won't go back to New York as long as Renaud is free," Sean said on a sigh.

"Which is why Adam will keep an eye on him at his place." I'd never seen Cole so upset. So ready to commit murder. I didn't think he'd actually go through with it, but then again, I'd also held a gun to a teenage boy and threatened to kill him for ever thinking he could touch me without permission. Was there a killer in all of us?

Perhaps crying myself to sleep would have to wait. I needed to face him, to talk to him like I'd wanted to after learning the news from Harrison yesterday.

Maybe Sebastian had indeed manipulated me. Or perhaps we were missing key pieces to this puzzle and just didn't know it yet. I didn't have a bloody clue, and I wouldn't if I didn't confront him.

"We need to call an emergency vote on Monday and get him removed from the board." Adam's statement had me standing even though my knees were wobbly once on foot.

"And tell them what?" Sean faced him. "The truth could be dangerous."

"There is one way," I spoke up. "The Limerick deal. He promised he'll be gone after the land is sold. I'm presenting a new deal to Paulson Incorporated next week, one that doesn't involve the sale of our land. If he accepts, Sebastian will leave us alone."

"Have you forgotten who actually owns Paulson?" Adam pushed away from the windows and came closer to me. "No way am I going to let you talk to Drake Anderson. Donovan was his brother-in-law, remember?"

"First of all, you left the company, so the decision is not up to you." I turned Sean's way. "And secondly, the meeting isn't with Anderson himself. The shell company has a CEO."

"We can't trust Sebastian will keep his word and leave us alone." And that was a no from Sean, but . . .

"Then if he refuses to leave, we'll have to come up with a

plan to have the board vote him off," I proposed, trying to remain confident despite everything that'd gone down tonight.

"If anything happens to you—"

"I know," I interrupted Adam. "I love you both." My gaze went back and forth between them.

My brothers wouldn't hesitate to retaliate against anyone who hurt me, and that included killing if it came to it. I had no doubt Sebastian put down whoever murdered his sister.

And the crazy thing?

I wasn't so sure if I could blame him for it.

CHAPTER TWENTY-SIX

HOLLY

IT WAS LATE, BUT HERE I WAS, IN THE LOBBY OF SEBASTIAN'S hotel waiting for the lift. I had no idea if Sebastian was even there, but I had to talk to him one-on-one to get answers.

When the lift doors slid open, I nearly bumped into Luca.

"Holly." He remained inside instead of exiting as I entered.

I'd never given him my name when we'd met, but clearly, he knew me.

"You sure you want to go see him right now?" He extended his arm to prevent the doors from closing, cocked his head, and raked his eyes over my body. The covetous way he looked at me had a chill whipping down my spine.

I didn't like him, that was for damn sure.

"Were you just with him?" I moved to the back, instinctively putting space between us as he pulled his hand away from the doors, allowing them to close. *Shit.* I shouldn't have trapped myself in there.

"He wouldn't let me inside, so I'm betting he'll send you away as well." He closed one eye for a moment, a predatory smile crossed his lips. "Or maybe not. Maybe you're exactly what he needs."

I swallowed as his gaze traveled over my body as if he were imagining what I was wearing beneath the coat.

"You know, Sebastian used to need a good fuck after beating someone up. Usually with more than one woman." He casually blocked the panel of buttons with his back, and I sucked in a sharp breath, my pulse quickening.

"Let me out." My words fell flat as fear took over.

He snickered. "I won't touch you, don't worry."

But he was now inches away, and I had nowhere to go but up against the side wall. "Please." When he didn't budge, I lifted my knee and connected it with his groin as hard as possible, one move Adam hadn't needed to teach me at the gym last weekend.

"Bitch." He grabbed hold of my upper arms and spun me around, forcing me flat against the wall. He tugged at my hair as his mouth went to my ear, and tears pricked my eyes. "I would never want his seconds. His little pet. You're his obsession now, and you'll be the one to ruin him. We were best friends before—"

I brought my elbow back into his ribs and tried to spin free, but he yanked on my hair so hard I yelped from the pain.

Just as I reared my elbow back to strike again, the doors dinged and whooshed open. Luca abruptly let go of me, and when I turned, I realized why.

Sebastian was standing outside the lift, his chest rising and falling with heavy breaths as if he'd raced to get to us.

He looked at me, then at Luca. "Get out," he said in a low but commanding voice. I assumed he was talking to me, so I hurried around Luca as Sebastian entered the lift.

The doors closed, and the last thing I heard was a loud thud before they began to ascend.

I bent forward and pressed my hands to my thighs, fighting to catch my breath.

I never should have come, and if Sean woke up and discovered I'd slipped out of his flat without telling him . . .

"You okay?" I looked up to see a woman on approach, and since we were alone in the lobby, her words were clearly meant for me. "Mr. Renaud asked me to ring him if you showed up." She wrapped a hand over my shoulder when I was fully upright. "I've never seen him look so upset before. I've been working for him for years, but when he came flying down the stairs because the elevator—"

"I'm fine."

Her brows slanted. "You want something to drink, honey?"

"You're American?"

"Yes. The name's Piper." She smiled. "I moved here for love, but the man I came for wasn't who I thought he was. He kicked me out onto the street with no money and no place to go."

Wow, she was forthcoming. "And Sebastian helped you?"

"Yes, ma'am." She must've realized I was on the verge of collapsing because she guided me to a nearby seating area. "That man gets a bad rap." She sat next to me. "He's not as heartless as he lets everyone think."

I eyed the lift, my heart still pounding like something fierce. "Will they both walk out of there alive?"

Before Piper could respond, the doors dinged again, and Luca flew out, landing on his hands and knees. Blood spattered the floor beneath him, and he jerked his chin to the right, seeking my eyes.

Vicious. Evil. He was nothing like Sebastian.

Sebastian knelt next to him and said something too low for me to hear, then Luca stood and ambled through the lobby, holding on to his arm as if it'd been dislocated from the shoulder.

His gaze held me in some type of trance as he stalked past, and I was unable to look away until Sebastian stood before me.

"Holly." There was a touch of blood below his bottom lip. A cut on his brow. Luca had gotten in a few shots as well. "Thank you," he said to Piper.

"Can I have anything sent to your room?" she asked upon rising.

"I'll be fine," he assured her as I surveyed the damage Luca had inflicted. My lips parted in surprise when I spotted a rip in his black tee.

I jumped to my feet and lifted his shirt to reveal what appeared to be a knife cut, a few centimeters in size, on his side.

Sebastian wrapped a palm around my wrist. "It's nothing."

"If you need anything, let me know," Piper commented, her soft, Southern accent almost soothing my nerves.

"Just a cleaning crew," he instructed.

"Did he hurt you?" Sebastian asked, anger fueling his voice. My gaze went to his palm now pressed to the side of his torso where he was bleeding.

"He, um." I blinked and pulled my focus to his eyes. "No, he just scared me."

"I'm sorry." His jaw tightened. "He won't bother you again."

"He's your best friend."

"Not anymore." I trailed alongside as he walked toward the lift even though I knew I should go back to Sean's flat. I also had a feeling Sebastian wouldn't let me leave his hotel alone after what had happened with Luca, so he must've known I'd follow him.

"Why'd you ask Piper to alert you if I arrived? How'd you know I'd come?"

"I didn't know." We stepped inside the lift, and my attention darted to the massive dent in one wall. Blood dotted the floor as well.

"He's a good fighter." His voice was calmer as he pushed the button for his floor.

"But you're better?" I knew the answer, but I wanted to hear his.

"I'm more motivated." He paused for a moment. "When Piper told me you got into the lift and Luca was in there with you . . ."

I took a step closer, unable to stop myself. "Promise me that Luca won't come after you because of me."

"After what happened in the club earlier, what do I matter to ya?" His brows drew together. "Why are you even here?" A touch of pain moved through his tone, and I absorbed some of it in my heart.

"Maybe you are dangerous. But I care about you, and I can't just turn that off."

"You need to. Your brothers are right to hate me." When the doors parted, we went to his suite without another word.

Once inside, Sebastian headed directly to his bedroom while I removed my coat and boots, taking my time to process what had happened in the lift with Luca and how Sebastian so quickly threw away his friendship to protect me.

I moved with slow steps to his bedroom and having never been inside that room before, I was nervous. It probably had the same expensive gray bedding, matching window treatments, and pictures on the wall as every other suite in the hotel.

The difference? *He* slept in that bed. Got dressed in there. Put his cologne on in the bedroom—the smell still lingering from the last time he'd done so.

Water was running in the en-suite bathroom, and I didn't bother to knock.

He was in front of the sink, shirtless, cleaning the wound on his side.

"You need help?" I leaned against the doorframe, unable to take my eyes off of his body.

He didn't respond and continued to fix himself up as if he'd done it a million times before, and given his scars, he probably had.

He turned off the sink and grabbed another shirt from the closet off to his right in the en suite and pulled it over his head, his wall of muscles flexing in the process.

My hand went to my heart. It was as if my ribs were collapsing onto my lungs, making it hard to breathe. "I wish I didn't care about you," I admitted when he pressed a palm to the wall at his side, his eyes holding mine. "And you feel the same, don't you?"

Obsession. Little pet. Sex after . . . Luca's horrible words rolled around in my mind.

"I told you people who care about me die. My mother. Sister." He paused. "Alessia was killed as a punishment for something I did. It was payback."

"What'd you do? I don't understand." I stepped in front of him, but he brought his hand between us as a shield.

"And you don't need to. All you need to know is that being around me is—"

"Dangerous, I know." And I was sick of everyone telling

me this without any real context.

"How'd you find out about The Alliance and Donovan's association with them?"

There were still a lot of blank spots, so everything was a stretch but . . . "Harrison had concerns about you, and he, um, found out some stuff."

Some stuff? I was as vague as him now. There was a lot to talk about, from the land in Limerick to his sister's death, but I wasn't sure how to even begin the conversation.

"The next time you talk to Reed, tell him to stay the bloody hell out of my business."

"He was trying to protect me," I protested. "Something it sounds like you've been doing as well, right?"

The angry tic of his jaw was the only response I got.

"Talk to me. I deserve that much."

"You deserve so much more." And now my heart was going to split as well.

My fingers feathered his chest, and he didn't stop me, even when his pec muscle jumped beneath my touch. "Luca said you're, um, obsessed with me."

"I am." His voice was low, growly. "From the moment I saw you at the nightclub five years ago, I've wanted to make you mine."

"I'm not anyone's to own," I challenged, trying to stand my ground, though a strong part of me wanted to be his in every possible way. But I wanted to give him more than my body; I wanted to give him my heart.

"You're right," he said, his voice softer.

"But?" I could feel the word breathing down my neck from a kilometer away.

His brown eyes, flecked with gold, or maybe stardust—

call me a romantic—narrowed on mine. "*But* that doesn't change the effect you have on me every time we're in a room together, how I want to fecking worship you. Guard you forever."

Worship. Guard. My knees grew weaker, and my back hit the wall.

His hands landed above my shoulders, his biceps tightening. He was fighting for control, again, trying to behave around me when it was clear every part of him— mind, body, and soul (and yes, I believed he had one) —wanted me.

I set my hands on the planes of his chest and took a steadying breath. "I have so many questions. Donovan. Your sister. How were you able to protect us?"

He stared deep into my eyes. "Tonight's not the night for questions." He was quiet before adding, "You shouldn't even be here. I'll have my driver take you home to make sure you get there safely."

"You shouldn't worry about my safety."

He angled his head. "There are a lot of things I shouldn't do, but I can't seem to stop myself." His eyes lowered to my mouth.

I was wrong when I'd told him I couldn't be owned. He owned me in every possible way. I didn't know the truth or have my answers, but I couldn't stop wishing he'd take me into his arms.

His eyes grew dark, his body rigid as if he wanted to—

Had Luca been right? Did Sebastian usually have sex after fighting? And who the hell did he fight? Or, oh God, kill?

"You're trying to convince yourself to forgive me." His gaze tightened on me, and my breath hitched. We were so close. His body nearly pressed to mine. "But you can't forgive what you don't understand."

"Then tell me," I pleaded.

"I'm a killer, Holly."

His words stole my breath. A jumbled mess of thoughts swirled around in my mind.

"Alessia forgave me. She believed I wasn't an animal on the inside. A killer." His words bled with regret. "She looked at me the same as you are now, and she died."

My shoulders began to tremble, and I couldn't find my voice this time. I removed my hands from his chest only to have him seize hold of my arms.

"But there is one promise I can make you. I'll move heaven and hell to protect you, even if that means—"

"Not being happy?" He was right that I didn't know his full story, but deep in my gut, I knew there had to be an explanation for everything he'd ever done. "Everyone deserves another chance. Your sister would want that for you."

"You don't know anything about what I deserve." A pair of forlorn eyes moved from mine to my lips, and lastly, to his grip on my bicep, and then he let me go. "And I had a second chance. I don't get another one." Defeat like I'd never witnessed before washed over him, and chills raked my spine. "I'm going to ring Nick so he can take you home."

This wasn't over. I still needed answers. But yeah, we were done for tonight. We both needed space. And it was quite possible I wasn't ready to hear what he had to say.

"I'm, um, staying at Sean's. He doesn't know I came here," I finally spoke up as he brought his mobile to his ear to call his driver.

"Good," he said with a nod. "Maybe he can talk some sense into you," he added after ending his call.

We walked in silence to the front door. I pulled on my boots, and he helped me into my coat. He untucked my hair from the collar, and when his fingers skirted my neck, my body responded to his touch.

How would I ever turn this thing off between us?

Time?

Another man?

An achy hollowness, a void of sorts, bloomed in my chest at the idea of anyone other than Sebastian ever touching me.

"What is it?" he asked once he'd opened the door.

My hands tensed at my sides, the warmth of his eyes settling on my mouth as if he could read my thoughts. "Will you kiss me?" My chest tightened with anticipation.

"You really want to kiss a killer?" He let go of the door, allowing it to shut on its own.

It was insane, but since he'd come into my life nothing made sense, had it?

"No." I shook my head. "I want to kiss you."

He had my back to the door before I knew it, trapping me against the heat of his body. His mouth slanted over mine, and I immediately lost every rational thought like always.

He kissed me with such a fierce intensity that my knees buckled, and my hands dove into his thick hair.

His tongue slid into my mouth, and his hard length pressed against me, a reminder of how strong and powerful he was—how complete I'd felt when he'd been inside of me in Limerick.

I moaned against his mouth, my nipples hardening to points even beneath the heavy weight of my shirt and coat. My center grew hot and wet. My body wasn't getting the memo this man was supposed to be off-limits.

His lips moved from my mouth to my cheek, and on to my ear. He lightly bit my earlobe and whispered, "You're the real deal, my sweet Holly." He paused, the touch of his breath on my skin created a tingling sensation throughout my body. "No matter what happens between us, don't ever change."

CHAPTER TWENTY-SEVEN

Sebastian

A day and a half passed since Cole McGregor had shown up at my nightclub. Thirty-three hours since I'd ended my friendship with Luca and sent Holly away from my hotel room.

Once the deal in Limerick was finalized, I'd be out of her life for good. I wouldn't be able to stop myself from keeping an eye on her to ensure The Alliance held up their end of the bargain, but crossing paths with Holly again was out of the question.

I dialed up Édouard Moreau's number, not sure why he'd yet to call me since Luca hobbled out of my hotel on Friday. I had to ensure the bad blood between his nephew and me wouldn't spill to him as well.

"I'm sorry," I said when he answered, "but Luca shouldn't have gone anywhere near Holly."

"What are you talking about? Did something happen with Luca?"

Why hadn't Luca run to his uncle after we fought? It didn't make sense. "Luca and I had an argument."

"Are you okay?"

Am I okay? I dropped down onto the couch. "I'm fine, but our friendship won't be. I need assurances Luca won't seek retribution."

He was quiet for a moment. "Against you? Or Holly McGregor?"

I could handle myself. "Holly." I glanced at my knuckles and eyed the bruises, a result of fighting with Luca and Cole, both in the same night.

I hadn't left my suite since Friday, and I was supposed to be taking Declan and Samuel to Holly's tonight for a home-cooked meal. I wasn't sure how to let them down, but I'd have to soon.

"I'll talk to him. We'll figure this out. You're like brothers."

"I'm afraid the damage is done. His actions are irredeemable."

"You're sure?" Moreau asked, his voice soft.

"I'm sure," I said without hesitation. "Please let him know he's no longer welcome in Ireland."

This was still my country, and if I gave the word someone was banned, The League would uphold my order.

"There's a reason I never considered offering him my position," Moreau said after a moment. "I didn't trust his ability to lead."

Luca in power? We'd talked about it when we were younger. He'd control France, and I'd be his right-hand man. Then I inherited the money and took over Ireland, and he remained a fixer.

"I'll handle my nephew. Don't you worry, my son."

"Thank you." I ended the call and was about to phone

Declan to let him know about the change in plans when a text alert from Holly popped up on my phone.

Holly: *Can you have Nick drop the boys off at Sean's flat? I want to keep my word and make dinner for them tonight.*

I wasn't sure if that was such a good idea. Her brother hated me, had every reason to, and I doubted he wanted anyone even remotely connected to me at his flat.

Me: *Maybe reschedule.*

Holly: *I already bought the food. I have no intention of disappointing them. They've been let down enough in their lives.*

Me: *Are you sure?*

Holly: *Absolutely.*

Me: *Is Cole okay?*

I probably shouldn't have asked. I didn't need to fuel her belief I maybe—possibly—did have a soul.

Holly: *He's fine. Bruised ego. Still angry, though. I think my brothers have convinced him to stay away from you for now.*

Me: *Good. And have they finally convinced you of the same?*

The bubbles popped then disappeared. This went on for a few more minutes.

I stood as I waited, my chest growing heavy from worry, but her response never came.

CHAPTER TWENTY-EIGHT

Sebastian

"WHY AREN'T YOU COMING TO DINNER WITH US?" DECLAN remained outside the limo and shut the door when it was clear I wasn't joining him inside.

"I can't. Too busy."

"You're a horrible liar." He pressed a palm to the limo window at his side. "What'd you do to piss Holly off, because if you hurt her . . ."

He let his threat go, knowing it'd be wasted on me, and I almost smiled. Good for him for coming to her defense. "She needs some space," I admitted, not sure why I was getting into this with an eighteen-year-old kid.

"No, what I assume she needs is an apology." His blue eyes thinned. "And flowers. Best in the city." He flicked his free hand. "We'll get them on the way."

"Trust me, that's not what she needs."

He dropped his arm, his nostrils flaring a touch. "She

likes you, I promise. Whatever gobshite thing you've done, you can make it right."

Yeah, this conversation was over his head. I'd also prefer him not to know how truly messed up I was.

"Her brother hates me. You're going to his place." No way would I bend to Declan's demands, but I found myself offering up lame excuses.

"Oh come on, man. Of course her brother ain't gonna like ya. No brother wants his sister shifting with some guy."

Shifting? Was this slang for sex? Or did it mean kissing? After bouncing around so many countries for so many years, I couldn't keep track of what was what.

I blinked a few times, trying to reset my focus. Declan was a stubborn arse, and I'd come to realize that quickly. He was too much like me, which meant we'd already butted heads a few times since he'd moved into the hotel and began training at the bar with Ola.

"Samuel really likes Holly, so if he thinks something is wrong, you'll break his bloody heart."

He really had to use the kid against me? I lightly dropped my head, doing my best not to waver.

I'd not only send mixed signals to Holly by showing up tonight, I'd probably have to block Sean's punches in the process. Samuel certainly didn't need to see a fight.

"I can't. I'm sorry. Her brother will really kill me."

He scoffed. "Funny. You could probably drop the guy with one of those looks of yours." He opened the door, and Samuel poked his head out, a smile on his face, his blue eyes lighting up.

Feck me. "I'm sorry."

Samuel brought his hands in prayer position. "I won't go without you, and I am dying to eat her food. A home-cooked meal. I haven't had one of those since Ma . . ." His hands dropped like weights to his lap, and his eyes nearly froze over.

He was worried about his ma, and now I had to disappoint him, too.

"Please." Declan tilted his head. "At least try." His lips tipped into a smile. "She'll forgive you, I promise."

"Flowers and chocolate always work," Samuel said as if he had a clue as to what we were talking about.

But hell, maybe he did? He'd stopped by the suite yesterday and this morning, asking to hang out with me, and I'd been in such a damn foul mood I hadn't even been able to look him in the eyes.

Declan rubbed his hands together, his smile stretching. "Come on, what do you say?"

CHAPTER TWENTY-NINE

HOLLY

SEAN WAS INTENTLY MURDERING AN ONION, WITH THE sleeves of his blue dress shirt loosely rolled to the elbows and a scowl on his face as he wielded a chef's knife. His eyes glistened with unshed tears, fighting not to let the onion win as if his manhood was in jeopardy.

He'd been stone-cold silent to me all day, and he'd only come near me because he knew the kids were coming over for dinner and assumed I'd need help preparing the food.

Adam had stopped by with Cole yesterday, and I was pretty sure we talked Cole off the revenge cliff for now. But Adam was tripping over guilt about ever getting involved with Donovan in the first place and blaming himself for bringing Sebastian into our lives, though we didn't quite fully understand any of it.

"I really do think Sebastian has been looking out for us. I don't think he lied at the club," I decided to voice my thoughts, even if they were a repeat from this morning, yesterday, and Friday night after Cole stormed the club.

"The fact you continue to defend him rips me apart." Sean faced me, his jaw clenching beneath his beard. "He's a murderer, Holly." His voice more pleading than angry this time.

"I know," I whispered, part of me still dying on the inside at the fact, the other part wanting to absolve his sins. "But maybe I'm not that much different from Sebastian."

"Funny," he grumbled.

I braced a hand on the marble at my side for support. "Remember Eddie?"

The blood drained from his face at the mention of my ex.

"I stole Da's gun and confronted him. I threatened to kill him if he ever touched another woman again without permission." My cheeks grew warm at the admission. I could feel the color rising up my neck, too. "I've been keeping tabs on him over the years to make sure he hasn't stepped out of line."

He brought a palm to his face, stealing his eyes from view.

"See? You can't even look at me." I turned toward the counter, unable to handle the disappointment.

Sean caught my arm with a gentle touch. "I know."

"I don't understand."

"I followed you to his house that night," he confessed. "I was worried you'd do something dangerous. You were as upset as I was." His lower lip momentarily rolled inward. "I watched through the window, ensuring he didn't hurt you."

"Why didn't you say anything?"

"Because I went in after you left, and I broke his arm."

My mouth gaped at his admission. The shocking and unexpected truth settled between us for a solid minute.

"You think I'm not like Adam, but maybe we are similar, and I just wear a better disguise."

"Then how can you—"

"I'm still nothing like Sebastian," he interrupted. "And neither are you."

The sound of the buzzer for the front door of the building killed any chance at finishing the conversation. I tapped the button on his security system to let them into the flat complex.

I glanced back on my way to the front door. "We'll talk about this later."

I checked myself in the mirror by the door even though I knew Sebastian wouldn't be coming.

I was dressed casually—jeans and a jumper, cranberry-red lip gloss a shade lighter than the jumper. My green eyes appeared darker, most likely due to all the crying I'd done in the last few days.

Laughing at what could only be the boys knocking at the same time, I swung open the door. The air whooshed free of my lungs at the sight before me.

Declan and Samuel were in faded denim jeans with matching khaki jackets open to a white pressed shirt. A bouquet of gorgeously arranged flowers were in Declan's hands, a box of chocolates in Samuel's, and . . . Sebastian stood behind them with a bottle of Proper Twelve.

My heart grew heavy in my chest, and memories of our night in Limerick flew to mind.

"Hi," I mouthed in disbelief. "You came."

"We made him." Samuel's slightly crooked teeth showed as his lips spread into a broad smile.

Declan's gaze moved behind me, and when I tracked his eyes, I knew Sean must've been there, and oh God, this wasn't going to end well.

I whirled around to face my brother, holding my hands in the air, prepared to protest, when he cocked his head and said in a deep, cutting voice, "Renaud, we weren't expecting you." Sean thanked the boys for the flowers and chocolate. "Want to help out in the kitchen?" he asked them, and I blinked in surprise.

Samuel sidestepped me to go inside. "Wow, what a place!"

I couldn't tear my eyes off Sebastian, bottle clutched between his palms like he didn't have a damn clue what to do. And that made the two of us. "Give him a break," Declan whispered into my ear as he passed. "He's clearly in love with ya."

I tried to hide the shock on my face at his words as Sean told the boys, "We'll be right in." He urged me into the hall and closed the door, so the three of us were alone.

"I didn't want to come," Sebastian said, his voice flat. "I can go."

"But they want you here?" I asked before Sean could say whatever angry words he no doubt had queued up and ready to fire at Sebastian.

He nodded. "They don't exactly give up."

"You have balls showing up," Sean said, and Sebastian turned to leave, but then he asked, "Were you really looking out for my family?"

I looked at my brother in surprise as Sebastian faced us. "Yes, and I'd do it again without hesitation."

"Holly wants these kids to have a nice dinner, and they clearly want you here . . . but don't think for one second—"

"Sean," I scolded.

He shook his head but went back into his flat.

"My being here is confusing," Sebastian said when we were alone, "and for that, I'm sorry."

"Only for that?" I asked while accepting the bottle.

"No." He removed his overcoat and draped it over his arm, revealing a relaxed look. A white cotton button-down, jeans, and brown oxfords. "I'm sorry for much more."

"Well." I bit into my lip for a second. "You know how to cook?"

"Not really."

"Know how to use a knife, at least?" My heart jumped into my throat. He probably knew how to use one very well, didn't he?

Reality. Truth. They tried to fight and push for a winning place in my mind, but his seductive brown eyes and the crook of lips into a slight smile shut them down.

"I think I can manage," he answered, a slight rasp to his tone.

"Then let's go." I opened the door and motioned him inside. "You can keep your shoes on here."

Sean's place was an open concept design and bare-bones decorated, much to Ma's dismay. White columns delineated the living room and kitchen on the first floor, which included an office and the guest room where I'd been staying. The second level housed his master suite, a guest room, and a workout area. Declan was already lounging on the couch, and Samuel stood at the breakfast bar, chatting with Sean in the kitchen.

"I couldn't decide on what to make, so I kind of got everything." I entered the kitchen and set the Proper Twelve on the counter. "We'll be having bacon and cabbage, Irish stew, and smoked salmon. And since I didn't have time to make my own, I got the best soda bread this side of Dublin." I'd hit up the Moore Street Market. Vendors lined up along the cobblestone street, offering their local produce and meat, plus a few delicious imported items. It was one of my favorite places to shop on the rare occasions I actually cooked.

Samuel pressed his palms to the counter and lifted his nose, excitement in his eyes. "So, this is what heaven is like?"

"Don't go gettin' used to it," Declan called out. "When Ma's back we're going home."

"No." Sebastian set his coat on the armchair by the couch and faced him. "She'll stay at the hotel. I'm not having you go back to that place. She can work there if she wants."

Declan stood and faced him. "You're serious?"

"I think that'd be best. And maybe you'll consider going back to school?"

I looked back and forth between Declan and Sebastian, and Sean observed the exchange as well. He didn't know what to make of this side of Sebastian, did he? Maybe him coming to dinner was exactly what was needed to prove to Sean he wasn't a bad guy. Maybe I needed this night, too.

"I don't know about school. The club has its perks." Declan plopped back onto the brown leather couch and reached for the remote to flip on the telly.

"You're going to school next year," Sebastian said with a father-like tone.

"Well, I love school," Samuel chimed in as Sebastian came up next to him and mussed up his hair. "I want to go to New York for uni." He beamed. "But Declan, nope, he's in love with Ola. No way will he leave that club."

"Ola?" Sebastian folded his arms and turned to the side to observe both boys.

Samuel eagerly nodded. "That's what I heard him tell his friend on the mobile last night. And when I met her yesterday she—"

"Shut up," Declan said, his voice low but playful. He was

on his feet, eyeing his brother with a shake of the head, a plea not to continue.

"Did you take Samuel to the club yesterday?" Sebastian asked, more so surprise than anger in his tone.

Declan rubbed at his forehead as if pushing away a headache. "He followed me there when you wouldn't hang out with him. Too busy sulking in your suite." He lifted his head, and there was a smile in his eyes, a threat to back off.

Out of the corner of my eye, Sean stilled for a brief moment, most likely digesting Declan's words, same as me. "And Ola, who is she?" I asked.

Declan smiled. Yup, teenage love, for sure. He'd fallen hard and fast. I knew a thing or two about that. "She's Polish. Blonde. Funny and smart. Wants to be a nurse but I've heard her singing in the back while stocking the liquor, and damn that woman has a voice."

"Oh, I think we met her, and I can see why you like her." I prepped the bacon as Sebastian cleared his throat and pivoted my direction.

"Don't go to the club again. It's not a place for a kid." He slapped a hand to Samuel's shoulder and squeezed. "And Ola's too old for you." He casually tossed the words over his shoulder, and Declan rolled his eyes, then faced the telly.

"Want to help?" I asked Sebastian as he eyed the food on the counter.

"Sure."

"Wash up first," I ordered.

"Yes, ma'am." He winked, but it was meant for Samuel, and the kid's broad smile showed he was eating it up.

Sean continued prepping the salmon, observing the scene discreetly while doing his best to maintain distance and not engage with Sebastian.

Declan flipped on the music channel on the telly and

turned up the volume. He stood and began bopping his head, mouthing the lyrics. I'd expected a sour mood after being told not to pursue his new love interest, but he appeared unshakeable.

"Who is this singing?" I asked as Sebastian pushed up his sleeves and began to wash his hands next to me.

"Rag'n'Bone Man," Declan answered.

Sebastian dried his hands and went back to the other side of the island, snagging a chopping board and knife on his way. I'd prepared the veggies for the stew to be diced, and he started in on the job.

I couldn't rip my eyes off his strong forearms to save my life. The muscles tightening with every move of the knife, the veins prominent. Each cut and slice was done with precision. The man did know his way around a knife.

My eyes dragged from the knife to Sebastian's chest and up to his tan throat. Finally to his mouth.

His lips were in a flat line, his eyes dedicated to the work in front of him.

"So, what makes you want to go to New York for school?" I needed to fill the silence before it became too damn awkward.

Samuel sat on the stool and rested his cheeks in his palms, elbows on the counter. "I want to be a writer. I think New York would be great for that."

"He's got the poor part down of being a writer." Declan lowered the music and joined us, standing off to the side of his brother, eyeing the food like he'd never seen so much in his life. "Writers don't make much money, kid."

"I don't care about that." Samuel's blue eyes moved his way. "And do you think wannabe singers do?"

"There's nothing 'wannabe' about me, bro." Declan

glimpsed me, a touch of red at the base of his throat. Was he embarrassed? He had more sides to him than I realized.

I leaned over the counter a little. "How about you write the songs and your brother sings them?"

"He needs to experience life more before he can write music." Declan snatched a raw carrot and took a bite.

I was pretty sure they'd both already experienced more than their fair share.

"You ever been to New York?" Samuel asked, choosing to ignore his brother's jab.

I turned on the double ovens and came back to the counter. "Our cousins, Cole and Bree, live in New York. One of them is even an actress."

"Oh, can I see her?" he asked, and Sebastian looked up at the mention of Cole's name.

Sean also froze, his hand hovering above the faucet handle.

We can do this. We can survive the night. I cleaned my hands and grabbed my mobile. "Here." I showed him some saved images I had of her.

Sebastian went back to cutting. Sean went back to being quiet and fixing the salmon. And I watched with a smile as Samuel swiped through the photos.

"She's pretty!" His eyes bulged when he flipped to the next image. "Is-is that Iron Man next to her?" He almost dropped my mobile from excitement. "I can't believe it."

"She's pretty lucky." Maybe Bree would even audition for Harrison's film. Well, if he still wanted to work with us.

Samuel handed me back my phone. "Maybe we can take a trip there?"

"And what, leave Ma behind?" Declan snapped, and Samuel flinched.

Sebastian set his knife down as if not sure how to handle

the situation. That'd make two of us. Adam had a lot more experience with kids than me, and I didn't want to say the wrong thing.

"She may never come back." Samuel dropped his palms to the counter and slouched.

"She will." Sean's words had my focus winging his way in surprise, and all the knots in my stomach seemed to loosen.

Sebastian looked his way too, and Sean's eyes went straight for him. Sebastian tipped his head ever so slightly as if in thanks, and I remained glued in place like a bloody idiot, terrified I was imagining what almost felt like a truce of sorts.

"Tell me about her," Sean said after placing the salmon in the oven, and he brought his hands to the counter to observe the boys.

Declan scratched at the stubble on his jaw as if torn between wanting to talk and maybe run away.

"She's wicked pretty," Samuel said with a laugh.

"'Wicked'?" Sean smiled.

"He's been watching a lot of American movies while at the hotel, and he's picking up their slang," Declan explained. "We didn't exactly have a telly where we lived before."

Samuel jerked a thumb Sebastian's way. "He even teared up while we watched the movie *Marley & Me*."

Marley & Me? Oh, I remembered that film. I ugly cried about the dog.

But wow, I had no clue he'd been spending time with the boys. Well, other than the night they played rugby.

"I didn't cry." Sebastian slid the cutting board across the counter, all the veggies now prepped.

I bit into my lip, drawing up a visual of Sebastian and Samuel on the couch watching a movie. Would Sebastian have slung his arm around his shoulder? Had there been popcorn and candy?

"Anyway, Ma is an artist. She paints." Samuel looked down at his hands. "She used to paint."

"You got any games here?" Declan asked out of the blue, and he was clearly coming in for the save to prevent his brother from growing depressed about the absence of his mother.

"Dinner has to cook for a bit," Sean began, "how about we play Twenty-Five?"

"Sure," Declan answered. "Where are the cards?"

Sean pointed to the coffee table in front of the couch. "In the drawer over there."

Declan wrapped an arm around Samuel and guided him out of the kitchen.

I poured the veggies into the pot on the stove. "I'm finished here for now. I'll join you all while I keep an eye on the food." I glimpsed the boys sitting at the table between the living room and kitchen area as Declan shuffled the cards.

Sean nodded and walked past me, then paused and looked at Sebastian. "You coming?"

His brows drew together. "Uh, yeah."

Was that an olive branch? Was I hallucinating?

But after thirty minutes of playing cards, and Samuel managing to drag three hilarious stories out of Sebastian, I realized this night was real.

And the ice around Sean's heart toward Sebastian began to thaw even more over dinner as well.

"Do you make it a habit of helping people like this?" Sean asked when the three of us adults were alone in the kitchen cleaning up after dinner while Declan and Samuel selected a movie to watch.

Sean folded his arms and pressed his back to the counter, his focus on Sebastian.

My heart jumped. Hell, it took a giant-size leap as hope

latched on to me that I was pulling Sean to my side, to believing Sebastian wasn't a bad man.

"I do what I can to help people. Don't you?" Sebastian asked, keeping his voice low so the boys wouldn't hear.

Sean looked my way, hesitation or maybe confusion in his eyes, then left the kitchen without another word. And what could he say? Everything he thought he knew about the man had probably gone out the window tonight, seeing how Sebastian had acted with the kids.

"Hey," I said softly and moved in closer to him. "You okay?"

Sebastian dragged his gaze from the floor to my eyes. "Thank you for giving the boys this night. They needed it. It may not seem like a big thing, but trust me, it is."

And he knew firsthand what it was like to be those boys, so yeah, I could imagine he was speaking from experience. "They're good kids. I never thought I'd be happy to be almost mugged," I pretty much whispered, "but I am, or they wouldn't be here. They wouldn't have you in their corner."

"I'll find their ma," he said as if he needed to hear the words himself, to believe them to be true.

"I'm sure you will." And God did I hope so. The boys deserved a happy ending, and maybe, somehow, I'd even get my own, too.

CHAPTER THIRTY

HOLLY

HARRISON STOOD IN THE DOORWAY OF MY OFFICE DRESSED IN jeans and a brown cable-knit jumper, his stance tense, his lips drawn tight. Eyes warily observing me as if unsure whether to accept my invitation to enter.

I stood and smoothed my hands along the sides of my red jumpsuit. "Hi." Yup, that was the brilliance I came up with.

He leaned into the frame, clearly not interested in joining me. "I have to catch a flight back to L.A. in two hours. I wanted to check on you and say goodbye."

I hoped after all of this was over we could stay friends, regardless of whether our companies ultimately worked together.

"How are you?" His brows drew together as I wiped my finger beneath my eye, a dampness there.

Shit, tears? I was supposed to remain steady and strong. Well, during daytime work hours, at least. After? It'd be about retail therapy on Grafton, followed by a candlelit bath with sappy tunes, and a glass of red (or three).

"I, um." I still didn't know what to say. So much had happened since he'd laid the truth on me on Thursday.

"I would've stopped by sooner, but I heard how Cole reacted to the information I gave you and what happened at the club. I guess I felt responsible." He stood at his full height and finally entered. Only two steps. Two very afraid-to-be-near-me steps.

"Not your fault at all. You were trying to help." I was pretty sure trying to defend Sebastian right now would go horribly, so I refrained. I finally circled my desk to stand before him. "Thank you for coming and—"

"I need time to think things through," he interrupted.

About the deal? Our friendship? What? But I held my questions at bay.

"I'll call you." He gently grabbed hold of my bicep, leaned in, and pressed his lips to my cheek and left.

I turned to my desk but lifted my eyes to the bookshelf. The books were color-coded by their spines, and it reminded me of Sebastian's alcohol arrangement—color-coded, as well.

I approached the bookshelf, my eyes falling upon *The Count of Monte Cristo*. I pulled the first edition from the shelf and opened it, thumbing through the pages.

Edmond Dantes. A sailor. Wrongly accused and imprisoned. A vengeance seeker.

Was Sebastian like Dantes?

I brought the book to my chest, leaned my back to the bookshelf, and closed my eyes. My skin grew warm as heat blazed up my spine. He was there, wasn't he?

"Sebastian," I whispered, taking the chance it was him and not Bella or Sean.

"One of my favorites." The deep timbre of Sebastian's voice had me opening my eyes.

"I, uh, was just thinking about you," I admitted and turned to put the book back in its place.

"Last night went differently than I'd expected." Sean didn't exactly shake his hand or pat him on the back before Sebastian left after the movie with the kids, but he didn't yell or punch, either.

When I faced him, he was working the top button free of his blue dress shirt. He leaned back against the glass wall alongside my closed door.

It was warmer today, and he'd probably come sans coat. *Sans? Great, I'm speaking French now.* The effect this man had on me . . . I knew all of twenty words in the language before he French kissed me that first time, and it was as if he'd infused the entire language into every crevice of my being with that hot tongue of his.

"Thank you again for last night."

"You don't need to thank me. I had a good time."

"I don't have long, I just wanted to stop by and let you know I need to catch a flight to London." He remained against the wall as if space between us was necessary. "The CEO at Paulson Incorporated isn't open to the new deal. I spoke with him this morning."

"Because he has no intention of creating jobs in Limerick." My body grew tense. This conversation was a reminder that there were still secrets and lies between us. "Because Paulson is a shell company of Drake Anderson's, and he's Alliance."

This time, he did push away from the wall, but instead of coming closer, he tucked his hands into his pockets. "Harrison also told you that?"

I crossed my arms, hoping I could maintain my footing,

worried my knees would buckle during a conversation I hadn't been prepared to have. I'd hoped to cling to the fantasy of last night a touch longer, before the reality of our situation set back in.

"I have no idea why Anderson wants your land, it could quite possibly be just to piss me off since I had his brother-in-law killed."

"I'm so confused." And maybe I wouldn't be if I didn't have Harrison's words in my head and a few comments here and there from Sebastian since then. We needed to set the record straight. But here?

"Earlier this year, Donovan decided to come out of whatever hole he'd been hiding in to exact his revenge against your family. I was short on time and out of town, so I struck a deal. Basically, a blank check in favors owed to Anderson to keep your family safe."

"I still don't—"

"Anderson agreed to let me have Donovan killed without consequences."

"But now you owe him because of it?" I looked away, struggling to process everything.

"Yes, and one of the favors is getting you to sell your land in Limerick." My gaze flew back his way. "I joined your company long before he called in his request. I was truly trying to help you out when your stock took a dive after Anna's kidnapping."

I wanted to believe him, but there were still so many unknowns.

"If I don't sell the land, what happens?" My palms went flat against my abdomen.

"If I don't hold up my end of the deal, then he won't hold up his."

"My safety?" He remained quiet, but I took his silence as a yes. "This can't be the only favor you owe him, am I right?"

"I'm sorry." He shook his head, refusing to answer my question. "I'm sorry how everything turned out." Regret floated through his words. "I'm heading to London to try and reason with him, but I don't think he'll bend." His voice was flat, tight—a struggle to keep his emotions in check and maintain a steady resolve to get through this conversation.

My shoulders sank, my thoughts collapsing as well.

"I promise I'll do whatever I can to change his mind."

And I wanted to argue that it was a waste of time to go talk to him given Anderson was a criminal, but I couldn't seem to get the words out.

He avoided my eyes, then turned.

"Be safe," I sputtered. "And maybe when you're home, we can talk more?"

Home. Why'd Sebastian feel like home to me now?

He glanced back, a painfully sad look in his eyes, then nodded and left without a word.

CHAPTER THIRTY-ONE

LONDON, ENGLAND

SEBASTIAN

HE'D FOLLOWED ME. *FECKING HELL.*

I took a quick turn down an alley between two buildings and spun around. I grabbed Cole McGregor by the shoulders and forcefully pinned him to the brick wall. "Are you out of your damn mind?"

"Someone has to make my cousin open her eyes, to see the truth about who you really are." He shoved at my chest, but I didn't budge.

My fingertips bit into his brown leather jacket as I maintained a firm grip. "I'm trying to protect you. Don't you get that? Alessia would want you safe."

His eyes darkened and narrowed, guilt present in the draw of his lips. "Alessia wanted a brother and look what happened."

I released him and backed up, and he shook out his arms at his sides but kept his back to the wall.

"I'd give anything to trade my life for hers," I admitted, my tone softer now. "And you're right, she is dead because of me. Dead because someone wanted me to suffer unimaginable pain, knowing how much she meant to me." Something inside of me wanted to snap. To break in half and just open up to a stranger who seemed to be sharing my grief. "She didn't deserve what happened." I could barely get the words out, my throat dry. "I warned her I was dangerous, that nothing good would come of her associating herself with me, but she was stubborn."

He dropped his gaze to the wet pavement beneath his shoes. The rain had let up only minutes ago.

"I did my best to protect her, to keep her safe," I added. "And I failed. I'll never forgive myself for that."

He was quiet as if finally absorbing the truth of my words, perhaps believing me.

"And the men who killed her are dead?" His voice was low. Weak. The sound of defeat an echo in the alley.

"Human traffickers from Serbia. All dead."

His gaze moved to my face. "How'd they die?"

I drew up the memory of that night as if it were fresh, the wound at my side still bleeding. "My knife," I said, swallowing hard. "But the people connected with Donovan Hannigan are far more dangerous than those men." I took a step closer since it appeared he didn't plan to swing. "You have to stay out of my way while I work to keep Holly and your family safe. Please, go home."

He ran his palm over his face, both eyes still a little swollen. Bruises on his jawline and around his mouth.

"Alessia . . . she regretted leaving you behind." She hadn't directly admitted it, but the night we bought the club,

I'd seen the change in her mood. The effect even the mention of his name had on her. She'd mourned the loss of their friendship as if he'd died. "How close were you two?"

His lips twitched into a near smile, but it quickly faded. The happy memories I had of her, of my ma, had a way of doing that to me as well before the pain took over. "I looked after her when it was clear she had no one else." He lowered his eyes to the ground again. "But after she learned about you, she began partying even more than normal, and one night we got into a fight." He turned to the side, facing the back of the alley. "The last time we talked was the night of that fight, and now . . ."

"When Alessia made up her mind about something, she refused to back down. You couldn't have stopped her from coming for me if, um, if that's why you were fighting."

I glanced at my watch. I only had a few minutes to make it to my meeting with Anderson, but I couldn't have Cole shadowing my every move.

"I still want to kill you, but what do I need to do to keep my cousins safe?"

He was going to be a stubborn thorn in my side, wasn't he? "You should go back to New York and let me handle things."

"I can't turn my back on my family." His voice thickened with anger, a contrast to the sadness gripping his tone a few moments ago. "And Dublin is still my home, so like hell will I let some corrupt group try and rip it apart if that's what's happening."

"There's only one way you take down this enemy," I informed him, "and you're not equipped to handle it, trust me."

He cocked his head. "And what way is that?"

"From the inside." The only reason I was even keeping up

this conversation was out of respect for Alessia, and because he'd stepped in for her before I'd known she existed. I owed him for that. And I always paid my debts.

"Will you take them down?"

I thought about Emilia Calibrisi, and her desire to go after The Alliance, but I didn't see a way to do that without innocent people getting hurt. "If I go after them, a target will be placed on Holly's head." My fingers tore through my hair, my muscles locking tight. A sense of helplessness wasn't something I was used to. "I need to go."

"You know no one will ever be safe as long as these arseholes are still out there, right?" He turned on his heel and started back for the street. And damn how much I hated that he was right.

DRAKE ANDERSON TIGHTENED THE KNOT OF HIS BLUE SILK tie, his eyes laser-focused on me from where he sat behind his desk. One green eye. One blue. And I was doing my best not to lunge forward and strangle the life out of the fifty-five-year-old bastard.

"This is it. I'm done after this. Done with your games." I'd lied to Holly, told her I was going to London to reason with this arsehole about the land, but in reality, the son of a bitch had summoned me.

Months of bullshit favors. Little things here and there. But his more recent request to force the McGregors to sell their land had nearly pushed me over the edge.

"One more favor, and we're done."

My hands knotted on my thighs. "What do you want?"

"Before that, let's put an end to this ridiculous proposal of yours to buy a different plot of land in Limerick." He lifted his tumbler and took a drink.

"You don't give a damn about the McGregors' land, you just enjoy pulling my strings."

"I do have plans for it, but part of me wants to burn the entire plot just to see how much it makes your lovely Holly cry." His words were cold and calculated. Heartless. "I'm moving up the deadline to Friday. The McGregors need to sell by then, or our arrangement is over."

He set his drink down and smoothed both hands along the edges of his ice-blond hair. He looked like a damn vampire with his pale skin. A fecking bloodsucker.

I had to bite my tongue. I'd survived this long doing his bidding, I could get through this last meeting if it meant ensuring Holly's safety.

"Tell me, is she as good in bed as she looks?" He closed one eye, his bottom lip catching between his teeth, and I gripped the chair arms. "I bet that one likes to scream. Does she like it rough? I bet you like it rough."

I shot to my feet, the blood pulsing straight to my hands as I locked them tight at my sides in preparation. My fuse had been lit, and I was on fire.

"There you are," he crooned, his gaze tightening on me. "Let the beast out. Let loose the dangerous man The Alliance has feared for years." He grinned. His skin barely moved in the process. Lines absent from Botox. "But no, you have a new woman to care for. You'd do anything to keep Holly from dying like your sister, so you won't let him out to play, will you?"

The sick fuck was attempting to bait me, but if I played into his hands, it would be as bad as if I handed Holly over to him.

How the hell did he even know how much she meant to me? I closed my eyes and took a breath, fighting for control.

"I honestly didn't know if the plan would work, if you'd truly give up everything for a woman, *again,* I might add, but it looks to be true."

Plan? I opened my eyes.

"I never knew my arsehole brother-in-law's life could be worth so much. Thank you for helping me eliminate the idiot."

"Thank you?" I bit down on my back teeth and repeated the words.

If I'd had Donovan eliminated without Anderson's permission, war between our organizations would have been immediate. So, I followed protocol, laid out my case against Donovan to Anderson and sought his approval. The gobshite made me believe he cared about the pact between The League and The Alliance and wanted to maintain peace. Made me believe he gave a feck about his brother-in-law by making a show of taking his time to consider my request. In the end, he reluctantly agreed Donovan was a loose cannon and should be killed. But in return for such a loss, I would owe Anderson some favors. Turns out the fecker played me.

Édouard Moreau had warned me about making a deal with Anderson, but what choice did I have? He didn't want war between our organizations, either, and I couldn't very well let the McGregors get slaughtered because Donovan was a vengeful son of a bitch who'd harbored a grudge.

"The land is yours," I finally said even though the words were painful. I hated myself so much for making Holly give up the land she loved in Limerick, but I didn't see any other way.

"The final favor then." He leaned back in his leather desk chair and pressed his hands to his abdomen, far too relaxed for a conversation with a man who wanted to kill him. "You are to give up your position as League leader in Ireland."

"Are you out of your damn mind?"

"Oh, come on, did you really think the favors I've asked in the last few months would be it? You didn't even get blood on your hands."

"This was the real deal? Your real plan all along?" I circled the desk, fisted the material of his dress shirt and forced him to his feet, my jaw straining. "You think I'll just step down, let you swoop in and destroy my city?"

He smirked, knowing he'd pulled one over on me. I wanted to wipe the smile off his face, then break his teeth and force him to swallow them one by one.

"Your choice. Holly's safety or remain League leader and protect Ireland."

I let go of his shirt and stepped back. His face was flushed, his body tense. He was pissed I'd had the audacity to touch him but refused to acknowledge I'd gotten to him. Trying to pull off *casual,* Anderson flicked at the material of his shirt with his manicured nails and pressed it back in place.

My throat thickened. The choice unfathomable.

Crime had drastically reduced after I came into power in Dublin, but now this arsehole would move in if I left.

He'd take advantage of my absence. Danforth, the leader in the U.K., wouldn't be able to stop him, either, and Anderson knew that. Danforth had always been the weakest link in The League.

"And don't go running to your League chaps either about the deal. You wouldn't want them to convince you to stay and let your precious pet die."

I could end him now. Take his goddamn life with my bare hands.

But The Alliance would come after me. Come after Holly.

Hell, they'd take their revenge on everyone who knew me, wouldn't they?

If I killed him in his office and on his turf, it'd be game over and war between our organizations.

"You left The League for your sister," he said as if reading my thoughts, noting the turmoil of my decision on my face. "It's time you do the same for Holly."

"The McGregors were under my protection. Donovan was going to break the pact by having them killed. He should've been fair game."

"Life isn't always fair, and you were faced with a choice." He shrugged. "And you chose to make a deal with me."

A deal with the devil. I'd sold my soul, and he was there to collect.

But he was wrong. Leaving The League didn't save Alessia, it got her killed. And like hell would I make that mistake again.

"Friday," he said as I started for the door, worried I'd grab his letter opener and slice his throat.

I opened the door and looked back at him. "The land, or my decision to step down?"

He casually tipped his head to the side and closed one eye. "Let's call it both."

My pulse raced as I tore out of his office building, my thoughts scrambled. I checked my mobile to find two voicemails as I hurried down the footpath. I needed to get to the airport and head back to Dublin ASAP.

I listened to the first voicemail, a message from The League member I had looking into Declan and Samuel's mother.

"The boys' ma is in the hospital," my associate said straight away. "She overdosed. Heroine." He rattled off more information, then added, "I couldn't reach you, so I went to

261

the hotel and talked to the boys. I dropped them off with her ten minutes ago. The doctor doesn't know if she'll wake up."

I halted at the message, at the fact I'd been too late in finding their mother. They couldn't lose her, not the same way I lost mine.

My heartbeat jumped with worry at the realization the next message was from the mobile I'd bought Samuel.

"Declan just left the hospital." Samuel's voice was breathy and low. "He's so angry. He's gonna try and kill the man who sold Ma drugs. He-he went back to our flat to get his gun. Please-please help."

No. Damn it. The call came five minutes ago. I tried Declan, but his mobile was off. I started to phone my League associate, but Declan would never listen to him, so I hailed a taxi and called Holly.

"I didn't expect to hear from you so soon," she said upon answering. "You okay?"

"No," I rushed out. "Declan's in trouble, and I'm still in London. Can you do me a favor?" I couldn't believe I was asking her this, but if Declan would listen to anyone, maybe it'd be her.

"Anything," she said softly.

"The boys' mother is in the hospital. Drug overdose. She may not make it, and Declan went back to his flat to get a gun. He's going to try and track down the man he thinks is his ma's dealer," I rushed to explain. "You might be able to get to him in time. I-I don't want him becoming a killer. Please, Holly." Without waiting for her answer, I rattled off the address to the flat.

"I, um, I'm on my way."

"Can you take Sean with you?" Hopefully, he was at the office with her. The idea of her heading to Declan's flat alone, and when he had a weapon, had my stomach flipping. "I'm catching the next flight back, but—"

"I'll stop him. You have my word."

"Thank you," I said under my breath as I got into the taxi. "Heathrow," I ordered after ending the call.

I dug my hand into my pocket and grasped Alessia's cross. I tightened my hand into a fist around it and closed my eyes, praying to God Declan didn't become like me.

CHAPTER THIRTY-TWO

HOLLY

"I NEED YOU," I SNAPPED OUT, INTERRUPTING SEAN MID-sentence in front of a group of stiff-shirt investors in the boardroom. "Now."

Sean stared at me in surprise, then motioned to one of the managers to take over as he stood. He placed his palm on my back, ushering me out of the room and into the hall. "What's wrong?"

"We need to get to Declan's flat and stop him from committing murder."

"What?" He stopped in the hall, but I grabbed his arm, urging him to continue.

"I'll explain on the way."

A million thoughts whirled around in my head, but I had to focus on preventing Declan from killing or getting himself killed.

"Their mother overdosed," I said once in my car. I fumbled with the key, trying to get it into the ignition as my hand shook. "She's in the hospital." I hurriedly buckled in and threw the Range Rover into reverse. "Declan's going after the dealer he believes sold her the drugs."

His brows drew together, worry in his eyes. I'd had a feeling he was growing attached to the kids during our time together last night. "He wants revenge?"

"Yes."

"Who called? Samuel?"

"Samuel called Sebastian." I jerked the wheel and pulled out onto the main road.

"And why isn't he helping?"

"He's on his way back from London."

"Damn it. I gotta call Adam." He dialed our brother and brought the mobile to his ear. "It's me. I think I know where Cole disappeared to."

"Wait, he's gone?" Why hadn't Sean told me this?

"He slipped out of Adam's house this morning, but I didn't know Renaud went out of town. I bet Cole followed him there," he quickly explained. "Yeah, okay," he said to Adam a second later. "Touch base when you know something."

"Is Cole out of his mind following Sebastian there?" I asked after he ended the call.

"Yes," he hissed. "We're all out of our minds lately."

I couldn't argue with that.

"Why was he in London?" Sean asked after a minute of awkward silence had passed.

"Sebastian stopped by the office earlier," I began, and had Sean not been in meetings all day, I probably would've caught him up sooner and explained what Sebastian had told me about Drake Anderson.

I gave him a quick recap about Donovan's intention to

seek revenge on Adam by targeting our family and Sebastian's deal with Anderson to protect us.

He dropped his head forward. "Adam's gonna lose his mind."

Part of me wanted to keep all of this from my brother because the guilt would rip him apart. But he'd never forgive me if I didn't let him know the danger we faced and how Sebastian was trying to help.

Sean remained quiet as we drove. He was probably as torn up as I was about all of this.

"His flat's on the second floor," I said as we neared the address Sebastian had provided.

"Shit." Sean pointed out the front window. "He's on the move."

Declan got into the back of a taxi, and the vehicle pulled away from the curb. I floored the pedal to keep up with him.

"Wherever he's going, you need to let me take the lead when we get there." Sean glimpsed me out of the corner of his eye as we crossed deeper into a part of town I'd never even been to before. Buildings with boarded-up windows. Homeless people on the streets. "I can't imagine what he's going through."

"Declan's a strong kid, but he's angry and hurting." I gripped the wheel, my palms slick from a nervous sweat. "He's got a good heart, I can tell. But Sebastian doesn't want him—"

"Turning out like him?"

Before I could respond, my mobile began ringing. An unknown number. I handed it to Sean so I could focus on driving.

He brought the phone to his ear. "This is Sean McGregor." He paused to listen. "Samuel?" He looked my way and gave a slight nod. "I'm glad to hear. We're about to pick up your brother now. Hang in there, kid." He ended the call. "Their mother is awake. She's gonna make it."

I swallowed the lump down my throat and held the wheel even tighter, tears springing in my eyes.

"They're pulling over," he announced.

I parked behind the taxi and unbuckled my seatbelt. "He's getting out."

"Wait here," Sean ordered, then climbed out of the SUV. "Declan!"

Declan spun around, a look of surprise on his face. He stared at Sean with wide eyes, then turned his attention to my SUV. Upon seeing me behind the wheel, he tightened his arms across his coat, as if worried I'd see the gun hidden beneath.

Sean took cautious steps Declan's way. "Let's talk. Please."

Declan was going to run, wasn't he?

I flung open the door and circled the front of the SUV. "Declan, please. Wait!"

"No." He turned and stalked off down the footpath. I started to follow, but my heel caught, and I flew forward to my knees, groaning upon impact.

Sean stopped his pursuit of Declan and whirled around to come to my aid.

"Your mother is okay!" I cried out, and he stopped and faced me.

His eyes moved back and forth between the direction he'd been heading and back to me as if he couldn't decide which route to choose.

"Declan," I whispered when he began heading my way.

"Are you okay?" He looked down at my legs, remorse in his tone and in his eyes.

"You came back." On reflex, I pulled him in for a hug. "You scared us. Sebastian, too."

At the feel of Declan lifting his hands to my back and returning my hug, I nearly cried. "She's really okay?"

"Samuel called," Sean responded. "She's going to be alright."

"I was so mad," he said, his voice hoarse. "I-I thought she was going to die."

The same way as Sebastian's mother. "I know." I caught Sean's eyes from over Declan's shoulder a moment later, but I wasn't ready to let go. I had to protect him, even though he was only eight years younger than me, he was still a kid. A child who almost lost his ma. "We'll get her into rehab, and then you can all be together. I promise."

* * *

"Sebastian!" Samuel jumped to his feet at the sight of Sebastian entering the hospital room that night.

I pushed away from the window where I'd been leaning, my pulse racing at his presence.

"Ma is sleeping," Samuel added in a lower voice, "but she's going to be okay."

Sebastian crouched, and Samuel threw his arms around his neck. He looked uncomfortable as if he wasn't sure how to hug him back. His body was stiff, his eyes moving to Declan who was now on his feet, arms hanging restlessly at his sides.

Samuel whispered something into Sebastian's ear, and it was then that he finally returned the hug.

"Thank you," he mouthed my way when Samuel had let go.

I nodded, my heart on the verge of exploding with relief.

Declan strode closer to Sebastian. "Sorry about scaring you."

Sebastian raked a hand through his dark hair at Declan's apology. I crossed the room to stand next to him and addressed Declan. "We're here for you." I smiled, and Declan shot me a crooked one back.

"We'll get her the help she needs." Sebastian glimpsed Declan's mother, and he had to have been wishing the medics had gotten to his own mother in time. "I promise." He reset his focus on Declan. "Do you mind if I steal Holly for a moment?"

"I won't go anywhere. You have my word," he responded.

"Thank you." He patted him on the shoulder, and he motioned for me to go out into the hall. "Maybe we should talk in private?"

Three doors down, we found an empty room and went inside. My palms were clammy, my heart almost wild in my chest, and all I wanted to do was copy Samuel and throw my arms around him, but I resisted.

I kept my back to the closed door as Sebastian went to the window. Darkness now draped over Dublin, no stars in sight. A few lights from nearby buildings were the only visible light from outside. "Thank you for helping out today."

"Of course." His eyes met mine in the reflection, and I pushed away from the door, a ball of nerves in my stomach when he faced me. "How was London?"

"It didn't go well." He leaned against the window, hands diving into his pockets, his ankle crossed over the other. Exhaustion in his eyes. "I'm in trouble, and I honestly don't know what to do."

I sucked in a sharp breath at his words. "And I take it admitting that to me isn't so easy?" I closed the space between us, and he lifted one hand from his pocket and placed it on my cheek.

His touch always calmed me, as well as inspired an entire sonata of other emotions. "Perhaps we should finish this conversation at my place? Come over later?" His eyes moved over my shoulder, and he dropped his hand.

I turned to see Sean and Adam entering the room. Both casually dressed in jeans and long-sleeved shirts. Sean had gone home to change an hour ago, and apparently, he'd brought Adam back with him.

My brothers stayed next to each other in front of the closed door, and I honestly had no idea what would happen next.

Adam scratched at the nape of his neck, his eyes dropping closed for only a second before he said, "Thank you for watching out for my family after I put us in such a dangerous position."

Sean told you?

"I don't know why you did it, but you kept us safe. You kept Holly safe when I couldn't, and I-I don't know what we would have done if we ever lost her," Adam continued, his voice low. "Cole said you killed the men responsible for your sister's death. He told us about the kind of people they were."

Kind of people?

"Human traffickers," Adam said as if reading the confused look on my face. "If Donovan killed Holly because of my actions, I would've broken every bone in his body and ended his life myself."

"I promised Alessia I'd never kill again." Sebastian's voice was deep. His words laced with pain. "I broke that promise when I had Donovan killed. I didn't take his life with my own hands, but his death was the only way . . ."

Adam looked straight at me, guilt crossing his face like I'd never seen before.

"Everything I've ever done has been about keeping people safe." He turned toward me. "I should get back to the boys, though."

I watched him leave, no protest from my brothers at his quick exit. "I don't know what to say." I stood before them. "Why the change of heart?"

"I'm still not sure what to think," Sean said. "But the way he was with the kids and . . ."

"And what he did for you. For us," Adam added. "Plus, there's Cole to consider. He wants to go after The Alliance, but he doesn't think it's possible without Renaud's help."

"And you're going to let Cole go after them?" I asked in surprise.

"I honestly don't know." Adam reached for my arm and squeezed. "But I got our family involved in this mess by fighting for Donovan years ago, and I need to figure out a way to make things right."

"And you think going against an evil group will be your chance at redemption?" I challenged.

"No," Adam answered. "But it would be a start."

CHAPTER THIRTY-THREE

Sebastian

She was still in the red jumpsuit she had on earlier when I opened my door. My gaze shouldn't have gone straight to the curves of her body, to her lips painted with a light gloss. And I shouldn't have reached for her and pulled her against me, but I did.

Maybe it was the two drinks I'd told myself not to have while I waited for her to come that had me unable to restrain myself. Most likely, it was just my need to be near her, to feel her soft breathing as her breasts rose and fell against my chest while I held on to her.

Holly looked up at me as I kept my greedy hands on the curve of her arse, holding her closely. "You greet everyone like this?"

I remembered the last time she'd asked me that when I'd opened the door and my dick was as hard as a titanium pole.

"Only for you." I wanted to kiss her, devour her, taste the flavor of her gloss so I could savor it when she pulled away.

Her long, black lashes framed her light green eyes, traces of blue there as well.

I wanted to take her away to my boat in Sicily, get her out of the evil world, and just lose myself in her. Maybe we could be safe on the run. But I couldn't ask her to leave her family and her life behind. And I couldn't turn my back on my home.

I let go of her and took two steps back. "No coat?"

Her eyes flicked to the bottle of Jameson and my glass by the armchair in the seating area. "It's not that cold out." She stepped out of her black heels, padded over to my drink, and poured herself a refill.

Her long, slender neck stretched as she raised the drink to her lips and tipped the entire thing back. "The conversation with my brothers was unexpected." She lowered the glass to the table, and I remained in place across the room from her.

I buried my hands into my pockets to prevent myself from reaching for her, ripping off that jumpsuit, and making love to her.

"What happened in London? What'd that arsehole say to you?" Her fiery spirit had my heart pumping harder. I loved that about her.

I was going to do something I hadn't even done with Alessia, and, God help me, I was terrified.

The real story. Could I tell it to her?

"Before we talk about Anderson, I owe you the truth." I'd always wondered if I'd told Alessia the truth, would she have asked me to leave The League? That question haunted me every day, and I'd never know the answer.

"What'd Reed already tell you?" And how much of it had been bullshit?

She collapsed back onto the armchair and braced her thighs. "He mentioned people have died who have known you." Her throat moved with a hard swallow. "Not just Alessia—he didn't know she was your sister—but other people. Some guy jumped from a window after meeting with you, for instance." Her beautiful eyes lifted to my face, and I did my best to remain rooted in place. "The money? Name changes? Was that when your sister found you?" She paused for a moment. "Cole had tried to stop her from going after you, but he obviously failed."

"Sometimes I hate myself for how much I can't regret she came into my life, because she'd still be alive if she hadn't."

"She was family." Her brows slanted inward as her shoulders relaxed with understanding.

I lifted my hands from my pockets and took a steady breath. "When I was eighteen," I began, hoping to steady my pulse to get through this, "a man recruited me into a group known as The League of Brothers, an organization created by rich and powerful men who wanted to use their money and influence to make a difference. They started as a group of five billionaires in charge, now there are sixteen. They recruit young men, known as fixers, to work for them and be their eyes and ears on the streets. To get the kind of results needed when the system can't."

"You were one of those men?" Her eyes fell to the carpet but only for a moment before she looked up at me.

I nodded. "I started as a fixer, training in martial arts and weaponry from some of the best masters in the world," I explained. "But we always gave people a choice to do the right thing. That man who jumped did that on his own after I'd shown him evidence of his crimes we'd uncovered." I scratched at my jaw, hoping I could get through this.

"But if they didn't make the right choice, what would happen?" She rose but didn't approach.

I brought my palms together and stared at my hands—hands that'd taken lives.

"Why not turn them over to the police?" she asked when I'd yet to voice the ugly truth of what I'd done, not sure how she'd handle what I had to say. Forgiving me for Donovan and for murdering Alessia's killers was one thing, but the others, I wasn't so sure.

I kept my eyes on my hands. "Because the courts failed in many cases. A lot of these men were released even without trial. They had too many influential people on their payroll. When justice wasn't served, we stepped in."

"And you're certain everyone deserved to die?"

"Death wasn't always the outcome." Her bare feet were in my line of sight, her pink toenail polish drawing my eye. She was directly in front of me.

Why didn't she run?

"If someone ever hurt my family, and they got away with it, I don't think I could bear for them to walk free." She lifted her palm to my cheek, and her touch had me flinching in surprise. "I don't necessarily agree with murdering for justice, but the alternative doesn't seem so great, either."

I closed my eyes at the sight of her quivering lip.

"I left for Alessia, but she never knew the truth of what I'd done, and I rejoined The League to get my revenge. I didn't become a fixer again. I came back as the leader of Ireland."

At the loss of her touch, I opened my eyes to find her standing in front of the window, a palm on the glass with her back to me.

"And it kills me because I couldn't have even assumed this position had she not shared her inheritance with me." My abdominal muscles squeezed with guilt. "You think she'd hate me?"

"No." She faced me, and I crouched to push up the material on my right leg to show her my tattoo. "This is the ink I received when I became a leader."

She came closer and bent forward for a better look. "A Celtic shield knot between two dragons."

"Norse serpents actually, but yeah, Viking dragons."

"Does everyone have the same ink?" Her fingers smoothed over my leg, and I instinctively tightened my muscles with her hand on me.

"Same meaning but different symbols based on the country. A symbol of protection surrounded by something feared to ward off danger." I pushed the denim back in place and stood. "And Drake Anderson is now demanding I relinquish my position."

She pushed upright and brought her thumbnail between her teeth. "So, he wanted a lot more than my land, he wants you gone."

"I never anticipated he'd make such a bold move. I should've, I guess."

"Not that I want you to give in to this animal, but would it be such a bad thing if you left?"

"Yes," I admitted. "If I step down without another leader in place, Anderson will swoop in and take over all the criminal activity in Dublin. A massive increase in illegal arms sales, prostitution, and drugs."

"But as leader you prevent that from happening?"

"A few years ago, the leaders of The League signed a pact with The Alliance, an agreement we'd stop hunting them in exchange for the reduction of their activities in our cities." I swiped a hand up and down the back of my head. "I hated the deal, but a lot of blood was being shed and . . ."

She covered a palm to her face and slowly dragged it down as she absorbed my words. "You can't leave then."

"But I can't risk them coming after you because I didn't hold up my end of the deal."

She shook her head, her eyes narrowing. "I won't have you sacrificing the city for me. I'm only one person." Tears slipped down her cheeks, and I cupped her face between my palms.

"Please don't cry." I kissed away her tears, willing her pain to become mine. Her unhappiness was like a million knives slicing me open.

Her chin wobbled, and I brought my mouth to hers, unable to stop myself from stealing a kiss. Her tongue swept across my bottom lip before dipping into my mouth. Soft. So fucking soft. And sweet.

"Sebastian," she cried against my mouth, an almost painful sound. One of need and love.

Before I knew what I was doing, I drew down the zipper at the side of her jumpsuit. And she fumbled with the buttons of my shirt and pushed it back.

With every touch, every stroke of her tongue matching mine, I could feel her forgiveness. Her forgiveness for what I'd done in the past. She only saw the light, the good in me, and I'd give anything to see what she saw because it was so damn hard to see anything other than the darkness when I looked in the mirror.

The pain of my losses. Lives taken.

She stepped back to finish stripping, and my heart hammered in my chest as she stood bare except a red G-string.

I removed the rest of my clothes. Even if this was a bad idea and the wrong damn time, I couldn't back down if this was what she wanted, too.

I slipped my finger beneath the red string that followed along the curve of her arse and snapped it.

She moaned when my finger continued to dip to the pucker of her arse before journeying to the flesh of her cheek, squeezing tightly.

I was going to lose my bloody mind. I needed my fill of her.

I shoved the red material down to her thighs so she could hit her sensitive spot against me as she rotated her hips, rubbing harder and harder with frenzied need.

I lowered to my knees, taking her with me, then went flat to my back, assisting her so she could better position herself on top of me.

With her legs straddling me, her hands on my chest, she continued to grind and move against me, her lip between her teeth, her eyes set on me with such a beautiful intensity it was enough to make even a man like me cry.

Her tits were full in my palms as she moved, and I did my best not to slide inside of her without rubber between us.

"Oh, God, yes," she cried.

"You're right there, love."

She moved harder and faster, shifting a bit too low and . . .

Her eyes snapped shut, her short nails buried deep into my pecs, and the back of my skull hit the floor when she sank down and took all of my rock-hard length.

I'd never been inside anyone without a condom. Never. And holy fuck.

"Holly," I warned, needing her to be the one to come to her senses, because I couldn't move to save my life, especially when she lifted up and slammed back down again, her pelvic bone hitting me.

"I can't stop," she sputtered, continuously moving. "You feel too good. I don't want to get off you." Her lids parted, and tears were in her eyes when she looked at me.

My chest tightened, and I gripped her hips and held on to her.

"Are you on the pill?" I asked, my voice hoarse, my words barely audible with her continuing to ride me, her wetness sheathing my length.

She nodded. "I've never done this and—"

"Me either," I admitted, and a strange lump of emotion gathered in my throat at the idea that we were two adults experiencing something intimate together for the first time.

I flipped her around without losing our connection a moment later, unable to stop myself. If she wanted to do this, I wasn't going to stop it from happening. We were living in a world of crazy, but this moment still felt so damn right.

With her back flat to the carpet and her spread out naked beneath me, I took control. She raised her pelvis to meet my cock, moving her arse up and down, and I swallowed her moans with my kiss.

"You feel so amazing," I murmured when pulling my mouth from hers.

Tears slipped out of the corners of her eyes, and when she cried out my name as she climaxed, bringing her thighs tightly together, the position created an even deeper penetration with each of my thrusts.

"I'm falling so hard for you," she said as I came, and my chest tightened as I locked eyes with her.

Emotion thickened my throat, cutting off my ability to beg her not to fall for me.

But how could I ask her that when I fell a long damn time ago?

* * *

SHE SMELLED LIKE JASMINE, EVERY PART OF HER. THE SOAP

from our shower together lingered on her body as I worked my mouth over her navel and up to her lips.

"Promise me we'll do that again before I have to go."

"Do what?" I wanted to hear her say it. Needed to hear the naughty words from her mouth. To know how much she'd enjoyed me inside of her.

Three times in the last two hours wouldn't be enough to satiate my need of her tonight. And I was grateful she felt the same.

She swirled a finger in the air when I pressed up on my elbows to support my weight above her. "The backward, upside-down—"

"You making a helicopter blade with your finger?"

She chuckled and swatted my chest. "Funny." Her brow lifted. "Whatever you want to call it, it was incredible. *You* are incredible." She chewed on her lip, a touch of nervousness showing. "That training you went through include Kama Sutra, too?" Her smile deepened.

I circled her nipple with my fingertip and lightly squeezed before licking her areola with the flat part of my tongue.

"I never believed it when I'd heard there was a connection between the nerves in my clitoris and nipples, but . . . yeah, I'm a believer now." She pressed on my shoulders as she squeezed her thighs closed. "You're way more experienced than me."

I lifted my mouth to find her eyes. "Out of practice, actually."

"Hard to believe."

"Honestly," I admitted and rolled to the side of her. "It's been a long time. I've only wanted you, so."

"Well, I'm not feeling so bad about my extremely long dry spell then. I haven't been with anyone either."

This made me absurdly happy, and maybe it shouldn't

have, but it did. Over the last several months, it'd killed me to wonder if she'd been out with anyone else. And although she'd been under my protection, I wasn't exactly keeping tabs on her dating life like some jerk stalker.

Her lips flattened, and darkness cut across her face a moment later. I propped my head up with my elbow and palm. She mimicked my move and gathered a sheet to cover her body.

"What is it?" I asked.

"I hate my mind just took a quick trip back to reality, and I'd much rather stay in this bed with you."

I sat upright since it appeared we'd be resuming our discussion from earlier tonight. "You know the thing that's been bothering me is how Anderson knows how much I care about you." I draped a sheet over my lower half and pressed my back to the headboard. "I mean, he knew I was willing to do whatever I had to to keep your family safe, but it's like he was expecting my moves. He knew which buttons to push."

"Have you told anyone in The League of Brothers about the deal for you to step down?"

I peeked over at her. "I forgot to mention, we're only known as The League now. A woman took over as leader in Italy when her father died, and we changed the name."

Her mouth rounded as a sense of understanding appeared on her face. "Your friend in Italy, the trip you took, it was about that?"

"Yeah." I expelled a breath. "But no, I haven't told anyone yet. I was too focused on Declan and Samuel. Plus, Anderson warned me not to say anything."

"And you don't seem like someone who'd bow down to a man like him."

For you, I'd do anything, but I kept my thoughts to

myself. She didn't need to burden herself with guilt for my actions.

"Anderson knew you placed my family under protection, but you don't think that's why he knows how much, I, um, matter to you?"

I squeezed the bridge of my nose. "He knew we were having sex. He called you my pet. It was just—"

"Pet?" she said under her breath. "Luca called me that in the lift." She reached for my hand and clasped it, and that simple touch somehow steadied my racing heart, but I pulled my hand free shortly after to stand.

I needed my feet on the ground as I worked through my thoughts. "Luca's the only one who knows how I feel about you."

"You think he's working with Anderson? Is that possible?"

"Luca's uncle is in charge in France. Luca's a fixer for The League, but shit, I don't know. He's been different lately."

"Wait, his uncle is a leader?" Disbelief colored her tone. "You hurt him in that lift. Are you in trouble?"

"No. His uncle is closer to me than him. In fact, he has no intention of turning his money or power over to Luca upon his death. He was going to offer it to me had I not met Alessia."

Her fingers dove through her dark locks. "And Luca doesn't have a grudge against you because of it?"

"He's always lived on the edge. Wild and a bit reckless, his behaviors overlooked because of his uncle." I stared at the floor as I tried to wrap my head around the possible betrayal. "We'd been like brothers before Alessia came into my life."

I grabbed a pair of sweats, pulled them on, and paced

alongside the window, which was covered in floor-to-ceiling drapes, blocking the view of the city.

She circled the bed to stand before me. "But is it possible he became envious of your position, and the way his uncle feels about you? Maybe he wants you gone from Ireland so he can have it himself."

"No. He wants France. Always has." I looked up at her and swallowed. "But that doesn't mean he doesn't want me out of his way to try and get it." Even if he knew I had no intention of ever becoming the leader of France, I'd block any type of coup against his uncle. "It could be the real reason he's in Dublin. Maybe he knew Anderson was preparing to make his final move." I lifted my eyes to the ceiling in thought.

"What is it? What are you thinking?"

"I talked to Luca before I called Anderson to try and make a deal. The idea of owing Anderson killed me, but he convinced me to do it, that it'd be the only way to get the results I wanted." Had I been so blinded by my friendship that I hadn't been able to see the truth?

She chewed on her lip and tightened the sheet to her chest.

I closed my eyes, trying to control my anger so I could think clearly. "I need to talk to Moreau. He'll know what to do. He might be able to help find a way out of this."

"A way that we can be together?" The sheet fell to the floor and pooled at her feet.

"I don't know." I wanted to reach for her, to pull her into my arms and tell her everything would be okay, but how could I? "I have to go."

She slung her arms around my body, giving me her trust. Her love. I didn't understand it, but I couldn't turn her away, not anymore.

I hugged her back, placing my chin on her head as I hung on to her like a lifeline.

"Let me go with you," she murmured into my chest, and I hated the break in her voice. "I'm safer with you than without you."

Alessia probably would have been too, and I messed everything up. "Okay."

She stepped out of my arms. "Really?"

I nodded and brought her cheeks between my palms. "Moreau should meet you. He should remember what we're fighting for—*who* we're fighting for. Why we exist in the first place."

She pressed up on her toes, her lips making a soft pass over mine before I banded her waist and tightened her against me to deepen the kiss. "I'm yours," she said a heartbeat later. "If you'll let me be."

"After everything you know about me . . .?"

She traced the line of my jaw with her finger, liquid in her eyes. "After everything I know," she whispered back with a nod, her eyes tight on me. "I want *you*, Sebastian Ryan."

CHAPTER THIRTY-FOUR

SICILY, ITALY

HOLLY

LITTLE DROPS OF SUNLIGHT STARTED TO APPEAR AS THE heavy pull of clouds parted above us on the deck of Sebastian's yacht. Plans had changed at the last minute, and instead of meeting Édouard Moreau in Paris, we took a flight to Italy.

He gathered me in his arms, and I tipped my chin to keep my head from being buried against his chest, even if that was a delicious position to be in. With one hand around my waist, he smoothed the other up and down my back over my lightweight rain jacket.

"You think your associate will be able to locate Luca? The idea of him out there somewhere creeps me out." I shuddered as if he were watching us now. Of course, we still didn't know if he was working with Anderson. It could all be speculation.

"If Luca doesn't want to be found, he won't be. He's a professional at disappearing people, including himself." He released me, walked over to the edge of the boat, and set his gaze on the water.

More beams of sunlight streamed down from overhead. Maybe it was a sign things would get better.

"I told you we don't always kill people."

"And that means?" I lifted a brow when he peeked back at me.

"Sorry. I'm new to this sharing thing." He gave me a small smile, then returned his focus to the water. "The League has sites set up around the world. Each top-level League fixer operates a prison. It has to be off-the-grid and unknown to anyone other than the operator and guards. Not even the leaders know the locations."

"Why not?"

"To keep them safer. They can't be tortured for information." He lifted his shoulders as if this was all so normal. "Most leaders are older, and they'd prefer their fixers to handle everything for them."

"But not you, right?" I arched a brow.

His lips crooked at the edges, and he rubbed the sides of my arms. "No, I'm not as trusting, nor have I worried about my own safety like that, but it's probably because I started out as a fixer, unlike any other leaders."

"I guess I still don't quite understand all of it." I chewed on my lip. "A bit over my head."

"One of the reasons you need to be rich to be a leader is to have the financial means to do what's necessary to execute justice. Top-level fixers, like Luca, are given funds by the leaders to construct their prisons as they see fit. And the fixers are in charge of hiring men to guard the sites."

"I see why you're different than the rest."

Ideas of cruel and unusual punishment inside some torture chamber came to mind, and it wasn't something I wanted to think about. "And you think Luca might be at his, um, prison hiding out?"

"If he wanted to hide somewhere not even I could find, then yes."

"And did you manage a site when you were a fixer?" I tried to hide the distress at such an idea from my voice, but when he turned to face me with narrowed eyes and lips drawn tight, I knew I'd failed.

His eyes cut to the deck. "Yes, but it's not what you're thinking. They're more like heavily guarded multi-room mansions. Much better than a prison." He cupped the back of my head, his gaze returning to mine.

"Well, for your sake, I hope he's not working with Anderson. You've been friends for so long, I can't imagine what you must be feeling." My hand went to his chest, and he circled my wrist, flattening my palm over his heart.

My pulse quickened beneath his grip as his eyes held mine. "Luca, and his uncle, they were the closest thing to family I had before Alessia. But he's changed into someone I don't recognize in the last few years." He shook his head. "Unless he's always been a bad person, and I just never noticed." He let go of me and looked back at the water.

He pressed his forearms to the railing and leaned forward, resetting his attention on the navy-blue water, softly lapping against the sides of the boat.

"You know how many times I imagined making love to you here?"

A change of subject and I couldn't blame him. I'd rather talk about making love than Luca's possible betrayal, too.

"Mm. No, but that doesn't mean I wouldn't like to hear it." I circled my arms around his body from behind and pressed my cheek to his back.

"Well, when I was here last week, that's all I could think about."

The fresh air did nothing to combat the heat now inside me.

"One of my fantasies was to have you naked on my bed down below, hands tied above your head, legs spread—"

"Am I interrupting?"

A female voice from behind had Sebastian immediately letting go of his words, and he stiffened but didn't yet turn.

"Not like you to let someone sneak up on you," the woman added, and I detected a smile in her tone.

"I knew you were coming, Emilia."

"Sure."

I slowly turned to put a face to a voice. She was the Italian version of Angelina Jolie starring in a *Lara Croft* film. Even her outfit made her look like she was prepared to raid tombs for treasure—tight dark leather trousers, matching leather boots, and a fitted jacket. Plus, was that a sword, or bow staff, stowed at her back? Her long dark hair was in a braid, and her full lips quirked into a smile when she saw me.

"Well, you going to introduce me to the woman that stole your heart?" she asked.

I took a hesitant step and extended a hand. "Holly."

"You're stunning. I guess I should've expected that. But I hear you have brains, too." She winked at Sebastian when I pulled my hand free from her strong grip. "I approve."

I wasn't about to offer a thank you, still not quite sure how I felt about the goddess standing before me. Jealousy wasn't really my thing. But ever since I'd met Sebastian, I'd been all sorts of not myself, and it was only recently that I realized I liked the woman I was when I was with him. The woman I let myself finally be. Fewer chains binding me, a bit more of the type to throw caution to the wind.

"Where's Moreau?" Sebastian stepped alongside me, claiming me as his, his hand swooping around to pull me against his side.

There was no jealousy in her eyes, more so admiration, and that made me feel a little better.

"We're going to meet at my home instead. I came to get you." Her eyes lingered on my jacket before dipping to my jeans and checkered-pattern rain boots. "It won't rain. You'll be fine."

"Your English is perfect." My thoughts jumped free, but when she'd spoken, I couldn't even make out an Italian accent.

"I studied at Oxford for a few years. And spent another two living in the devil's playground."

"The what?"

"Vegas," Sebastian explained. "We should get going."

Emilia didn't move, though. "I didn't expect you to take me up on my suggestion quite so soon to go against The Alliance."

Sebastian released his arm from my back. "Things have changed."

"So it would seem," she answered, a hint of curiosity returning to her eyes, and I felt as though I was some mysterious creature being studied under a lens as she observed me.

"Come on." Sebastian patted my back, urging me to walk when all I wanted to do was go back to hearing him describe the sinful but sweet things he wanted to do to me on his boat.

"How far do we have to go?" I hopped into the back of her black Range Rover, which felt too big for the winding, narrow roads there.

"Just a few kilometers. The home is on a mountain overlooking the coast."

Sebastian probably should've sat up front with her, but he'd opted to sit with me. To hold my hand as the vehicle climbed a steep hill. "How, um, high up on this mountain?" I swallowed as we continued to go up and freaking up.

Emilia caught my eyes in the rearview mirror. "Very."

"Great view of Mount Etna, too," Sebastian added and squeezed my hand, and the warmth of his touch relaxed me.

A few minutes later, we reached the gated entrance to the mansion. At the center, a pair of ancient-looking doors parted. Fit for a kingdom, they looked to be made of steel with crisscrossing iron rods. A few other cars were parked in the driveway that curved around a beautiful fountain in front of the home. Well, more like a castle. Touches of Roman history embedded in the stone features of the design, from turrets down to the pillars alongside the double doors at the front.

Sebastian helped me out of the back. "You'll be okay." His voice was soft. As calming as the sounds of the water lapping against his boat.

His words should have made me feel better, but I was about to meet not only Luca's uncle but a man who helped create an organization that condoned murder in the name of justice, a man who'd brought Sebastian into the life.

He stopped outside the front door and pushed his sunglasses to the top of his head. "You okay?" he mouthed, sensing I was still uneasy.

I gulped, knowing my eyes were wide, but I managed a nod.

"Let's go." Emilia strode through the front door, which

had been opened by someone on her staff. "Moreau's in Papa's study."

"I'm so sorry about your father." I'd meant to offer my condolences in the car, but I'd been tongue-tied upon meeting her.

She slowed her brisk pace and caught my eyes, walking alongside me. "He lived a full and happy life. Thank you."

I nodded, not sure what else to say.

When we entered the study, the room reminded me a bit of Ma's library. All four walls were covered in books. Not a single window in the room, and maybe you didn't need one. Books were supposed to be like windows to another world, right? Maybe someday Samuel would write a novel, and it'd end up here alongside other great works of literature.

I pulled my focus to the man on the other side of the room in a red leather armchair. Hints of vanilla-flavored cigars met my nose even though I didn't see one lit. Most likely, Emilia's late father had been a smoker.

"Sebastian." The man set his drink on the table next to him and rose. If Luca had been a cross between Johnny Depp and James Dean, well, now I knew why. His uncle was the James Dean side of the equation. He smoothed his hands over the lapels of his navy jacket, his eyes catching mine in the process. "Holly McGregor."

The way he said my name was as if he knew me on a personal level. It was all so strange.

"Thank you for flying here on such short notice." Sebastian walked me closer, inviting me to shake the man's hand.

Moreau kissed both my cheeks then held on to my arms. "I see why he cares so much for you."

"It's more than looks." Sebastian's words caught me by

surprise, and I made a note to thank him for his comment later.

"Well, let's talk, shall we?" Moreau motioned for us to sit on the couch across from the armchair, and Emilia remained standing. "Emilia has filled me in."

Jacket now off, hands on my legs, I scooted closer to Sebastian on the couch, trying to calm my nerves. He covered my hand with his, and Moreau's eyes lingered for a moment on our linked palms.

"You really believe my nephew to be working with Anderson?" he asked when Sebastian had yet to speak up.

"It's hard for me to believe such betrayal, but if he's jealous or wants power, then maybe." Emotions layered heavy and thick in Sebastian's voice, no doubt making the words harder to get out. "When Alessia came into my life, and Luca discovered the truth about her being my family, he didn't take it so well. He thought she was dangerous, a weakness to be used against me." He paused for a breath. "After she died, Luca helped me get my vengeance. Things were normal between us for a while, but this year, he started acting differently again. I-I don't know." Uncertainty gripped his tone.

Moreau's gaze cut to the floor, his face aging ten years before my eyes. "I promised Luca's mother I'd always look out for him before she and my brother got onto that plane. They never made it to their destination, but I've always tried to keep that promise." He stood. "He was seven at the time his parents died. Did I fail him?"

He was accepting Sebastian's words as fact. As the gospel truth. And if he could so easily believe Luca's culpability, it had to mean Luca was, in fact, working with The Alliance.

"Luca has always been, well, Luca." Sebastian cupped his jaw, his eyes moving to Emilia and back to me. A forlorn look crossed his face before he set his attention on Moreau. "And if he's working with the enemy, well, that's on him. Not you."

"What we do know is that Anderson wants Ireland without League leadership to make it more vulnerable," Emilia said, talking for the first time.

"If I don't follow through with the deal I made with Anderson, he'll come after Holly." Every muscle in Sebastian's body visibly grew rigid. I knew I wasn't responsible for his pain, but it was hard not to feel that way when Anderson had preyed upon a perceived weakness of his to get to him—me.

"There's a chance Anderson didn't inform the rest of The Alliance about this deal. He's done it before. Either way, we'll propose a new deal." Moreau kept his voice calm and steady. His experience was evident in the way he spoke, in his confidence.

"And that means?" I asked, feeling totally out of my element.

"War, if they don't agree to new terms," Emilia responded.

"I don't want anyone dying because of me. Or for me." At my words, Sebastian tightened his hold of my hand.

"I'll give The Alliance a choice: Anderson or the pact," Moreau said.

"And what of Luca?" Emilia asked.

"He's my nephew. If he's involved, please let me handle his punishment."

In one of the very prisons Luca operated, maybe?

"The Alliance needs to be taken down," Emilia noted with grit to her voice. "Maybe not now, but eventually."

"I agree." Sebastian released my hand and stood, and I followed suit and moved to my feet to stand at his side.

"This new deal is just to buy us time until we are strong enough to strike," Emilia added.

"I guess it's time for the new generation to make the decisions." Moreau extended his hand to Sebastian. "I have your back. Always."

CHAPTER THIRTY-FIVE

HOLLY

"EMILIA'S HERE," SEBASTIAN ANNOUNCED, HIS EYES ON HIS mobile. We were at Sean's flat, and it was the night of Anderson's deadline for Sebastian to give up his position in The League.

When we returned from Italy, Sebastian opened up and explained everything to my brothers and Cole. It was mutually decided it'd be best for Adam to take Anna out of town, and for our parents to leave Dublin as well. Cole and Sean chose to stay to try and help. Sebastian had said no, at first, but us McGregors, well, we could be a stubborn bunch.

Sebastian brought Emilia into the flat a minute later and made the introductions. Emilia grasped my brother's hand, and Sean stood frozen, a gobsmacked look on his face. Yeah, she had that effect on people.

"Is it a go?" Cole asked her as she unzipped her leather jacket, showing the tight fit of a black tank top that hugged her curves.

"The Alliance has agreed to sacrifice Anderson to keep the truce intact."

"Sacrifice? Does that mean kill?" I stood, my legs shaky, and Sebastian came up beside me and secured a hand around my waist, holding me against him.

"He'll be punished for violating the pact and nearly causing a war." Emilia's answer was vague.

"In a League prison, right? You wouldn't trust The Alliance to keep him locked up, would you?" I asked her, and Emilia shot a surprised look Sebastian's way.

I caught him nod out of my peripheral view as if saying *She knows*.

"Yes," Emilia finally answered. "Anderson is in transit now."

"But how will we really know he's there if you don't even know the location?" I had to be sure this guy wouldn't be a threat to my family.

"My people will confirm upon arrival with photographic evidence. I'll also get monthly reports on his condition." Her lips teased into a smile. "We are the good guys, remember? We're not animals like them."

"I have no bloody idea what you're talking about," Sean said while holding up his palms, "but hey, if it means this arsehole is gone, I'm good with that."

"Unfortunately, The Alliance only agreed to continue the truce if Sebastian stepped down." Her words were like one of Adam's infamous left hooks. A hard blow to the cheek. A dizzy effect after.

Sebastian let go of me at her words and strode to the window. His back muscles pinched tight, drawing material of his shirt together as he palmed the glass. "Why am I not surprised?"

"A life for a life, so to speak," she added as if ensuring us outsiders understood.

"So, Anderson has been prevented from taking over Dublin, but whoever replaces him surely will." The base of Cole's throat grew red from anger.

"We can't agree to that, right?" I asked, frantically looking around at everyone in the room.

"It's already been done. Moreau had no choice. It was that or war. But"—Emilia looked back and forth between where Cole and Sean stood—"we came up with a solution."

"You can't be serious." Sebastian whirled around in one fast move to face the room.

"What am I missing?" I gripped my chest, my heart moving too hard, and the fluttering sensation in my stomach had me growing ill.

"We do have two eligible men who could adopt the role of leader to make certain Dublin remains safe from The Alliance." She held her palms open toward my brother and cousin.

"No," Sebastian and I both said in unison.

Sean brought his palm over his mouth.

Cole, though, he stood firm. Unrelenting in his pursuit of justice toward a group not even responsible for taking a woman he once cared for. "I'll do it. I'll stay in Dublin until The Alliance has been taken down." He shifted to the side to catch Sebastian's eyes. "You said it would require someone on the inside to take them down, then use me. Let me do this." There was a hardness to his words, a darkness taking over. "I can earn their trust. Build a bridge before we burn it."

"You're confident. I like that." Emilia cocked her head, casting an approving nod. "We can train you. Prepare you. And then as leader, you can replace Sebastian, and your family will remain under League protection. As long as they are in Ireland, no one will be able to come after them without severe consequences."

"Wait, what?" My world was spinning now. Sebastian and I would finally be free to be together, but that put Cole in the line of fire . . . I didn't know what to think. "Is this true?"

Sebastian crossed the room to get to me. He held on to my biceps while staring into my eyes. He was as scared and confused as me, wasn't he? "Yes, we'd be safe," he practically breathed out. "But I can't ask you to do this, Cole." He let go of me to look at my cousin. "It's too dangerous. And the man you'd have to be, I don't think you have it in you."

"No more killing," I sputtered. "It doesn't have to be that way. The League can use those prisons, right? Or, let the Garda handle things."

"Killing is never the goal we set out for. Often, death happens in self-defense. Refusing to free a kidnapped girl and turn themselves in, for instance." Emilia stepped closer to me, her eyes warm, and yet, there was a fierce intensity there, too.

"The people who killed Alessia," Sebastian began, "I murdered them in cold blood. And I'm sorry, but I don't regret that."

Human traffickers, I reminded myself. I'd probably want them dead, too, even if they weren't responsible for Alessia's murder.

"You did what you had to," Cole said, his tone so dark and low it was as if he'd already stepped into Sebastian's shoes.

Was this really happening?

I needed to sit.

To breathe.

Sebastian took my hand. "Give us a minute." He guided

me past the kitchen and down the hall to the guest room I'd been staying in before I'd gone to Italy with him.

"What do you want?" he asked as I took a seat on the bed.

I looked up at him. "You're asking me?"

He knelt in front of me. No mask. No hidden agenda. Commitment in the depths of his brown eyes. "Yes." He held my hand on my lap and intertwined our fingers.

"I want you. Dublin safe. My family free of harm." A simple but honest list.

"And what of your dreams?"

I smiled, unable to stop the tiny act from happening. "Thanks to you, I can see a bit farther ahead now. I can see so many great things in my future, but I don't want any of them without you." Tears began a journey down my cheeks. "My dreams can only exist in a world where we're together."

The pad of his thumb traced the line between my bottom and top lips.

He pushed upright, dipped his hand into his pocket, and produced a silver cross. "This was Alessia's. It was all I found of hers in my home after the fire. All that survived." He knelt once again and uncurled my fingertips and placed the Celtic cross in my palm. It was an exact match to the tattoo on his back.

"Whatever happens tonight," he said, his eyes becoming glossy as he closed my hand around the necklace, "you should know I'm in love with you."

CHAPTER THIRTY-SIX

Sebastian

"Luca just approached your front door," Emilia reported over the comm in my ear. "He's alone from what I can tell.

I poured myself a scotch as I waited for Luca to enter the club. His betrayal was more than I could handle, but after what he did to Holly in the lift at my hotel, I'd slowly been coming to terms with the fact he was no longer who I thought he was.

The guy who I jumped out of a plane with at nineteen.

The man who trained alongside me in the Himalayas.

The friend who broke me out of jail in Cuba when I had a little too much fun on my twenty-second birthday.

I would have to let go of seventeen years of memories. Mostly good ones, too.

I downed my drink in two swallows then stepped away from the bar in preparation for Luca's appearance. The club had been closed down. A sign hung outside: **Water Main**

Break. Ola was at the hotel with Samuel and Declan to ensure they didn't show up, even though she had no damn clue what was going down tonight.

Luca had guts showing up here alone. Then again, his arrogance knew no bounds. But it was one of the conditions of the new deal with The Alliance. Anderson was forced to call Luca and order him to meet with me on his behalf under the guise of accepting my "resignation" as League leader.

Luca was walking right into a trap, but it all felt too easy.

Luca was smart. Cunning. And I had to remember that he'd probably have a backup plan if things went south when he presented himself as working for The Alliance, which we'd confirmed was true with Anderson before our people carted him off to one of our prisons.

Apparently, after I had called Anderson requesting to take down Donovan Hannigan earlier this year, two months later, Luca approached him with an idea. He'd help take me out of power in exchange for Anderson's assistance to take over France. The deals would appear legit. No hostile takeovers. No reason for war between the organizations. He'd presented the plan to use Holly to get me to step down. But as for how Luca would assume his uncle's position and wealth without it being an outright overthrow, I had no clue. And it didn't matter because it'd never happen. Tonight, he'd be stopped. One way or another.

I couldn't see Luca yet, but with the club empty and no DJ blaring music, the door scraping open on the concrete floors was audible even from where I stood by the bar.

Luca was removing his coat when he came into sight, and he tossed it onto the satin couch off to his left. "I don't see any water damage," he said with a sly smile. "You fake that so you could have the place cleared out for some reason tonight?"

"What are you doing here?" Dumb didn't exactly suit me, and Luca knew that.

A cocky grin touched his lips, and he spread open his palms as he crossed the room. "I'm sorry about what happened at the hotel with Holly." He pushed his sleeves to the elbows as if prepping for round two from that night, a clear contradiction to his apology.

I had my hands casually at my sides as I attempted to go along with the plan and not lose my bloody mind being alone with him. "And why is that? Because you lost?"

He went up the two steps to get to the raised platform of the dance area. "I never liked this place." His eyes went to the bar. "You let your sister dictate everything. Even the damn arrangement of liquor."

I'd keep a handle on my temper for this charade, but if he started bad-mouthing Alessia, I wouldn't be able to remain calm for long. And he was counting on that. He knew me well enough to know exactly what buttons to push.

"She changed you."

He'd told me this before, but for the first time, I could see he truly believed it. He hated her, didn't he?

My pulse picked up, and I swallowed, fighting for control.

"Want us to move in now?" Emilia asked in my ear. She must've realized Luca was pushing me to my breaking point.

"No," I responded to Emilia while directing the word at Luca so he would think it was for him. "No, she made me a better person. She was family."

He pounded a fist on his chest, his brows snapping together. "I was family. Your brother. You didn't need some trust fund brat." His hands settled on his hips as he let go of a deep breath, his chest lifting and falling from another attempt at control.

Shit, did he really think he had a right to be upset with me?

"I-I tried to get you to see the truth. She didn't accept you for you. She wanted to change you. What kind of person does that make her?" He stabbed the air now, an angry hiss following.

"I know you wanted to talk to him first," Emilia popped into my ear, "but I don't think we should waste time."

He pissed on seventeen years of friendship in his pursuit for power, so yeah, I needed fecking answers.

"You left The League for her. My uncle offered you the position of a lifetime, but Alessia snapped her fingers, and you left."

I went onto the raised platform, my heart beating out of control, and I stood before him. Face to fucking face.

Moreau wants him alive—I had to remind myself as he tossed his hand through his hair. "Were you jealous? You had to be, right? He wanted to give me what you believed to be rightfully yours." I could push back, too. I knew his damn buttons.

He grinned. "Nah," he said, waving a finger between us. "You're not going to bait me."

"Damn it, Sebastian," Emilia said into my ear. "Luca has company."

"Take them out," I ordered, not giving a damn Luca could hear me, but when his smile stretched from ear to ear, I knew why.

His backup plan.

"Three tangos. One hostage," Emilia said. "Holly."

I lunged for Luca and fisted his shirt, and he held both palms in the air. "I'm not the only one on comms." He winked. "Make a move, and she dies."

"What do you want me to do?" Emilia asked from

overwatch. "I don't have a clear shot. I could take out two of the men, but the one with a knife to Holly's throat, I can't take the risk."

I let go of Luca and stepped back. "Let them in," I ordered as Luca pushed his shirt back in place.

"Did you hurt her?" I seethed.

"Not yet, but I can't say the same about the others."

"What'd you do?" Holly had been at Sean's flat with her brother and Cole. I had three guards with them, too.

"Insurance policy." He smiled. "You agree to the deal with Anderson as promised, and you let me leave here—and your precious pet and her family will live. A deal is a deal." Luca's gaze moved over my shoulder, and I turned to see Holly being shoved into the club.

"Holly." I wanted to go for her, but three men stood by her with weapons drawn.

"What do you want me to do?" Emilia asked. "Go after Cole and Sean?"

"I have it covered here," I gave the command, my heart racing, as I let her know to leave with her men and rescue Holly's family.

"Copy that," she answered.

Holly's mouth was covered with tape, her hands bound as well. Tears cut down her cheeks, but there didn't appear to be any physical damage.

"Let her go," I directed the order to The Alliance assassins. "You're in direct violation of the pact. Leave, or the consequence will be death." By my fecking hand, and I wouldn't hesitate.

"Afraid they can't do that."

I turned to the side to keep both Luca and Holly in my line of sight. "Stand down." I had to buy myself time to ensure Emilia got to Cole and Sean before I made my move on Luca. I couldn't have him ordering their deaths before she got there.

Thankfully, Sean's flat was only a few blocks away.

"Why do you want me gone?"

He scratched at his beard. "When Alessia died, you were supposed to come back to The League. You were supposed to become a killer again, the man I knew you could be. You'd get your vengeance and step back in as a fixer. Everything would be back to normal."

"What the fuck are you talking about?" I closed the space between us, nearly nose to nose.

"I wanted my friend back. She ruined everything, and if she was gone . . ." He cupped his mouth and turned to the side, and my heart leaped into my throat at the realization of what he was saying.

"Tell me it wasn't you." Chills crashed over my skin, and every nerve in my body twitched. "Tell me you didn't have Alessia killed to get me back into The League," I roared, unable to stop the anger from surfacing.

He lowered his head and took a breath before facing me. "It's your fault, really. You should never have chosen her over us." He stabbed at my chest. "Over the family we gave you. You were nothing before my uncle took you off the street."

"Don't attack," Emilia warned. "Wait for me to secure Sean and Cole." She could hear me, but I could only hear her when she clicked onto the line.

Her words were what I needed because I had been on the verge of snapping Luca's neck. Five different ways to kill him in a split second had played out in my mind before Emilia's voice came into my ear.

I looked back at Holly to remain steady. Grounded. She was so strong. Chin lifted. No flinching. She was staying put together for me, to keep me from acting on my emotions and charging the men around her.

"You've never killed a woman," I whispered, feeling defeated. "Did you really start with my sister?"

"You don't know me anymore." Genuine pain crossed his face, but no way in hell would I feel sorry for him. He was mourning the loss of our friendship, but he ruined my damn life.

"How'd you do it?" My hands tightened at my sides, my breathing was uneven, my temper close to snapping.

"I went to Italy. Drugged her. Brought her back to your home. And had the Serbians waiting outside for my order to burn the place down." His words were too calculated. Too practiced. A nervous tic in his eye that said he was bluffing.

"You're lying."

"Why would I lie about that?" He snickered. "I set up the Serbians. I had to make sure you'd get your revenge, too. To remember who you are."

I brought my fist to my chest and spread my fingers, my palm going flat over my heart. "No." I shook my head. "I don't believe you."

"Sebastian," Emilia came over the line. "Cole and Sean are secure. You can make your move now."

Relief should've cut through at Emilia's words, but Luca's confession about Alessia's death had blindsided me. Logically, the details added up. But no matter how much Luca had changed, he wouldn't kill a woman, and I had to believe that.

"The Alliance cut a new deal," I informed him and the three men still surrounding Holly. "Drake Anderson is now in League custody, and you no longer report to him. If you don't withdraw your weapons and leave, you will be terminated." I tipped my chin. "Call. Find out for yourself."

"You're the one lying now." Luca brought his mobile to his ear and distanced himself with a few steps.

"Not what you expected to hear?" I asked when Luca lowered the mobile a moment later and tossed it to the ground in anger. "Go!" I yelled to the three guards, "or I will make your deaths long and drawn out." I looked straight at the man with the dagger close to Holly. "You know who I am and what I'm capable of."

The moment the men lowered their arms, I jumped from the platform and rushed for Holly. I pulled the tape from her lips and whispered, "Are you okay?"

"Yes, but Sean and Cole . . ."

"Emilia's with them. They're okay. I'm so sorry." I snatched my knife to work at her wrists, keeping my focus on Luca who appeared to be frozen in shock. Once I freed her, I brought my mouth to her ear, "I need you to get out of here. Please."

"I don't want to leave you."

"I'm fine," I promised, then gestured for her to exit, my heart unable to handle her in the club any longer. "Holly's exiting. Have one of our people meet her outside," I told Emilia.

Luca slowly stepped down from the platform.

"It's over," I said at the sight of the blade in his hand. The knife, his preferred weapon. Mine, too. "Your uncle doesn't want you to die, but I'm not sure if I can let you walk out of here alive."

He lunged for me, and I sidestepped his sloppy attempt to come after me. I wielded my own blade, holding it tight when he came back at me. I blocked his efforts, knocking his knife free.

"I'm not going to rot in a League prison! You'll have to kill me first." He rushed me with a flying knee kick, catching me in the side this time, throwing me off my balance.

"You act like you're fearless, but you're not. You love life too much to want to die," I shot back as my right fist connected with his cheekbone.

"I hate you," he hissed. "I-I just wanted my friend back." He leaned forward, panting after we'd gone at it for another few minutes as if inside a UFC cage. We knew each other's moves. Trained together. "Then you traded one woman for another. A new obsession. Someone else you'd give up everything for." His top lip lifted in a snarl as I pressed my palms to my thighs for a second, catching my own breath. It'd been a while since I'd fought an opponent like him. Inside the lift, he hadn't put up a fight like this. He had everything to lose tonight.

"Stand down. Please."

"No," he hollered, and I charged him, needing to end this now. I pushed off my feet and extended both my legs at once, hooking my right leg around his neck to take him to the ground, employing an ancient Silat martial arts technique.

I squeezed his throat between my legs until he eventually tapped out. The bastard didn't have a death wish. He'd lied.

"You're right," he said after coughing. He dropped flat to his back, his palms going to his chest as he struggled to find his breath. "I didn't kill Alessia. I wanted to. I had planned on it. Even the Serbians thought it was her body burning inside the house."

I was still on the ground, sitting off to the side of him, and I shifted to my knees, knife still in hand. "What are you saying?"

He rolled his head to the side to view me, his chest puffing out from the deep breaths he kept taking. "All the resources I had, the contacts—people loyal to me . . . I swapped the dead woman's dental records for Alessia's. I left your sister's cross beneath a block of steel in hopes it'd survive. I never broke the sacred League rule. I've never killed a woman." He shifted to his knees. "You let me go, and I'll tell you where you can find her."

"I don't believe you." I slowly stood and anchored my feet to the ground.

"She's in my facility under another name." He looked me straight in the eyes, and I knew then he was telling the truth.

"All these years—you kept her locked up?"

I wanted to believe she was alive, but what kind of hell had she been through?

"I'm not letting you go until I confirm she's okay." I held a palm between us.

He pointed to the platform. "Can I get my phone?"

I nodded, unable to speak. Hell, I could barely remember to breathe.

He handed me his mobile a minute later and lifted his chin, urging me to take it.

I kept my knife in one hand while bringing the mobile to my ear. "Who is this?"

"Sebastian," a soft voice met my ear. "Is that really you?"

My lungs were going to collapse, and I nearly lost my footing at the sound of Alessia's voice. "It's me," I choked out a response. "You're alive? This is real?"

"Yes, it's real. I-I never thought I'd hear from you again."

"I'm coming for you, okay?" My voice rattled. "I promise."

The call ended a moment later, and I tucked the mobile into my pocket and shot my hand out, gripping Luca by the throat. "You belong in hell."

He brought a hand over mine and closed his eyes.

"And I don't need you to find her. I can trace the call."

"Sebastian, don't!"

I stilled at the sound of Holly's voice, but I couldn't let go. What Luca did, how could I?

"Don't do this." She touched my back. "Alessia wouldn't want this."

"I don't know," I replied and finally let Luca go. He fell back onto the ground, gasping for breath.

I turned to face Holly, and she wrapped her arms around me. I stole a glimpse of The League guard who'd escorted her into the club, which he shouldn't have done.

"Alessia's alive," I whispered into her ear, hoping if I said the words aloud, it'd ensure they were true. "She's alive," I repeated, then sank to my knees and fecking sobbed.

CHAPTER THIRTY-SEVEN

SEBASTIAN

"WHAT ARE YOU DOING HERE?" I HANDED OFF MY LUGGAGE and looked back at Cole.

"You're taking the McGregor jet to Russia to find your sister. You actually expected I'd stay behind?" He brushed past me and climbed the stairs to board the plane.

Getting Holly to stay behind had been a challenge, but the idea of her going into a League prison housing criminals had made me insane. And the idea my sister had spent years there . . .

I strapped in across from him. "You're pretty banged up."

One eye swollen. A gash through his brow. And I was pretty sure the rest of his body looked like someone had taken a bow staff to him like he was a piñata.

"It's been three hours since you got your arse handed to you." Luca's Alliance buddies had done a number on him and Sean, as well as my guards. Thankfully, everyone survived. "You should be in a hospital."

"What I need is to be there for Alessia."

"I'm her brother."

"I know." His gaze flipped from his lap to my face, and his jaw clenched.

I leaned back in my seat, trying to get a read on him. "Alessia's alive. I don't know what kind of hell she's been through, but she doesn't need us fighting when we arrive. So, if you really want to come with me—"

"For years, I thought she was out there somewhere partying, doing God knows what. I convinced myself she was happy because she would've come back home if she wasn't. I tried finding her, and then again after she sent me some cagey apologetic goodbye email—and to find out she was hiding in plain fecking sight in Dublin . . ." He gripped the arms of his chair as we started to move down the runway once we were cleared for takeoff. "But for the last several years, she was in a prison in Russia, for Christ's sake. I was living my life, trying to forget her, and she was locked away." He bowed his head.

"Imagine your guilt and multiply it by a thousand." I looked out the small window off to my left. "She was under my nose this entire time. Hidden away by my best friend. I don't even know how to process that, but I'm focusing on the fact she's alive." I dipped a hand into my pocket and reached for the Celtic cross Holly had given me back.

"That's hers," Cole said. "I gave it to her for her eighteenth birthday."

I fought back the emotion trying to break to the surface and extended my palm. "Then you be the one to put it back on her."

He closed his hand around the cross.

"She was in love with Ireland long before she met me," I admitted. "Now I know why."

His eyes shot to my face.

"Why'd she leave you?"

His forehead tightened, a touch of self-loathing in his eyes at whatever memory he may have latched on to. "She wanted a brother, but she didn't want it to be me."

"She had feelings for you." Clearly beyond friendship.

"She was only twenty and in a fragile state, but I can't help but wonder what would've happened had I just said *Screw age*."

"You did the right thing." Maybe he could be leader after all.

He relaxed back into his seat once the jet had reached cruising altitude. "She was so mad at her father when she found out about you. I guess when her mother died, he tried to track down your ma, only to discover she'd passed as well. He decided you wouldn't want to know him after what he did, so he didn't try to find you."

"Alessia never told me." We both grew quiet after that. I had no clue what to say, and I was certain he didn't know either. Our guilt could fill the plane and then some. It weighed us both down.

But Alessia was alive, and Holly was now safe, so I had to focus on that.

"You still want to be leader?" I asked a few hours later.

"Now more than ever." His eyes tightened. "It's the best way to keep her safe." His gaze cut to the window. "I lost her once, I'm not losing her again."

CHAPTER THIRTY-EIGHT

OFF-THE-GRID, RUSSIA

SEBASTIAN

THE HIGHEST PEAK OF THE URAL MOUNTAINS, MOUNT Narodnaya, was the only thing of view from The League prison. The slope of the mountain was covered in highland tundra.

The tires, covered in chains, crunched over the snow. The wind whistled outside and our windows rattled.

The prison, more like a much smaller version of the Palace of Versailles, wasn't what I'd been expecting at all. I knew some League prisons were more like mansions than jails, but this had to double as Luca's hideout, his place to escape.

"She's in there?" Cole tapped at the window in surprise. "You've never been here, right?"

"No." I blinked a few times. "The location of each prison

is known only to the fixer. I tracked down the prison using Luca's phone, and someone new is being placed in charge of the site as we speak."

"And the guards know we're coming?" he asked as we rolled up to the first security checkpoint.

"I spoke with them, as well as another League leader. They're prepared for our arrival."

"Tell me the prison Luca's going to won't look like this?" he asked once we'd passed through security.

I bit down on my back teeth. "No, the place he's going to will make Guantanamo Bay look like a day spa." We had two locations we reserved for the worst offenders, and one of them had been mine when I'd been a fixer.

I'd called Moreau after Holly had stopped me from killing Luca and made a new deal. Once I'd recounted what Luca had done to my sister, I stipulated the only way I would allow Luca to live was if he rotted in my old facility.

Our driver parked in the circular driveway, which had been cleared of snow. Two armed guards in heavy coats with automatic weapons slung over their shoulders opened our doors.

I tightened my jacket and grabbed the winter coat I'd brought with me for Alessia off the seat and stepped out of the vehicle, a cold snap of air whipped me in the face and cut to my bones.

"Mr. Renaud," the guard by my door began with a bow of the head, "we had no idea prisoner seven-nine-eight was your —" The Russian guard let go of his words and muttered an apology for referring to my sister by her number.

"Where is she?" My breath was visible as I spoke, the frigid air grabbing on to my words and turning them into a cloud. I peered at the ivory structure with threads of gold crisscrossing the windows like bars.

"We brought her down to the guards' living quarters," he answered, terror in his eyes as if worried I'd punish him.

I wanted to pump him for intel to learn how she'd been treated, but I didn't want to waste time. I had to get to her.

I motioned for Cole to follow me to the main doors.

"Take us to her now." Without a word, the guard led us into the mansion.

The place was elegant, draped in red and gold linens, and other finery, but I highly doubted the prison rooms were quite as nice. And so help me, I didn't care whose orders these men were under, if anyone ever touched Alessia, I'd end them.

Cole's breathing was a bit labored as he tried to keep up with my pace, clutching his side as we moved down the hall.

The guard stopped outside a dark door that looked old enough to have belonged during the reign of Louis the Fourteenth. Clearly, Luca had spent his uncle's money to build his own personal palace and sanctuary under the guise of a League facility.

"You ready?" the guard asked, and I nodded, my lips sealed the feck shut. I was too damn nervous. Afraid we'd come all this way, gotten our hopes up, only to discover it was some other woman and not my sister.

He pushed the door in to reveal a living room. Unexpectedly modern compared to what I'd seen so far. Two large flat-screen TVs side by side on the far side wall with leather couches and armchairs for viewing. But where was—

I let go of my thoughts when I moved farther into the space to find a nook off to the left and a fireplace. A dark-haired woman was on a blanket in front of a lit fire, her knees to her chest.

Please, be her.

"Alessia, is that you?" Cole spoke first. I'd been too

entranced by the sight, nearly paralyzed by fear, worried this was another one of Luca's games.

The woman slowly rose and turned to face us. "Sebastian."

It was her.

Oh, God.

Alessia and I were both frozen in the moment.

Her hair was nearly to her hips, her body fitter, more muscle tone as if she'd been working out. She hadn't aged much in her face, but she had in her eyes. Hell, her eyes were decades older.

Her gaze slowly moved off to my side where Cole stood as shocked as me. "Cole?"

I dropped the coat I'd been clutching to the ground and sidestepped it to get to her, still in a daze, but I needed to get closer, to ensure she wasn't a mirage.

"It's really you?" I asked as she met me halfway.

"Yes," she cried, and I pulled her into my arms. She buried her face in my chest, and I expected a sob, but it didn't come. Had being locked up hardened her?

"I'm so sorry." I repeated those words over and over again until I finally let go of her.

Cole was next to us now, his eyes shadowed by years of guilt and longing. "Aless-Alessia." Her name was like a broken whisper of regret.

"How? Why?" She blinked a few times before flinging her arms around his neck. He closed his eyes and held on to her tight. "Are you okay?" she asked. "You look hurt?"

"I'm fine," he responded, his voice cutting out again from emotion.

"Cole and I . . . we're working together now," I explained.

One thing was for damn certain—he loved my sister even

if he'd never told her. We had that in common, too. "Luca's gone. You're okay now."

"I'm so sorry you thought I was dead. I wrote you hundreds of letters over the years, wishing I could send them to you." Alessia pulled back from Cole and turned to me. "The both of you."

Cole looked down at the burgundy carpet, the only clue we were still inside the Versailles rip-off of a mansion slash prison, and his shoulders sloped with guilt.

"I should've told you the truth about everything," I responded, my tone an echo of my grief. "What happened to you, it's on me."

"It's on Luca." Cole's words held venom as he lifted his gaze.

"Let's get you out of here." I looked to Cole, who nodded as if saying *We have her back.*

He snatched the coat from the floor and helped her put it on, then we went into the hall. Part of me wanted to burn the place to the ground before I left. But there were *real* criminals inside, and hopefully, under new leadership, the site would be run properly. As part of my last business as a League leader, I'd be ordering an audit of the prison to ensure everyone inside actually belonged there.

Cole halted in the foyer and turned toward one of the guards. "Surely she told you who she really was, why didn't you look into it?" It was a valid point. Had these men been more loyal to Luca than to the laws of The League?

"I didn't know," the Russian answered, his red mustache, perched over thin lips, moved as his face tightened.

"I don't believe you." I let go of Alessia to confront him.

"He's not lying," Alessia came to his defense. "And the guards treated me exceptionally well, too."

I looked between the guard and Alessia, and his shoulders relaxed.

"My first month here, I convinced a guard I was your sister, and he believed me. Luca had him killed." She squeezed her eyes tight. "I convinced another guard, and he died, too. Luca told me their deaths were on my hands, and if I told anyone else, he'd keep killing them to protect the truth. And then-then he said he'd also have you killed." Her lip trembled. "The guards were nice. They treated me really well. Those men didn't deserve to die, and I couldn't risk anything happening to you."

Fuck. I pulled her back into my arms.

"Let's go," Cole said after a moment. "Let's get you the hell out of here."

We helped her into the back of the car and started for the airport. Cole slipped his hand into his jacket pocket, then took Alessia's and gently placed her necklace in her palm. "You should have this back."

"Will you put it on me?" she asked, her voice fragile, the vibrancy I remembered gone, but hopefully she'd find her way back to who she was before Luca stole her away.

She pivoted to the side on the backseat in the limo, and Cole shifted her hair, longer than ever, over her shoulder to her chest, then clasped the necklace. That cross was tattooed on my back, a cross given to her by a McGregor.

It was strange how we were connected.

I'd never been a big believer in fate, but I guess if I could change, anything was possible.

CHAPTER THIRTY-NINE

HOLLY

FIVE DAYS HAD GONE BY SINCE SEBASTIAN AND COLE HAD returned from Russia, bringing Alessia back with them.

Five very intense days.

Alessia hadn't wanted to talk much about her time in Russia. She'd provided enough details to prevent Sebastian from being totally beside himself with guilt, though.

Her living quarters had been rather nice. The guards had taken to her right away and given her free rein of the house whenever Luca wasn't around. But she'd never risked telling them the truth again after Luca had killed two guards and threatened Sebastian's life.

I couldn't begin to imagine what she'd been through. Of course, she was Sebastian's sister, which meant she was probably tough like him. Resilient. And I believed she would get through this; she would persevere same as he had. But she didn't have to do it alone this time. She had him and the entire McGregor clan as well.

"Here's some tea." I held out the cup for Alessia, but her gaze was fixed on the window.

She looked so much like her brother. Naturally golden skin from her Italian ancestry, brown eyes, prominent cheekbones, dark hair, and full lips. About my height. Above average but not runway tall like Bella. Simply stunning.

She pulled her focus my way when I sat on the couch next to her inside Sebastian's suite. "Oh, um, thanks." She took the cup between her palms, and she stared down at the earl grey.

She grew up in America, so maybe she didn't like tea? "Not a tea person?"

She smiled, and it was the first one I'd seen. "What gave it away?"

"That slight crinkling of your nose as if you were convincing yourself to be nice and drink it." I took the cup from her and set it on the table.

"Will Sebastian be back soon?" She wrapped a throw blanket around her shoulders and tightened it to her chest.

"Yeah, he's just going over some stuff with Cole."

"About taking over?"

I nodded, not sure what to say. Sebastian had explained everything to her, but I was still trying to understand it all. "Yeah," I finally answered. "The League voted yes last night at the meeting, so there's a lot for Cole to learn, I suppose."

"I hate that he's going to leave his sister." She shot a shy smile my way. "Your cousin, I mean."

"I'm surprised we never met when I visited New York."

"And if we had, and you recognized me in Dublin before Luca . . ." Her attention whipped back to the windows.

"I would've told Cole," I finished for her. "Because he'd spent a long time looking for you."

"The first nine or so months after I found Sebastian, I'd been traveling with him sort of off-the-grid as I tried to convince him letting me into his life wasn't a mistake. I'm not surprised Cole didn't find me."

"And yet, you somehow found Sebastian."

She looked back at me. "My dad sort of helped me, I guess. He clued me in that a family friend was in the CIA. High-ranking, too. He asked him to help me before he died." She closed her eyes, a familiar pull of guilt on her face. Like brother like sister. "I kept the details from Cole."

I wanted to ask why, but the woman was held captive for years, and I hoped she'd open up when she was ready. I cared about my cousin, too, and I knew how distraught he'd been when he'd lost her. I only hoped they'd get a fresh start if that's what they wanted, at least.

I reached for two chocolate truffles from the bowl on the table and offered her one.

She toyed with the candy between her fingers but didn't open it.

Me? I needed the chocolate to cope with this all. I was probably in need of a size up in jeans from all the "coping" I'd been doing in the last five days, too.

Her dark brown eyes shifted to my face as I popped the chocolate ball into my mouth, and the smooth milky center touched my tongue. "I don't know if Cole can be the person he needs to be, the man my brother was or still is."

"And what kind of person is that?"

She set the candy back down and pulled the blanket tight to her body again. "A justice seeker. A vigilante. Whatever you want to call it. That's not Cole."

Now wouldn't be the best time to tell her Cole had attacked Sebastian when he'd discovered the truth, and how he'd been out for blood. "People can surprise you. Your brother surprised me."

"And you love him, don't you?" Her lip tucked between her teeth. "My brother in love with Cole's cousin. Small, small world."

"I guess it is," I whispered. "Or maybe we were all meant to do something great, something bigger than ourselves."

CHAPTER FORTY

Holly

"You don't have to do this." I slipped off Sebastian's bed and grabbed my black silk robe. The conversation wouldn't last long if I stood naked in front of him.

He pulled on a pair of gray pajama bottoms and faced me. "The land in Limerick is safe. More importantly, you're safe. You don't need me at the company."

The next board meeting was tomorrow. I could hardly believe three weeks had passed since the board had agreed to reconvene to vote on the sale of the land to Paulson Incorporated, a bogus freaking shell company.

"I'll announce my resignation at the meeting. Your family can have their shares back." He braced my arms, and his palms slid over the silk up and down my biceps.

"Are you doing this to ensure the Reed deal doesn't fall through?" I'd yet to speak to Harrison since he left Dublin, no bloody clue what to say. I'd also been a bit preoccupied with taking down evil people. Who would've thought I'd become a real-life Supergirl?

"I'm doing this because it's what's right." He brought his lips to mine for a gentle kiss.

We'd had to quietly make love this week with Alessia sleeping in the other room. But it was well worth it to have her home and safe.

"I was thinking maybe we could go on holiday once Alessia is settled. Get away for a few days. My boat. The sea. No one to hear you cry out my name while you come." He stared at me with heavy-lidded eyes.

Sounds like heaven. "You sure you're ready to leave her?"

"No, but it was her idea. She's sort of stubborn and thinks we need this. We'll wait a bit, but . . . I, um, trust Cole to protect her."

"I don't think they've talked much. There's guilt, or something, between them."

"I know a thing or two about that."

I placed a palm on his naked chest. "I also know that trusting Cole with her life, well, that's not easy for you to do."

"Yeah." He leaned in and nipped my lip. "But I'm learning I can't quite control everything. I sure as hell failed trying to stop myself from falling in love with you."

"Thank God." I gasped when he scooped me into his arms and tossed me back onto the bed.

He removed his pajama bottoms and moved on top of me, then worked at the knot of my robe, pushed the material to the side, and drank me in with that smoldering look I loved.

I squirmed beneath him, anxious for what he was going to do next. "Do me a favor," I murmured. "I know you've been holding back, restraining yourself in bed, but you don't need to do that anymore."

He looked at me, his eyes glinting with passion. "Oh, really?"

I nodded.

His lips crooked at the edges. "Well, then, yes, ma'am . . ." he said as he pinned my arms over my head and buried himself deep inside of me.

* * *

"WELL, MAYBE NOW I DON'T WANT TO LEAVE YOUR company." Sebastian faked a pout as he leaned against the window in my office, arms across his chest. I'd never seen the man pout, but even on him, he made it look sexy.

He was a different person since Alessia had returned. Freer. More relaxed. And maybe it also had to do with stepping down as League leader.

Of course, we still had The Alliance to go after, but Emilia said we had months before we had to begin strategizing, so yeah, right now, I wanted to spend my time with the man I loved.

I traced my tongue over my red bottom lip, then nibbled at the side.

He took the bait. Two quick strides and he had me up against the bookshelf behind my desk. "If you were as naughty as you were in the boardroom earlier today, the last two times we'd had meetings, I would've lost my bloody mind."

I lifted my chin to find his eyes. "And if I was touching your crotch beneath the table and playing footsie with you three weeks ago, you should have charged me with sexual harassment since we weren't together then."

"I like how that sounds."

I chuckled. "The harassment part?"

He shook his head. "The together part." He brushed his lips over mine. "I've wanted you to be mine for years. How'd I get so lucky?"

"And if you try and get lucky in my building, I'll forget we're now on the same side."

Sean's words had Sebastian bowing his forehead to mine, and given the erection he was sporting, he was probably trying to calm his dick down before he turned to face my brother.

"I thought with all of your Batman-like skills you would've heard me open the door," Sean taunted. Damn him.

I shifted my head to the right to catch my brother's eyes and glare at him.

"Oh come on, it was funny." He held his palms open. "Billionaire vigilante?" He shut the door behind him.

I rolled my eyes. "He doesn't go out and fight crime at night." I pulled my focus back to Sebastian, and his lips stretched. "You don't, do you?"

"No." He lifted a brow, and he fought a smile. "Do you want me to?"

"Not at all."

He let go of me and turned around. My attention dipped to his navy-blue trousers, the signs of his hard-on gone. Phew.

"Nice speech you gave in the meeting." Sean kept his back to the door, and it was obvious he still wasn't comfortable with the new arrangement—the one where we'd be working with a man he used to hate. Yeah, even I had to pinch myself a few times a day to believe it.

"Was that a compliment?" I perched a hip against my desk as Sebastian moved back to the window. He positioned his back to the glass and kept his eyes steady on my brother.

And yeah, he was uncomfortable, too. It'd take time for all of us, I supposed.

"Anyway, I'm here to let you know I just got off the phone with Reed." He strode farther into the room and closer to my desk. "I know you've been avoiding a conversation with him, so I thought I'd make the call for you."

My heartbeat quickened, and my palms grew sweaty almost instantly. "And what'd you tell him?"

"A watered-down version of the truth. Sebastian's not in bed with The Alliance, but he's stepping down from the company as promised. His sister is alive."

It was the first time Sean called Sebastian by his first name, and I'd take that as a win. A step forward. "And what'd he say?"

"He needs time to think about everything, especially since I went ahead and threw the gut shot—the one about you dating Sebastian."

"I probably should've been the one to tell him that."

"Why? You were always friends, right?" Sean challenged, and I couldn't help but wonder if Sebastian was thinking the same thing now.

"We are friends, which is why it should have been me." I glimpsed Sebastian out of the corner of my eye, and he didn't look jealous or angry.

"We still on for tonight?" he asked Sebastian, and he nodded. "I can't believe Ethan's really going to stay in New York to help out there with Cole gone. Maybe Uncle William can whip some sense into him. Da's been too easy on him." He started for the door and casually waved goodbye. "See you two later."

I took a seat in front of my desk, and Sebastian sat next to me once the door was closed. He reached across the short space between us and held my hand. "You need me to finalize one last deal before I go?"

"Is that code for sex?" I grinned, unable to stop myself.

He looked over at the glass walls then back at me. "I was thinking I could talk to Reed. I have been known to be convincing when I want to be."

"Thank you, but I think I know a thing or two about closing deals." I wet my lips. "After all, I learned from the best."

He grabbed the chair arm and yanked it, so my seat bumped into his, then he fisted my hair and brought my mouth closer but didn't kiss me.

"What about the glass—" He swallowed my question with a kiss, and when I pulled back a minute later to catch my breath, I tracked his amused expression to the three employees standing outside my office with shocked looks on their faces.

He reached for the remote off my desk and commanded the blinds to scroll down. "Guess it's a good thing you're the boss."

CHAPTER FORTY-ONE

Sebastian

Alessia's hand raced along the bar counter as she walked behind it. "You didn't change anything. Not even the arrangement of the liquor."

It was only nine at night, so the club wasn't open yet. It was also the first time Alessia had requested to come. "Why mess with perfection?"

"It's good to be back."

"The club is yours. Always has been and always will be. And now you'll be running it as Alessia. If you want it, that is."

"Well, Josie died that day. Not me." She forced a smile as if she were trying to reclaim that innocence she used to naturally carry, but I was worried Luca may have stolen it. "And I don't want to run this place alone." She circled the bar to stand closer to me. "Run it with me?"

How the hell could I say no to her? After everything she'd

been through, I'd do pretty much whatever she asked. "Of course."

Her eyes widened. "Really?" She draped her arms over my shoulders, taking me back to the night she appeared on my dock, invited herself onto my boat, and somehow convinced me to let her into my life, and then she hugged me.

"I love you, Sis," I said near her ear before she stepped out of my hold.

Unshed tears had her eyes glistening. "I love you, too." She reached for the cross at her neck and smoothed it between her thumb and forefinger. "We have time to make up for, don't we?"

I nodded. "If you don't want me going on the trip with Holly, I can postpone."

"Absolutely not. How can your special Christmas surprise happen if you don't take that trip first?" She placed a palm over my chest and patted me a few times as if in a sudden daze, or at a loss for words. "Reconnecting with you has been so easy, but Cole . . . the way we left things six years ago, I don't know what to say to him."

He was due any minute with his cousins. Emilia, too.

"He cares about you," I offered the reminder. "He's happy to have you back. More than happy. Maybe words aren't needed right now?"

"Maybe." She stepped to the side of me when Holly entered the club with Cole, Sean, and Adam.

The sight of Holly took my breath away. Another killer red pantsuit that had me envisioning peeling it off and running my mouth over her entire body.

"Hi." I met her halfway and went in for a quick kiss.

"Well, since this is my first official secret meeting, are there any protocols we're supposed to follow?" Sean asked in a teasing voice. "Like talking over champagne, for instance?"

I rolled my eyes.

"Any special initiation for Cole?" Adam sat on one of the satin couches off to the side of the dance floor and braced his ankle over his knee.

"Actually, there is, right?" Holly glimpsed Cole sitting next to Adam. "A tattoo."

"I need to get ink?" Cole guffawed. "You serious? Why didn't you say something sooner?" His gaze cut to Alessia as she crossed the room to get closer, and his mouth tightened.

There was a lot that needed to be said between them, but I think I was right—they'd need some time first. Well, Alessia needed time, at least.

"You got a problem with tattoos?" Adam's lips gathered into a smile.

"No, but I feckin' hate needles." Cole raced a hand over his head.

"I can hold your hand," Sean offered as he plopped down on the sofa opposite him.

"Any luck finding a home?" Holly asked as she joined them on the couches. And a nice touch at her art of deflection.

"Yeah, I made an offer on a flat a few blocks from here," Cole answered.

Alessia would be living in the hotel for now, but at some point, she'd need a real place to call home.

"How's Bree handling the news of you moving here?" Holly asked.

"She's shooting a new movie in Montreal while dealing with the divorce from Derek, so I may even be back before her."

I doubted that. This wouldn't be a few-months-and-be-done kind of thing, but I didn't want to tell him that now. We all needed a bit of a reprieve from the heavy stuff before we moved forward.

"Starting without me?" Emilia asked on approach. She'd traded in her typical leather look for something a bit more casual. Jeans, black boots, and a plain black jumper.

Sean stood at the sight of her and smoothed a hand over his black dress shirt. "You're here."

"I am." She smiled. "Once you're settled in, we should begin training," she said to Cole, then she focused on Sean as he sat back down.

"Can I steal you away for a minute?" I asked Emilia, and she nodded. I kissed Holly on the cheek and motioned for Emilia to follow me to the other side of the club. "Can you stay in town while I'm gone?" I asked once we were out of earshot of everyone.

"Of course." She gripped my arm. "I'm glad you're doing this. You need to get away."

"Just one thing," I said, unable to hold back a smile. "Don't take it too easy on Sean."

"Sean? You mean if I train him, too?"

"Yeah."

She pulled her hand free of my arm. "Shouldn't you be telling me the opposite instead?"

I glanced back at Sean. "If he's gonna become my brother-in-law, he needs to toughen up."

She smirked. "And how soon will this possibly happen?"

I looked at Holly. "Hopefully, very soon."

CHAPTER FORTY-TWO

MEDITERRANEAN SEA

SEBASTIAN

HOLLY CLAWED AT THE BED BENEATH US AS I PUMPED IN AND out of her from behind.

"Harder," she commanded, her words nearly drowned out by the crackling of lightning and thunder outside on the water. We were halfway between Italy and Greece with absolutely nothing around us. I had her all to myself, and it was perfect.

"You sure?" I asked, needing to hear the confirmation.

I pulled out and leaned back to view her perfect arse, then slapped a hand to her backside and palmed her soaking wet sex.

She looked back at me, her eyes half-lidded and drowsy with lust. "Make me scream."

Fuck. I secured my hands back onto her hips and thrust back inside of her and moved like an animal, pounding hard and fast.

She tossed her head, her silky hair cascading over her back. My name tore free from her lips as I relished in her slickness all over my cock as I moved in and out of her.

Back in Dublin, she'd said to me I'd been holding back, and she'd been right. Not emotionally, but physically, worried I'd be too rough. But she was as wild as me when we made love. Maybe one of these days she'd even let me take her "virgin ass" as she called it. A man could hope.

She moaned as she climaxed a minute later, then I flipped her to her back and finished while on top so I could see her face.

A growl-like sound left my mouth as her eyes locked with mine, and she buried her fingernails into my chest as I came hard.

I kept my hands braced alongside her, not ready to separate our bodies.

She traced the line of the scar at my side, the one I'd gotten when taking down the men I'd thought were responsible for Alessia's murder. Of course, technically, they did play a part, but they'd been manipulated by Luca, same as me.

I tipped my head to the side, studying her. Worry grew inside of me. "You okay?" I collapsed off to the side of her, my eyes going to my cum on her pussy.

She positioned her hand behind her head, her tits lifting a touch in the process. Her nipples still erect.

"I just hate how many times you've been hurt," she said softly.

"It won't happen again."

"You sure?" She turned to her side to better face me.

"Yes," I promised, and it was a promise I planned on keeping.

I'd just gotten my sister back, and I was so damn in love with Holly it actually hurt at times . . . no way was I going to ever jeopardize losing either one.

* * *

"FAVORITE FOOD?" I POPPED THE PISTACHIO FROM ITS SHELL, sitting opposite of her at the table in the mini kitchen area on the boat.

"Any type of pasta with cheese." She smiled and grabbed the stem of her wine glass. "Your turn."

"Fish and chips. I'm really a simple guy at heart."

"Ha." She swatted a hand into the air. "Nothing simple about you." She squinted. "Okay, my turn. Celebrity crush?"

I wasn't sure if I was thrilled with this game anymore. Because feck me, I couldn't hear her response. If Harrison Reed was her answer, I'd have a mild heart attack.

"Oh, come on. Who?" She rolled her eyes, and she must've sensed what was on my mind.

"I'm not much into movies. My life has plenty of adventure."

She snatched a nut and threw it my way, but I caught it. "Fine. Favorite superhero? Everyone has to have one of those, right?" She set her glass down and leaned over the table. "You totally want to say Batman, but my brother ruined that for you, huh?"

I laughed. "No, I'm actually more of a Superman fan. I always loved the idea of flying as a kid."

"Well, you're my superhero." She lifted her shoulders.

"Can I roll my eyes now?" I pushed the bowl of

pistachios off to the side and reached for her hand. "Next question." I smiled. "Why do you want to make the movie so much?"

She sat back but kept her eyes on me. "My cousin Bree is the actress in the family, but I've always had an interest in the TV and movie business. I used to go on set of the productions of some of the local shows our company produced when I was a kid, and I always loved it." She was beaming. So gorgeous. "I like the magic of what happens behind the scenes. All the little bits that go on that no one knows about, but without them, there'd be no show or movie."

"And you really want this movie deal with Reed, huh?"

"To make a movie in my own city," she began, and I'd swear there were stars in her eyes, "would be amazing."

"So, do it anyway. If he backs out, why not? What's stopping you?"

The side of her mouth crooked. "You'd prefer that, right?"

I shook my head. "I fell in love with a dreamer, and all I want is to see her dreams come true." God, I was becoming a romantic, wasn't I? I'd become anything to see her smiling and happy.

"So, we've been asking questions for about thirty minutes now. I think we've covered all the major topics and officially know everything about each other."

"Maybe one more." I slipped my hand into the pocket of my jeans, which was all I had on. No trunks beneath.

"Yeah?"

I took a deep breath and tried to steady my pulse. I was pretty sure this was the most nervous I'd been in my life. "How about a Christmas wedding?" I tightened my hand around the diamond but kept it on my lap. *This* Christmas."

Her eyes narrowed as if she didn't quite grasp my words, and her mind was busy trying to make sense of what I'd said.

"Will you be my wife in two weeks?" I cleared my throat, moved off the seat, and dropped to one knee next to her. I reached for her hand and brought the 2-carat princess cut diamond in a platinum setting to the top of her ring finger and held it there as I waited for an answer.

Every second of waiting had my heart diving into my stomach.

She closed her eyes, and a tear escaped.

Was it going to be a no?

My body tensed, and I closed my eyes as I tried not to lose my balance in my crouched position as worry took hold of me.

"Look at me." Her command was whisper-soft, and I swallowed the lump in my throat at the feel of her other hand on my cheek.

I slowly opened my eyes. More tears dampened her cheeks.

"We only started dating last month, and I spent most of the year before that trying to hate you." She kept her palm in place, and I sucked in a sharp breath of disappointment. I'd thought for sure she felt the same, but . . . "None of that matters because I love you more than anything." She looked down at the ring then back at me. "I want to be Holly Ryan, though, if that's okay with you?"

She bowed her head to mine, and I fought back the rise of emotion, the threat of something I'd never felt before—happy tears.

My real name paired with hers.

I'd once envisioned League leader of Ireland as my dream. I'd been wrong.

This woman sitting before me was it. My ma had loved

my father, arsehole or not, with everything she had, and she'd never been able to love another man. I understood that now because my heart belonged to Holly. Forever.

"I'd love nothing more." I blinked back the tears and slid the ring on her finger. "It's simple, like me."

She sniffled and wiped more tears from her cheeks. "It's perfect." She brought her mouth to mine. "I love you."

"I love you more," I whispered against her lips and kissed her again.

"Two weeks, huh?" she asked a few minutes later after we both got our hearts to work at the proper speeds.

"I asked your father. He said *Feck off,* at first, but Adam managed to convince him. And Anna has offered to help plan a lightning-fast wedding. Emilia even offered to help, and she hates weddings."

She half laughed, half cried. "Adam really gave his blessing?"

"Sean, too." I stood all the way up, and she rose as well. "I, uh, don't know Ethan all that well, so I didn't ask. Sorry."

"I really love you." She looped her hands around my neck. "Christmas, though? Are you trying to use that day so you'll never forget our anniversary?"

I laughed. "No, but damn, that would've been smart thinking."

"Then why?" She lifted a brow. "I mean, aside from your desire to marry me ASAP because I'm awesome." She nibbled on her bottom lip as she observed me, her beautiful green eyes glossy.

"Christmas was my favorite time of the year when Ma was alive. Christmas in Paris was even better," I admitted.

"Then let's do a Christmas wedding in Paris."

I swallowed, my breath catching. "You're serious?"

"What girl wouldn't want a Christmas wedding in Paris and to the man of her dreams?"

"I do know a guy who owns a hotel there."

She brought her lips close to mine. "Maybe fairy tales really do exist," she murmured before kissing me.

EPILOGUE

PARIS, FRANCE

HOLLY

FIFTY GUESTS ON CHRISTMAS EVE, I HADN'T EXPECTED SO many family members and close friends would be able to pop over to Paris for a last-minute wedding, but I was one lucky woman.

I glanced at my husband as I danced with Da for my second time that evening. He was standing on the other side of the cozy reception salon talking with my brothers, all three of them, and they were laughing—so much so that Adam had to bend forward as he clutched his stomach. I had no idea who had caused the laughter, but it was one of the best wedding gifts I could ask for.

I wasn't sure where Cole was, but I didn't see Alessia either, so maybe they stole a moment alone on the terrace to talk.

"You as surprised as I am that this night happened so fast?" Da stepped back when the band changed over to a new song.

"Well, I'm beginning to think Anna should open her own party planning business. I couldn't have pulled this off without her."

"It helps your husband owns the hotel."

And we're worth billions, but I kept that to myself. I didn't want to verbalize my guilt that not everyone could experience a fairy tale ceremony in front of the Champs-Élysées beneath the moonlight on Christmas Eve.

And beyond where we were now was the Eiffel Tower. Sebastian had great taste in hotel locations, that was for sure. And the reception was intimate and cozy, just how I'd imagined.

Snowy white and silver colors with a hint of Christmas. Twinkling lights, garlands, amaryllis flowers with pine branches and silver leaves with candles for centerpieces. Eggnog for the signature cocktail, and a strawberry Nutcracker-themed wedding cake. Oh, and it was a minor detail, but it was spot on—glass ornaments with the guest names stenciled on them to identify their place at one of the eight tables off to the side of the dance floor.

Da took my hand and guided me to where Ma sat with my cousin Bree, her son, Jack, and Anna. Sebastian had opted not to invite many friends. Emilia, Édouard Moreau, his bartender Ola, as well as Declan and Samuel, were in attendance. The boys' mother had a month left at rehab before she moved into the hotel for a fresh start, all thanks to my incredible husband.

Ma stood at the sight of me, her eyes sparkling as she eyed my ball gown, which was every bit Cinderella-like. An Ines di Santi Gracie dress with a cathedral train that had been bustled. I still had no idea how Ma pulled off the miracle to not only get the dress in time but ensure it fit. And it did fit to perfection. A strapless neckline, natural waist, silk and tulle fabric with gorgeous beads on the bodice, as well as detachable embroidered sleeves. It was stunning, and when I first stood in front of Sebastian to say our vows, he'd been speechless. Tears in his eyes.

"There's something your mother and I would like to tell you. A bit of a wedding gift, if you will." Da motioned for the terrace.

"Be back," I said to the others at the table with a smile.

Ma pushed in the white infinity seat to the table. Two overlapping circles were at the back of the chair to represent love being eternal. Anna had thought of everything.

"Save a dance for me!" Bree's son, Jack, exclaimed, and I blew him a kiss, then followed my parents to the terrace. Heaters were outside to keep the area warm so we didn't have to wear jackets.

. . . And that's where Cole and Alessia had gone. Cole's hand was on her back as they looked at the view. The intimate gesture had my heart palpitating.

Da cleared his throat, making our presence known, and he immediately lowered his hand from Alessia's back as they both faced us.

"So damn stunning, cuz." Cole strode closer and placed a kiss on both my cheeks. When in France, right?

"You clean up nice yourself," I teased.

He was in the same tuxedo as Sebastian and my brothers. All men wore Brioni. Of course. Tuxedo jackets with satin collars, suspenders, and a black bow tie.

"Thanks for picking a bridesmaid dress that's not hideous." Alessia looked stunning and ethereal in her pink halter sequin dress embellished with metallic beads on the bodice.

"I wanted to avoid any bridal payback later when I wear a bridesmaid dress at your wedding," I joked.

She reached for my arm and squeezed. "I'm so glad to have a sister."

Cole tipped his head goodbye, and they went back into the reception area inside.

"So." I rubbed my palms together and faced Ma and Da.

Da laced his hand with Ma's and looked up at me. "We've called off the divorce. We're staying together."

I leapt toward them, unable to stop myself, doing my best not to trip in my gown, and hugged them tightly.

"You reminded us what it means to love again," Ma said when pulling back. It was honestly her fault I loved fairy tales since she used to be a professor of literature at Trinity, and I grew up hearing stories of happily ever afters.

"Mind if I steal your daughter for a moment?"

I stepped back to find Harrison there. If anyone should steal me, it ought to be my husband, but I was glad he showed up. Extremely surprised, but thankful, because I hoped it meant he wanted to continue our friendship.

"Save me another dance." Da patted Harrison on the shoulder, then took Ma's hand and escorted her back inside.

Harrison tipped his head, motioning to go closer to the balcony. "You came," I said under my breath, my eyes on the Eiffel Tower.

"It was unexpected news, and I'll be flying home early to get to my family for Christmas dinner, but I couldn't miss your wedding." He set his forearms over the railing, leaning forward. "We are friends, right?"

"I'd like to be," I admitted.

"I doubt you'd marry a guy you didn't trust and so fast, so

. . . what I'm trying to say is that we have a deal." He stood tall and extended his hand. "If you still want to work together, that is?"

First, my brothers bonded with Sebastian. Then, my parents reconciled. Now this? The gifts kept coming. "One condition. You, at least, let my cousin audition for a role in the film. You don't have to say yes, but she's a brilliant actress."

"Bree?"

"Yeah. She'd have to get the all clear from her soon-to-be ex-husband to come over here with her son if she lands a role, but it'd mean a lot if she could audition."

"She does have the look."

"Are looks all that matter?" I challenged, fighting a smile. "And why, Harrison, are you blushing?"

His hand raced through his hair, and he shook his head, but then a smirk stretched his lips. "You McGregor women apparently have that effect on me."

"Hm." And if Anna had heard him, she'd be planning their wedding next in her head. But I knew better. Bree would never fall for a Hollywood player, and I was pretty sure Harrison had sworn off actresses, so nope, no wedding for them. It was too bad. It'd be kind of nice to have him as part of the family.

We went back inside a few moments later, and everyone was crowded on the dance floor as a traditional Irish folk song was playing by the band. "Wedding may be in Paris, but we had to bring a little home with us," Sebastian said, catching me by surprise from behind. "Reed," he greeted and shook his hand. "Thanks for coming."

"Well, you did call and make a convincing argument for it."

"Wait, what?" I lifted my brows in surprise, and

Sebastian smiled. "Who are you, and what have you done with my husband?" I whispered into his ear, and he laughed.

"Excuse us." He pulled me to the dance floor and secured his hands around me. "Your husband would very much like to rip that dress off you."

I blushed, worried someone on the dance floor overheard him. "I thought you said I looked beautiful in this dress. Like an angel. A tempting goddess."

"All of those things." He pulled me tighter so our bodies were flush. "And more. But I still prefer you *sans vêtements*."

"Yeah, you look pretty damn hot without clothes, too," I said as he spun and dipped me. "Is this real? This night, I mean?"

"Want me to pinch you?" He flashed his white teeth, and his smile met his eyes.

I startled when he pinched my arse. "Not there!"

He bit into his lip as we moved, as we danced together. I didn't know what would happen with The Alliance next year, but I knew for sure we'd be okay. We could get through anything if we stuck together as a family.

Family was everything, and now mine felt complete.

"Alessia seems to be doing well, right?"

"I think she's doing amazing." *Especially after everything she's been through.* "I wish your ma could have been here tonight."

"I can feel her here. Is that crazy?" His Adam's apple moved with a swallow.

"Not at all," I answered softly.

His eyes tightened on me, and I brought my lips to his for a soft kiss, but he deepened it when his tongue dipped into my mouth.

At the feel of someone tugging on my gown, I forced my

lips from my husband and glimpsed back to see Jack there. "My turn!"

"Can this little guy cut in?"

Sebastian crouched to eye level with Jack and gave him a high five. "For you, of course." He stood again and brought his mouth to my ear. "Maybe we'll try for one of those, at some point."

"One of those?" I laughed and swatted his chest before lifting Jack up to dance.

I looked over at Anna dancing with Adam not far away. They were so happy and with a child on the way. I had Sebastian now, but maybe after The Alliance matter was settled, we could try for kids.

Sebastian took Jack a few minutes later, as if knowing my arms were growing tired. Sean motioned for him to hand him over, and he hoisted Jack over his shoulders and carried him around the room, which had Jack cracking up.

"Your brother has a surprise for you." Sebastian took my hand and guided me toward the band. "Which brother?" And another surprise? I was far too spoiled tonight.

Sebastian pulled me tight to his side as Ethan dropped onto a stool in front of a mic, then winked at me. "This song is for you two. Hope you like it."

It'd been years since I'd heard Ethan sing, and when the background music began, I realized he was going to sing a song by one of my all-time favorite artists who I'd forever mourn, Avicii.

I grinned from ear to ear when he began singing the song *Broken Arrows*. Ethan stood when the beats intensified, and every lyric captured my heart and moved right to my soul . . . it was perfect. This entire night was heaven.

Sebastian turned me to face him as Ethan continued to sing, and emotion swelled in my chest. He held on to my

347

cheeks and stared deep into my eyes, and I wanted to cry. Happy tears, of course, because in this moment, something became as clear as day. "You," I mouthed, my eyes blurry. "You're it. My dream," I cried, hoping he could hear me over the music.

"You, too, my love." He kissed me, and the entire room erupted into applause just as the song finished. "You. Always."

I hugged my brother after the song, then Sebastian took my hand, guided me to the balcony, and closed the door behind us.

"Cold?" I shook my head no, and he tossed his jacket, got rid of the bow tie, then knelt before me and lifted my skirt. I braced my hands on his shoulders, not sure what he was doing, then laughed when I realized he was getting rid of my heels. "Don't want you in pain." He tossed my shoes over his shoulder.

I nearly moaned from the relief at losing the heels.

"I've been waiting to get you alone all night," he said, his voice husky. He set his eyes on me, and I was fairly certain the world stopped at that moment. Just for one blink of an eye, absolutely everything stopped.

He brought his thumb to my lip and pulled it down before cupping the back of my head.

"I need you to know I'll never let anything happen to you. You're my wife. My family. My everything." His voice was hoarse with emotion.

I arched a brow. "Well, our relationship began with you trying to protect me. I guess I can't expect you to stop now."

His mouth edged closer to mine. "Never."

I held a finger in front of my lips before he could kiss me. "As long as you let me have your back, too, then I guess we have a deal," I said before his mouth slanted over mine.

As far as happily ever afters go?

Yeah, our story may have had some bumps and a few twists and turns, but I couldn't have asked for more. And all I could hope was the rest of my family would find happiness and love, too . . .

*CONTINUE FOR A SPECIAL BONUS EPILOGUE FROM ALESSIA'S point-of-view.

SPECIAL BONUS EPILOGUE

The Wedding Night

Alessia

"This a new Taylor Swift song?" I asked as I danced with my brother. I missed out on years of new music, and if I was going to run a club, I had my homework cut out for me on catching up.

He smiled. "I wouldn't know."

"Right. Why would you?" The song was a bit too romantic given I was dancing with my brother, but it was his wedding night, and wow, we were together again, and he was married. It was insane.

He hadn't aged much since I'd been gone. Handsome as ever. Less broody, and I was pretty sure I had Holly to thank for that.

But I'd lost so much time and . . .

My throat constricted, and my chest grew heavy.

I pulled back and stopped dancing. "I'm gonna grab some air if you don't mind." I kissed both his cheeks. "And before you ask to join me, or worry about me, I'm fine."

I would be, at least. Eventually.

His brows knitted, concern apparent, and that was the last thing I wanted tonight.

"I promise," I added and fixed a killer smile to close the deal.

"Yeah, uh, okay." He left my side, taking hesitant steps, and I made a beeline for the outdoors.

The terrace had multiple heaters, but the dress was sleeveless, so I was still cold. I hugged my body as I walked to the edge of the balcony and marveled at the view.

How many times had I visited Sebastian in Paris and stood in this very spot before Luca had taken me?

He'd believed I was dead for so long, and a part of me had died on the inside. I had to figure out how to become me again.

"I wanted to offer my apologies, I hope you don't mind."

I stilled at the French-accented voice behind me. "Moreau?" I'd heard a lot about him. Luca had vented to me like I was his own personal therapist whenever he visited. If only I'd been able to talk Luca off the cliff of crazy, I could've come home sooner.

"You don't owe me an apology." I wrung my hands together, brought them to my abdomen, and turned to face him.

"What my nephew did to you . . ." His brows drew together with regret.

"Everything okay?" Cole asked on approach.

"I'm fine," I finally answered, holding Cole's eyes as if Moreau wasn't outside with us.

"You sure you're ready for the challenge of leadership?" he asked Cole.

I wasn't ready. The idea of him filling Sebastian's shoes scared me to death.

"Everyone will be safe, right?" Worry moved through his voice, his focus on Moreau.

"*Oui*," he answered.

"Then I'm ready."

Moreau nodded goodbye and left us.

Surprisingly, it was the first time Cole and I had actually been alone together since my return. Even when Sebastian had been on vacation with Holly, someone had always been in the room.

I might have done that on purpose, too nervous for whatever conversation needed to happen between us that I hadn't been prepared for.

He removed his tux jacket and hung it over my shoulders, and I tipped my head in thanks.

"When Bree saw you tonight, I haven't seen her cry like that since she told me about Derek cheating. I'd even pre-warned her she'd see you, but still."

Derek, I remembered him. Bree had been dating him before I left, and I'd never liked the guy. "Will Bree ever forgive me for taking off without saying goodbye?" I swallowed. "And will you?" The fight we'd had before I left, the guilt of it had haunted me for years.

"Of course," he said after a moment. "Both of us."

"I'm not sure if I deserve that." My shoulders sagged. "I'm so sorry about the fight, and how I acted before and—"

"Don't." He held a hand between us. "You don't owe me any explanations. I'm so damn glad you're okay." He was even more handsome in his maturity.

I reached for his arm, and his jacket slipped from my

shoulders in the process. We knelt at the same time to grab it, our heads nearly colliding. "Thank you," I said softly when he handed it back to me once we were both upright.

I clutched the jacket between my palms. "Can we just stand here? Look at this beautiful view and not say anything?" I wasn't ready to open up old wounds, not yet, at least.

"For you?" He placed a hand on the small of my back, and I closed my eyes at the touch. "Anything."

THE INSIDE MAN, FEATURING COLE AND ALESSIA, RELEASES spring 2020.

PLAYLIST

Human, Rag'n'Bone Man
Easier, 5 Seconds of Summer
Diamonds, Rihanna
Thunder, Imagine Dragons
Slow Hands, Niall Horan
Blame, Calvin Harris, John Newman
Save the World- Zedd Remix - Swedish House Mafia
Let me Love You, DJ Snake, Justin Bieber
Never Be Alone (feat. Aloe Black), David Guetta
Broken Arrows, Avicii

Spotify Playlist: *The Real Deal,* Brittney Sahin

ALSO BY BRITTNEY SAHIN

Dublin Nights

On the Edge - Travel to Dublin and get swept up in this romantic suspense starring an Irish businessman by day…and fighter by night.

On the Line - novella

The Inside Man - Alessia & Cole

Stand-alone (with a connection to *On the Edge*):

The Story of Us– Sports columnist Maggie Lane has 1 rule: never fall for a player. One mistaken kiss with Italian soccer star Marco Valenti changes everything…

Stealth Ops Series: Bravo Team

Finding His Mark - Luke & Eva (feat. Harrison Reed)

Finding Justice - Owen & Samantha

Finding the Fight - Asher & Jessica

Finding Her Chance - Liam & Emily

Finding the Way Back - Knox & Adriana

Stealth Ops Series: Echo Team

Chasing the Knight - Wyatt Pierson (2/20/2020)

Becoming Us

Someone Like You - A former Navy SEAL. A father. And off-limits.
(Noah Dalton)

My Every Breath - A sizzling and suspenseful romance.
Businessman Cade King has fallen for the wrong woman. She's the
daughter of a hitman - and he's the target.

Hidden Truths

The Safe Bet – Begin the series with the Man-of-Steel lookalike
Michael Maddox.

Beyond the Chase - Fall for the sexy Irishman, Aiden O'Connor, in
this romantic suspense.

The Hard Truth – Read Connor Matthews' story in this second-
chance romantic suspense novel.

Surviving the Fall – Jake Summers loses the last 12 years of his life
in this action-packed romantic thriller.

The Final Goodbye - Friends-to-lovers romantic mystery

WHERE ELSE TO FIND ME

Thank you for reading Sebastian and Holly's story. If you don't mind taking a minute to leave a short review, I would greatly appreciate it. Reviews are incredibly helpful to keeping the series going. Thank you!

www.brittneysahin.com
brittneysahin@emkomedia.net
FB Reader Group - Brittney's Book Babes
FB - Stealth Ops Spoiler Room
FB- Dublin Nights Spoiler Room
Bonus Content - website

3855

Made in the USA
Middletown, DE
04 December 2019

79997066R00217